Robert Louis Stevenson

THE STRANGE CASE OF DR. JEKYLL AND MR. HYDE

and

THE DYNAMITER

CLASSICS OF
Mystery & Suspense

CLASSICS OF
Mystery & Suspense

Published by Trident Press International
801 12th Avenue South
Suite 302
Naples Florida 34102 USA
www.trident-international.com
email: tridentpress@worldnet.att.net

Copyright © Trident Press International 2001
Printed in Australia
ISBN: 1582791880

THE STRANGE CASE
OF DR. JEKYLL
AND MR. HYDE

Story of the Door

Mr. Utterson the lawyer was a man of a rugged countenance that was never lighted by a smile; cold, scanty and embarrassed in discourse; backward in sentiment; lean, long, dusty, dreary and yet somehow lovable. At friendly meetings, and when the wine was to his taste, something eminently human beaconed from his eye; something indeed which never found its way into his talk, but which spoke not only in these silent symbols of the after-dinner face, but more often and loudly in the acts of his life. He was austere with himself; drank gin when he was alone, to mortify a taste for vintages; and though he enjoyed the theater, had not crossed the doors of one for twenty years. But he had an approved tolerance for others; sometimes wondering, almost with envy, at the high pressure of spirits involved in their misdeeds; and in any extremity inclined to help rather than to reprove. "I incline to Cain's heresy," he used to say quaintly: "I let my brother go to the devil in his own way." In this character, it was frequently his fortune to be the last reputable acquaintance and the last good influence in the lives of downgoing men. And to such as these, so long as they came about his chambers, he never marked a shade of change in his demeanour.

No doubt the feat was easy to Mr. Utterson; for he was undemonstrative at the best, and even his friendship seemed to be founded in a similar catholicity of good-nature. It is the mark of a modest man to accept his friendly circle ready-made from the hands of opportunity; and that was the lawyer's way. His friends were those of his own blood or those whom he had known the longest; his affections, like ivy, were the growth of time, they implied no aptness in the object. Hence, no doubt the bond that united him to Mr. Richard Enfield, his distant kinsman, the well-known man about town. It was a nut to crack for many, what these two could see in each other, or what subject they could find in common. It was reported by those who encountered them in their Sunday walks, that they said nothing, looked singularly dull and would hail with obvious relief the appearance of a friend. For all that, the two men put the greatest store by these excursions, counted them the chief jewel of each week, and not only set aside occasions of pleasure, but even resisted the calls of business, that they might enjoy them uninterrupted.

It chanced on one of these rambles that their way led them down a by-street in a busy quarter of London. The street was small and what is called quiet, but it drove a thriving trade on the weekdays. The inhabitants were all doing well, it seemed and all emulously hoping to do better still, and laying out the surplus of their grains in coquetry; so that the shop fronts stood along that thoroughfare with an air of invitation, like rows of smiling saleswomen. Even on Sunday, when it veiled its more florid charms and lay comparatively empty of passage, the street shone out in contrast to its dingy neighbourhood, like a fire in a forest; and with its freshly painted shutters, well-polished brasses, and general cleanliness and gaiety of note, instantly caught and pleased the eye of the passenger.

Two doors from one corner, on the left hand going east the line was broken by the entry of a court; and just at that point a certain sinister block of building thrust forward its gable on the street. It was two storeys high; showed no window, nothing but a door on the lower storey and a blind forehead of discoloured wall on the upper; and bore in every feature, the marks of prolonged and sordid negligence. The door, which was equipped with neither bell nor knocker, was blistered and distained. Tramps slouched into the recess and struck matches on the panels; children kept shop upon the steps; the schoolboy had tried his knife on the mouldings; and for close on a generation, no one had appeared to drive away these random visitors or to repair their ravages.

Mr. Enfield and the lawyer were on the other side of the by-street; but when they came abreast of the entry, the former lifted up his cane and pointed.

"Did you ever remark that door?" he asked; and when his companion had replied in the affirmative. "It is connected in my mind," added he, "with a very odd story."

"Indeed?" said Mr. Utterson, with a slight change of voice, "and what was that?"

"Well, it was this way," returned Mr. Enfield: "I was coming home from some place at the end of the world, about three o'clock of a black winter morning, and my way lay through a part of town where there was literally nothing to be seen but lamps. Street after street and all the folks asleep—street after street, all lighted up as if for a procession and all as empty as a church—till at last I got into that state of mind when a man listens and listens and begins to long for the sight of a policeman. All at once, I saw two figures: one a little man who was stumping along eastward at a good walk, and the other a girl of maybe eight or ten who was running as hard as she was able down a cross street. Well, sir, the two ran into one another naturally enough at the corner; and then came the horrible part of the thing; for the man trampled calmly over the child's body and left her screaming on the ground. It sounds nothing to hear, but it was hellish to see. It wasn't like a man; it was like some damned Juggernaut. I gave a few halloa, took to my heels, collared my gentleman, and brought him back to where there was already quite a group about the screaming child. He was perfectly cool and made no resistance, but gave me one look, so ugly that it brought out the sweat on me like running. The people who had turned out were the girl's own family; and pretty soon, the doctor, for whom she had been sent put in his appearance. Well, the child was not much the worse, more frightened, according to the Sawbones; and there you might have supposed would be an end to it. But there was one curious circumstance. I had taken a loathing to my gentleman at first sight. So had the child's family, which was only natural. But the doctor's case was what struck me. He was the usual cut and dry apothecary, of no particular age and colour, with a strong Edinburgh accent and about as emotional as a bagpipe. Well, sir, he was like the rest of us; every time he looked at my prisoner, I saw that Sawbones turn sick and white with desire to kill him. I knew what was in his mind, just as he knew what was in mine; and killing being out of the question, we did the next best. We told the man we could and would make such a scandal out of this as should make his name stink from one end of London to the other. If he had any friends or any credit, we undertook that he should lose them. And all the time, as we were pitching it in red hot, we were keeping the women off him as best we could for they were as wild as harpies. I never saw a circle of such hateful faces; and there was the man in the middle, with a kind of black sneering coolness—frightened to, I could see that—but carrying it off, sir, really like Satan. 'If you choose to make capital out of this accident,' said he, 'I am naturally helpless. No gentleman but wishes to avoid a scene,' says he. 'Name your figure.' Well, we screwed him up to a hundred pounds for the child's family; he would have clearly liked to stick out; but there was something about the lot of us that meant mischief, and at last he struck. The next thing was to get the money; and where do you think he carried us but to that place with the door?—whipped out a key, went in, and presently came back with the matter of ten pounds in gold and a cheque for the balance on Coutts's, drawn payable to bearer and signed with a name that I can't mention, though it's one of the points of my story, but it was a name at least very well known and often printed. The figure was stiff; but the signature was good for more than that if it was only genuine. I took the liberty of pointing out to my gentleman that the whole business looked apocryphal, and that a man does not, in real life, walk into a cellar door at four in the morning and come out with another man's cheque for close upon a hundred pounds. But he was quite easy and sneering. 'Set your mind at rest,' says he, 'I will stay with you till the banks open and cash the cheque myself.' So we all set off, the doctor, and the child's father, and our friend and myself, and passed the rest of the night in my chambers; and next day, when we had breakfasted, went in a body to the bank. I gave in the cheque myself, and said I had every reason to believe it was a forgery. Not a bit of it. The cheque was genuine."

"Tut-tut," said Mr. Utterson.

"I see you feel as I do," said Mr. Enfield. "Yes, it's a bad story. For my man was a fellow that nobody could have to do with, a really damnable man; and the person that drew the cheque is the very pink of the proprieties, celebrated too, and (what makes it worse) one of your fellows who do what they call good. Black mail I suppose; an honest man paying through the nose for some of the capers of his youth. Black Mail House is what I call the place with the door, in consequence. Though even that, you know, is far from explaining all," he added, and with the words fell into a vein of musing.

From this he was recalled by Mr. Utterson asking rather suddenly: "And you don't know if the drawer of the cheque lives there?"

"A likely place, isn't it?" returned Mr. Enfield. "But I happen to have noticed his address; he lives in some square or other."

"And you never asked about the—place with the door?" said Mr. Utterson.

"No, sir: I had a delicacy," was the reply. "I feel very strongly about putting questions; it partakes too much of the style of the day of judgment. You start a question, and it's like starting a stone. You sit quietly on the top of a hill; and away the stone goes, starting others; and presently some bland old bird (the last you would have thought of) is knocked on the head in his own back garden and the family have to change their name. No sir, I make it a rule of mine: the more it looks like Queer Street, the less I ask."

"A very good rule, too," said the lawyer.

"But I have studied the place for myself," continued Mr. Enfield. "It seems scarcely a house. There is no other door, and nobody goes in or out of that one but, once in a great while, the gentleman of my adventure. There are three windows looking on the court on the first floor; none below; the windows are always shut but they're clean. And then there is a chimney which is generally smoking; so somebody must live there. And yet it's not so sure; for the buildings are so packed together about the court, that it's hard to say where one ends and another begins."

The pair walked on again for a while in silence; and then "Enfield," said Mr. Utterson, "that's a good rule of yours."

"Yes, I think it is," returned Enfield.

"But for all that," continued the lawyer, "there's one point I want to ask: I want to ask the name of that man who walked over the child."

"Well," said Mr. Enfield, "I can't see what harm it would do. It was a man of the name of Hyde."

"Hm," said Mr. Utterson. "What sort of a man is he to see?"

"He is not easy to describe. There is something wrong with his appearance; something displeasing, something down-right detestable. I never saw a man I so disliked, and yet I scarce know why. He must be deformed somewhere; he gives a strong feeling of deformity, although I couldn't specify the point. He's an extraordinary looking man, and yet I really can name nothing out of the way. No, sir; I can make no hand of it; I can't describe him. And it's not want of memory; for I declare I can see him this moment."

Mr. Utterson again walked some way in silence and obviously under a weight of consideration. "You are sure he used a key?" he inquired at last.

"My dear sir . . ." began Enfield, surprised out of himself.

"Yes, I know," said Utterson; "I know it must seem strange. The fact is, if I do not ask you the name of the other party, it is because I know it already. You see, Richard, your tale has gone home. If you have been inexact in any point you had better correct it."

"I think you might have warned me," returned the other with a touch of sullenness. "But I have been pedantically exact, as you call it. The fellow had a key; and what's more, he has it still. I saw him use it not a week ago."

Mr. Utterson sighed deeply but said never a word; and the young man presently resumed. "Here is another lesson to say nothing," said he. "I am ashamed of my long tongue. Let us make a bargain never to refer to this again."

"With all my heart," said the lawyer. I shake hands on that, Richard."

Search for Mr. Hyde

That evening Mr. Utterson came home to his bachelor house in sombre spirits and sat down to dinner without relish. It was his custom of a Sunday, when this meal was over, to sit close by the fire, a volume of some dry divinity on his reading desk, until the clock of the neighbouring church rang out the hour of twelve, when he would go soberly and gratefully to bed. On this night however, as soon as the cloth was taken away, he took up a candle and went into his business room. There he opened his safe, took from the most private part of it a document endorsed on the envelope as Dr. Jekyll's Will and sat down with a clouded brow to study its contents. The will was holograph, for Mr. Utterson though he took charge of it now that it was made, had refused to lend the least assistance in the making of it; it provided not only that, in case of the decease of Henry Jekyll, M.D., D.C.L., L.L.D., F.R.S., etc., all his possessions were to pass into the hands of his "friend and benefactor Edward Hyde," but that in case of Dr. Jekyll's "disappearance or unexplained absence for any period exceeding three calendar months," the said Edward Hyde should step into the said Henry Jekyll's shoes without further delay and free from any burthen or obligation beyond the payment of a few small sums to the members of the doctor's household. This document had long been the lawyer's eyesore. It offended him both as a lawyer and as a lover of the sane and customary sides of life, to whom the fanciful was the immodest. And hitherto it was his ignorance of Mr. Hyde that had swelled his indignation; now, by a sudden turn, it was his knowledge. It was already bad enough when the name was but a name of which he could learn no more. It was worse when it began to be clothed upon with detestable attributes; and out of the shifting, insubstantial mists that had so long baffled his eye, there leaped up the sudden, definite presentment of a fiend.

"I thought it was madness," he said, as he replaced the obnoxious paper in the safe, "and now I begin to fear it is disgrace."

With that he blew out his candle, put on a greatcoat, and set forth in the direction of Cavendish Square, that citadel of medicine, where his friend, the great Dr. Lanyon, had his house and received his crowding patients. "If anyone knows, it will be Lanyon," he had thought.

The solemn butler knew and welcomed him; he was subjected to no stage of delay, but ushered direct from the door to the dining-room where Dr. Lanyon sat alone over his wine. This was a hearty, healthy, dapper, red-faced gentleman, with a shock of hair prematurely white, and a boisterous and decided manner. At sight of Mr. Utterson, he sprang up from his chair and welcomed him with both hands. The geniality, as was the way of the man, was somewhat theatrical to the eye; but it reposed on genuine feeling. For these two were old friends, old mates both at school and college, both thorough respectors of themselves and of each other, and what does not always follow, men who thoroughly enjoyed each other's company.

After a little rambling talk, the lawyer led up to the subject which so disagreeably preoccupied his mind.

"I suppose, Lanyon," said he, "you and I must be the two oldest friends that Henry Jekyll has?"

"I wish the friends were younger," chuckled Dr. Lanyon. "But I suppose we are. And what of that? I see little of him now."

"Indeed?" said Utterson. "I thought you had a bond of common interest."

"We had," was the reply. "But it is more than ten years since Henry Jekyll became too fanciful for me. He began to go wrong, wrong in mind; and though of course I continue to take an interest in him for old sake's sake, as they say, I see and I have seen devilish little of the man. Such unscientific balderdash," added the doctor, flushing suddenly purple, "would have estranged Damon and Pythias."

This little spirit of temper was somewhat of a relief to Mr. Utterson. "They have only differed on some point of science," he thought; and being a man of no scientific passions (except in the matter of conveyancing), he even added: "It is nothing worse than that!" He gave his friend a few seconds to recover his composure, and then approached the question he had come to put. Did you ever come across a protege of his—one Hyde?" he asked.

"Hyde?" repeated Lanyon. "No. Never heard of him. Since my time."

That was the amount of information that the lawyer carried back with him to the great, dark bed on which he tossed to and fro, until the small hours of the morning began to grow large. It was a night of little ease to his toiling mind, toiling in mere darkness and beseiged by questions.

Six o'clock stuck on the bells of the church that was so conveniently near to Mr. Utterson's dwelling, and still he was digging at the problem. Hitherto it had touched him on the intellectual side alone; but now his imagination also was engaged, or rather enslaved; and as he lay and tossed in the gross darkness of the night and the curtained room, Mr. Enfield's tale went by before his mind in a scroll of lighted pictures. He would be aware of the great field of lamps of a nocturnal city; then of the figure of a man walking swiftly; then of a child running from the doctor's; and then these met, and that human Juggernaut trod the child down and passed on regardless of her screams. Or else he would see a room in a rich house, where his friend lay asleep, dreaming and smiling at his dreams; and then the door of that room would be opened, the curtains of the bed plucked apart, the sleeper recalled, and lo! there would stand by his side a figure to whom power was given, and even at that dead hour, he must rise and do its bidding. The figure in these two phases haunted the lawyer all night; and if at any time he dozed over, it was but to see it glide more stealthily through sleeping houses, or move the more swiftly and still the more swiftly, even to dizziness, through wider labyrinths of lamp-lighted city, and at every street corner crush a child and leave her screaming. And still the figure had no face by which he might know it; even in his dreams, it had no face, or one that baffled him and melted before his eyes; and thus it was that there sprang up and grew apace in the lawyer's mind a singularly strong, almost an inordinate, curiosity to behold the features of the real Mr. Hyde. If he could but once set eyes on him, he thought the mystery would lighten and perhaps roll altogether away, as was the habit of mysterious things when well examined. He might see a reason for his friend's strange preference or bondage (call it which you please) and even for the startling clause of the will. At least it would be a face worth seeing: the face of a man who was without bowels of mercy: a face which had but to show itself to raise up, in the mind of the unimpressionable Enfield, a spirit of enduring hatred.

From that time forward, Mr. Utterson began to haunt the door in the by-street of shops. In the morning before office hours, at noon when business was plenty, and time scarce, at night under the face of the fogged city moon, by all lights and at all hours of solitude or concourse, the lawyer was to be found on his chosen post.

"If he be Mr. Hyde," he had thought, "I shall be Mr. Seek."

And at last his patience was rewarded. It was a fine dry night; frost in the air; the streets as clean as a ballroom floor; the lamps, unshaken by any wind, drawing a regular pattern of light and shadow. By ten o'clock, when the shops were closed the by-street was very solitary and, in spite of the low growl of London from all round, very silent. Small sounds carried far; domestic sounds out of the houses were clearly audible on either side of the roadway; and the rumour of the approach of any passenger preceded him by a long time. Mr. Utterson had been some minutes at his post, when he was aware of an odd light footstep drawing near. In the course of his nightly patrols, he had long grown accustomed to the quaint effect with which the footfalls of a single person, while he is still a great way off, suddenly spring out distinct from the vast hum and clatter of the city. Yet his attention had never before been so sharply and decisively arrested; and it was with a strong, superstitious prevision of success that he withdrew into the entry of the court.

The steps drew swiftly nearer, and swelled out suddenly louder as they turned the end of the street. The lawyer, looking forth from the entry, could soon see what manner of man he had to deal with. He was small and very plainly dressed and the look of him, even at that distance, went somehow strongly against the watcher's inclination. But he made straight for the door, crossing the roadway to save time; and as he came, he drew a key from his pocket like one approaching home.

Mr. Utterson stepped out and touched him on the shoulder as he passed. "Mr. Hyde, I think?"

Mr. Hyde shrank back with a hissing intake of the breath. But his fear was only momentary; and though he did not look the lawyer in the face, he answered coolly enough: "That is my name. What do you want?"

"I see you are going in," returned the lawyer. "I am an old friend of Dr. Jekyll's—Mr. Utterson of Gaunt Street—you must have heard of my name; and meeting you so conveniently, I thought you might admit me."

"You will not find Dr. Jekyll; he is from home," replied Mr. Hyde, blowing in the key. And then suddenly, but still without looking up, "How did you know me?" he asked.

"On your side," said Mr. Utterson "will you do me a favour?"

"With pleasure," replied the other. "What shall it be?"

"Will you let me see your face?" asked the lawyer.

Mr. Hyde appeared to hesitate, and then, as if upon some sudden reflection, fronted about with an air of defiance; and the pair stared at each other pretty fixedly for a few seconds. "Now I shall know you again," said Mr. Utterson. "It may be useful."

"Yes," returned Mr. Hyde, "It is as well we have met; and apropos, you should have my address." And he gave a number of a street in Soho.

"Good God!" thought Mr. Utterson, "can he, too, have been thinking of the will?" But he kept his feelings to himself and only grunted in acknowledgment of the address.

"And now," said the other, "how did you know me?"

"By description," was the reply.

"Whose description?"

"We have common friends," said Mr. Utterson.

"Common friends," echoed Mr. Hyde, a little hoarsely. "Who are they?"

"Jekyll, for instance," said the lawyer.

"He never told you," cried Mr. Hyde, with a flush of anger. "I did not think you would have lied."

"Come," said Mr. Utterson, "that is not fitting language."

The other snarled aloud into a savage laugh; and the next moment, with extraordinary quickness, he had unlocked the door and disappeared into the house.

The lawyer stood awhile when Mr. Hyde had left him, the picture of disquietude. Then he began slowly to mount the street, pausing every step or two and putting his hand to his brow like a man in mental perplexity. The problem he was thus debating as he walked, was one of a class that is rarely solved. Mr. Hyde was pale and dwarfish, he gave an impression of deformity without any nameable malformation, he had a displeasing smile, he had borne himself to the lawyer with a sort of murderous mixture of timidity and boldness, and he spoke with a husky, whispering and somewhat broken voice; all these were points against him, but not all of these together could explain the hitherto unknown disgust, loathing and fear with which Mr. Utterson regarded him. "There must be something else," said the perplexed gentleman. "There is something more, if I could find a name for it. God bless me, the man seems hardly human! Something troglodytic, shall we say? or can it be the old story of Dr. Fell? or is it the mere radience of a foul soul that thus transpires through, and transfigures, its clay continent? The last,I think; for, O my poor old Harry Jekyll, if ever I read Satan's signature upon a face, it is on that of your new friend."

Round the corner from the by-street, there was a square of ancient, handsome houses, now for the most part decayed from their high estate and let in flats and chambers to all sorts and conditions of men; map-engravers, architects, shady lawyers and the agents of obscure enterprises. One house, however, second from the corner, was still occupied entire; and at the door of this, which wore a great air of wealth and comfort, though it was now plunged in darkness except for the fanlight, Mr. Utterson stopped and knocked. A well-dressed, elderly servant opened the door.

"Is Dr. Jekyll at home, Poole?" asked the lawyer.

"I will see, Mr. Utterson," said Poole, admitting the visitor, as he spoke, into a large, low-roofed, comfortable hall paved with flags, warmed (after the fashion of a country house) by a bright, open fire, and furnished with costly cabinets of oak. "Will you wait here by the fire, sir? or shall I give you a light in the dining-room?"

"Here, thank you," said the lawyer, and he drew near and leaned on the tall fender. This hall, in which he was now left alone, was a pet fancy of his friend the doctor's; and Utterson himself was wont to speak of it as the pleasantest room in London. But tonight there was a shudder in his blood; the face of Hyde sat heavy on his memory; he felt (what was rare with him) a nausea and distaste of life; and in the gloom of his spirits, he seemed to read a menace in the flickering of the firelight on the polished cabinets and the uneasy starting of the shadow on the roof. He was ashamed of his relief, when Poole presently returned to announce that Dr. Jekyll was gone out.

"I saw Mr. Hyde go in by the old dissecting room, Poole," he said. "Is that right, when Dr. Jekyll is from home?"

"Quite right, Mr. Utterson, sir," replied the servant. "Mr. Hyde has a key."

"Your master seems to repose a great deal of trust in that young man, Poole," resumed the other musingly.

"Yes, sir, he does indeed," said Poole. "We have all orders to obey him."

"I do not think I ever met Mr. Hyde?" asked Utterson.

"O, dear no, sir. He never dines here," replied the butler. Indeed we see very little of him on this side of the house; he mostly comes and goes by the laboratory."

"Well, good-night, Poole."

"Good-night, Mr. Utterson."

And the lawyer set out homeward with a very heavy heart. "Poor Harry Jekyll," he thought, "my mind misgives me he is in deep waters! He was wild when he was young; a long while ago to be sure; but in the law of God, there is no statute of limitations. Ay, it must be that; the ghost of some old sin, the cancer of some concealed disgrace: punishment coming, PEDE CLAUDO, years after memory has forgotten and self-love condoned the fault." And the lawyer, scared by the thought, brooded awhile on his own past, groping in all the corners of memory, least by chance some Jack-in-the-Box of an old iniquity should leap to light there. His past was fairly blameless; few men could read the rolls of their life with less apprehension; yet he was humbled to the dust by the many ill things he had done, and raised up again into a sober and fearful gratitude by the many he had come so near to doing yet avoided. And then by a return on his former subject, he conceived a spark of hope. "This Master Hyde, if he were studied," thought he, "must have secrets of his own; black secrets, by the look of him; secrets compared to which poor Jekyll's worst would be like sunshine. Things cannot continue as they are. It turns me cold to think of this creature stealing like a thief to Harry's bedside; poor Harry, what a wakening! And the danger of it; for if this Hyde suspects the existence of the will, he may grow impatient to inherit. Ay, I must put my shoulders to the wheel—if Jekyll will but let me," he added, "if Jekyll will only let me." For once more he saw before his mind's eye, as clear as transparency, the strange clauses of the will.

Dr. Jekyll Was Quite at Ease

A fortnight later, by excellent good fortune, the doctor gave one of his pleasant dinners to some five or six old cronies, all intelligent, reputable men and all judges of good wine; and Mr. Utterson so contrived that he remained behind after the others had departed. This was no new arrangement, but a thing that had befallen many scores of times. Where Utterson was liked, he was liked well. Hosts loved to detain the dry lawyer, when the light-hearted and loose-tongued had already their foot on the threshold; they liked to sit a while in his unobtrusive company, practising for solitude, sobering their minds in the man's rich silence after the expense and strain of gaiety. To this rule, Dr. Jekyll was no exception; and as he now sat on the opposite side of the fire—a large, well-made, smooth-faced man of fifty, with something of a stylish cast perhaps, but every mark of capacity and kindness—you could see by his looks that he cherished for Mr. Utterson a sincere and warm affection.

"I have been wanting to speak to you, Jekyll," began the latter. "You know that will of yours?"

A close observer might have gathered that the topic was distasteful; but the doctor carried it off gaily. "My poor Utterson," said he, "you are unfortunate in such a client. I never saw a man so distressed as you were by my will; unless it were that hide-bound pedant, Lanyon, at what he called my scientific heresies. O, I know he's a good fellow—you needn't frown—an excellent fellow, and I always mean to see more of him; but a hide-bound pedant for all that; an ignorant, blatant pedant. I was never more disappointed in any man than Lanyon."

"You know I never approved of it," pursued Utterson, ruthlessly disregarding the fresh topic.

"My will? Yes, certainly, I know that," said the doctor, a trifle sharply. "You have told me so."

"Well, I tell you so again," continued the lawyer. "I have been learning something of young Hyde."

The large handsome face of Dr. Jekyll grew pale to the very lips, and there came a blackness about his eyes. "I do not care to hear more," said he. "This is a matter I thought we had agreed to drop."

"What I heard was abominable," said Utterson.

"It can make no change. You do not understand my position," returned the doctor, with a certain incoherency of manner. "I am painfully situated, Utterson; my position is a very strange—a very strange one. It is one of those affairs that cannot be mended by talking."

"Jekyll," said Utterson, "you know me: I am a man to be trusted. Make a clean breast of this in confidence; and I make no doubt I can get you out of it."

"My good Utterson," said the doctor, "this is very good of you, this is downright good of you, and I cannot find words to thank you in. I believe you fully; I would trust you before any man alive, ay, before myself, if I could make the choice; but indeed it isn't what you fancy; it is not as bad as that; and just to put your good heart at rest, I will tell you one thing: the moment I choose, I can be rid of Mr. Hyde. I give you my hand upon that; and I thank you again and again; and I will just add one little word, Utterson, that I'm sure you'll take in good part: this is a private matter, and I beg of you to let it sleep."

Utterson reflected a little, looking in the fire.

"I have no doubt you are perfectly right," he said at last, getting to his feet.

"Well, but since we have touched upon this business, and for the last time I hope," continued the doctor, "there is one point I should like you to understand. I have really a very great interest in poor Hyde. I know you have seen him; he told me so; and I fear he was rude. But I do sincerely take a great, a very great interest in that young man; and if I am taken away, Utterson, I wish you to promise me that you will bear with him and get his rights for him. I think you would, if you knew all; and it would be a weight off my mind if you would promise."

"I can't pretend that I shall ever like him," said the lawyer.

"I don't ask that," pleaded Jekyll, laying his hand upon the other's arm; "I only ask for justice; I only ask you to help him for my sake, when I am no longer here."

Utterson heaved an irrepressible sigh. "Well," said he, "I promise."

The Carew Murder Case

Nearly a year later, in the month of October, 18—, London was startled by a crime of singular ferocity and rendered all the more notable by the high position of the victim. The details were few and startling. A maid servant living alone in a house not far from the river, had gone upstairs to bed about eleven. Although a fog rolled over the city in the small hours, the early part of the night was cloudless, and the lane, which the maid's window overlooked, was brilliantly lit by the full moon. It seems she was romantically given, for she sat down upon her box, which stood immediately under the window, and fell into a dream of musing. Never (she used to say, with streaming tears, when she narrated that experience), never had she felt more at peace with all men or thought more kindly of the world. And as she so sat she became aware of an aged beautiful gentleman with white hair, drawing near along the lane; and advancing to meet him, another and very small gentleman, to whom at first she paid less attention. When they had come within speech (which was just under the maid's eyes) the older man bowed and accosted the other with a very pretty manner of politeness. It did not seem as if the subject of his address were of great importance; indeed, from his pointing, it some times appeared as if he were only inquiring his way; but the moon shone on his face as he spoke, and the girl was pleased to watch it, it seemed to breathe such an innocent and old-world kindness of disposition, yet with something high too, as of a well-founded self-content. Presently her eye wandered to the other, and she was surprised to recognise in him a certain Mr. Hyde, who had once visited her master and for whom she had conceived a dislike. He had in his hand a heavy cane, with which he was trifling; but he answered never a word, and seemed to listen with an ill-contained impatience. And then all of a sudden he broke out in a great flame of anger, stamping with his foot, brandishing the cane, and carrying on (as the maid described it) like a madman. The old gentleman took a step back, with the air of one very much surprised and a trifle hurt; and at that Mr. Hyde broke out of all bounds and clubbed him to the earth. And next moment, with ape-like fury, he was trampling his victim under foot and hailing down a storm of blows, under which the bones were audibly shattered and the body jumped upon the roadway. At the horror of these sights and sounds, the maid fainted.

It was two o'clock when she came to herself and called for the police. The murderer was gone long ago; but there lay his victim in the middle of the lane, incredibly mangled. The stick with which the deed had been done, although it was of some rare and very tough and heavy wood, had broken in the middle under the stress of this insensate cruelty; and one splintered half had rolled in the neighbouring gutter—the other, without doubt, had been carried away by the murderer. A purse and gold watch were found upon the victim: but no cards or papers, except a sealed and stamped envelope, which he had been probably carrying to the post, and which bore the name and address of Mr. Utterson.

This was brought to the lawyer the next morning, before he was out of bed; and he had no sooner seen it and been told the circumstances, than he shot out a solemn lip. "I shall say nothing till I have seen the body," said he; "this may be very serious. Have the kindness to wait while I dress." And with the same grave countenance he hurried through his breakfast and drove to the police station, whither the body had been carried. As soon as he came into the cell, he nodded.

"Yes," said he, "I recognise him. I am sorry to say that this is Sir Danvers Carew."

"Good God, sir," exclaimed the officer, "is it possible?" And the next moment his eye lighted up with professional ambition. "This will make a deal of noise," he said. "And perhaps you can help us to the man." And he briefly narrated what the maid had seen, and showed the broken stick.

Mr. Utterson had already quailed at the name of Hyde; but when the stick was laid before him, he could doubt no longer; broken and battered as it was, he recognized it for one that he had himself presented many years before to Henry Jekyll.

"Is this Mr. Hyde a person of small stature?" he inquired.

"Particularly small and particularly wicked-looking, is what the maid calls him," said the officer.

Mr. Utterson reflected; and then, raising his head, "If you will come with me in my cab," he said, "I think I can take you to his house."

It was by this time about nine in the morning, and the first fog of the season. A great chocolate-coloured pall lowered over heaven, but the wind was continually charging and routing these embattled vapours; so that as the cab crawled from street to street, Mr. Utterson beheld a marvelous number of degrees and hues of twilight; for here it would be dark like the back-end of evening; and there would be a glow of a rich, lurid brown, like the light of some strange conflagration; and here, for a moment, the fog would be quite broken up, and a haggard shaft of daylight would glance in between the swirling wreaths. The dismal quarter of Soho seen under these changing glimpses, with its muddy ways, and slatternly passengers, and its lamps, which had never been extinguished or had been kindled afresh to combat this mournful reinvasion of darkness, seemed, in the lawyer's eyes, like a district of some city in a nightmare. The thoughts of his mind, besides, were of the gloomiest dye; and when he glanced at the companion of his drive, he was conscious of some touch of that terror of the law and the law's officers, which may at times assail the most honest.

As the cab drew up before the address indicated, the fog lifted a little and showed him a dingy street, a gin palace, a low French eating house, a shop for the retail of penny numbers and twopenny salads, many ragged children huddled in the doorways, and many women of many different nationalities passing out, key in hand, to have a morning glass; and the next moment the fog settled down again upon that part, as brown as umber, and cut him off from his blackguardly surroundings. This was the home of Henry Jekyll's favourite; of a man who was heir to a quarter of a million sterling.

An ivory-faced and silvery-haired old woman opened the door. She had an evil face, smoothed by hypocrisy: but her manners were excellent. Yes, she said, this was Mr. Hyde's, but he was not at home; he had been in that night very late, but he had gone away again in less than an hour; there was nothing strange in that; his habits were very irregular, and he was often absent; for instance, it was nearly two months since she had seen him till yesterday.

"Very well, then, we wish to see his rooms," said the lawyer; and when the woman began to declare it was impossible, "I had better tell you who this person is," he added. "This is Inspector Newcomen of Scotland Yard."

A flash of odious joy appeared upon the woman's face. "Ah!" said she, "he is in trouble! What has he done?"

Mr. Utterson and the inspector exchanged glances. "He don't seem a very popular character," observed the latter. "And now, my good woman, just let me and this gentleman have a look about us."

In the whole extent of the house, which but for the old woman remained otherwise empty, Mr. Hyde had only used a couple of rooms; but these were furnished with luxury and good taste. A closet was filled with wine; the plate was of silver, the napery elegant; a good picture hung upon the walls, a gift (as Utterson supposed) from Henry Jekyll, who was much of a connoisseur; and the carpets were of many plies and agreeable in colour. At this moment, however, the rooms bore every mark of having been recently and hurriedly ransacked; clothes lay about the floor, with their pockets inside out; lock-fast drawers stood open; and on the hearth there lay a pile of grey ashes, as though many papers had been burned. From these embers the inspector disinterred the butt end of a green cheque book, which had resisted the action of the fire; the other half of the stick was found behind the door; and as this clinched his suspicions, the officer declared himself delighted. A visit to the bank, where several thousand pounds were found to be lying to the murderer's credit, completed his gratification.

"You may depend upon it, sir," he told Mr. Utterson: "I have him in my hand. He must have lost his head, or he never would have left the stick or, above all, burned the cheque book. Why, money's life to the man. We have nothing to do but wait for him at the bank, and get out the handbills."

This last, however, was not so easy of accomplishment; for Mr. Hyde had numbered few familiars—even the master of the servant maid had only seen him twice; his family could nowhere be traced; he had never been photographed; and the few who could describe him differed widely, as common observers will. Only on one point were they agreed; and that was the haunting sense of unexpressed deformity with which the fugitive impressed his beholders.

Incident of the Letter

It was late in the afternoon, when Mr. Utterson found his way to Dr. Jekyll's door, where he was at once admitted by Poole, and carried down by the kitchen offices and across a yard which had once been a garden, to the building which was indifferently known as the laboratory or dissecting rooms. The doctor had bought the house from the heirs of a celebrated surgeon; and his own tastes being rather chemical than anatomical, had changed the destination of the block at the bottom of the garden. It was the first time that the lawyer had been received in that part of his friend's quarters; and he eyed the dingy, windowless structure with curiosity, and gazed round with a distasteful sense of strangeness as he crossed the theatre, once crowded with eager students and now lying gaunt and silent, the tables laden with chemical apparatus, the floor strewn with crates and littered with packing straw, and the light falling dimly through the foggy cupola. At the further end, a flight of stairs mounted to a door covered with red baize; and through this, Mr. Utterson was at last received into the doctor's cabinet. It was a large room fitted round with glass presses, furnished, among other things, with a cheval-glass and a business table, and looking out upon the court by three dusty windows barred with iron. The fire burned in the grate; a lamp was set lighted on the chimney shelf, for even in the houses the fog began to lie thickly; and there, close up to the warmth, sat Dr. Jekyll, looking deathly sick. He did not rise to meet his visitor, but held out a cold hand and bade him welcome in a changed voice.

"And now," said Mr. Utterson, as soon as Poole had left them, "you have heard the news?"

The doctor shuddered. "They were crying it in the square," he said. "I heard them in my dining-room."

"One word," said the lawyer. "Carew was my client, but so are you, and I want to know what I am doing. You have not been mad enough to hide this fellow?"

"Utterson, I swear to God," cried the doctor, "I swear to God I will never set eyes on him again. I bind my honour to you that I am done with him in this world. It is all at an end. And indeed he does not want my help; you do not know him as I do; he is safe, he is quite safe; mark my words, he will never more be heard of."

The lawyer listened gloomily; he did not like his friend's feverish manner. "You seem pretty sure of him," said he; "and for your sake, I hope you may be right. If it came to a trial, your name might appear."

"I am quite sure of him," replied Jekyll; "I have grounds for certainty that I cannot share with any one. But there is one thing on which you may advise me. I have—I have received a letter; and I am at a loss whether I should show it to the police. I should like to leave it in your hands, Utterson; you would judge wisely, I am sure; I have so great a trust in you."

"You fear, I suppose, that it might lead to his detection?" asked the lawyer.

"No," said the other. "I cannot say that I care what becomes of Hyde; I am quite done with him. I was thinking of my own character, which this hateful business has rather exposed."

Utterson ruminated awhile; he was surprised at his friend's selfishness, and yet relieved by it. "Well," said he, at last, let me see the letter."

The letter was written in an odd, upright hand and signed "Edward Hyde": and it signified, briefly enough, that the writer's benefactor, Dr. Jekyll, whom he had long so unworthily repaid for a thousand generosities, need labour under no alarm for his safety, as he had means of escape on which he placed a sure dependence. The lawyer liked this letter well enough; it put a better colour on the intimacy than he had looked for; and he blamed himself for some of his past suspicions.

"Have you the envelope?" he asked.

"I burned it," replied Jekyll, "before I thought what I was about. But it bore no postmark. The note was handed in."

"Shall I keep this and sleep upon it?" asked Utterson.

"I wish you to judge for me entirely," was the reply. "I have lost confidence in myself."

"Well, I shall consider," returned the lawyer. "And now one word more: it was Hyde who dictated the terms in your will about that disappearance?"

The doctor seemed seized with a qualm of faintness; he shut his mouth tight and nodded.

"I knew it," said Utterson. "He meant to murder you. You had a fine escape."

"I have had what is far more to the purpose," returned the doctor solemnly: "I have had a lesson—O God, Utterson, what a lesson I have had!" And he covered his face for a moment with his hands.

On his way out, the lawyer stopped and had a word or two with Poole. "By the bye," said he, "there was a letter handed in to-day: what was the messenger like?" But Poole was positive nothing had come except by post; "and only circulars by that," he added.

This news sent off the visitor with his fears renewed. Plainly the letter had come by the laboratory door; possibly, indeed, it had been written in the cabinet; and if that were so, it must be differently judged, and handled with the more caution. The newsboys, as he went, were crying themselves hoarse along the footways: "Special edition. Shocking murder of an M.P." That was the funeral oration of one friend and client; and he could not help a certain apprehension lest the good name of another should be sucked down in the eddy of the scandal. It was, at least, a ticklish decision that he had to make; and self-reliant as he was by habit, he began to cherish a longing for advice. It was not to be had directly; but perhaps, he thought, it might be fished for.

Presently after, he sat on one side of his own hearth, with Mr. Guest, his head clerk, upon the other, and midway between, at a nicely calculated distance from the fire, a bottle of a particular old wine that had long dwelt unsunned in the foundations of his house. The fog still slept on the wing above the drowned city, where the lamps glimmered like carbuncles; and through the muffle and smother of these fallen clouds, the procession of the town's life was still rolling in through the great arteries with a sound as of a mighty wind. But the room was gay with firelight. In the bottle the acids were long ago resolved; the imperial dye had softened with time, as the colour grows richer in stained windows; and the glow of hot autumn afternoons on hillside vineyards, was ready to be set free and to disperse the fogs of London. Insensibly the lawyer melted. There was no man from whom he kept fewer secrets than Mr. Guest; and he was not always sure that he kept as many as he meant. Guest had often been on business to the doctor's; he knew Poole; he could scarce have failed to hear of Mr. Hyde's familiarity about the house; he might draw conclusions: was it not as well, then, that he should see a letter which put that mystery to right? and above all since Guest, being a great student and critic of handwriting, would consider the step natural and obliging? The clerk, besides, was a man of counsel; he could scarce read so strange a document without dropping a remark; and by that remark Mr. Utterson might shape his future course.

"This is a sad business about Sir Danvers," he said.

"Yes, sir, indeed. It has elicited a great deal of public feeling," returned Guest. "The man, of course, was mad."

"I should like to hear your views on that," replied Utterson. "I have a document here in his handwriting; it is between ourselves, for I scarce know what to do about it; it is an ugly business at the best. But there it is; quite in your way: a murderer's autograph."

Guest's eyes brightened, and he sat down at once and studied it with passion. "No sir," he said: "not mad; but it is an odd hand."

"And by all accounts a very odd writer," added the lawyer.

Just then the servant entered with a note.

"Is that from Dr. Jekyll, sir?" inquired the clerk. "I thought I knew the writing. Anything private, Mr. Utterson?

"Only an invitation to dinner. Why? Do you want to see it?"

"One moment. I thank you, sir;" and the clerk laid the two sheets of paper alongside and sedulously compared their contents. "Thank you, sir," he said at last, returning both; "it's a very interesting autograph."

There was a pause, during which Mr. Utterson struggled with himself. "Why did you compare them, Guest?" he inquired suddenly.

"Well, sir," returned the clerk, "there's a rather singular resemblance; the two hands are in many points identical: only differently sloped."

"Rather quaint," said Utterson.

"It is, as you say, rather quaint," returned Guest.

"I wouldn't speak of this note, you know," said the master.

"No, sir," said the clerk. "I understand."

But no sooner was Mr. Utterson alone that night, than he locked the note into his safe, where it reposed from that time forward. "What!" he thought. "Henry Jekyll forge for a murderer!" And his blood ran cold in his veins.

Remarkable Incident of Dr. Lanyon

Time ran on; thousands of pounds were offered in reward, for the death of Sir Danvers was resented as a public injury; but Mr. Hyde had disappeared out of the ken of the police as though he had never existed. Much of his past was unearthed, indeed, and all disreputable: tales came out of the man's cruelty, at once so callous and violent; of his vile life, of his strange associates, of the hatred that seemed to have surrounded his career; but of his present whereabouts, not a whisper. From the time he had left the house in Soho on the morning of the murder, he was simply blotted out; and gradually, as time drew on, Mr. Utterson began to recover from the hotness of his alarm, and to grow more at quiet with himself. The death of Sir Danvers was, to his way of thinking, more than paid for by the disappearance of Mr. Hyde. Now that that evil influence had been withdrawn, a new life began for Dr. Jekyll. He came out of his seclusion, renewed relations with his friends, became once more their familiar guest and entertainer; and whilst he had always been known for charities, he was now no less distinguished for religion. He was busy, he was much in the open air, he did good; his face seemed to open and brighten, as if with an inward consciousness of service; and for more than two months, the doctor was at peace.

On the 8th of January Utterson had dined at the doctor's with a small party; Lanyon had been there; and the face of the host had looked from one to the other as in the old days when the trio were inseparable friends. On the 12th, and again on the 14th, the door was shut against the lawyer. "The doctor was confined to the house," Poole said, "and saw no one." On the 15th, he tried again, and was again refused; and having now been used for the last two months to see his friend almost daily, he found this return of solitude to weigh upon his spirits. The fifth night he had in Guest to dine with him; and the sixth he betook himself to Dr. Lanyon's.

There at least he was not denied admittance; but when he came in, he was shocked at the change which had taken place in the doctor's appearance. He had his death-warrant written legibly upon his face. The rosy man had grown pale; his flesh had fallen away; he was visibly balder and older; and yet it was not so much these tokens of a swift physical decay that arrested the lawyer's notice, as a look in the eye and quality of manner that seemed to testify to some deep-seated terror of the mind. It was unlikely that the doctor should fear death; and yet that was what Utterson was tempted to suspect. "Yes," he thought; he is a doctor, he must know his own state and that his days are counted; and the knowledge is more than he can bear." And yet when Utterson remarked on his ill-looks, it was with an air of great firmness that Lanyon declared himself a doomed man.

"I have had a shock," he said, "and I shall never recover. It is a question of weeks. Well, life has been pleasant; I liked it; yes, sir, I used to like it. I sometimes think if we knew all, we should be more glad to get away."

"Jekyll is ill, too," observed Utterson. "Have you seen him?"

But Lanyon's face changed, and he held up a trembling hand. "I wish to see or hear no more of Dr. Jekyll," he said in a loud, unsteady voice. "I am quite done with that person; and I beg that you will spare me any allusion to one whom I regard as dead."

"Tut-tut," said Mr. Utterson; and then after a considerable pause, "Can't I do anything?" he inquired. "We are three very old friends, Lanyon; we shall not live to make others."

"Nothing can be done," returned Lanyon; "ask himself."

"He will not see me," said the lawyer.

"I am not surprised at that," was the reply. "Some day, Utterson, after I am dead, you may perhaps come to learn the right and wrong of this. I cannot tell you. And in the meantime, if you can sit and talk with me of other things, for God's sake, stay and do so; but if you cannot keep clear of this accursed topic, then in God's name, go, for I cannot bear it."

As soon as he got home, Utterson sat down and wrote to Jekyll, complaining of his exclusion from the house, and asking the cause of this unhappy break with Lanyon; and the next day brought him a long answer, often very pathetically worded, and sometimes darkly mysterious in drift. The quarrel with Lanyon was incurable. "I do not blame our old friend," Jekyll wrote, but I share his view that we must never meet. I mean from henceforth to lead a life of extreme seclusion; you must not be surprised, nor must you doubt my friendship, if my door is often shut even to you. You must suffer me to go my own dark way. I have brought on myself a punishment and a danger that I cannot name. If I am the chief of sinners, I am the chief of sufferers also. I could not think that this earth contained a place for sufferings and terrors so unmanning; and you can do but one thing, Utterson, to lighten this destiny, and that is to respect my silence." Utterson was amazed; the dark influence of Hyde had been withdrawn, the doctor had returned to his old tasks and amities; a week ago, the prospect had smiled with every promise of a cheerful and an honoured age; and now in a moment, friendship, and peace of mind, and the whole tenor of his life were wrecked. So great and unprepared a change pointed to madness; but in view of Lanyon's manner and words, there must lie for it some deeper ground.

A week afterwards Dr. Lanyon took to his bed, and in something less than a fortnight he was dead. The night after the funeral, at which he had been sadly affected, Utterson locked the door of his business room, and sitting there by the light of a melancholy candle, drew out and set before him an envelope addressed by the hand and sealed with the seal of his dead friend. "PRIVATE: for the hands of G. J. Utterson ALONE, and in case of his predecease to be destroyed unread," so it was emphatically superscribed; and the lawyer dreaded to behold the contents. "I have buried one friend to-day," he thought: "what if this should cost me another?" And then he condemned the fear as a disloyalty, and broke the seal. Within there was another enclosure, likewise sealed, and marked upon the cover as "not to be opened till the death or disappearance of Dr. Henry Jekyll." Utterson could not trust his eyes. Yes, it was disappearance; here again, as in the mad will which he had long ago restored to its author, here again were the idea of a disappearance and the name of Henry Jekyll bracketted. But in the will, that idea had sprung from the sinister suggestion of the man Hyde; it was set there with a purpose all too plain and horrible. Written by the hand of Lanyon, what should it mean? A great curiosity came on the trustee, to disregard the prohibition and dive at once to the bottom of these mysteries; but professional honour and faith to his dead friend were stringent obligations; and the packet slept in the inmost corner of his private safe.

It is one thing to mortify curiosity, another to conquer it; and it may be doubted if, from that day forth, Utterson desired the society of his surviving friend with the same eagerness. He thought of him kindly; but his thoughts were disquieted and fearful. He went to call indeed; but he was perhaps relieved to be denied admittance; perhaps, in his heart, he preferred to speak with Poole upon the doorstep and surrounded by the air and sounds of the open city, rather than to be admitted into that house of voluntary bondage, and to sit and speak with its inscrutable recluse. Poole had, indeed, no very pleasant news to communicate. The doctor, it appeared, now more than ever confined himself to the cabinet over the laboratory, where he would sometimes even sleep; he was out of spirits, he had grown very silent, he did not read; it seemed as if he had something on his mind. Utterson became so used to the unvarying character of these reports, that he fell off little by little in the frequency of his visits.

Incident at the Window

It chanced on Sunday, when Mr. Utterson was on his usual walk with Mr. Enfield, that their way lay once again through the by-street; and that when they came in front of the door, both stopped to gaze on it.

"Well," said Enfield, "that story's at an end at least. We shall never see more of Mr. Hyde."

"I hope not," said Utterson. "Did I ever tell you that I once saw him, and shared your feeling of repulsion?"

"It was impossible to do the one without the other," returned Enfield. "And by the way, what an ass you must have thought me, not to know that this was a back way to Dr. Jekyll's! It was partly your own fault that I found it out, even when I did."

"So you found it out, did you?" said Utterson.

"But if that be so, we may step into the court and take a look at the windows. To tell you the truth, I am uneasy about poor Jekyll; and even outside, I feel as if the presence of a friend might do him good."

The court was very cool and a little damp, and full of premature twilight, although the sky, high up overhead, was still bright with sunset. The middle one of the three windows was half-way open; and sitting close beside it, taking the air with an infinite sadness of mien, like some disconsolate prisoner, Utterson saw Dr. Jekyll.

"What! Jekyll!" he cried. "I trust you are better."

"I am very low, Utterson," replied the doctor drearily, "very low. It will not last long, thank God."

"You stay too much indoors," said the lawyer. "You should be out, whipping up the circulation like Mr. Enfield and me. (This is my cousin—Mr. Enfield—Dr. Jekyll.) Come now; get your hat and take a quick turn with us."

"You are very good," sighed the other. "I should like to very much; but no, no, no, it is quite impossible; I dare not. But indeed, Utterson, I am very glad to see you; this is really a great pleasure; I would ask you and Mr. Enfield up, but the place is really not fit."

"Why, then," said the lawyer, good-naturedly, "the best thing we can do is to stay down here and speak with you from where we are."

"That is just what I was about to venture to propose," returned the doctor with a smile. But the words were hardly uttered, before the smile was struck out of his face and succeeded by an expression of such abject terror and despair, as froze the very blood of the two gentlemen below. They saw it but for a glimpse for the window was instantly thrust down; but that glimpse had been sufficient, and they turned and left the court without a word. In silence, too, they traversed the by-street; and it was not until they had come into a neighbouring thoroughfare, where even upon a Sunday there were still some stirrings of life, that Mr. Utterson at last turned and looked at his companion. They were both pale; and there was an answering horror in their eyes.

"God forgive us, God forgive us," said Mr. Utterson.

But Mr. Enfield only nodded his head very seriously, and walked on once more in silence.

The Last Night

Mr. Utterson was sitting by his fireside one evening after dinner, when he was surprised to receive a visit from Poole.

"Bless me, Poole, what brings you here?" he cried; and then taking a second look at him, "What ails you?" he added; is the doctor ill?"

"Mr. Utterson," said the man, "there is something wrong."

"Take a seat, and here is a glass of wine for you," said the lawyer. "Now, take your time, and tell me plainly what you want."

"You know the doctor's ways, sir," replied Poole, "and how he shuts himself up. Well, he's shut up again in the cabinet; and I don't like it, sir—I wish I may die if I like it. Mr. Utterson, sir, I'm afraid."

"Now, my good man," said the lawyer, "be explicit. What are you afraid of?"

"I've been afraid for about a week," returned Poole, doggedly disregarding the question, "and I can bear it no more."

The man's appearance amply bore out his words; his manner was altered for the worse; and except for the moment when he had first announced his terror, he had not once looked the lawyer in the face. Even now, he sat with the glass of wine untasted on his knee, and his eyes directed to a corner of the floor. "I can bear it no more," he repeated.

"Come," said the lawyer, "I see you have some good reason, Poole; I see there is something seriously amiss. Try to tell me what it is."

"I think there's been foul play," said Poole, hoarsely.

"Foul play!" cried the lawyer, a good deal frightened and rather inclined to be irritated in consequence. "What foul play! What does the man mean?"

"I daren't say, sir," was the answer; but will you come along with me and see for yourself?"

Mr. Utterson's only answer was to rise and get his hat and greatcoat; but he observed with wonder the greatness of the relief that appeared upon the butler's face, and perhaps with no less, that the wine was still untasted when he set it down to follow.

It was a wild, cold, seasonable night of March, with a pale moon, lying on her back as though the wind had tilted her, and flying wrack of the most diaphanous and lawny texture. The wind made talking difficult, and flecked the blood into the face. It seemed to have swept the streets unusually bare of passengers, besides; for Mr. Utterson thought he had never seen that part of London so deserted. He could have wished it otherwise; never in his life had he been conscious of so sharp a wish to see and touch his fellow-creatures; for struggle as he might, there was borne in upon his mind a crushing anticipation of calamity. The square, when they got there, was full of wind and dust, and the thin trees in the garden were lashing themselves along the railing. Poole, who had kept all the way a pace or two ahead, now pulled up in the middle of the pavement, and in spite of the biting weather, took off his hat and mopped his brow with a red pocket-handkerchief. But for all the hurry of his coming, these were not the dews of exertion that he wiped away, but the moisture of some strangling anguish; for his face was white and his voice, when he spoke, harsh and broken.

"Well, sir," he said, "here we are, and God grant there be nothing wrong."

"Amen, Poole," said the lawyer.

Thereupon the servant knocked in a very guarded manner; the door was opened on the chain; and a voice asked from within, "Is that you, Poole?"

"It's all right," said Poole. "Open the door."

The hall, when they entered it, was brightly lighted up; the fire was built high; and about the hearth the whole of the servants, men and women, stood huddled together like a flock of sheep. At the sight of Mr. Utterson, the housemaid broke into hysterical whimpering; and the cook, crying out "Bless God! it's Mr. Utterson," ran forward as if to take him in her arms.

"What, what? Are you all here?" said the lawyer peevishly. "Very irregular, very unseemly; your master would be far from pleased."

"They're all afraid," said Poole.

Blank silence followed, no one protesting; only the maid lifted her voice and now wept loudly.

"Hold your tongue!" Poole said to her, with a ferocity of accent that testified to his own jangled nerves; and indeed, when the girl had so suddenly raised the note of her lamentation, they had all started and turned towards the inner door with faces of dreadful expectation. "And now," continued the butler, addressing the knife-boy, "reach me a candle, and we'll get this through hands at once." And then he begged Mr. Utterson to follow him, and led the way to the back garden.

"Now, sir," said he, "you come as gently as you can. I want you to hear, and I don't want you to be heard. And see here, sir, if by any chance he was to ask you in, don't go."

Mr. Utterson's nerves, at this unlooked-for termination, gave a jerk that nearly threw him from his balance; but he recollected his courage and followed the butler into the laboratory building through the surgical theatre, with its lumber of crates and bottles, to the foot of the stair. Here Poole motioned him to stand on one side and listen; while he himself, setting down the candle and making a great and obvious call on his resolution, mounted the steps and knocked with a somewhat uncertain hand on the red baize of the cabinet door.

"Mr. Utterson, sir, asking to see you," he called; and even as he did so, once more violently signed to the lawyer to give ear.

A voice answered from within: "Tell him I cannot see anyone," it said complainingly.

"Thank you, sir," said Poole, with a note of something like triumph in his voice; and taking up his candle, he led Mr. Utterson back across the yard and into the great kitchen, where the fire was out and the beetles were leaping on the floor.

"Sir," he said, looking Mr. Utterson in the eyes, "Was that my master's voice?"

"It seems much changed," replied the lawyer, very pale, but giving look for look.

"Changed? Well, yes, I think so," said the butler. "Have I been twenty years in this man's house, to be deceived about his voice? No, sir; master's made away with; he was made away with eight days ago, when we heard him cry out upon the name of God; and who's in there instead of him, and why it stays there, is a thing that cries to Heaven, Mr. Utterson!"

"This is a very strange tale, Poole; this is rather a wild tale my man," said Mr. Utterson, biting his finger. "Suppose it were as you suppose, supposing Dr. Jekyll to have been—well, murdered what could induce the murderer to stay? That won't hold water; it doesn't commend itself to reason."

"Well, Mr. Utterson, you are a hard man to satisfy, but I'll do it yet," said Poole. "All this last week (you must know) him, or it, whatever it is that lives in that cabinet, has been crying night and day for some sort of medicine and cannot get it to his mind. It was sometimes his way—the master's, that is—to write his orders on a sheet of paper and throw it on the stair. We've had nothing else this week back; nothing but papers, and a closed door, and the very meals left there to be smuggled in when nobody was looking.

Well, sir, every day, ay, and twice and thrice in the same day, there have been orders and complaints, and I have been sent flying to all the wholesale chemists in town. Every time I brought the stuff back, there would be another paper telling me to return it, because it was not pure, and another order to a different firm. This drug is wanted bitter bad, sir, whatever for."

"Have you any of these papers?" asked Mr. Utterson.

Poole felt in his pocket and handed out a crumpled note, which the lawyer, bending nearer to the candle, carefully examined. Its contents ran thus: "Dr. Jekyll presents his compliments to Messrs. Maw. He assures them that their last sample is impure and quite useless for his present purpose. In the year 18—, Dr. J. purchased a somewhat large quantity from Messrs. M. He now begs them to search with most sedulous care, and should any of the same quality be left, forward it to him at once. Expense is no consideration. The importance of this to Dr. J. can hardly be exaggerated." So far the letter had run composedly enough, but here with a sudden splutter of the pen, the writer's emotion had broken loose. "For God's sake," he added, "find me some of the old."

"This is a strange note," said Mr. Utterson; and then sharply, "How do you come to have it open?"

"The man at Maw's was main angry, sir, and he threw it back to me like so much dirt," returned Poole.

"This is unquestionably the doctor's hand, do you know?" resumed the lawyer.

"I thought it looked like it," said the servant rather sulkily; and then, with another voice, "But what matters hand of write?" he said. "I've seen him!"

"Seen him?" repeated Mr. Utterson. "Well?"

"That's it!" said Poole. "It was this way. I came suddenly into the theater from the garden. It seems he had slipped out to look for this drug or whatever it is; for the cabinet door was open, and there he was at the far end of the room digging among the crates. He looked up when I came in, gave a kind of cry, and whipped upstairs into the cabinet. It was but for one minute that I saw him, but the hair stood upon my head like quills. Sir, if that was my master, why had he a mask upon his face? If it was my master, why did he cry out like a rat, and run from me? I have served him long enough. And then . . ." The man paused and passed his hand over his face.

"These are all very strange circumstances," said Mr. Utterson, "but I think I begin to see daylight. Your master, Poole, is plainly seized with one of those maladies that both torture and deform the sufferer; hence, for aught I know, the alteration of his voice; hence the mask and the avoidance of his friends; hence his eagerness to find this drug, by means of which the poor soul retains some hope of ultimate recovery—God grant that he be not deceived! There is my explanation; it is sad enough, Poole, ay, and appalling to consider; but it is plain and natural, hangs well together, and delivers us from all exorbitant alarms."

"Sir," said the butler, turning to a sort of mottled pallor, "that thing was not my master, and there's the truth. My master"—here he looked round him and began to whisper— "is a tall, fine build of a man, and this was more of a dwarf." Utterson attempted to protest. "O, sir," cried Poole, "do you think I do not know my master after twenty years? Do you think I do not know where his head comes to in the cabinet door, where I saw him every morning of my life? No, sir, that thing in the mask was never Dr. Jekyll—God knows what it was, but it was never Dr. Jekyll; and it is the belief of my heart that there was murder done."

"Poole," replied the lawyer, "if you say that, it will become my duty to make certain. Much as I desire to spare your master's feelings, much as I am puzzled by this note which seems to prove him to be still alive, I shall consider it my duty to break in that door."

"Ah, Mr. Utterson, that's talking!" cried the butler.

"And now comes the second question," resumed Utterson: "Who is going to do it?"

"Why, you and me, sir," was the undaunted reply.

"That's very well said," returned the lawyer; "and whatever comes of it, I shall make it my business to see you are no loser."

"There is an axe in the theatre," continued Poole; "and you might take the kitchen poker for yourself."

The lawyer took that rude but weighty instrument into his hand, and balanced it. "Do you know, Poole," he said, looking up, "that you and I are about to place ourselves in a position of some peril?"

"You may say so, sir, indeed," returned the butler.

"It is well, then that we should be frank," said the other. "We both think more than we have said; let us make a clean breast. This masked figure that you saw, did you recognise it?"

"Well, sir, it went so quick, and the creature was so doubled up, that I could hardly swear to that," was the answer. "But if you mean, was it Mr. Hyde?—why, yes, I think it was! You see, it was much of the same bigness; and it had the same quick, light way with it; and then who else could have got in by the laboratory door? You have not forgot, sir, that at the time of the murder he had still the key with him? But that's not all. I don't know, Mr. Utterson, if you ever met this Mr. Hyde?"

"Yes," said the lawyer, "I once spoke with him."

"Then you must know as well as the rest of us that there was something queer about that gentleman—something that gave a man a turn—I don't know rightly how to say it, sir, beyond this: that you felt in your marrow kind of cold and thin."

"I own I felt something of what you describe," said Mr. Utterson.

"Quite so, sir," returned Poole. "Well, when that masked thing like a monkey jumped from among the chemicals and whipped into the cabinet, it went down my spine like ice. O, I know it's not evidence, Mr. Utterson; I'm book-learned enough for that; but a man has his feelings, and I give you my bible-word it was Mr. Hyde!"

"Ay, ay," said the lawyer. "My fears incline to the same point. Evil, I fear, founded—evil was sure to come—of that connection. Ay truly, I believe you; I believe poor Harry is killed; and I believe his murderer (for what purpose, God alone can tell) is still lurking in his victim's room. Well, let our name be vengeance. Call Bradshaw."

The footman came at the summons, very white and nervous.

"Put yourself together, Bradshaw," said the lawyer. "This suspense, I know, is telling upon all of you; but it is now our intention to make an end of it. Poole, here, and I are going to force our way into the cabinet. If all is well, my shoulders are broad enough to bear the blame. Meanwhile, lest anything should really be amiss, or any malefactor seek to escape by the back, you and the boy must go round the corner with a pair of good sticks and take your post at the laboratory door. We give you ten minutes, to get to your stations."

As Bradshaw left, the lawyer looked at his watch. "And now, Poole, let us get to ours," he said; and taking the poker under his arm, led the way into the yard. The scud had banked over the moon, and it was now quite dark. The wind, which only broke in puffs and draughts into that deep well of building, tossed the light of the candle to and fro about their steps, until they came into the shelter of the theatre, where they sat down silently to wait. London hummed solemnly all around; but nearer at hand, the stillness was only broken by the sounds of a footfall moving to and fro along the cabinet floor.

"So it will walk all day, sir," whispered Poole; "ay, and the better part of the night. Only when a new sample comes from the chemist, there's a bit of a break. Ah, it's an ill conscience that's such an enemy to rest! Ah, sir, there's blood foully shed in every step of it! But hark again, a little closer—put your heart in your ears, Mr. Utterson, and tell me, is that the doctor's foot?"

The steps fell lightly and oddly, with a certain swing, for all they went so slowly; it was different indeed from the heavy creaking tread of Henry Jekyll. Utterson sighed. "Is there never anything else?" he asked.

Poole nodded. "Once," he said. "Once I heard it weeping!"

"Weeping? how that?" said the lawyer, conscious of a sudden chill of horror.

"Weeping like a woman or a lost soul," said the butler. "I came away with that upon my heart, that I could have wept too."

But now the ten minutes drew to an end. Poole disinterred the axe from under a stack of packing straw; the candle was set upon the nearest table to light them to the attack; and they drew near with bated breath to where that patient foot was still going up and down, up and down, in the quiet of the night. "Jekyll," cried Utterson, with a loud voice, "I demand to see you." He paused a moment, but there came no reply. "I give you fair warning, our suspicions are aroused, and I must and shall see you," he resumed; "if not by fair means, then by foul—if not of your consent, then by brute force!"

"Utterson," said the voice, "for God's sake, have mercy!"

"Ah, that's not Jekyll's voice—it's Hyde's!" cried Utterson. "Down with the door, Poole!"

Poole swung the axe over his shoulder; the blow shook the building, and the red baize door leaped against the lock and hinges. A dismal screech, as of mere animal terror, rang from the cabinet. Up went the axe again, and again the panels crashed and the frame bounded; four times the blow fell; but the wood was tough and the fittings were of excellent workmanship; and it was not until the fifth, that the lock burst and the wreck of the door fell inwards on the carpet.

The besiegers, appalled by their own riot and the stillness that had succeeded, stood back a little and peered in. There lay the cabinet before their eyes in the quiet lamplight, a good fire glowing and chattering on the hearth, the kettle singing its thin strain, a drawer or two open, papers neatly set forth on the business table, and nearer the fire, the things laid out for tea; the quietest room, you would have said, and, but for the glazed presses full of chemicals, the most commonplace that night in London.

Right in the middle there lay the body of a man sorely contorted and still twitching. They drew near on tiptoe, turned it on its back and beheld the face of Edward Hyde. He was dressed in clothes far to large for him, clothes of the doctor's bigness; the cords of his face still moved with a semblance of life, but life was quite gone: and by the crushed phial in the hand and the strong smell of kernels that hung upon the air, Utterson knew that he was looking on the body of a self-destroyer.

"We have come too late," he said sternly, "whether to save or punish. Hyde is gone to his account; and it only remains for us to find the body of your master."

The far greater proportion of the building was occupied by the theatre, which filled almost the whole ground storey and was lighted from above, and by the cabinet, which formed an upper story at one end and looked upon the court. A corridor joined the theatre to the door on the by-street; and with this the cabinet communicated separately by a second flight of stairs. There were besides a few dark closets and a spacious cellar. All these they now thoroughly examined. Each closet needed but a glance, for all were empty, and all, by the dust that fell from their doors, had stood long unopened. The cellar, indeed, was filled with crazy lumber, mostly dating from the times of the surgeon who was Jekyll's predecessor; but even as they opened the door they were advertised of the uselessness of further search, by the fall of a perfect mat of cobweb which had for years sealed up the entrance. No where was there any trace of Henry Jekyll dead or alive.

Poole stamped on the flags of the corridor. "He must be buried here," he said, hearkening to the sound.

"Or he may have fled," said Utterson, and he turned to examine the door in the by-street. It was locked; and lying near by on the flags, they found the key, already stained with rust.

"This does not look like use," observed the lawyer.

"Use!" echoed Poole. "Do you not see, sir, it is broken? much as if a man had stamped on it."

"Ay," continued Utterson, "and the fractures, too, are rusty." The two men looked at each other with a scare. "This is beyond me, Poole," said the lawyer. "Let us go back to the cabinet."

They mounted the stair in silence, and still with an occasional awestruck glance at the dead body, proceeded more thoroughly to examine the contents of the cabinet. At one table, there were traces of chemical work, various measured heaps of some white salt being laid on glass saucers, as though for an experiment in which the unhappy man had been prevented.

"That is the same drug that I was always bringing him," said Poole; and even as he spoke, the kettle with a startling noise boiled over.

This brought them to the fireside, where the easy-chair was drawn cosily up, and the tea things stood ready to the sitter's elbow, the very sugar in the cup. There were several books on a shelf; one lay beside the tea things open, and Utterson was amazed to find it a copy of a pious work, for which Jekyll had several times expressed a great esteem, annotated, in his own hand with startling blasphemies.

Next, in the course of their review of the chamber, the searchers came to the cheval-glass, into whose depths they looked with an involuntary horror. But it was so turned as to show them nothing but the rosy glow playing on the roof, the fire sparkling in a hundred repetitions along the glazed front of the presses, and their own pale and fearful countenances stooping to look in.

"This glass has seen some strange things, sir," whispered Poole.

"And surely none stranger than itself," echoed the lawyer in the same tones. "For what did Jekyll"—he caught himself up at the word with a start, and then conquering the weakness— "what could Jekyll want with it?" he said.

"You may say that!" said Poole.

Next they turned to the business table. On the desk, among the neat array of papers, a large envelope was uppermost, and bore, in the doctor's hand, the name of Mr. Utterson. The lawyer unsealed it, and several enclosures fell to the floor. The first was a will, drawn in the same eccentric terms as the one which he had returned six months before, to serve as a testament in case of death and as a deed of gift in case of disappearance; but in place of the name of Edward Hyde, the lawyer, with indescribable amazement read the name of Gabriel John Utterson. He looked at Poole, and then back at the paper, and last of all at the dead malefactor stretched upon the carpet.

"My head goes round," he said. "He has been all these days in possession; he had no cause to like me; he must have raged to see himself displaced; and he has not destroyed this document."

He caught up the next paper; it was a brief note in the doctor's hand and dated at the top. "O Poole!" the lawyer cried, "he was alive and here this day. He cannot have been disposed of in so short a space; he must be still alive, he must have fled! And then, why fled? and how? and in that case, can we venture to declare this suicide? O, we must be careful. I foresee that we may yet involve your master in some dire catastrophe."

"Why don't you read it, sir?" asked Poole.

"Because I fear," replied the lawyer solemnly. "God grant I have no cause for it!" And with that he brought the paper to his eyes and read as follows:

"My dear Utterson,—When this shall fall into your hands, I shall have disappeared, under what circumstances I have not the penetration to foresee, but my instinct and all the circumstances of my nameless situation tell me that the end is sure and must be early. Go then, and first read the narrative which Lanyon warned me he was to place in your hands; and if you care to hear more, turn to the confession of

"Your unworthy and unhappy friend,

"HENRY JEKYLL."

"There was a third enclosure?" asked Utterson.

"Here, sir," said Poole, and gave into his hands a considerable packet sealed in several places.

The lawyer put it in his pocket. "I would say nothing of this paper. If your master has fled or is dead, we may at least save his credit. It is now ten; I must go home and read these documents in quiet; but I shall be back before midnight, when we shall send for the police."

They went out, locking the door of the theatre behind them; and Utterson, once more leaving the servants gathered about the fire in the hall, trudged back to his office to read the two narratives in which this mystery was now to be explained.

Dr. Lanyon's Narrative

On the ninth of January, now four days ago, I received by the evening delivery a registered envelope, addressed in the hand of my colleague and old school companion, Henry Jekyll. I was a good deal surprised by this; for we were by no means in the habit of correspondence; I had seen the man, dined with him, indeed, the night before; and I could imagine nothing in our intercourse that should justify formality of registration. The contents increased my wonder; for this is how the letter ran:

"10th December, 18—.

"Dear Lanyon,—You are one of my oldest friends; and although we may have differed at times on scientific questions, I cannot remember, at least on my side, any break in our affection. There was never a day when, if you had said to me, 'Jekyll, my life, my honour, my reason, depend upon you,' I would not have sacrificed my left hand to help you. Lanyon my life, my honour, my reason, are all at your mercy; if you fail me to-night, I am lost. You might suppose, after this preface, that I am going to ask you for something dishonourable to grant. Judge for yourself.

"I want you to postpone all other engagements for to-night— ay, even if you were summoned to the bedside of an emperor; to take a cab, unless your carriage should be actually at the door; and with this letter in your hand for consultation, to drive straight to my house. Poole, my butler, has his orders; you will find him waiting your arrival with a locksmith. The door of my cabinet is then to be forced: and you are to go in alone; to open the glazed press (letter E) on the left hand, breaking the lock if it be shut; and to draw out, with all its contents as they stand, the fourth drawer from the top or (which is the same thing) the third from the bottom. In my extreme distress of mind, I have a morbid fear of misdirecting you; but even if I am in error, you may know the right drawer by its contents: some powders, a phial and a paper book. This drawer I beg of you to carry back with you to Cavendish Square exactly as it stands.

"That is the first part of the service: now for the second. You should be back, if you set out at once on the receipt of this, long before midnight; but I will leave you that amount of margin, not only in the fear of one of those obstacles that can neither be prevented nor foreseen, but because an hour when your servants are in bed is to be preferred for what will then remain to do. At midnight, then, I have to ask you to be alone in your consulting room, to admit with your own hand into the house a man who will present himself in my name, and to place in his hands the drawer that you will have brought with you from my cabinet. Then you will have played your part and earned my gratitude completely. Five minutes afterwards, if you insist upon an explanation, you will have understood that these arrangements are of capital importance; and that by the neglect of one of them, fantastic as they must appear, you might have charged your conscience with my death or the shipwreck of my reason.

"Confident as I am that you will not trifle with this appeal, my heart sinks and my hand trembles at the bare thought of such a possibility. Think of me at this hour, in a strange place, labouring under a blackness of distress that no fancy can exaggerate, and yet well aware that, if you will but punctually serve me, my troubles will roll away like a story that is told. Serve me, my dear Lanyon and save

"Your friend,
"H.J.

"P.S.—I had already sealed this up when a fresh terror struck upon my soul. It is possible that the post-office may fail me, and this letter not come into your hands until to-morrow morning. In that case, dear Lanyon, do my errand when it shall be most convenient for you in the course of the day; and once more expect my messenger at midnight. It may then already be too late; and if that night passes without event, you will know that you have seen the last of Henry Jekyll."

Upon the reading of this letter, I made sure my colleague was insane; but till that was proved beyond the possibility of doubt, I felt bound to do as he requested. The less I understood of this farrago, the less I was in a position to judge of its importance; and an appeal so worded could not be set aside without a grave responsibility. I rose accordingly from table, got into a hansom, and drove straight to Jekyll's house. The butler was awaiting my arrival; he had received by the same post as mine a registered letter of instruction, and had sent at once for a locksmith and a carpenter. The tradesmen came while we were yet speaking; and we moved in a body to old Dr. Denman's surgical theatre, from which (as you are doubtless aware) Jekyll's private cabinet is most conveniently entered. The door was very strong, the lock excellent; the carpenter avowed he would have great trouble and have to do much damage, if force were to be used; and the locksmith was near despair. But this last was a handy fellow, and after two hour's work, the door stood open. The press marked E was unlocked; and I took out the drawer, had it filled up with straw and tied in a sheet, and returned with it to Cavendish Square.

Here I proceeded to examine its contents. The powders were neatly enough made up, but not with the nicety of the dispensing chemist; so that it was plain they were of Jekyll's private manufacture: and when I opened one of the wrappers I found what seemed to me a simple crystalline salt of a white colour. The phial, to which I next turned my attention, might have been about half full of a blood-red liquor, which was highly pungent to the sense of smell and seemed to me to contain phosphorus and some volatile ether. At the other ingredients I could make no guess. The book was an ordinary version book and contained little but a series of dates. These covered a period of many years, but I observed that the entries ceased nearly a year ago and quite abruptly. Here and there a brief remark was appended to a date, usually no more than a single word: "double" occurring perhaps six times in a total of several hundred entries; and once very early in the list and followed by several marks of exclamation, "total failure!!!" All this, though it whetted my curiosity, told me little that was definite. Here were a phial of some salt, and the record of a series of experiments that had led (like too many of Jekyll's investigations) to no end of practical usefulness. How could the presence of these articles in my house affect either the honour, the sanity, or the life of my flighty colleague? If his messenger could go to one place, why could he not go to another? And even granting some impediment, why was this gentleman to be received by me in secret? The more I reflected the more convinced I grew that I was dealing with a case of cerebral disease; and though I dismissed my servants to bed, I loaded an old revolver, that I might be found in some posture of self-defence.

Twelve o'clock had scarce rung out over London, ere the knocker sounded very gently on the door. I went myself at the summons, and found a small man crouching against the pillars of the portico.

"Are you come from Dr. Jekyll?" I asked.

He told me "yes" by a constrained gesture; and when I had bidden him enter, he did not obey me without a searching backward glance into the darkness of the square. There was a policeman not far off, advancing with his bull's eye open; and at the sight, I thought my visitor started and made greater haste.

These particulars struck me, I confess, disagreeably; and as I followed him into the bright light of the consulting room, I kept my hand ready on my weapon. Here, at last, I had a chance of clearly seeing him. I had never set eyes on him before, so much was certain. He was small, as I have said; I was struck besides with the shocking expression of his face, with his remarkable combination of great muscular activity and great apparent debility of constitution, and—last but not least—with the odd, subjective disturbance caused by his neighbourhood. This bore some resemblance to incipient rigour, and was accompanied by a marked sinking of the pulse. At the time, I set it down to some idiosyncratic, personal distaste, and merely wondered at the acuteness of the symptoms; but I have since had reason to believe the cause to lie much deeper in the nature of man, and to turn on some nobler hinge than the principle of hatred.

This person (who had thus, from the first moment of his entrance, struck in me what I can only, describe as a disgustful curiosity) was dressed in a fashion that would have made an ordinary person laughable; his clothes, that is to say, although they were of rich and sober fabric, were enormously too large for him in every measurement—the trousers hanging on his legs and rolled up to keep them from the ground, the waist of the coat below his haunches, and the collar sprawling wide upon his shoulders. Strange to relate, this ludicrous accoutrement was far from moving me to laughter. Rather, as there was something abnormal and misbegotten in the very essence of the creature that now faced me— something seizing, surprising and revolting—this fresh disparity seemed but to fit in with and to reinforce it; so that to my interest in the man's nature and character, there was added a curiosity as to his origin, his life, his fortune and status in the world.

These observations, though they have taken so great a space to be set down in, were yet the work of a few seconds. My visitor was, indeed, on fire with sombre excitement.

"Have you got it?" he cried. "Have you got it?" And so lively was his impatience that he even laid his hand upon my arm and sought to shake me.

I put him back, conscious at his touch of a certain icy pang along my blood. "Come, sir," said I. "You forget that I have not yet the pleasure of your acquaintance. Be seated, if you please." And I showed him an example, and sat down myself in my customary seat and with as fair an imitation of my ordinary manner to a patient, as the lateness of the hour, the nature of my preoccupations, and the horror I had of my visitor, would suffer me to muster.

"I beg your pardon, Dr. Lanyon," he replied civilly enough. "What you say is very well founded; and my impatience has shown its heels to my politeness. I come here at the instance of your colleague, Dr. Henry Jekyll, on a piece of business of some moment; and I understood ..." He paused and put his hand to his throat, and I could see, in spite of his collected manner, that he was wrestling against the approaches of the hysteria— "I understood, a drawer . . ."

But here I took pity on my visitor's suspense, and some perhaps on my own growing curiosity.

"There it is, sir," said I, pointing to the drawer, where it lay on the floor behind a table and still covered with the sheet.

He sprang to it, and then paused, and laid his hand upon his heart: I could hear his teeth grate with the convulsive action of his jaws; and his face was so ghastly to see that I grew alarmed both for his life and reason.

"Compose yourself," said I.

He turned a dreadful smile to me, and as if with the decision of despair, plucked away the sheet. At sight of the contents, he uttered one loud sob of such immense relief that I sat petrified.

And the next moment, in a voice that was already fairly well under control, "Have you a graduated glass?" he asked.

I rose from my place with something of an effort and gave him what he asked.

He thanked me with a smiling nod, measured out a few minims of the red tincture and added one of the powders. The mixture, which was at first of a reddish hue, began, in proportion as the crystals melted, to brighten in colour, to effervesce audibly, and to throw off small fumes of vapour. Suddenly and at the same moment, the ebullition ceased and the compound changed to a dark purple, which faded again more slowly to a watery green. My visitor, who had watched these metamorphoses with a keen eye, smiled, set down the glass upon the table, and then turned and looked upon me with an air of scrutiny.

"And now," said he, "to settle what remains. Will you be wise? will you be guided? will you suffer me to take this glass in my hand and to go forth from your house without further parley? or has the greed of curiosity too much command of you? Think before you answer, for it shall be done as you decide. As you decide, you shall be left as you were before, and neither richer nor wiser, unless the sense of service rendered to a man in mortal distress may be counted as a kind of riches of the soul. Or, if you shall so prefer to choose, a new province of knowledge and new avenues to fame and power shall be laid open to you, here, in this room, upon the instant; and your sight shall be blasted by a prodigy to stagger the unbelief of Satan."

"Sir," said I, affecting a coolness that I was far from truly possessing, "you speak enigmas, and you will perhaps not wonder that I hear you with no very strong impression of belief. But I have gone too far in the way of inexplicable services to pause before I see the end."

"It is well," replied my visitor. "Lanyon, you remember your vows: what follows is under the seal of our profession. And now, you who have so long been bound to the most narrow and material views, you who have denied the virtue of transcendental medicine, you who have derided your superiors—behold!"

He put the glass to his lips and drank at one gulp. A cry followed; he reeled, staggered, clutched at the table and held on, staring with injected eyes, gasping with open mouth; and as I looked there came, I thought, a change—he seemed to swell—his face became suddenly black and the features seemed to melt and alter—and the next moment, I had sprung to my feet and leaped back against the wall, my arms raised to shield me from that prodigy, my mind submerged in terror.

"O God!" I screamed, and "O God!" again and again; for there before my eyes—pale and shaken, and half fainting, and groping before him with his hands, like a man restored from death—there stood Henry Jekyll!

What he told me in the next hour, I cannot bring my mind to set on paper. I saw what I saw, I heard what I heard, and my soul sickened at it; and yet now when that sight has faded from my eyes, I ask myself if I believe it, and I cannot answer. My life is shaken to its roots; sleep has left me; the deadliest terror sits by me at all hours of the day and night; and I feel that my days are numbered, and that I must die; and yet I shall die incredulous. As for the moral turpitude that man unveiled to me, even with tears of penitence, I can not, even in memory, dwell on it without a start of horror. I will say but one thing, Utterson, and that (if you can bring your mind to credit it) will be more than enough. The creature who crept into my house that night was, on Jekyll's own confession, known by the name of Hyde and hunted for in every corner of the land as the murderer of Carew.

HASTIE LANYON

Henry Jekyll's Full Statement of the Case

I was born in the year 18—to a large fortune, endowed besides with excellent parts, inclined by nature to industry, fond of the respect of the wise and good among my fellowmen, and thus, as might have been supposed, with every guarantee of an honorurable and distinguished future. And indeed the worst of my faults was a certain impatient gaiety of disposition, such as has made the happiness of many, but such as I found it hard to reconcile with my imperious desire to carry my head high, and wear a more than commonly grave countenance before the public. Hence it came about that I concealed my pleasures; and that when I reached years of reflection, and began to look round me and take stock of my progress and position in the world, I stood already committed to a profound duplicity of me. Many a man would have even blazoned such irregularities as I was guilty of; but from the high views that I had set before me, I regarded and hid them with an almost morbid sense of shame. It was thus rather the exacting nature of my aspirations than any particular degradation in my faults, that made me what I was, and, with even a deeper trench than in the majority of men, severed in me those provinces of good and ill which divide and compound man's dual nature. In this case, I was driven to reflect deeply and inveterately on that hard law of life, which lies at the root of religion and is one of the most plentiful springs of distress. Though so profound a double-dealer, I was in no sense a hypocrite; both sides of me were in dead earnest; I was no more myself when I laid aside restraint and plunged in shame, than when I laboured, in the eye of day, at the futherance of knowledge or the relief of sorrow and suffering. And it chanced that the direction of my scientific studies, which led wholly towards the mystic and the transcendental, reacted and shed a strong light on this consciousness of the perennial war among my members. With every day, and from both sides of my intelligence, the moral and the intellectual, I thus drew steadily nearer to that truth, by whose partial discovery I have been doomed to such a dreadful shipwreck: that man is not truly one, but truly two. I say two, because the state of my own knowledge does not pass beyond that point. Others will follow, others will outstrip me on the same lines; and I hazard the guess that man will be ultimately known for a mere polity of multifarious, incongruous and independent denizens. I, for my part, from the nature of my life, advanced infallibly in one direction and in one direction only. It was on the moral side, and in my own person, that I learned to recognise the thorough and primitive duality of man; I saw that, of the two natures that contended in the field of my consciousness, even if I could rightly be said to be either, it was only because I was radically both; and from an early date, even before the course of my scientific discoveries had begun to suggest the most naked possibility of such a miracle, I had learned to dwell with pleasure, as a beloved daydream, on the thought of the separation of these elements. If each, I told myself, could be housed in separate identities, life would be relieved of all that was unbearable; the unjust might go his way, delivered from the aspirations and remorse of his more upright twin; and the just could walk steadfastly and securely on his upward path, doing the good things in which he found his pleasure, and no longer exposed to disgrace and penitence by the hands of this extraneous evil. It was the curse of mankind that these incongruous faggots were thus bound together—that in the agonised womb of consciousness, these polar twins should be continuously struggling. How, then were they dissociated?

I was so far in my reflections when, as I have said, a side light began to shine upon the subject from the laboratory table. I began to perceive more deeply than it has ever yet been stated, the trembling immateriality, the mistlike transience, of this seemingly so solid body in which we walk attired. Certain agents I found to have the power to shake and pluck back that fleshly vestment, even as a wind might toss the curtains of a pavilion. For two good reasons, I will not enter deeply into this scientific branch of my confession. First, because I have been made to learn that the doom and burthen of our life is bound for ever on man's shoulders, and when the attempt is made to cast it off, it but returns upon us with more unfamiliar and more awful pressure. Second, because, as my narrative will make, alas! too evident, my discoveries were incomplete. Enough then, that I not only recognised my natural body from the mere aura and effulgence of certain of the powers that made up my spirit, but managed to compound a drug by which these powers should be dethroned from their supremacy, and a second form and countenance substituted, none the less natural to me because they were the expression, and bore the stamp of lower elements in my soul.

I hesitated long before I put this theory to the test of practice. I knew well that I risked death; for any drug that so potently controlled and shook the very fortress of identity, might, by the least scruple of an overdose or at the least inopportunity in the moment of exhibition, utterly blot out that immaterial tabernacle which I looked to it to change. But the temptation of a discovery so singular and profound at last overcame the suggestions of alarm. I had long since prepared my tincture; I purchased at once, from a firm of wholesale chemists, a large quantity of a particular salt which I knew, from my experiments, to be the last ingredient required; and late one accursed night, I compounded the elements, watched them boil and smoke together in the glass, and when the ebullition had subsided, with a strong glow of courage, drank off the potion.

The most racking pangs succeeded: a grinding in the bones, deadly nausea, and a horror of the spirit that cannot be exceeded at the hour of birth or death. Then these agonies began swiftly to subside, and I came to myself as if out of a great sickness. There was something strange in my sensations, something indescribably new and, from its very novelty, incredibly sweet. I felt younger, lighter, happier in body; within I was conscious of a heady recklessness, a current of disordered sensual images running like a millrace in my fancy, a solution of the bonds of obligation, an unknown but not an innocent freedom of the soul. I knew myself, at the first breath of this new life, to be more wicked, tenfold more wicked, sold a slave to my original evil; and the thought, in that moment, braced and delighted me like wine. I stretched out my hands, exulting in the freshness of these sensations; and in the act, I was suddenly aware that I had lost in stature.

There was no mirror, at that date, in my room; that which stands beside me as I write, was brought there later on and for the very purpose of these transformations. The night however, was far gone into the morning—the morning, black as it was, was nearly ripe for the conception of the day—the inmates of my house were locked in the most rigorous hours of slumber; and I determined, flushed as I was with hope and triumph, to venture in my new shape as far as to my bedroom. I crossed the yard, wherein the constellations looked down upon me, I could have thought, with wonder, the first creature of that sort that their unsleeping vigilance had yet disclosed to them; I stole through the corridors, a stranger in my own house; and coming to my room, I saw for the first time the appearance of Edward Hyde.

I must here speak by theory alone, saying not that which I know, but that which I suppose to be most probable. The evil side of my nature, to which I had now transferred the stamping efficacy, was less robust and less developed than the good which I had just deposed. Again, in the course of my life, which had been, after all, nine tenths a life of effort, virtue and control, it had been much less exercised and much less exhausted. And hence, as I think, it came about that Edward Hyde was so much smaller, slighter and younger than Henry Jekyll. Even as good shone upon the countenance of the one, evil was written broadly and plainly on the face of the other. Evil besides (which I must still believe to be the lethal side of man) had left on that body an imprint of deformity and decay. And yet when I looked upon that ugly idol in the glass, I was conscious of no repugnance, rather of a leap of welcome. This, too, was myself. It seemed natural and human. In my eyes it bore a livelier image of the spirit, it seemed more express and single, than the imperfect and divided countenance I had been hitherto accustomed to call mine. And in so far I was doubtless right. I have observed that when I wore the semblance of Edward Hyde, none could come near to me at first without a visible misgiving of the flesh. This, as I take it, was because all human beings, as we meet them, are commingled out of good and evil: and Edward Hyde, alone in the ranks of mankind, was pure evil.

I lingered but a moment at the mirror: the second and conclusive experiment had yet to be attempted; it yet remained to be seen if I had lost my identity beyond redemption and must flee before daylight from a house that was no longer mine; and hurrying back to my cabinet, I once more prepared and drank the cup, once more suffered the pangs of dissolution, and came to myself once more with the character, the stature and the face of Henry Jekyll.

That night I had come to the fatal cross-roads. Had I approached my discovery in a more noble spirit, had I risked the experiment while under the empire of generous or pious aspirations, all must have been otherwise, and from these agonies of death and birth, I had come forth an angel instead of a fiend. The drug had no discriminating action; it was neither diabolical nor divine; it but shook the doors of the prisonhouse of my disposition; and like the captives of Philippi, that which stood within ran forth. At that time my virtue slumbered; my evil, kept awake by ambition, was alert and swift to seize the occasion; and the thing that was projected was Edward Hyde. Hence, although I had now two characters as well as two appearances, one was wholly evil, and the other was still the old Henry Jekyll, that incongruous compound of whose reformation and improvement I had already learned to despair. The movement was thus wholly toward the worse.

Even at that time, I had not conquered my aversions to the dryness of a life of study. I would still be merrily disposed at times; and as my pleasures were (to say the least) undignified, and I was not only well known and highly considered, but growing towards the elderly man, this incoherency of my life was daily growing more unwelcome. It was on this side that my new power tempted me until I fell in slavery. I had but to drink the cup, to doff at once the body of the noted professor, and to assume, like a thick cloak, that of Edward Hyde. I smiled at the notion; it seemed to me at the time to be humourous; and I made my preparations with the most studious care. I took and furnished that house in Soho, to which Hyde was tracked by the police; and engaged as a housekeeper a creature whom I knew well to be silent and unscrupulous. On the other side, I announced to my servants that a Mr. Hyde (whom I described) was to have full liberty and power about my house in the square; and to parry mishaps, I even called and made myself a familiar object, in my second character. I next drew up that will to which you so much objected; so that if anything befell me in the person of Dr. Jekyll, I could enter on that of Edward Hyde without pecuniary loss. And thus fortified, as I supposed, on every side, I began to profit by the strange immunities of my position.

Men have before hired bravos to transact their crimes, while their own person and reputation sat under shelter. I was the first that ever did so for his pleasures. I was the first that could plod in the public eye with a load of genial respectability, and in a moment, like a schoolboy, strip off these lendings and spring headlong into the sea of liberty. But for me, in my impenetrable mantle, the safely was complete. Think of it—I did not even exist! Let me but escape into my laboratory door, give me but a second or two to mix and swallow the draught that I had always standing ready; and whatever he had done, Edward Hyde would pass away like the stain of breath upon a mirror; and there in his stead, quietly at home, trimming the midnight lamp in his study, a man who could afford to laugh at suspicion, would be Henry Jekyll.

The pleasures which I made haste to seek in my disguise were, as I have said, undignified; I would scarce use a harder term. But in the hands of Edward Hyde, they soon began to turn toward the monstrous. When I would come back from these excursions, I was often plunged into a kind of wonder at my vicarious depravity. This familiar that I called out of my own soul, and sent forth alone to do his good pleasure, was a being inherently malign and villainous; his every act and thought centered on self; drinking pleasure with bestial avidity from any degree of torture to another; relentless like a man of stone. Henry Jekyll stood at times aghast before the acts of Edward Hyde; but the situation was apart from ordinary laws, and insidiously relaxed the grasp of conscience. It was Hyde, after all, and Hyde alone, that was guilty. Jekyll was no worse; he woke again to his good qualities seemingly unimpaired; he would even make haste, where it was possible, to undo the evil done by Hyde. And thus his conscience slumbered.

Into the details of the infamy at which I thus connived (for even now I can scarce grant that I committed it) I have no design of entering; I mean but to point out the warnings and the successive steps with which my chastisement approached. I met with one accident which, as it brought on no consequence, I shall no more than mention. An act of cruelty to a child aroused against me the anger of a passer-by, whom I recognised the other day in the person of your kinsman; the doctor and the child's family joined him; there were moments when I feared for my life; and at last, in order to pacify their too just resentment, Edward Hyde had to bring them to the door, and pay them in a cheque drawn in the name of Henry Jekyll. But this danger was easily eliminated from the future, by opening an account at another bank in the name of Edward Hyde himself; and when, by sloping my own hand backward, I had supplied my double with a signature, I thought I sat beyond the reach of fate.

Some two months before the, murder of Sir Danvers, I had been out for one of my adventures, had returned at a late hour, and woke the next day in bed with somewhat odd sensations. It was in vain I looked about me; in vain I saw the decent furniture and tall proportions of my room in the square; in vain that I recognised the pattern of the bed curtains and the design of the mahogany frame; something still kept insisting that I was not where I was, that I had not wakened where I seemed to be, but in the little room in Soho where I was accustomed to sleep in the body of Edward Hyde. I smiled to myself, and in my psychological way, began lazily to inquire into the elements of this illusion, occasionally, even as I did so, dropping back into a comfortable morning doze. I was still so engaged when, in one of my more wakeful moments, my eyes fell upon my hand. Now the hand of Henry Jekyll (as you have often remarked) was professional in shape and size: it was large, firm, white and comely. But the hand which I now saw, clearly enough, in the yellow light of a mid-London morning, lying half shut on the bedclothes, was lean, corder, knuckly, of a dusky pallor and thickly shaded with a swart growth of hair. It was the hand of Edward Hyde.

I must have stared upon it for near half a minute, sunk as I was in the mere stupidity of wonder, before terror woke up in my breast as sudden and startling as the crash of cymbals; and bounding from my bed I rushed to the mirror. At the sight that met my eyes, my blood was changed into something exquisitely thin and icy. Yes, I had gone to bed Henry Jekyll, I had awakened Edward Hyde. How was this to be explained? I asked myself; and then, with another bound of terror—how was it to be remedied? It was well on in the morning; the servants were up; all my drugs were in the cabinet—a long journey down two pairs of stairs, through the back passage, across the open court and through the anatomical theatre, from where I was then standing horror-struck. It might indeed be possible to cover my face; but of what use was that, when I was unable to conceal the alteration in my stature? And then with an overpowering sweetness of relief, it came back upon my mind that the servants were already used to the coming and going of my second self. I had soon dressed, as well as I was able, in clothes of my own size: had soon passed through the house, where Bradshaw stared and drew back at seeing Mr. Hyde at such an hour and in such a strange array; and ten minutes later, Dr. Jekyll had returned to his own shape and was sitting down, with a darkened brow, to make a feint of breakfasting.

Small indeed was my appetite. This inexplicable incident, this reversal of my previous experience, seemed, like the Babylonian finger on the wall, to be spelling out the letters of my judgment; and I began to reflect more seriously than ever before on the issues and possibilities of my double existence. That part of me which I had the power of projecting, had lately been much exercised and nourished; it had seemed to me of late as though the body of Edward Hyde had grown in stature, as though (when I wore that form) I were conscious of a more generous tide of blood; and I began to spy a danger that, if this were much prolonged, the balance of my nature might be permanently overthrown, the power of voluntary change be forfeited, and the character of Edward Hyde become irrevocably mine. The power of the drug had not been always equally displayed. Once, very early in my career, it had totally failed me; since then I had been obliged on more than one occasion to double, and once, with infinite risk of death, to treble the amount; and these rare uncertainties had cast hitherto the sole shadow on my contentment. Now, however, and in the light of that morning's accident, I was led to remark that whereas, in the beginning, the difficulty had been to throw off the body of Jekyll, it had of late gradually but decidedly transferred itself to the other side. All things therefore seemed to point to this; that I was slowly losing hold of my original and better self, and becoming slowly incorporated with my second and worse.

Between these two, I now felt I had to choose. My two natures had memory in common, but all other faculties were most unequally shared between them. Jekyll (who was composite) now with the most sensitive apprehensions, now with a greedy gusto, projected and shared in the pleasures and adventures of Hyde; but Hyde was indifferent to Jekyll, or but remembered him as the mountain bandit remembers the cavern in which he conceals himself from pursuit. Jekyll had more than a father's interest; Hyde had more than a son's indifference. To cast in my lot with Jekyll, was to die to those appetites which I had long secretly indulged and had of late begun to pamper. To cast it in with Hyde, was to die to a thousand interests and aspirations, and to become, at a blow and forever, despised and friendless. The bargain might appear unequal; but there was still another consideration in the scales; for while Jekyll would suffer smartingly in the fires of abstinence, Hyde would be not even conscious of all that he had lost. Strange as my circumstances were, the terms of this debate are as old and commonplace as man; much the same inducements and alarms cast the die for any tempted and trembling sinner; and it fell out with me, as it falls with so vast a majority of my fellows, that I chose the better part and was found wanting in the strength to keep to it.

Yes, I preferred the elderly and discontented doctor, surrounded by friends and cherishing honest hopes; and bade a resolute farewell to the liberty, the comparative youth, the light step, leaping impulses and secret pleasures, that I had enjoyed in the disguise of Hyde. I made this choice perhaps with some unconscious reservation, for I neither gave up the house in Soho, nor destroyed the clothes of Edward Hyde, which still lay ready in my cabinet. For two months, however, I was true to my determination; for two months, I led a life of such severity as I had never before attained to, and enjoyed the compensations of an approving conscience. But time began at last to obliterate the freshness of my alarm; the praises of conscience began to grow into a thing of course; I began to be tortured with throes and longings, as of Hyde struggling after freedom; and at last, in an hour of moral weakness, I once again compounded and swallowed the transforming draught.

I do not suppose that, when a drunkard reasons with himself upon his vice, he is once out of five hundred times affected by the dangers that he runs through his brutish, physical insensibility; neither had I, long as I had considered my position, made enough allowance for the complete moral insensibility and insensate readiness to evil, which were the leading characters of Edward Hyde. Yet it was by these that I was punished. My devil had been long caged, he came out roaring. I was conscious, even when I took the draught, of a more unbridled, a more furious propensity to ill. It must have been this, I suppose, that stirred in my soul that tempest of impatience with which I listened to the civilities of my unhappy victim; I declare, at least, before God, no man morally sane could have been guilty of that crime upon so pitiful a provocation; and that I struck in no more reasonable spirit than that in which a sick child may break a plaything. But I had voluntarily stripped myself of all those balancing instincts by which even the worst of us continues to walk with some degree of steadiness among temptations; and in my case, to be tempted, however slightly, was to fall.

Instantly the spirit of hell awoke in me and raged. With a transport of glee, I mauled the unresisting body, tasting delight from every blow; and it was not till weariness had begun to succeed, that I was suddenly, in the top fit of my delirium, struck through the heart by a cold thrill of terror. A mist dispersed; I saw my life to be forfeit; and fled from the scene of these excesses, at once glorying and trembling, my lust of evil gratified and stimulated, my love of life screwed to the topmost peg. I ran to the house in Soho, and (to make assurance doubly sure) destroyed my papers; thence I set out through the lamplit streets, in the same divided ecstasy of mind, gloating on my crime, light-headedly devising others in the future, and yet still hastening and still hearkening in my wake for the steps of the avenger. Hyde had a song upon his lips as he compounded the draught, and as he drank it, pledged the dead man. The pangs of transformation had not done tearing him, before Henry Jekyll, with streaming tears of gratitude and remorse, had fallen upon his knees and lifted his clasped hands to God. The veil of self-indulgence was rent from head to foot. I saw my life as a whole: I followed it up from the days of childhood, when I had walked with my father's hand, and through the self-denying toils of my professional life, to arrive again and again, with the same sense of unreality, at the damned horrors of the evening. I could have screamed aloud; I sought with tears and prayers to smother down the crowd of hideous images and sounds with which my memory swarmed against me; and still, between the petitions, the ugly face of my iniquity stared into my soul. As the acuteness of this remorse began to die away, it was succeeded by a sense of joy. The problem of my conduct was solved. Hyde was thenceforth impossible; whether I would or not, I was now confined to the better part of my existence; and O, how I rejoiced to think of it! with what willing humility I embraced anew the restrictions of natural life! with what sincere renunciation I locked the door by which I had so often gone and come, and ground the key under my heel!

The next day, came the news that the murder had been over-looked, that the guilt of Hyde was patent to the world, and that the victim was a man high in public estimation. It was not only a crime, it had been a tragic folly. I think I was glad to know it; I think I was glad to have my better impulses thus buttressed and guarded by the terrors of the scaffold. Jekyll was now my city of refuge; let but Hyde peep out an instant, and the hands of all men would be raised to take and slay him.

I resolved in my future conduct to redeem the past; and I can say with honesty that my resolve was fruitful of some good. You know yourself how earnestly, in the last months of the last year, I laboured to relieve suffering; you know that much was done for others, and that the days passed quietly, almost happily for myself. Nor can I truly say that I wearied of this beneficent and innocent life; I think instead that I daily enjoyed it more completely; but I was still cursed with my duality of purpose; and as the first edge of my penitence wore off, the lower side of me, so long indulged, so recently chained down, began to growl for licence. Not that I dreamed of resuscitating Hyde; the bare idea of that would startle me to frenzy: no, it was in my own person that I was once more tempted to trifle with my conscience; and it was as an ordinary secret sinner that I at last fell before the assaults of temptation.

There comes an end to all things; the most capacious measure is filled at last; and this brief condescension to my evil finally destroyed the balance of my soul. And yet I was not alarmed; the fall seemed natural, like a return to the old days before I had made my discovery. It was a fine, clear, January day, wet under foot where the frost had melted, but cloudless overhead; and the Regent's Park was full of winter chirrupings and sweet with spring odours. I sat in the sun on a bench; the animal within me licking the chops of memory; the spiritual side a little drowsed, promising subsequent penitence, but not yet moved to begin. After all, I reflected, I was like my neighbours; and then I smiled, comparing myself with other men, comparing my active good-will with the lazy cruelty of their neglect. And at the very moment of that vainglorious thought, a qualm came over me, a horrid nausea and the most deadly shuddering. These passed away, and left me faint; and then as in its turn faintness subsided, I began to be aware of a change in the temper of my thoughts, a greater boldness, a contempt of danger, a solution of the bonds of obligation. I looked down; my clothes hung formlessly on my shrunken limbs; the hand that lay on my knee was corded and hairy. I was once more Edward Hyde. A moment before I had been safe of all men's respect, wealthy, beloved—the cloth laying for me in the dining-room at home; and now I was the common quarry of mankind, hunted, houseless, a known murderer, thrall to the gallows.

My reason wavered, but it did not fail me utterly. I have more than once observed that in my second character, my faculties seemed sharpened to a point and my spirits more tensely elastic; thus it came about that, where Jekyll perhaps might have succumbed, Hyde rose to the importance of the moment. My drugs were in one of the presses of my cabinet; how was I to reach them? That was the problem that (crushing my temples in my hands) I set myself to solve. The laboratory door I had closed. If I sought to enter by the house, my own servants would consign me to the gallows. I saw I must employ another hand, and thought of Lanyon. How was he to be reached? how persuaded? Supposing that I escaped capture in the streets, how was I to make my way into his presence? and how should I, an unknown and displeasing visitor, prevail on the famous physician to rifle the study of his colleague, Dr. Jekyll? Then I remembered that of my original character, one part remained to me: I could write my own hand; and once I had conceived that kindling spark, the way that I must follow became lighted up from end to end.

Thereupon, I arranged my clothes as best I could, and summoning a passing hansom, drove to an hotel in Portland Street, the name of which I chanced to remember. At my appearance (which was indeed comical enough, however tragic a fate these garments covered) the driver could not conceal his mirth. I gnashed my teeth upon him with a gust of devilish fury; and the smile withered from his face—happily for him—yet more happily for myself, for in another instant I had certainly dragged him from his perch. At the inn, as I entered, I looked about me with so black a countenance as made the attendants tremble; not a look did they exchange in my presence; but obsequiously took my orders, led me to a private room, and brought me wherewithal to write. Hyde in danger of his life was a creature new to me; shaken with inordinate anger, strung to the pitch of murder, lusting to inflict pain. Yet the creature was astute; mastered his fury with a great effort of the will; composed his two important letters, one to Lanyon and one to Poole; and that he might receive actual evidence of their being posted, sent them out with directions that they should be registered. Thenceforward, he sat all day over the fire in the private room, gnawing his nails; there he dined, sitting alone with his fears, the waiter visibly quailing before his eye; and thence, when the night was fully come, he set forth in the corner of a closed cab, and was driven to and fro about the streets of the city. He, I say—I cannot say, I. That child of Hell had nothing human; nothing lived in him but fear and hatred. And when at last, thinking the driver had begun to grow suspicious, he discharged the cab and ventured on foot, attired in his misfitting clothes, an object marked out for observation, into the midst of the nocturnal passengers, these two base passions raged within him like a tempest. He walked fast, hunted by his fears, chattering to himself, skulking through the less frequented thoroughfares, counting the minutes that still divided him from midnight. Once a woman spoke to him, offering, I think, a box of lights. He smote her in the face, and she fled.

When I came to myself at Lanyon's, the horror of my old friend perhaps affected me somewhat: I do not know; it was at least but a drop in the sea to the abhorrence with which I looked back upon these hours. A change had come over me. It was no longer the fear of the gallows, it was the horror of being Hyde that racked me. I received Lanyon's condemnation partly in a dream; it was partly in a dream that I came home to my own house and got into bed. I slept after the prostration of the day, with a stringent and profound slumber which not even the nightmares that wrung me could avail to break. I awoke in the morning shaken, weakened, but refreshed. I still hated and feared the thought of the brute that slept within me, and I had not of course forgotten the appalling dangers of the day before; but I was once more at home, in my own house and close to my drugs; and gratitude for my escape shone so strong in my soul that it almost rivalled the brightness of hope.

I was stepping leisurely across the court after breakfast, drinking the chill of the air with pleasure, when I was seized again with those indescribable sensations that heralded the change; and I had but the time to gain the shelter of my cabinet, before I was once again raging and freezing with the passions of Hyde. It took on this occasion a double dose to recall me to myself; and alas! six hours after, as I sat looking sadly in the fire, the pangs returned, and the drug had to be re-administered. In short, from that day forth it seemed only by a great effort as of gymnastics, and only under the immediate stimulation of the drug, that I was able to wear the countenance of Jekyll. At all hours of the day and night, I would be taken with the premonitory shudder; above all, if I slept, or even dozed for a moment in my chair, it was always as Hyde that I awakened. Under the strain of this continually impending doom and by the sleeplessness to which I now condemned myself, ay, even beyond what I had thought possible to man, I became, in my own person, a creature eaten up and emptied by fever, languidly weak both in body and mind, and solely occupied by one thought: the horror of my other self. But when I slept, or when the virtue of the medicine wore off, I would leap almost without transition (for the pangs of transformation grew daily less marked) into the possession of a fancy brimming with images of terror, a soul boiling with causeless hatreds, and a body that seemed not strong enough to contain the raging energies of life. The powers of Hyde seemed to have grown with the sickliness of Jekyll. And certainly the hate that now divided them was equal on each side. With Jekyll, it was a thing of vital instinct. He had now seen the full deformity of that creature that shared with him some of the phenomena of consciousness, and was co-heir with him to death: and beyond these links of community, which in themselves made the most poignant part of his distress, he thought of Hyde, for all his energy of life, as of something not only hellish but inorganic. This was the shocking thing; that the slime of the pit seemed to utter cries and voices; that the amorphous dust gesticulated and sinned; that what was dead, and had no shape, should usurp the offices of life. And this again, that that insurgent horror was knit to him closer than a wife, closer than an eye; lay caged in his flesh, where he heard it mutter and felt it struggle to be born; and at every hour of weakness, and in the confidence of slumber, prevailed against him, and deposed him out of life. The hatred of Hyde for Jekyll was of a different order. His terror of the gallows drove him continually to commit temporary suicide, and return to his subordinate station of a part instead of a person; but he loathed the necessity, he loathed the despondency into which Jekyll was now fallen, and he resented the dislike with which he was himself regarded. Hence the ape-like tricks that he would play me, scrawling in my own hand blasphemies on the pages of my books, burning the letters and destroying the portrait of my father; and indeed, had it not been for his fear of death, he would long ago have ruined himself in order to involve me in the ruin. But his love of me is wonderful; I go further: I, who sicken and freeze at the mere thought of him, when I recall the abjection and passion of this attachment, and when I know how he fears my power to cut him off by suicide, I find it in my heart to pity him.

It is useless, and the time awfully fails me, to prolong this description; no one has ever suffered such torments, let that suffice; and yet even to these, habit brought—no, not alleviation—but a certain callousness of soul, a certain acquiescence of despair; and my punishment might have gone on for years, but for the last calamity which has now fallen, and which has finally severed me from my own face and nature. My provision of the salt, which had never been renewed since the date of the first experiment, began to run low. I sent out for a fresh supply and mixed the draught; the ebullition followed, and the first change of colour, not the second; I drank it and it was without efficiency. You will learn from Poole how I have had London ransacked; it was in vain; and I am now persuaded that my first supply was impure, and that it was that unknown impurity which lent efficacy to the draught.

About a week has passed, and I am now finishing this statement under the influence of the last of the old powders. This, then, is the last time, short of a miracle, that Henry Jekyll can think his own thoughts or see his own face (now how sadly altered!) in the glass. Nor must I delay too long to bring my writing to an end; for if my narrative has hitherto escaped destruction, it has been by a combination of great prudence and great good luck. Should the throes of change take me in the act of writing it, Hyde will tear it in pieces; but if some time shall have elapsed after I have laid it by, his wonderful selfishness and circumscription to the moment will probably save it once again from the action of his ape-like spite. And indeed the doom that is closing on us both has already changed and crushed him. Half an hour from now, when I shall again and forever reindue that hated personality, I know how I shall sit shuddering and weeping in my chair, or continue, with the most strained and fearstruck ecstasy of listening, to pace up and down this room (my last earthly refuge) and give ear to every sound of menace. Will Hyde die upon the scaffold? or will he find courage to release himself at the last moment? God knows; I am careless; this is my true hour of death, and what is to follow concerns another than myself. Here then, as I lay down the pen and proceed to seal up my confession, I bring the life of that unhappy Henry Jekyll to an end.

THE DYNAMITER

To messrs. Cole and Cox, Police Officers:

GENTLEMEN,—In the volume now in your hands, the authors have touched upon that ugly devil of crime, with which it is your glory to have contended. It were a waste of ink to do so in a serious spirit. Let us dedicate our horror to acts of a more mingled strain, where crime preserves some features of nobility, and where reason and humanity can still relish the temptation. Horror, in this case, is due to Mr. Parnell: he sits before posterity silent, Mr. Forster's appeal echoing down the ages. Horror is due to ourselves, in that we have so long coquetted with political crime; not seriously weighing, not acutely following it from cause to consequence; but with a generous, unfounded heat of sentiment, like the schoolboy with the penny tale, applauding what was specious. When it touched ourselves (truly in a vile shape), we proved false to the imaginations; discovered, in a clap, that crime was no less cruel and no less ugly under sounding names; and recoiled from our false deities.

But seriousness comes most in place when we are to speak of our defenders. Whoever be in the right in this great and confused war of politics; whatever elements of greed, whatever traits of the bully, dishonour both parties in this inhuman contest;—your side, your part, is at least pure of doubt. Yours is the side of the child, of the breeding woman, of individual pity and public trust. If our society were the mere kingdom of the devil (as indeed it wears some of his colours) it yet embraces many precious elements and many innocent persons whom it is a glory to defend. Courage and devotion, so common in the ranks of the police, so little recognised, so meagerly rewarded, have at length found their commemoration in an historical act. History, which will represent Mr. Parnell sitting silent under the appeal of Mr. Forster, and Gordon setting forth upon his tragic enterprise, will not forget Mr. Cole carrying the dynamite in his defenceless hands, nor Mr. Cox coming coolly to his aid.

Robert Louis Stevenson & Fanny Van De Grift Stevenson

A Note for the Reader

IT is within the bounds of possibility that you may take up this volume, and yet be unacquainted with its predecessor: the first series of NEW ARABIAN NIGHTS. The loss is yours—and mine; or to be more exact, my publishers'. But if you are thus unlucky, the least I can do is to pass you a hint. When you shall find a reference in the following pages to one Theophilus Godall of the Bohemian Cigar Divan in Rupert Street, Soho, you must be prepared to recognise, under his features, no less a person than Prince Florizel of Bohemia, formerly one of the magnates of Europe, now dethroned, exiled, impoverished, and embarked in the tobacco trade.

    R. L. S.

Prologue of the Cigar Divan

IN the city of encounters, the Bagdad of the West, and, to be more precise, on the broad northern pavement of Leicester Square, two young men of five- or six-and-twenty met after years of separation. The first, who was of a very smooth address and clothed in the best fashion, hesitated to recognise the pinched and shabby air of his companion.

'What!' he cried, 'Paul Somerset!'

'I am indeed Paul Somerset,' returned the other, 'or what remains of him after a well-deserved experience of poverty and law. But in you, Challoner, I can perceive no change; and time may be said, without hyperbole, to write no wrinkle on your azure brow.'

'All,' replied Challoner, 'is not gold that glitters. But we are here in an ill posture for confidences, and interrupt the movement of these ladies. Let us, if you please, find a more private corner.'

'If you will allow me to guide you,' replied Somerset, 'I will offer you the best cigar in London.'

And taking the arm of his companion, he led him in silence and at a brisk pace to the door of a quiet establishment in Rupert Street, Soho. The entrance was adorned with one of those gigantic Highlanders of wood which have almost risen to the standing of antiquities; and across the window-glass, which sheltered the usual display of pipes, tobacco, and cigars, there ran the gilded legend: 'Bohemian Cigar Divan, by T. Godall.' The interior of the shop was small, but commodious and ornate; the salesman grave, smiling, and urbane; and the two young men, each puffing a select regalia, had soon taken their places on a sofa of mouse-coloured plush and proceeded to exchange their stories.

'I am now,' said Somerset, 'a barrister; but Providence and the attorneys have hitherto denied me the opportunity to shine. A select society at the Cheshire Cheese engaged my evenings; my afternoons, as Mr. Godall could testify, have been generally passed in this divan; and my mornings, I have taken the precaution to abbreviate by not rising before twelve. At this rate, my little patrimony was very rapidly, and I am proud to remember, most agreeably expended.

Since then a gentleman, who has really nothing else to recommend him beyond the fact of being my maternal uncle, deals me the small sum of ten shillings a week; and if you behold me once more revisiting the glimpses of the street lamps in my favourite quarter, you will readily divine that I have come into a fortune.'

'I should not have supposed so,' replied Challoner. 'But doubtless I met you on the way to your tailors.'

'It is a visit that I purpose to delay,' returned Somerset, with a smile. 'My fortune has definite limits. It consists, or rather this morning it consisted, of one hundred pounds.'

'That is certainly odd,' said Challoner; 'yes, certainly the coincidence is strange. I am myself reduced to the same margin.'

'You!' cried Somerset. 'And yet Solomon in all his glory—'

'Such is the fact. I am, dear boy, on my last legs,' said Challoner. 'Besides the clothes in which you see me, I have scarcely a decent trouser in my wardrobe; and if I knew how, I would this instant set about some sort of work or commerce. With a hundred pounds for capital, a man should push his way.'

'It may be,' returned Somerset; 'but what to do with mine is more than I can fancy. Mr. Godall,' he added, addressing the salesman, 'you are a man who knows the world: what can a young fellow of reasonable education do with a hundred pounds?'

'It depends,' replied the salesman, withdrawing his cheroot. 'The power of money is an article of faith in which I profess myself a sceptic. A hundred pounds will with difficulty support you for a year; with somewhat more difficulty you may spend it in a night; and without any difficulty at all you may lose it in five minutes on the Stock Exchange. If you are of that stamp of man that rises, a penny would be as useful; if you belong to those that fall, a penny would be no more useless. When I was myself thrown unexpectedly upon the world, it was my fortune to possess an art: I knew a good cigar. Do you know nothing, Mr. Somerset?'

'Not even law,' was the reply.

'The answer is worthy of a sage,' returned Mr. Godall. 'And you, sir,' he continued, turning to Challoner, 'as the friend of Mr. Somerset, may I be allowed to address you the same question?'

'Well,' replied Challoner, 'I play a fair hand at whist.'

'How many persons are there in London,' returned the sales-man, 'who have two-and-thirty teeth? Believe me, young gentle-man, there are more still who play a fair hand at whist. Whist, sir, is wide as the world; 'tis an accomplishment like breathing. I once knew a youth who announced that he was studying to be Chancel-lor of England; the design was certainly ambitious; but I find it less excessive than that of the man who aspires to make a liveli-hood by whist.'

'Dear me,' said Challoner, 'I am afraid I shall have to fall to be a working man.'

'Fall to be a working man?' echoed Mr. Godall. 'Suppose a rural dean to be unfrocked, does he fall to be a major? suppose a captain were cashiered, would he fall to be a puisne judge? The ignorance of your middle class surprises me. Outside itself, it thinks the world to lie quite ignorant and equal, sunk in a com-mon degradation; but to the eye of the observer, all ranks are seen to stand in ordered hierarchies, and each adorned with its particu-lar aptitudes and knowledge. By the defects of your education you are more disqualified to be a working man than to be the ruler of an empire. The gulf, sir, is below; and the true learned arts—those which alone are safe from the competition of insurgent laymen— are those which give his title to the artisan.'

'This is a very pompous fellow,' said Challoner, in the ear of his companion.

'He is immense,' said Somerset.

Just then the door of the divan was opened, and a third young fellow made his appearance, and rather bashfully requested some tobacco. He was younger than the others; and, in a somewhat meaningless and altogether English way, he was a handsome lad. When he had been served, and had lighted his pipe and taken his place upon the sofa, he recalled himself to Challoner by the name of Desborough.

'Desborough, to be sure,' cried Challoner. 'Well, Desborough, and what do you do?'

'The fact is,' said Desborough, 'that I am doing nothing.'

'A private fortune possibly?' inquired the other.

'Well, no,' replied Desborough, rather sulkily. 'The fact is that I am waiting for something to turn up.'

'All in the same boat!' cried Somerset. 'And have you, too, one hundred pounds?'

'Worse luck,' said Mr. Desborough.

'This is a very pathetic sight, Mr. Godall,' said Somerset: 'Three futiles.'

'A character of this crowded age,' returned the salesman.

'Sir,' said Somerset, 'I deny that the age is crowded; I will admit one fact, and one fact only: that I am futile, that he is futile, and that we are all three as futile as the devil. What am I? I have smattered law, smattered letters, smattered geography, smattered mathematics; I have even a working knowledge of judicial astrology; and here I stand, all London roaring by at the street's end, as impotent as any baby. I have a prodigious contempt for my maternal uncle; but without him, it is idle to deny it, I should simply resolve into my elements like an unstable mixture. I begin to perceive that it is necessary to know some one thing to the bottom—were it only literature. And yet, sir, the man of the world is a great feature of this age; he is possessed of an extraordinary mass and variety of knowledge; he is everywhere at home; he has seen life in all its phases; and it is impossible but that this great habit of existence should bear fruit. I count myself a man of the world, accomplished, CAP-A-PIE. So do you, Challoner. And you, Mr. Desborough?'

'Oh yes,' returned the young man.

'Well then, Mr. Godall, here we stand, three men of the world, without a trade to cover us, but planted at the strategic centre of the universe (for so you will allow me to call Rupert Street), in the midst of the chief mass of people, and within ear-shot of the most continuous chink of money on the surface of the globe. Sir, as civilised men, what do we do? I will show you. You take in a paper?'

'I take,' said Mr. Godall solemnly, 'the best paper in the world, the STANDARD.'

'Good,' resumed Somerset. 'I now hold it in my hand, the voice of the world, a telephone repeating all men's wants. I open it, and where my eye first falls—well, no, not Morrison's Pills—but here, sure enough, and but a little above, I find the joint that I was seeking; here is the weak spot in the armour of society. Here is a want, a plaint, an offer of substantial gratitude: "TWO HUNDRED POUNDS REWARD. —The above reward will be paid to any person giving information as to the identity and whereabouts of a man observed yesterday in the neighbourhood of the Green Park. He was over six feet in height, with shoulders disproportionately broad, close shaved, with black moustaches, and wearing a sealskin great-coat." There, gentlemen, our fortune, if not made, is founded.'

'Do you then propose, dear boy, that we should turn detectives?' inquired Challoner.

'Do I propose it? No, sir,' cried Somerset. 'It is reason, destiny, the plain face of the world, that commands and imposes it. Here all our merits tell; our manners, habit of the world, powers of conversation, vast stores of unconnected knowledge, all that we are and have builds up the character of the complete detective. It is, in short, the only profession for a gentleman.'

'The proposition is perhaps excessive,' replied Challoner; 'for hitherto I own I have regarded it as of all dirty, sneaking, and ungentlemanly trades, the least and lowest.'

'To defend society?' asked Somerset; 'to stake one's life for others? to deracinate occult and powerful evil? I appeal to Mr. Godall. He, at least, as a philosophic looker-on at life, will spit upon such philistine opinions. He knows that the policeman, as he is called upon continually to face greater odds, and that both worse equipped and for a better cause, is in form and essence a more noble hero than the soldier. Do you, by any chance, deceive yourself into supposing that a general would either ask or expect, from the best army ever marshalled, and on the most momentous battle-field, the conduct of a common constable at Peckham Rye?'

'I did not understand we were to join the force,' said Challoner.

'Nor shall we. These are the hands; but here—here, sir, is the head,' cried Somerset. 'Enough; it is decreed. We shall hunt down this miscreant in the sealskin coat.'

'Suppose that we agreed,' retorted Challoner, 'you have no plan, no knowledge; you know not where to seek for a beginning.'

'Challoner!' cried Somerset, 'is it possible that you hold the doctrine of Free Will? And are you devoid of any tincture of philosophy, that you should harp on such exploded fallacies? Chance, the blind Madonna of the Pagan, rules this terrestrial bustle; and in Chance I place my sole reliance. Chance has brought us three together; when we next separate and go forth our several ways, Chance will continually drag before our careless eyes a thousand eloquent clues, not to this mystery only, but to the countless mysteries by which we live surrounded. Then comes the part of the man of the world, of the detective born and bred. This clue, which the whole town beholds without comprehension, swift as a cat, he leaps upon it, makes it his, follows it with craft and passion, and from one trifling circumstance divines a world.'

'Just so,' said Challoner; 'and I am delighted that you should recognise these virtues in yourself. But in the meanwhile, dear boy, I own myself incapable of joining. I was neither born nor bred as a detective, but as a placable and very thirsty gentleman; and, for my part, I begin to weary for a drink. As for clues and adventures, the only adventure that is ever likely to occur to me will be an adventure with a bailiff.'

'Now there is the fallacy,' cried Somerset. 'There I catch the secret of your futility in life. The world teems and bubbles with adventure; it besieges you along the street: hands waving out of windows, swindlers coming up and swearing they knew you when you were abroad, affable and doubtful people of all sorts and conditions begging and truckling for your notice. But not you: you turn away, you walk your seedy mill round, you must go the dullest way. Now here, I beg of you, the next adventure that offers itself, embrace it in with both your arms; whatever it looks, grimy or romantic, grasp it. I will do the like; the devil is in it, but at least we shall have fun; and each in turn we shall narrate the story of our fortunes to my philosophic friend of the divan, the great Godall, now hearing me with inward joy. Come, is it a bargain? Will you, indeed, both promise to welcome every chance that offers, to plunge boldly into every opening, and, keeping the eye wary and the head composed, to study and piece together all that happens? Come, promise: let me open to you the doors of the great profession of intrigue.'

'It is not much in my way,' said Challoner, 'but, since you make a point of it, amen.'

'I don't mind promising,' said Desborough, 'but nothing will happen to me.'

'O faithless ones!' cried Somerset. 'But at least I have your promises; and Godall, I perceive, is transported with delight.'

'I promise myself at least much pleasure from your various narratives,' said the salesman, with the customary calm polish of his manner.

'And now, gentlemen,' concluded Somerset, 'let us separate. I hasten to put myself in fortune's way. Hark how, in this quiet corner, London roars like the noise of battle; four million destinies are here concentred; and in the strong panoply of one hundred pounds, payable to the bearer, I am about to plunge into that web.'

Challoner's Adventure: The Squire of Dames

MR. EDWARD CHALLONER had set up lodgings in the suburb of Putney, where he enjoyed a parlour and bedroom and the sincere esteem of the people of the house. To this remote home he found himself, at a very early hour in the morning of the next day, condemned to set forth on foot. He was a young man of a portly habit; no lover of the exercises of the body; bland, sedentary, patient of delay, a prop of omnibuses. In happier days he would have chartered a cab; but these luxuries were now denied him; and with what courage he could muster he addressed himself to walk.

It was then the height of the season and the summer; the weather was serene and cloudless; and as he paced under the blinded houses and along the vacant streets, the chill of the dawn had fled, and some of the warmth and all the brightness of the July day already shone upon the city. He walked at first in a profound abstraction, bitterly reviewing and repenting his performances at whist; but as he advanced into the labyrinth of the south-west, his ear was gradually mastered by the silence. Street after street looked down upon his solitary figure, house after house echoed upon his passage with a ghostly jar, shop after shop displayed its shuttered front and its commercial legend; and meanwhile he steered his course, under day's effulgent dome and through this encampment of diurnal sleepers, lonely as a ship.

'Here,' he reflected, 'if I were like my scatter-brained companion, here were indeed the scene where I might look for an adventure. Here, in broad day, the streets are secret as in the blackest night of January, and in the midst of some four million sleepers, solitary as the woods of Yucatan. If I but raise my voice I could summon up the number of an army, and yet the grave is not more silent than this city of sleep.'

He was still following these quaint and serious musings when he came into a street of more mingled ingredients than was common in the quarter. Here, on the one hand, framed in walls and the green tops of trees, were several of those discreet, BIJOU residences on which propriety is apt to look askance. Here, too, were many of the brick-fronted barracks of the poor; a plaster cow, perhaps, serving as ensign to a dairy, or a ticket announcing the business of the mangler. Before one such house, that stood a little separate among walled gardens, a cat was playing with a straw, and Challoner paused a moment, looking on this sleek and solitary creature, who seemed an emblem of the neighbouring peace. With the cessation of the sound of his own steps the silence fell dead; the house stood smokeless: the blinds down, the whole machinery of life arrested; and it seemed to Challoner that he should hear the breathing of the sleepers.

As he so stood, he was startled by a dull and jarring detonation from within. This was followed by a monstrous hissing and simmering as from a kettle of the bigness of St. Paul's; and at the same time from every chink of door and window spirted an ill-smelling vapour. The cat disappeared with a cry. Within the lodging-house feet pounded on the stairs; the door flew back, emitting clouds of smoke; and two men and an elegantly dressed young lady tumbled forth into the street and fled without a word. The hissing had already ceased, the smoke was melting in the air, the whole event had come and gone as in a dream, and still Challoner was rooted to the spot. At last his reason and his fear awoke together, and with the most unwonted energy he fell to running.

Little by little this first dash relaxed, and presently he had resumed his sober gait and begun to piece together, out of the confused report of his senses, some theory of the occurrence. But the occasion of the sounds and stench that had so suddenly assailed him, and the strange conjunction of fugitives whom he had seen to issue from the house, were mysteries beyond his plummet. With an obscure awe he considered them in his mind, continuing, meanwhile, to thread the web of streets, and once more alone in morning sunshine.

In his first retreat he had entirely wandered; and now, steering vaguely west, it was his luck to light upon an unpretending street, which presently widened so as to admit a strip of gardens in the midst. Here was quite a stir of birds; even at that hour, the shadow of the leaves was grateful; instead of the burnt atmosphere of cities, there was something brisk and rural in the air; and Challoner paced forward, his eyes upon the pavement and his mind running upon distant scenes, till he was recalled, upon a sudden, by a wall that blocked his further progress. This street, whose name I have forgotten, is no thoroughfare.

He was not the first who had wandered there that morning; for as he raised his eyes with an agreeable deliberation, they alighted on the figure of a girl, in whom he was struck to recognise the third of the incongruous fugitives. She had run there, seemingly, blindfold; the wall had checked her career: and being entirely wearied, she had sunk upon the ground beside the garden railings, soiling her dress among the summer dust. Each saw the other in the same instant of time; and she, with one wild look, sprang to her feet and began to hurry from the scene.

Challoner was doubly startled to meet once more the heroine of his adventure, and to observe the fear with which she shunned him. Pity and alarm, in nearly equal forces, contested the possession of his mind; and yet, in spite of both, he saw himself condemned to follow in the lady's wake. He did so gingerly, as fearing to increase her terrors; but, tread as lightly as he might, his footfalls eloquently echoed in the empty street. Their sound appeared to strike in her some strong emotion; for scarce had he begun to follow ere she paused. A second time she addressed herself to flight; and a second time she paused. Then she turned about, and with doubtful steps and the most attractive appearance of timidity, drew near to the young man. He on his side continued to advance with similar signals of distress and bashfulness. At length, when they were but some steps apart, he saw her eyes brim over, and she reached out both her hands in eloquent appeal.

'Are you an English gentleman?' she cried.

The unhappy Challoner regarded her with consternation. He was the spirit of fine courtesy, and would have blushed to fail in his devoirs to any lady; but, in the other scale, he was a man averse from amorous adventures. He looked east and west; but the houses that looked down upon this interview remained inexorably shut; and he saw himself, though in the full glare of the day's eye, cut off from any human intervention. His looks returned at last upon the suppliant. He remarked with irritation that she was charming both in face and figure, elegantly dressed and gloved; a lady undeniable; the picture of distress and innocence; weeping and lost in the city of diurnal sleep.

'Madam,' he said, 'I protest you have no cause to fear intrusion; and if I have appeared to follow you, the fault is in this street, which has deceived us both.' An unmistakable relief appeared upon the lady's face. 'I might have guessed it!' she exclaimed. 'Thank you a thousand times! But at this hour, in this appalling silence, and among all these staring windows, I am lost in terrors—oh, lost in them!' she cried, her face blanching at the words. 'I beg you to lend me your arm,' she added with the loveliest, suppliant inflection. 'I dare not go alone; my nerve is gone—I had a shock, oh, what a shock! I beg of you to be my escort.'

'My dear madam,' responded Challoner heavily, 'my arm is at your service.'

'She took it and clung to it for a moment, struggling with her sobs; and the next, with feverish hurry, began to lead him in the direction of the city. One thing was plain, among so much that was obscure: it was plain her fears were genuine. Still, as she went, she spied around as if for dangers; and now she would shiver like a person in a chill, and now clutch his arm in hers. To Challoner her terror was at once repugnant and infectious; it gained and mastered, while it still offended him; and he wailed in spirit and longed for release.

'Madam,' he said at last, 'I am, of course, charmed to be of use to any lady; but I confess I was bound in a direction opposite to that you follow, and a word of explanation—'

'Hush!' she sobbed, 'not here—not here!'

The blood of Challoner ran cold. He might have thought the lady mad; but his memory was charged with more perilous stuff; and in view of the detonation, the smoke and the flight of the ill-assorted trio, his mind was lost among mysteries. So they continued to thread the maze of streets in silence, with the speed of a guilty flight, and both thrilling with incommunicable terrors. In time, however, and above all by their quick pace of walking, the pair began to rise to firmer spirits; the lady ceased to peer about the corners; and Challoner, emboldened by the resonant tread and distant figure of a constable, returned to the charge with more of spirit and directness.

'I thought,' said he, in the tone of conversation, 'that I had indistinctly perceived you leaving a villa in the company of two gentlemen.'

'Oh!' she said, 'you need not fear to wound me by the truth. You saw me flee from a common lodging-house, and my companions were not gentlemen. In such a case, the best of compliments is to be frank.'

'I thought,' resumed Challoner, encouraged as much as he was surprised by the spirit of her reply, 'to have perceived, besides, a certain odour. A noise, too—I do not know to what I should compare it—'

'Silence!' she cried. 'You do not know the danger you invoke. Wait, only wait; and as soon as we have left those streets, and got beyond the reach of listeners, all shall be explained. Meanwhile, avoid the topic. What a sight is this sleeping city!' she exclaimed; and then, with a most thrilling voice, '"Dear God," she quoted, "the very houses seem asleep, and all that mighty heart is lying still."'

'I perceive, madam,' said he, 'you are a reader.'

'I am more than that,' she answered, with a sigh. 'I am a girl condemned to thoughts beyond her age; and so untoward is my fate, that this walk upon the arm of a stranger is like an interlude of peace.'

They had come by this time to the neighbourhood of the Victoria Station and here, at a street corner, the young lady paused, withdrew her arm from Challoner's, and looked up and down as though in pain or indecision. Then, with a lovely change of countenance, and laying her gloved hand upon his arm—

'What you already think of me,' she said, 'I tremble to conceive; yet I must here condemn myself still further. Here I must leave you, and here I beseech you to wait for my return. Do not attempt to follow me or spy upon my actions. Suspend yet awhile your judgment of a girl as innocent as your own sister; and do not, above all, desert me. Stranger as you are, I have none else to look to. You see me in sorrow and great fear; you are a gentleman, courteous and kind: and when I beg for a few minutes' patience, I make sure beforehand you will not deny me.'

Challoner grudgingly promised; and the young lady, with a grateful eye-shot, vanished round the corner. But the force of her appeal had been a little blunted; for the young man was not only destitute of sisters, but of any female relative nearer than a great-aunt in Wales. Now he was alone, besides, the spell that he had hitherto obeyed began to weaken; he considered his behaviour with a sneer; and plucking up the spirit of revolt, he started in pursuit. The reader, if he has ever plied the fascinating trade of the noctambulist, will not be unaware that, in the neighbourhood of the great railway centres, certain early taverns inaugurate the business of the day. It was into one of these that Challoner, coming round the corner of the block, beheld his charming companion disappear. To say he was surprised were inexact, for he had long since left that sentiment behind him. Acute disgust and disappointment seized upon his soul; and with silent oaths, he damned this commonplace enchantress. She had scarce been gone a second, ere the swing-doors reopened, and she appeared again in company with a young man of mean and slouching attire. For some five or six exchanges they conversed together with an animated air; then the fellow shouldered again into the tap; and the young lady, with something swifter than a walk, retraced her steps towards Challoner. He saw her coming, a miracle of grace; her ankle, as she hurried, flashing from her dress; her movements eloquent of speed and youth; and though he still entertained some thoughts of flight, they grew miserably fainter as the distance lessened. Against mere beauty he was proof: it was her unmistakable gentility that now robbed him of the courage of his cowardice. With a proved adventuress he had acted strictly on his right; with one who, in spite of all, he could not quite deny to be a lady, he found himself disarmed. At the very corner from whence he had spied upon her interview, she came upon him, still transfixed, and—'Ah!' she cried, with a bright flush of colour. 'Ah! Ungenerous!'

The sharpness of the attack somewhat restored the Squire of Dames to the possession of himself.

'Madam,' he returned, with a fair show of stoutness, 'I do not think that hitherto you can complain of any lack of generosity; I have suffered myself to be led over a considerable portion of the metropolis; and if I now request you to discharge me of my office of protector, you have friends at hand who will be glad of the succession.'

She stood a moment dumb.

'It is well,' she said. 'Go! go, and may God help me! You have seen me—me, an innocent girl! fleeing from a dire catastrophe and haunted by sinister men; and neither pity, curiosity, nor honour move you to await my explanation or to help in my distress. Go!' she repeated. 'I am lost indeed.' And with a passionate gesture she turned and fled along the street.

Challoner observed her retreat and disappear, an almost intolerable sense of guilt contending with the profound sense that he was being gulled. She was no sooner gone than the first of these feelings took the upper hand; he felt, if he had done her less than justice, that his conduct was a perfect model of the ungracious; the cultured tone of her voice, her choice of language, and the elegant decorum of her movements, cried out aloud against a harsh

construction; and between penitence and curiosity he began
slowly to follow in her wake. At the corner he had her once more
full in view. Her speed was failing like a stricken bird's. Even as he
looked, she threw her arm out gropingly, and fell and leaned
against the wall. At the spectacle, Challoner's fortitude gave way.
In a few strides he overtook her and, for the first time removing
his hat, assured her in the most moving terms of his entire respect
and firm desire to help her. He spoke at first unheeded; but gradually it appeared that she began to comprehend his words; she
moved a little, and drew herself upright; and finally, as with a sudden movement of forgiveness, turned on the young man a countenance in which reproach and gratitude were mingled. 'Ah,
madam,' he cried, 'use me as you will!' And once more, but now
with a great air of deference, he offered her the conduct of his arm.
She took it with a sigh that struck him to the heart; and they began
once more to trace the deserted streets. But now her steps, as
though exhausted by emotion, began to linger on the way; she
leaned the more heavily upon his arm; and he, like the parent bird,
stooped fondly above his drooping convoy. Her physical distress
was not accompanied by any failing of her spirits; and hearing her
strike so soon into a playful and charming vein of talk, Challoner
could not sufficiently admire the elasticity of his companion's
nature. 'Let me forget,' she had said, 'for one half hour, let me forget;' and sure enough, with the very word, her sorrows appeared to
be forgotten. Before every house she paused, invented a name for
the proprietor, and sketched his character: here lived the old general whom she was to marry on the fifth of the next month, there
was the mansion of the rich widow who had set her heart on Challoner; and though she still hung wearily on the young man's arm,
her laughter sounded low and pleasant in his ears. 'Ah,' she sighed,
by way of commentary, 'in such a life as mine I must seize tight
hold of any happiness that I can find.'

   When they arrived, in this leisurely manner, at the head of
Grosvenor Place, the gates of the park were opening and the bed-
raggled company of night-walkers were being at last admitted into
that paradise of lawns. Challoner and his companion followed the
movement, and walked for awhile in silence in that tatterdemalion

crowd; but as one after another, weary with the night's patrolling of the city pavement, sank upon the benches or wandered into separate paths, the vast extent of the park had soon utterly swallowed up the last of these intruders; and the pair proceeded on their way alone in the grateful quiet of the morning.

Presently they came in sight of a bench, standing very open on a mound of turf. The young lady looked about her with relief.

'Here,' she said, 'here at last we are secure from listeners. Here, then, you shall learn and judge my history. I could not bear that we should part, and that you should still suppose your kindness squandered upon one who was unworthy.'

Thereupon she sat down upon the bench, and motioning Challoner to take a place immediately beside her, began in the following words, and with the greatest appearance of enjoyment, to narrate the story of her life.

Story of the Destroying Angel

MY father was a native of England, son of a cadet of a great, ancient, but untitled family; and by some event, fault or misfortune, he was driven to flee from the land of his birth and to lay aside the name of his ancestors. He sought the States; and instead of lingering in effeminate cities, pushed at once into the far West with an exploring party of frontiersmen. He was no ordinary traveller; for he was not only brave and impetuous by character, but learned in many sciences, and above all in botany, which he particularly loved. Thus it fell that, before many months, Fremont himself, the nominal leader of the troop, courted and bowed to his opinion.

They had pushed, as I have said, into the still unknown regions of the West. For some time they followed the track of Mormon caravans, guiding themselves in that vast and melancholy desert by the skeletons of men and animals. Then they inclined their route a little to the north, and, losing even these dire memorials, came into a country of forbidding stillness.

I have often heard my father dwell upon the features of that ride: rock, cliff, and barren moor alternated; the streams were very far between; and neither beast nor bird disturbed the solitude. On the fortieth day they had already run so short of food that it was judged advisable to call a halt and scatter upon all sides to hunt. A great fire was built, that its smoke might serve to rally them; and each man of the party mounted and struck off at a venture into the surrounding desert.

My father rode for many hours with a steep range of cliffs upon the one hand, very black and horrible; and upon the other an unwatered vale dotted with boulders like the site of some subverted city. At length he found the slot of a great animal, and from the claw-marks and the hair among the brush, judged that he was on the track of a cinnamon bear of most unusual size. He quickened the pace of his steed, and still following the quarry, came at last to the division of two watersheds. On the far side the country was exceeding intricate and difficult, heaped with boulders, and dotted here and there with a few pines, which seemed to indicate the neighbourhood of water. Here, then, he picketed his horse, and relying on his trusty rifle, advanced alone into that wilderness.

Presently, in the great silence that reigned, he was aware of the sound of running water to his right; and leaning in that direction, was rewarded by a scene of natural wonder and human pathos strangely intermixed. The stream ran at the bottom of a narrow and winding passage, whose wall-like sides of rock were sometimes for miles together unscalable by man. The water, when the stream was swelled with rains, must have filled it from side to side; the sun's rays only plumbed it in the hour of noon; the wind, in that narrow and damp funnel, blew tempestuously. And yet, in the bottom of this den, immediately below my father's eyes as he leaned over the margin of the cliff, a party of some half a hundred men, women, and children lay scattered uneasily among the rocks. They lay some upon their backs, some prone, and not one stirring; their upturned faces seemed all of an extraordinary paleness and emaciation; and from time to time, above the washing of the stream, a faint sound of moaning mounted to my father's ears.

While he thus looked, an old man got staggering to his feet, unwound his blanket, and laid it, with great gentleness, on a young girl who sat hard by propped against a rock. The girl did not seem to be conscious of the act; and the old man, after having looked upon her with the most engaging pity, returned to his former bed and lay down again uncovered on the turf. But the scene had not passed without observation even in that starving camp. From the very outskirts of the party, a man with a white beard and seemingly of venerable years, rose upon his knees, and came crawling stealthily among the sleepers towards the girl; and judge of my father's indignation, when he beheld this cowardly miscreant strip from her both the coverings and return with them to his original position. Here he lay down for a while below his spoils, and, as my father imagined, feigned to be asleep; but presently he had raised himself again upon one elbow, looked with sharp scrutiny at his companions, and then swiftly carried his hand into his bosom and thence to his mouth. By the movement of his jaws he must be eating; in that camp of famine he had reserved a store of nourishment; and while his companions lay in the stupor of approaching death, secretly restored his powers.

My father was so incensed at what he saw that he raised his rifle; and but for an accident, he has often declared, he would have shot the fellow dead upon the spot. How different would then have been my history! But it was not to be: even as he raised the barrel, his eye lighted on the bear, as it crawled along a ledge some way below him; and ceding to the hunters instinct, it was at the brute, not at the man, that he discharged his piece. The bear leaped and fell into a pool of the river; the canyon re-echoed the report; and in a moment the camp was afoot. With cries that were scarce human, stumbling, falling and throwing each other down, these starving people rushed upon the quarry; and before my father, climbing down by the ledge, had time to reach the level of the stream, many were already satisfying their hunger on the raw flesh, and a fire was being built by the more dainty.

His arrival was for some time unremarked. He stood in the midst of these tottering and clay-faced marionettes; he was surrounded by their cries; but their whole soul was fixed on the dead carcass; even those who were too weak to move, lay, half-turned over, with their eyes riveted upon the bear; and my father, seeing himself stand as though invisible in the thick of this dreary hub-bub, was seized with a desire to weep. A touch upon the arm restrained him. Turning about, he found himself face to face with the old man he had so nearly killed; and yet, at the second glance, recognised him for no old man at all, but one in the full strength of his years, and of a strong, speaking, and intellectual countenance stigmatised by weariness and famine. He beckoned my father near the cliff, and there, in the most private whisper, begged for brandy. My father looked at him with scorn: 'You remind me,' he said, 'of a neglected duty. Here is my flask; it contains enough, I trust, to revive the women of your party; and I will begin with her whom I saw you robbing of her blankets.' And with that, not heeding his appeals, my father turned his back upon the egoist.

The girl still lay reclined against the rock; she lay too far sunk in the first stage of death to have observed the bustle round her couch; but when my father had raised her head, put the flask to her lips, and forced or aided her to swallow some drops of the restorative, she opened her languid eyes and smiled upon him faintly. Never was there a smile of a more touching sweetness; never were eyes more deeply violet, more honestly eloquent of the soul! I speak with knowledge, for these were the same eyes that smiled upon me in the cradle. From her who was to be his wife, my father, still jealously watched and followed by the man with the grey beard, carried his attentions to all the women of the party, and gave the last drainings of his flask to those among the men who seemed in the most need.

'Is there none left? not a drop for me?' said the man with the beard.

'Not one drop,' replied my father; 'and if you find yourself in want, let me counsel you to put your hand into the pocket of your coat.'

'Ah!' cried the other, 'you misjudge me. You think me one who clings to life for selfish and commonplace considerations. But let me tell you, that were all this caravan to perish, the world would but be lightened of a weight. These are but human insects, pullulating, thick as May-flies, in the slums of European cities, whom I myself have plucked from degradation and misery, from the dung-heap and gin-palace door. And you compare their lives with mine!'

'You are then a Mormon missionary?' asked my father.

'Oh!' cried the man, with a strange smile, 'a Mormon missionary if you will! I value not the title. Were I no more than that, I could have died without a murmur. But with my life as a physician is bound up the knowledge of great secrets and the future of man. This it was, when we missed the caravan, tried for a short cut and wandered to this desolate ravine, that ate into my soul, and, in five days, has changed my beard from ebony to silver.'

'And you are a physician,' mused my father, looking on his face, 'bound by oath to succour man in his distresses.'

'Sir,' returned the Mormon, 'my name is Grierson: you will hear that name again; and you will then understand that my duty was not to this caravan of paupers, but to mankind at large.'

My father turned to the remainder of the party, who were now sufficiently revived to hear; told them that he would set off at once to bring help from his own party; 'and,' he added, 'if you be again reduced to such extremities, look round you, and you will see the earth strewn with assistance. Here, for instance, growing on the under side of fissures in this cliff, you will perceive a yellow moss. Trust me, it is both edible and excellent.'

'Ha!' said Doctor Grierson, 'you know botany!'

'Not I alone,' returned my father, lowering his voice; 'for see where these have been scraped away. Am I right? Was that your secret store?'

My father's comrades, he found, when he returned to the signal-fire, had made a good day's hunting. They were thus the more easily persuaded to extend assistance to the Mormon caravan; and the next day beheld both parties on the march for the frontiers of Utah. The distance to be traversed was not great; but the nature of the country, and the difficulty of procuring food, extended the time to nearly three weeks; and my father had thus ample leisure to know and appreciate the girl whom he had succoured. I will call my mother Lucy. Her family name I am not at liberty to mention; it is one you would know well. By what series of undeserved calamities this innocent flower of maidenhood, lovely, refined by education, ennobled by the finest taste, was thus cast among the horrors of a Mormon caravan, I must not stay to tell you. Let it suffice, that even in these untoward circumstances, she found a heart worthy of her own. The ardour of attachment which united my father and mother was perhaps partly due to the strange manner of their meeting; it knew, at least, no bounds either divine or human; my father, for her sake, determined to renounce his ambitions and abjure his faith; and a week had not yet passed upon the march before he had resigned from his party, accepted the Mormon doctrine, and received the promise of my mother's hand on the arrival of the party at Salt Lake.

The marriage took place, and I was its only offspring. My father prospered exceedingly in his affairs, remained faithful to my mother; and though you may wonder to hear it, I believe there were few happier homes in any country than that in which I saw the light and grew to girlhood. We were, indeed, and in spite of all our wealth, avoided as heretics and half-believers by the more precise and pious of the faithful: Young himself, that formidable tyrant, was known to look askance upon my father's riches; but of this I had no guess. I dwelt, indeed, under the Mormon system, with perfect innocence and faith. Some of our friends had many wives; but such was the custom; and why should it surprise me more than marriage itself? From time to time one of our rich acquaintances would disappear, his family be broken up, his wives and houses shared among the elders of the Church, and his memory only recalled with bated breath and dreadful headshakings. When I had been very still, and my presence perhaps was forgotten, some such topic would arise among my elders by the evening fire; I would see them draw the closer together and look behind them with scared eyes; and I might gather from their whisperings how some one, rich, honoured, healthy, and in the prime of his days, some one, perhaps, who had taken me on his knees a week before, had in one hour been spirited from home and family, and vanished like an image from a mirror, leaving not a print behind. It was terrible, indeed; but so was death, the universal law. And even if the talk should wax still bolder, full of ominous silences and nods, and I should hear named in a whisper the Destroying

Angels, how was a child to understand these mysteries? I heard of a Destroying Angel as some more happy child might hear in England of a bishop or a rural dean, with vague respect and without the wish for further information. Life anywhere, in society as in nature, rests upon dread foundations; I beheld safe roads, a garden blooming in the desert, pious people crowding to worship; I was aware of my parents' tenderness and all the harmless luxuries of my existence; and why should I pry beneath this honest seeming surface for the mysteries on which it stood?

We dwelt originally in the city; but at an early date we moved to a beautiful house in a green dingle, musical with splashing water, and surrounded on almost every side by twenty miles of poisonous and rocky desert. The city was thirty miles away; there was but one road, which went no further than my father's door; the rest were bridle-tracks impassable in winter; and we thus dwelt in a solitude inconceivable to the European. Our only neighbour was Dr. Grierson. To my young eyes, after the hair-oiled, chin-bearded elders of the city, and the ill-favoured and mentally stunted women of their harems, there was something agreeable in the correct manner, the fine bearing, the thin white hair and beard, and the piercing looks of the old doctor. Yet, though he was almost our only visitor, I never wholly overcame a sense of fear in his presence; and this disquietude was rather fed by the awful solitude in which he lived and the obscurity that hung about his occupations. His house was but a mile or two from ours, but very differently placed. It stood overlooking the road on the summit of a steep slope, and planted close against a range of overhanging bluffs. Nature, you would say, had here desired to imitate the works of man; for the slope was even, like the glacis of a fort, and the cliffs of a constant height, like the ramparts of a city. Not even spring could change one feature of that desolate scene; and the windows looked down across a plain, snowy with alkali, to ranges of cold stone sierras on the north. Twice or thrice I remember passing within view of this forbidding residence; and seeing it always shuttered, smokeless, and deserted, I remarked to my parents that some day it would certainly be robbed.

'Ah, no,' said my father, 'never robbed;' and I observed a strange conviction in his tone.

At last, and not long before the blow fell on my unhappy family, I chanced to see the doctor's house in a new light. My father was ill; my mother confined to his bedside; and I was suffered to go, under the charge of our driver, to the lonely house some twenty miles away, where our packages were left for us. The horse cast a shoe; night overtook us halfway home; and it was well on for three in the morning when the driver and I, alone in a light waggon, came to that part of the road which ran below the doctor's house. The moon swam clear; the cliffs and mountains in this strong light lay utterly deserted; but the house, from its station on the top of the long slope and close under the bluff, not only shone abroad from every window like a place of festival, but from the great chimney at the west end poured forth a coil of smoke so thick and so voluminous, that it hung for miles along the windless night air, and its shadow lay far abroad in the moonlight upon the glittering alkali. As we continued to draw near, besides, a regular and panting throb began to divide the silence. First it seemed to me like the beating of a heart; and next it put into my mind the thought of some giant, smothered under mountains and still, with incalculable effort, fetching breath. I had heard of the railway, though I had not seen it, and I turned to ask the driver if this resembled it. But some look in his eye, some pallor, whether of fear or moonlight on his face, caused the words to die upon my lips. We continued, therefore, to advance in silence, till we were close below the lighted house; when suddenly, without one premonitory rustle, there burst forth a report of such a bigness that it shook the earth and set the echoes of the mountains thundering from cliff to cliff. A pillar of amber flame leaped from the chimney-top and fell in multitudes of sparks; and at the same time the lights in the windows turned for one instant ruby red and then expired. The driver had checked his horse instinctively, and the echoes were still rumbling farther off among the mountains, when there broke from the now darkened interior a series of yells—whether of man or woman it was impossible to guess—the door flew open, and there ran forth into the moonlight, at the top of the long slope, a figure clad in white, which began to dance and leap and throw itself down, and roll as if in agony, before the house. I could no more restrain my cries; the driver laid his lash about the horse's flank, and we fled up the rough track at the peril of our lives; and did not draw rein till, turning the corner of the mountain, we beheld my father's ranch and deep, green groves and gardens, sleeping in the tranquil light.

This was the one adventure of my life, until my father had climbed to the very topmost point of material prosperity, and I myself had reached the age of seventeen. I was still innocent and merry like a child; tended my garden or ran upon the hills in glad simplicity; gave not a thought to coquetry or to material cares; and if my eye rested on my own image in a mirror or some sylvan spring, it was to seek and recognise the features of my parents. But the fears which had long pressed on others were now to be laid on my youth. I had thrown myself, one sultry, cloudy afternoon, on a divan; the windows stood open on the verandah, where my mother sat with her embroidery; and when my father joined her from the garden, their conversation, clearly audible to me, was of so startling a nature that it held me enthralled where I lay.

'The blow has come,' my father said, after a long pause.

I could hear my mother start and turn, but in words she made no reply.

'Yes,' continued my father, 'I have received to-day a list of all that I possess; of all, I say; of what I have lent privately to men whose lips are sealed with terror; of what I have buried with my own hand on the bare mountain, when there was not a bird in heaven. Does the air, then, carry secrets? Are the hills of glass? Do the stones we tread upon preserve the footprint to betray us? Oh, Lucy, Lucy, that we should have come to such a country!'

'But this,' returned my mother, 'is no very new or very threatening event. You are accused of some concealment. You will pay more taxes in the future, and be mulcted in a fine. It is disquieting, indeed, to find our acts so spied upon, and the most private known. But is this new? Have we not long feared and suspected every blade of grass?'

'Ay, and our shadows!' cried my father. 'But all this is nothing. Here is the letter that accompanied the list.'

I heard my mother turn the pages, and she was some time silent.

'I see,' she said at last; and then, with the tone of one reading: "'From a believer so largely blessed by Providence with this world's goods,'" she continued, "'the Church awaits in confidence some signal mark of piety." There lies the sting. Am I not right? These are the words you fear?'

'These are the words,' replied my father. 'Lucy, you remember Priestley? Two days before he disappeared, he carried me to the summit of an isolated butte; we could see around us for ten miles; sure, if in any quarter of this land a man were safe from spies, it were in such a station; but it was in the very ague-fit of terror that he told me, and that I heard, his story. He had received a letter such as this; and he submitted to my approval an answer, in which he offered to resign a third of his possessions. I conjured him, as he valued life, to raise his offering; and, before we parted, he had doubled the amount. Well, two days later he was gone—gone from the chief street of the city in the hour of noon—and gone for ever. O God!' cried my father, 'by what art do they thus spirit out of life the solid body? What death do they command that leaves no traces? that this material structure, these strong arms, this skeleton that can resist the grave for centuries, should be thus reft in a moment from the world of sense? A horror dwells in that thought more awful than mere death.'

'Is there no hope in Grierson?' asked my mother.

'Dismiss the thought,' replied my father. 'He now knows all that I can teach, and will do naught to save me. His power, besides, is small, his own danger not improbably more imminent than mine; for he, too, lives apart; he leaves his wives neglected and unwatched; he is openly cited for an unbeliever; and unless he buys security at a more awful price —but no; I will not believe it: I have no love for him, but I will not believe it.'

'Believe what?' asked my mother; and then, with a change of note, 'But oh, what matters it?' she cried. 'Abimelech, there is but one way open: we must fly!'

'It is in vain,' returned my father. 'I should but involve you in my fate. To leave this land is hopeless: we are closed in it as men are closed in life; and there is no issue but the grave.'

'We can but die then,' replied my mother. 'Let us at least die together. Let not Asenath and myself survive you. Think to what a fate we should be doomed!'

My father was unable to resist her tender violence; and though I could see he nourished not one spark of hope, he consented to desert his whole estate, beyond some hundreds of dollars that he had by him at the moment, and to flee that night, which promised to be dark and cloudy. As soon as the servants were asleep, he was to load two mules with provisions; two others were to carry my mother and myself; and, striking through the mountains by an unfrequented trail, we were to make a fair stroke for liberty and life. As soon as they had thus decided, I showed myself at the window, and, owning that I had heard all, assured them that they could rely on my prudence and devotion. I had no fear, indeed, but to show myself unworthy of my birth; I held my life in my hand without alarm; and when my father, weeping upon my neck, had blessed Heaven for the courage of his child, it was with a sentiment of pride and some of the joy that warriors take in war, that I began to look forward to the perils of our flight.

Before midnight, under an obscure and starless heaven, we had left far behind us the plantations of the valley, and were mounting a certain canyon in the hills, narrow, encumbered with great rocks, and echoing with the roar of a tumultuous torrent. Cascade after cascade thundered and hung up its flag of whiteness in the night, or fanned our faces with the wet wind of its descent. The trail was breakneck, and led to famine-guarded deserts; it had been long since deserted for more practicable routes; and it was now a part of the world untrod from year to year by human footing. Judge of our dismay, when turning suddenly an angle of the cliffs, we found a bright bonfire blazing by itself under an impending rock; and on the face of the rock, drawn very rudely with charred wood, the great Open Eye which is the emblem of the Mormon faith. We looked upon each other in the firelight; my mother broke into a passion of tears; but not a word was said. The mules were turned about; and leaving that great eye to guard the lonely canyon, we retraced our steps in silence. Day had not yet broken ere we were once more at home, condemned beyond reprieve.

What answer my father sent I was not told; but two days later, a little before sundown, I saw a plain, honest-looking man ride slowly up the road in a great pother of dust. He was clad in homespun, with a broad straw hat; wore a patriarchal beard; and had an air of a simple rustic farmer, that was, in my eyes, very reassuring. He was, indeed, a very honest man and pious Mormon; with no liking for his errand, though neither he nor any one in Utah dared to disobey; and it was with every mark of diffidence that he had had himself announced as Mr. Aspinwall, and entered the room where our unhappy family was gathered. My mother and me, he awkwardly enough dismissed; and as soon as he was alone with my father laid before him a blank signature of President Young's, and offered him a choice of services: either to set out as a missionary to the tribes about the White Sea, or to join the next day, with a party of Destroying Angels, in the massacre of sixty German immigrants. The last, of course, my father could not entertain, and the first he regarded as a pretext: even if he could consent to leave his wife defenceless, and to collect fresh victims for the tyranny under which he was himself oppressed, he felt sure he would never be suffered to return. He refused both; and Aspinwall, he said, betrayed sincere emotion, part religious, at the spectacle of such disobedience, but part human, in pity for my father and his family. He besought him to reconsider his decision; and at length, finding he could not prevail, gave him till the moon rose to settle his affairs, and say farewell to wife and daughter. 'For,' said he, 'then, at the latest, you must ride with me.'

I dare not dwell upon the hours that followed: they fled all too fast; and presently the moon out-topped the eastern range, and my father and Mr. Aspinwall set forth, side by side, on their nocturnal journey. My mother, though still bearing an heroic countenance, had hastened to shut herself in her apartment, thenceforward solitary; and I, alone in the dark house, and consumed by grief and apprehension, made haste to saddle my Indian pony, to ride up to the corner of the mountain, and to enjoy one farewell sight of my departing father. The two men had set forth at a deliberate pace; nor was I long behind them, when I reached the point of view. I was the more amazed to see no moving creature in the landscape. The moon, as the saying is, shone bright as day; and nowhere, under the whole arch of night, was there a growing tree, a bush, a farm, a patch of tillage, or any evidence of man, but one. From the corner where I stood, a rugged bastion of the line of bluffs concealed the doctor's house; and across the top of that projection the soft night wind carried and unwound about the hills a coil of sable smoke. What fuel could produce a vapour so sluggish to dissipate in that dry air, or what furnace pour it forth so copiously, I was unable to conceive; but I knew well enough that it came from the doctor's chimney; I saw well enough that my father had already disappeared; and in despite of reason, I connected in my mind the loss of that dear protector with the ribbon of foul smoke that trailed along the mountains.

Days passed, and still my mother and I waited in vain for news; a week went by, a second followed, but we heard no word of the father and husband. As smoke dissipates, as the image glides from the mirror, so in the ten or twenty minutes that I had spent in getting my horse and following upon his trail, had that strong and brave man vanished out of life. Hope, if any hope we had, fled with every hour; the worst was now certain for my father, the worst was to be dreaded for his defenceless family. Without weakness, with a desperate calm at which I marvel when I look back upon it, the widow and the orphan awaited the event. On the last day of the third week we rose in the morning to find ourselves alone in the house, alone, so far as we searched, on the estate; all our attendants, with one accord, had fled: and as we knew them to be gratefully devoted, we drew the darkest intimations from their flight. The day passed, indeed, without event; but in the fall of the evening we were called at last into the verandah by the approaching clink of horse's hoofs.

The doctor, mounted on an Indian pony, rode into the garden, dismounted, and saluted us. He seemed much more bent, and his hair more silvery than ever; but his demeanour was composed, serious, and not unkind.

'Madam,' said he, 'I am come upon a weighty errand; and I would have you recognise it as an effect of kindness in the President, that he should send as his ambassador your only neighbour and your husband's oldest friend in Utah.'

'Sir,' said my mother, 'I have but one concern, one thought. You know well what it is. Speak: my husband?'

'Madam,' returned the doctor, taking a chair on the verandah, 'if you were a silly child, my position would now be painfully embarrassing. You are, on the other hand, a woman of great intelligence and fortitude: you have, by my forethought, been allowed three weeks to draw your own conclusions and to accept the inevitable. Farther words from me are, I conceive, superfluous.'

My mother was as pale as death, and trembled like a reed; I gave her my hand, and she kept it in the folds of her dress and wrung it till I could have cried aloud. 'Then, sir,' said she at last, 'you speak to deaf ears. If this be indeed so, what have I to do with errands? What do I ask of Heaven but to die?'

'Come,' said the doctor, 'command yourself. I bid you dismiss all thoughts of your late husband, and bring a clear mind to bear upon your own future and the fate of that young girl.'

'You bid me dismiss—' began my mother. 'Then you know!' she cried.

'I know,' replied the doctor.

'You know?' broke out the poor woman. 'Then it was you who did the deed! I tear off the mask, and with dread and loathing see you as you are—you, whom the poor fugitive beholds in nightmares, and awakes raving—you, the Destroying Angel!'

'Well, madam, and what then?' returned the doctor. 'Have not my fate and yours been similar? Are we not both immured in this strong prison of Utah? Have you not tried to flee, and did not the Open Eye confront you in the canyon? Who can escape the watch of that unsleeping eye of Utah? Not I, at least. Horrible tasks have, indeed, been laid upon me; and the most ungrateful was the last; but had I refused my offices, would that have spared your husband? You know well it would not. I, too, had perished along with him; nor would I have been able to alleviate his last moments, nor could I to-day have stood between his family and the hand of Brigham Young.'

'Ah!' cried I, 'and could you purchase life by such concessions?'

'Young lady,' answered the doctor, 'I both could and did; and you will live to thank me for that baseness. You have a spirit, Asenath, that it pleases me to recognise. But we waste time. Mr. Fonblanque's estate reverts, as you doubtless imagine, to the Church; but some part of it has been reserved for him who is to marry the family; and that person, I should perhaps tell you without more delay, is no other than myself.'

At this odious proposal my mother and I cried out aloud, and clung together like lost souls.

'It is as I supposed,' resumed the doctor, with the same measured utterance. 'You recoil from this arrangement. Do you expect me to convince you? You know very well that I have never held the Mormon view of women. Absorbed in the most arduous studies, I have left the slatterns whom they call my wives to scratch and quarrel among themselves; of me, they have had nothing but my purse; such was not the union I desired, even if I had the leisure to pursue it. No: you need not, madam, and my old friend'—and here the doctor rose and bowed with something of gallantry—'you need not apprehend my importunities. On the contrary, I am rejoiced to read in you a Roman spirit; and if I am obliged to bid you follow me at once, and that in the name, not of my wish, but of my orders, I hope it will be found that we are of a common mind.'

So, bidding us dress for the road, he took a lamp (for the night had now fallen) and set off to the stable to prepare our horses.

'What does it mean?—what will become of us?' I cried.

'Not that, at least,' replied my mother, shuddering. 'So far we can trust him. I seem to read among his words a certain tragic promise. Asenath, if I leave you, if I die, you will not forget your miserable parents?'

Thereupon we fell to cross-purposes: I beseeching her to explain her words; she putting me by, and continuing to recommend the doctor for a friend. 'The doctor!' I cried at last; 'the man who killed my father?'

'Nay,' said she, 'let us be just. I do believe before, Heaven, he played the friendliest part. And he alone, Asenath, can protect you in this land of death.'

At this the doctor returned, leading our two horses; and when we were all in the saddle, he bade me ride on before, as he had matter to discuss with Mrs. Fonblanque. They came at a foot's pace, eagerly conversing in a whisper; and presently after the moon rose and showed them looking eagerly in each other's faces as they went, my mother laying her hand upon the doctor's arm, and the doctor himself, against his usual custom, making vigorous gestures of protest or asseveration.

At the foot of the track which ascended the talus of the mountain to his door, the doctor overtook me at a trot.

'Here,' he said, 'we shall dismount; and as your mother prefers to be alone, you and I shall walk together to my house.'

'Shall I see her again?' I asked.

'I give you my word,' he said, and helped me to alight. 'We leave the horses here,' he added. 'There are no thieves in this stone wilderness.'

The track mounted gradually, keeping the house in view. The windows were once more bright; the chimney once more vomited smoke; but the most absolute silence reigned, and, but for the figure of my mother very slowly following in our wake, I felt convinced there was no human soul within a range of miles. At the thought, I looked upon the doctor, gravely walking by my side, with his bowed shoulders and white hair, and then once more at his house, lit up and pouring smoke like some industrious factory. And then my curiosity broke forth. 'In Heaven's name,' I cried, 'what do you make in this inhuman desert?'

He looked at me with a peculiar smile, and answered with an evasion—

'This is not the first time,' said he, 'that you have seen my furnaces alight. One morning, in the small hours, I saw you driving past; a delicate experiment miscarried; and I cannot acquit myself of having startled either your driver or the horse that drew you.'

'What!' cried I, beholding again in fancy the antics of the figure, 'could that be you?'

'It was I,' he replied; 'but do not fancy that I was mad. I was in agony. I had been scalded cruelly.'

We were now near the house, which, unlike the ordinary houses of the country, was built of hewn stone and very solid. Stone, too, was its foundation, stone its background. Not a blade of grass sprouted among the broken mineral about the walls, not a flower adorned the windows. Over the door, by way of sole adornment, the Mormon Eye was rudely sculptured; I had been brought up to view that emblem from my childhood; but since the night of our escape, it had acquired a new significance, and set me shrinking. The smoke rolled voluminously from the chimney top, its edges ruddy with the fire; and from the far corner of the building, near the ground, angry puffs of steam shone snow-white in the moon and vanished.

The doctor opened the door and paused upon the threshold. 'You ask me what I make here,' he observed. 'Two things: Life and Death.' And he motioned me to enter.

'I shall await my mother,' said I.

'Child,' he replied, 'look at me: am I not old and broken? Of us two, which is the stronger, the young maiden or the withered man?'

I bowed, and passing by him, entered a vestibule or kitchen, lit by a good fire and a shaded reading-lamp. It was furnished only with a dresser, a rude table, and some wooden benches; and on one of these the doctor motioned me to take a seat; and passing by another door into the interior of the house, he left me to myself. Presently I heard the jar of iron from the far end of the building; and this was followed by the same throbbing noise that had startled me in the valley, but now so near at hand as to be menacing by loudness, and even to shake the house with every recurrence of the stroke. I had scarce time to master my alarm when the doctor returned, and almost in the same moment my mother appeared upon the threshold. But how am I to describe to you the peace and ravishment of that face? Years seemed to have passed over her head during that brief ride, and left her younger and fairer; her eyes shone, her smile went to my heart; she seemed no more a woman but the angel of ecstatic tenderness. I ran to her in a kind of terror; but she shrank a little back and laid her finger on her lips, with something arch and yet unearthly. To the doctor, on the contrary, she reached out her hand as to a friend and helper; and so strange was the scene that I forgot to be offended.

'Lucy,' said the doctor, 'all is prepared. Will you go alone, or shall your daughter follow us?'

'Let Asenath come,' she answered, 'dear Asenath! At this hour, when I am purified of fear and sorrow, and already survive myself and my affections, it is for your sake, and not for mine, that I desire her presence. Were she shut out, dear friend, it is to be feared she might misjudge your kindness.'

'Mother,' I cried wildly, 'mother, what is this?'

But my mother, with her radiant smile, said only 'Hush!' as though I were a child again, and tossing in some fever-fit; and the doctor bade me be silent and trouble her no more. 'You have made a choice,' he continued, addressing my mother, 'that has often strangely tempted me. The two extremes: all, or else nothing; never, or this very hour upon the clock —these have been my incongruous desires. But to accept the middle term, to be content with a half-gift, to flicker awhile and to burn out—never for an hour, never since I was born, has satisfied the appetite of my ambition.' He looked upon my mother fixedly, much of admiration and some touch of envy in his eyes; then, with a profound sigh, he led the way into the inner room.

It was very long. From end to end it was lit up by many lamps, which by the changeful colour of their light, and by the incessant snapping sounds with which they burned, I have since divined to be electric. At the extreme end an open door gave us a glimpse into what must have been a lean-to shed beside the chimney; and this, in strong contrast to the room, was painted with a red reverberation as from furnace-doors. The walls were lined with books and glazed cases, the tables crowded with the implements of chemical research; great glass accumulators glittered in the light; and through a hole in the gable near the shed door, a heavy driving-belt entered the apartment and ran overhead upon steel pulleys, with clumsy activity and many ghostly and fluttering sounds. In one corner I perceived a chair resting upon crystal feet, and curiously wreathed with wire. To this my mother advanced with a decisive swiftness.

'Is this it?' she asked.

The doctor bowed in silence.

'Asenath,' said my mother, 'in this sad end of my life I have found one helper. Look upon him: it is Doctor Grierson. Be not, oh my daughter, be not ungrateful to that friend!'

She sate upon the chair, and took in her hands the globes that terminated the arms.

'Am I right?' she asked, and looked upon the doctor with such a radiancy of face that I trembled for her reason. Once more the doctor bowed, but this time leaning hard against the wall. He must have touched a spring. The least shock agitated my mother where she sat; the least passing jar appeared to cross her features; and she sank back in the chair like one resigned to weariness. I was at her knees that moment; but her hands fell loosely in my grasp; her face, still beatified with the same touching smile, sank forward on her bosom: her spirit had for ever fled.

I do not know how long may have elapsed before, raising for a moment my tearful face, I met the doctor's eyes. They rested upon mine with such a depth of scrutiny, pity, and interest, that even from the freshness of my sorrow, I was startled into attention.

'Enough,' he said, 'to lamentation. Your mother went to death as to a bridal, dying where her husband died. It is time, Asenath, to think of the survivors. Follow me to the next room.'

I followed him, like a person in a dream; he made me sit by the fire, he gave me wine to drink; and then, pacing the stone floor, he thus began to address me—

'You are now, my child, alone in the world, and under the immediate watch of Brigham Young. It would be your lot, in ordinary circumstances, to become the fiftieth bride of some ignoble elder, or by particular fortune, as fortune is counted in this land, to find favour in the eyes of the President himself. Such a fate for a girl like you were worse than death; better to die as your mother died than to sink daily deeper in the mire of this pit of woman's degradation. But is escape conceivable? Your father tried; and you beheld yourself with what security his jailers

acted, and how a dumb drawing on a rock was counted a sufficient sentry over the avenues of freedom. Where your father
failed, will you be wiser or more fortunate? or are you, too, helpless in the toils?'

I had followed his words with changing emotion, but now I
believed I understood.

'I see,' I cried; 'you judge me rightly. I must follow where my
parents led; and oh! I am not only willing, I am eager!'

'No,' replied the doctor, 'not death for you. The flawed vessel
we may break, but not the perfect. No, your mother cherished a
different hope, and so do I. I see,' he cried, 'the girl develop to the
completed woman, the plan reach fulfilment, the promise—ay,
outdone! I could not bear to arrest so lively, so comely a process.
It was your mother's thought,' he added, with a change of tone,
'that I should marry you myself.' I fear I must have shown a perfect horror of aversion from this fate, for he made haste to quiet
me. 'Reassure yourself, Asenath,' he resumed. 'Old as I am, I have
not forgotten the tumultuous fancies of youth. I have passed my
days, indeed, in laboratories; but in all my vigils I have not forgotten the tune of a young pulse. Age asks with timidity to be
spared intolerable pain; youth, taking fortune by the beard,
demands joy like a right. These things I have not forgotten; none,
rather, has more keenly felt, none more jealously considered
them; I have but postponed them to their day. See, then: you
stand without support; the only friend left to you, this old inves-
tigator, old in cunning, young in sympathy. Answer me but one
question: Are you free from the entanglement of what the world
calls love? Do you still command your heart and purposes? or are
you fallen in some bond-slavery of the eye and ear?'

I answered him in broken words; my heart, I think I must
have told him, lay with my dead parents.

'It is enough,' he said. 'It has been my fate to be called on
often, too often, for those services of which we spoke to-night;
none in Utah could carry them so well to a conclusion; hence
there has fallen into my hands a certain share of influence which I
now lay at your service, partly for the sake of my dead friends,
your parents; partly for the interest I bear you in your own right. I

shall send you to England, to the great city of London, there to await the bridegroom I have selected. He shall be a son of mine, a young man suitable in age and not grossly deficient in that quality of beauty that your years demand. Since your heart is free, you may well pledge me the sole promise that I ask in return for much expense and still more danger: to await the arrival of that bridegroom with the delicacy of a wife.'

I sat awhile stunned. The doctor's marriages, I remembered to have heard, had been unfruitful; and this added perplexity to my distress. But I was alone, as he had said, alone in that dark land; the thought of escape, of any equal marriage, was already enough to revive in me some dawn of hope; and in what words I know not, I accepted the proposal.

He seemed more moved by my consent than I could reasonably have looked for. 'You shall see,' he cried; 'you shall judge for yourself.' And hurrying to the next room he returned with a small portrait somewhat coarsely done in oils. It showed a man in the dress of nearly forty years before, young indeed, but still recognisable to be the doctor. 'Do you like it?' he asked. 'That is myself when I was young. My— my boy will be like that, like but nobler; with such health as angels might condescend to envy; and a man of mind, Asenath, of commanding mind. That should be a man, I think; that should be one among ten thousand. A man like that— one to combine the passions of youth with the restraint, the force, the dignity of age—one to fill all the parts and faculties, one to be man's epitome—say, will that not satisfy the needs of an ambitious girl? Say, is not that enough?' And as he held the picture close before my eyes, his hands shook.

I told him briefly I would ask no better, for I was transpierced with this display of fatherly emotion; but even as I said the words, the most insolent revolt surged through my arteries. I held him in horror, him, his portrait, and his son; and had there been any choice but death or a Mormon marriage, I declare before Heaven I had embraced it.

'It is well,' he replied, 'and I had rightly counted on your spirit. Eat, then, for you have far to go.' So saying, he set meat before me; and while I was endeavouring to obey, he left the room and returned with an armful of coarse raiment. 'There,' said he, 'is your disguise. I leave you to your toilet.'

The clothes had probably belonged to a somewhat lubberly boy of fifteen; and they hung about me like a sack, and cruelly hampered my movements. But what filled me with uncontrollable shudderings, was the problem of their origin and the fate of the lad to whom they had belonged. I had scarcely effected the exchange when the doctor returned, opened a back window, helped me out into the narrow space between the house and the overhanging bluffs, and showed me a ladder of iron footholds mortised in the rock. 'Mount,' he said, 'swiftly. When you are at the summit, walk, so far as you are able, in the shadow of the smoke. The smoke will bring you, sooner or later, to a canyon; follow that down, and you will find a man with two horses. Him you will implicitly obey. And remember, silence! That machinery, which I now put in motion for your service, may by one word be turned against you. Go; Heaven prosper you!'

The ascent was easy. Arrived at the top of the cliff, I saw before me on the other side a vast and gradual declivity of stone, lying bare to the moon and the surrounding mountains. Nowhere was any vantage or concealment; and knowing how these deserts were beset with spies, I made haste to veil my movements under the blowing trail of smoke. Sometimes it swam high, rising on the night wind, and I had no more substantial curtain than its moon-thrown shadow; sometimes again it crawled upon the earth, and I would walk in it, no higher than to my shoulders, like some mountain fog. But, one way or another, the smoke of that ill-omened furnace protected the first steps of my escape, and led me unobserved to the canyon.

There, sure enough, I found a taciturn and sombre man beside a pair of saddle-horses; and thenceforward, all night long, we wandered in silence by the most occult and dangerous paths among the mountains. A little before the dayspring we took refuge in a wet and gusty cavern at the bottom of a gorge; lay there all day concealed; and the next night, before the glow had faded out of the west, resumed our wanderings. About noon we stopped again, in a lawn upon a little river, where was a screen of bushes; and here my guide, handing me a bundle from his pack, bade me change my dress once more. The bundle contained clothing of my own, taken from our house, with such necessaries as a comb and soap. I made my toilet by the mirror of a quiet pool; and as I was so doing, and smiling with some complacency to see myself restored to my own image, the mountains rang with a scream of far more than human piercingness; and while I still stood astonished, there sprang up and swiftly increased a storm of the most awful and earth-rending sounds. Shall I own to you, that I fell upon my face and shrieked? And yet this was but the overland train winding among the near mountains: the very means of my salvation: the strong wings that were to carry me from Utah!

When I was dressed, the guide gave me a bag, which contained, he said, both money and papers; and telling me that I was already over the borders in the territory of Wyoming, bade me follow the stream until I reached the railway station, half a mile below. 'Here,' he added, 'is your ticket as far as Council Bluffs. The East express will pass in a few hours.' With that, he took both horses, and, without further words or any salutation, rode off by the way that we had come.

Three hours afterwards, I was seated on the end platform of the train as it swept eastward through the gorges and thundered in tunnels of the mountain. The change of scene, the sense of escape, the still throbbing terror of pursuit— above all, the astounding magic of my new conveyance, kept me from any logical or melancholy thought. I had gone to the doctor's house two nights before prepared to die, prepared for worse than death; what had passed, terrible although it was, looked almost bright compared to my anticipations; and it was not till I had slept a full night in the flying palace car, that I awoke to the sense of my irreparable loss and to some reasonable alarm about the future. In this mood, I examined the contents of the bag. It was well supplied with gold; it contained tickets and complete directions for my journey as far as Liverpool, and a long letter from the doctor, supplying me with a fictitious name and story, recommending the most guarded silence, and bidding me to await faithfully the coming of his son. All then had been arranged beforehand: he had counted upon my consent, and what was tenfold worse, upon my mother's voluntary death. My horror of my only friend, my aversion for this son who was to marry me, my revolt against the whole current and conditions of my life, were now complete. I was sitting stupefied by my distress and helplessness, when, to my joy, a very pleasant lady offered me her conversation. I clutched at the relief; and I was soon glibly telling her the story in the doctor's letter: how I was a Miss Gould, of Nevada City, going to England to an uncle, what money I had, what family, my age, and so forth, until I had exhausted my instructions, and, as the lady still continued to ply me with questions, began to embroider on my own account. This soon carried one of my inexperience beyond her depth; and I had already remarked a shadow on the lady's face, when a gentleman drew near and very civilly addressed me.

'Miss Gould, I believe?' said he; and then, excusing himself to the lady by the authority of my guardian, drew me to the fore platform of the Pullman car. 'Miss Gould,' he said in my ear, 'is it possible that you suppose yourself in safety? Let me completely undeceive you. One more such indiscretion and you return to Utah. And, in the meanwhile, if this woman should again address you, you are to reply with these words: "Madam, I do not like you, and I will be obliged if you will suffer me to choose my own associates."'

Alas, I had to do as I was bid; this lady, to whom I already felt myself drawn with the strongest cords of sympathy, I dismissed with insult; and thenceforward, through all that day, I sat in silence, gazing on the bare plains and swallowing my tears. Let that suffice: it was the pattern of my journey. Whether on the train, at the hotels, or on board the ocean steamer, I never exchanged a friendly word with any fellow-traveller but I was certain to be interrupted. In every place, on every side, the most unlikely persons, man or woman, rich or poor, became protectors to forward me upon my journey, or spies to observe and regulate my conduct. Thus I crossed the States, thus passed the ocean, the Mormon Eye still following my movements; and when at length a cab had set me down before that London lodging-house from which you saw me flee this morning, I had already ceased to struggle and ceased to hope.

The landlady, like every one else through all that journey, was expecting my arrival. A fire was lighted in my room, which looked upon the garden; there were books on the table, clothes in the drawers; and there (I had almost said with contentment, and certainly with resignation) I saw month follow month over my head. At times my landlady took me for a walk or an excursion, but she would never suffer me to leave the house alone; and I, seeing that she also lived under the shadow of that widespread Mormon terror, felt too much pity to resist. To the child born on Mormon soil, as to the man who accepts the engagements of a secret order, no escape is possible; so I had clearly read, and I was thankful even for this respite. Meanwhile, I tried honestly to prepare my mind for my approaching nuptials. The day drew near when my bridegroom was to visit me, and gratitude and fear alike obliged me to consent. A son of Doctor Grierson's, be he what he pleased, must still be young, and it was even probable he should be handsome; on more than that, I felt I dared not reckon; and in moulding my mind towards consent I dwelt the more carefully on these physical attractions which I felt I might expect, and averted my eyes from moral or intellectual considerations. We have a great power upon our spirits; and as time passed I worked myself into a frame of acquiescence, nay, and I began to grow impatient for the hour. At night sleep forsook me; I sat all day by the fire, absorbed in dreams, conjuring up the features of my husband, and anticipating in fancy the touch of his hand and the sound of his voice. In the dead level and solitude of my existence, this was the one eastern window and the one door of hope. At last, I had so cultivated and prepared my will, that I began to be besieged with fears upon the other side. How if it was I that did not please? How if this unseen lover should turn from me with disaffection? And now I spent hours before the glass, studying and judging my attractions, and was never weary of changing my dress or ordering my hair.

When the day came I was long about my toilet; but at last, with a sort of hopeful desperation, I had to own that I could do no more, and must now stand or fall by nature. My occupation ended, I fell a prey to the most sickening impatience, mingled with alarms; giving ear to the swelling rumour of the streets, and at each change of sound or silence, starting, shrinking, and colouring to the brow. Love is not to be prepared, I know, without some knowledge of the object; and yet, when the cab at last rattled to the door and I heard my visitor mount the stairs, such was the tumult of hopes in my poor bosom that love itself might have been proud to own their parentage. The door opened, and it was Doctor Grierson that appeared. I believe I must have screamed aloud, and I know, at least, that I fell fainting to the floor.

When I came to myself he was standing over me, counting my pulse. 'I have startled you,' he said. 'A difficulty unforeseen—the impossibility of obtaining a certain drug in its full purity—has forced me to resort to London unprepared. I regret that I should have shown myself once more without those poor attractions which are much, perhaps, to you, but to me are no more considerable than rain that falls into the sea. Youth is but a state, as passing as that syncope from which you are but just awakened, and, if there be truth in science, as easy to recall; for I find, Asenath, that I must now take you for my confidant. Since my first years, I have devoted every hour and act of life to one ambitious task; and the time of my success is at hand. In these new countries, where I was so long content to stay, I collected indispensable ingredients; I have fortified myself on every side from the possibility of error; what was a dream now takes the substance of reality; and when I offered you a son of mine I did so in a figure. That son—that husband, Asenath, is myself—not as you now behold me, but restored to the first energy of youth. You think me mad? It is the customary attitude of ignorance. I will not argue; I will leave facts to speak. When you behold me purified, invigorated, renewed, restamped in the original image—when you recognise in me (what I shall be) the first perfect expression of the powers of mankind—I shall be able to laugh with a better grace at your passing and natural incredulity. To what can you aspire—fame, riches, power, the charm of youth, the dear-bought wisdom of age—that I shall not be able to afford you in perfection? Do not deceive yourself. I already excel you in every human gift but one: when that gift also has been restored to me you will recognise your master.'

Hereupon, consulting his watch, he told me he must now leave me to myself; and bidding me consult reason, and not girlish fancies, he withdrew. I had not the courage to move; the night fell and found me still where he had laid me during my faint, my face buried in my hands, my soul drowned in the darkest apprehensions. Late in the evening he returned, carrying a candle, and, with a certain irritable tremor, bade me rise and sup. 'Is it possible,' he added, 'that I have been deceived in your courage? A cowardly girl is no fit mate for me.'

I flung myself before him on my knees, and with floods of tears besought him to release me from this engagement, assuring him that my cowardice was abject, and that in every point of intellect and character I was his hopeless and derisible inferior.

'Why, certainly,' he replied. 'I know you better than yourself; and I am well enough acquainted with human nature to understand this scene. It is addressed to me,' he added with a smile, 'in my character of the still untransformed. But do not alarm yourself about the future. Let me but attain my end, and not you only, Asenath, but every woman on the face of the earth becomes my willing slave.'

Thereupon he obliged me to rise and eat; sat down with me to table; helped and entertained me with the attentions of a fashionable host; and it was not till a late hour, that, bidding me courteously good-night, he once more left me alone to my misery.

In all this talk of an elixir and the restoration of his youth, I scarce knew from which hypothesis I should the more eagerly recoil. If his hopes reposed on any base of fact, if indeed, by some abhorrent miracle, he should discard his age, death were my only refuge from that most unnatural, that most ungodly union. If, on the other hand, these dreams were merely lunatic, the madness of a life waxed suddenly acute, my pity would become a load almost as heavy to bear as my revolt against the marriage. So passed the night, in alternations of rebellion and despair, of hate and pity; and with the next morning I was only to comprehend more fully my enslaved position. For though he appeared with a very tranquil countenance, he had no sooner observed the marks of grief upon my brow than an answering darkness gathered on his own.

'Asenath.' he said, 'you owe me much already; with one finger I still hold you suspended over death; my life is full of labour and anxiety; and I choose,' said he, with a remarkable accent of command, 'that you shall greet me with a pleasant face.' He never needed to repeat the recommendation; from that day forward I was always ready to receive him with apparent cheerfulness; and he rewarded me with a good deal of his company, and almost more than I could bear of his confidence. He had set up a laboratory in the back part of the house, where he toiled day and night at his elixir, and he would come thence to visit me in my parlour: now with passing humours of discouragement; now, and far more often, radiant with hope. It was impossible to see so much of him, and not to recognise that the sands of his life were running low; and yet all the time he would be laying out vast fields of future, and planning, with all the confidence of youth, the most unbounded schemes of pleasure and ambition. How I replied I know not; but I found a voice and words to answer, even while I wept and raged to hear him.

A week ago the doctor entered my room with the marks of great exhilaration contending with pitiful bodily weakness. 'Asenath,' said he, 'I have now obtained the last ingredient. In one week from now the perilous moment of the last projection will draw nigh. You have once before assisted, although unconsciously, at the failure of a similar experiment. It was the elixir which so terribly exploded one night when you were passing my house; and it is idle to deny that the conduct of so delicate a process, among the million jars and trepidations of so great a city, presents a certain element of danger. From this point of view, I cannot but regret the perfect stillness of my house among the deserts; but, on the other hand, I have succeeded in proving that the singularly unstable equilibrium of the elixir, at the moment of projection, is due rather to the impurity than to the nature of the ingredients; and as all are now of an equal and exquisite nicety, I have little fear for the result. In a week then from to-day, my dear Asenath, this period of trial will be ended.' And he smiled upon me in a manner unusually paternal.

I smiled back with my lips, but at my heart there raged the blackest and most unbridled terror. What if he failed? And oh, tenfold worse! what if he succeeded? What detested and unnatural changeling would appear before me to claim my hand? And could there, I asked myself with a dreadful sinking, be any truth in his boasts of an assured victory over my reluctance? I knew him, indeed, to be masterful, to lead my life at a sign. Suppose, then, this experiment to succeed; suppose him to return to me, hideously restored, like a vampire in a legend; and suppose that, by some devilish fascination . . . My head turned; all former fears deserted me: and I felt I could embrace the worst in preference to this.

My mind was instantly made up. The doctor's presence in London was justified by the affairs of the Mormon polity. Often, in our conversation, he would gloat over the details of that great organisation, which he feared even while yet he wielded it; and would remind me, that even in the humming labyrinth of London, we were still visible to that unsleeping eye in Utah. His visitors, indeed, who were of every sort, from the missionary to the destroying angel, and seemed to belong to every rank of life, had, up to that moment, filled me with unmixed repulsion and alarm. I knew that if my secret were to reach the ear of any leader my fate were sealed beyond redemption; and yet in my present pass of horror and despair, it was to these very men that I turned for help. I waylaid upon the stair one of the Mormon missionaries, a man of a low class, but not inaccessible to pity; told him I scarce remember what elaborate fable to explain my application; and by his intermediacy entered into correspondence with my father's family. They recognised my claim for help, and on this very day I was to begin my escape.

Last night I sat up fully dressed, awaiting the result of the doctor's labours, and prepared against the worst. The nights at this season and in this northern latitude are short; and I had soon the company of the returning daylight. The silence in and around the house was only broken by the movements of the doctor in the laboratory; to these I listened, watch in hand, awaiting the hour of my escape, and yet consumed by anxiety about the strange experiment that was going forward overhead. Indeed, now that I was conscious of some protection for myself, my sympathies had turned more directly to the doctor's side; I caught myself even praying for his success; and when some hours ago a low, peculiar cry reached my ears from the laboratory, I could no longer control my impatience, but mounted the stairs and opened the door.

The doctor was standing in the middle of the room; in his hand a large, round-bellied, crystal flask, some three parts full of a bright amber-coloured liquid; on his face a rapture of gratitude and joy unspeakable. As he saw me he raised the flask at arm's length. 'Victory!' he cried. 'Victory, Asenath!' And then—whether the flask escaped his trembling fingers, or whether the explosion were spontaneous, I cannot tell—enough that we were thrown, I against the door-post, the doctor into the corner of the room; enough that we were shaken to the soul by the same explosion that must have startled you upon the street; and that, in the brief space of an indistinguishable instant, there remained nothing of the labours of the doctor's lifetime but a few shards of broken crystal and those voluminous and ill-smelling vapours that pursued me in my flight.

The Squire of Dames (concluded)

WHAT with the lady's animated manner and dramatic conduct of her voice, Challoner had thrilled to every incident with genuine emotion. His fancy, which was not perhaps of a very lively character, applauded both the matter and the style; but the more judicial functions of his mind refused assent. It was an excellent story; and it might be true, but he believed it was not. Miss Fonblanque was a lady, and it was doubtless possible for a lady to wander from the truth; but how was a gentleman to tell her so? His spirits for some time had been sinking, but they now fell to zero; and long after her voice had died away he still sat with a troubled and averted countenance, and could find no form of words to thank her for her narrative. His mind, indeed, was empty of everything beyond a dull longing for escape. From this pause, which grew the more embarrassing with every second, he was roused by the sudden laughter of the lady. His vanity was alarmed; he turned and faced her; their eyes met; and he caught from hers a spark of such frank merriment as put him instantly at ease.

'You certainly,' he said, 'appear to bear your calamities with excellent spirit.'

'Do I not?' she cried, and fell once more into delicious laughter. But from this access she more speedily recovered. 'This is all very well,' said she, nodding at him gravely, 'but I am still in a most distressing situation, from which, if you deny me your help, I shall find it difficult indeed to free myself.'

At this mention of help Challoner fell back to his original gloom.

'My sympathies are much engaged with you,' he said, 'and I should be delighted, I am sure. But our position is most unusual; and circumstances over which I have, I can assure you, no control, deprive me of the power—the pleasure— Unless, indeed,' he added, somewhat brightening at the thought, 'I were to recommend you to the care of the police?'

She laid her hand upon his arm and looked hard into his eyes; and he saw with wonder that, for the first time since the moment of their meeting, every trace of colour had faded from her cheek.

'Do so,' she said, 'and—weigh my words well—you kill me as certainly as with a knife.'

'God bless me!' exclaimed Challoner.

'Oh,' she cried, 'I can see you disbelieve my story and make light of the perils that surround me; but who are you to judge? My family share my apprehensions; they help me in secret; and you saw yourself by what an emissary, and in what a place, they have chosen to supply me with the funds for my escape. I admit that you are brave and clever and have impressed me most favourably; but how are you to prefer your opinion before that of my uncle, an ex-minister of state, a man with the ear of the Queen, and of a long political experience? If I am mad, is he? And you must allow me, besides, a special claim upon your help. Strange as you may think my story, you know that much of it is true; and if you who heard the explosion and saw the Mormon at Victoria, refuse to credit and assist me, to whom am I to turn?'

'He gave you money then?' asked Challoner, who had been dwelling singly on that fact.

'I begin to interest you,' she cried. 'But, frankly, you are condemned to help me. If the service I had to ask of you were serious, were suspicious, were even unusual, I should say no more. But what is it? To take a pleasure trip (for which, if you will suffer me, I propose to pay) and to carry from one lady to another a sum of money! What can be more simple?'

'Is the sum,' asked Challoner, 'considerable?'

She produced a packet from her bosom; and observing that she had not yet found time to make the count, tore open the cover and spread upon her knees a considerable number of Bank of England notes. It took some time to make the reckoning, for the notes were of every degree of value; but at last, and counting a few loose sovereigns, she made out the sum to be a little under 710 pounds sterling. The sight of so much money worked an immediate revolution in the mind of Challoner.

'And you propose, madam,' he cried, 'to intrust that money to a perfect stranger?'

'Ah!' said she, with a charming smile, 'but I no longer regard you as a stranger.'

'Madam,' said Challoner, 'I perceive I must make you a confession. Although of a very good family—through my mother, indeed, a lineal descendant of the patriot Bruce—I dare not conceal from you that my affairs are deeply, very deeply involved. I am in debt; my pockets are practically empty; and, in short, I am fallen to that state when a considerable sum of money would prove to many men an irresistible temptation.'

'Do you not see,' returned the young lady, 'that by these words you have removed my last hesitation? Take them.' And she thrust the notes into the young man's hand.

He sat so long, holding them, like a baby at the font, that Miss Fonblanque once more bubbled into laughter.

'Pray,' she said, 'hesitate no further; put them in your pocket; and to relieve our position of any shadow of embarrassment, tell me by what name I am to address my knight-errant, for I find myself reduced to the awkwardness of the pronoun.'

Had borrowing been in question, the wisdom of our ancestors had come lightly to the young man's aid; but upon what pretext could he refuse so generous a trust? Upon none he saw, that was not unpardonably wounding; and the bright eyes and the high spirits of his companion had already made a breach in the rampart of Challoner's caution. The whole thing, he reasoned, might be a mere mystification, which it were the height of solemn folly to resent. On the other hand, the explosion, the interview at the public-house, and the very money in his hands, seemed to prove beyond denial the existence of some serious danger; and if that were so, could he desert her? There was a choice of risks: the risk of behaving with extraordinary incivility and unhandsomeness to a lady, and the risk of going on a fool's errand. The story seemed false; but then the money was undeniable. The whole circumstances were questionable and obscure; but the lady was charming, and had the speech and manners of society. While he still hung in the wind, a recollection returned upon his mind with some of the dignity of prophecy. Had he not promised Somerset to break with the traditions of the commonplace, and to accept the first adventure offered? Well, here was the adventure.

He thrust the money into his pocket.

'My name is Challoner,' said he.

'Mr. Challoner,' she replied, 'you have come very generously to my aid when all was against me. Though I am myself a very humble person, my family commands great interest; and I do not think you will repent this handsome action.'

Challoner flushed with pleasure.

'I imagine that, perhaps, a consulship,' she added, her eyes dwelling on him with a judicial admiration, 'a consulship in some great town or capital—or else—But we waste time; let us set about the work of my delivery.'

She took his arm with a frank confidence that went to his heart; and once more laying by all serious thoughts, she entertained him, as they crossed the park, with her agreeable gaiety of mind. Near the Marble Arch they found a hansom, which rapidly conveyed them to the terminus at Euston Square; and here, in the hotel, they sat down to an excellent breakfast. The young lady's first step was to call for writing materials and write, upon one corner of the table, a hasty note; still, as she did so, glancing with smiles at her companion. 'Here,' said she, 'here is the letter which will introduce you to my cousin.' She began to fold the paper. 'My cousin, although I have never seen her, has the character of a very charming woman and a recognised beauty; of that I know nothing, but at least she has been very kind to me; so has my lord her father; so have you—kinder than all— kinder than I can bear to think of.' She said this with unusual emotion; and, at the same time, sealed the envelope. 'Ah!' she cried, 'I have shut my letter! It is not quite courteous; and yet, as between friends, it is perhaps better so. I introduce you, after all, into a family secret; and though you and I are already old comrades, you are still unknown to my uncle. You go then to this address, Richard Street, Glasgow; go, please, as soon as you arrive; and give this letter with your own hands into those of Miss Fonblanque, for that is the name by which she is to pass. When we next meet, you will tell me what you think of her,' she added, with a touch of the provocative.

'Ah,' said Challoner, almost tenderly, 'she can be nothing to me.'

'You do not know,' replied the young lady, with a sigh. 'By-the-bye, I had forgotten—it is very childish, and I am almost ashamed to mention it—but when you see Miss Fonblanque, you will have to make yourself a little ridiculous; and I am sure the part in no way suits you. We had agreed upon a watchword. You will have to address an earl's daughter in these words: "NIGGER, NIGGER, NEVER DIE;" but reassure yourself,' she added, laughing, 'for the fair patrician will at once finish the quotation. Come now, say your lesson.'

'"Nigger, nigger, never die,"' repeated Challoner, with undisguised reluctance.

Miss Fonblanque went into fits of laughter. 'Excellent,' said she, 'it will be the most humorous scene.' And she laughed again.

'And what will be the counterword?' asked Challoner stiffly.

'I will not tell you till the last moment,' said she; 'for I perceive you are growing too imperious.'

Breakfast over, she accompanied the young man to the platform, bought him the GRAPHIC, the ATHENAEUM, and a paper-cutter, and stood on the step conversing till the whistle sounded. Then she put her head into the carriage. 'BLACK FACE AND SHINING EYE!' she whispered, and instantly leaped down upon the platform, with a thrill of gay and musical laughter. As the train steamed out of the great arch of glass, the sound of that laughter still rang in the young man's ears.

Challoner's position was too unusual to be long welcome to his mind. He found himself projected the whole length of England, on a mission beset with obscure and ridiculous circumstances, and yet, by the trust he had accepted, irrevocably bound to persevere. How easy it appeared, in the retrospect, to have refused the whole proposal, returned the money, and gone forth again upon his own affairs, a free and happy man! And it was now impossible: the enchantress who had held him with her eye had now disappeared, taking his honour in pledge; and as she had failed to leave him an address, he was denied even the inglorious safety of retreat. To use the paper-knife, or even to read the periodicals with which she had presented him, was to renew the bitterness of his remorse; and as he was alone in the compartment, he passed the day staring at the landscape in impotent repentance, and long before he was landed on the platform of St. Enoch's, had fallen to the lowest and coldest zones of self-contempt.

As he was hungry, and elegant in his habits, he would have preferred to dine and to remove the stains of travel; but the words of the young lady, and his own impatient eagerness, would suffer no delay. In the late, luminous, and lamp-starred dusk of the summer evening, he accordingly set forward with brisk steps.

The street to which he was directed had first seen the day in the character of a row of small suburban villas on a hillside; but the extension of the city had long since, and on every hand, surrounded it with miles of streets. From the top of the hill a range of very tall buildings, densely inhabited by the poorest classes of the population and variegated by drying-poles from every second window, overplumbed the villas and their little gardens like a seaboard cliff. But still, under the grime of years of city smoke, these antiquated cottages, with their venetian blinds and rural porticoes, retained a somewhat melancholy savour of the past.

The street when Challoner entered it was perfectly deserted. From hard by, indeed, the sound of a thousand footfalls filled the ear; but in Richard Street itself there was neither light nor sound of human habitation. The appearance of the neighbourhood weighed heavily on the mind of the young man; once more, as in the streets of London, he was impressed with the sense of city deserts; and as he approached the number indicated, and somewhat falteringly rang the bell, his heart sank within him.

The bell was ancient, like the house; it had a thin and garrulous note; and it was some time before it ceased to sound from the rear quarters of the building. Following upon this an inner door was stealthily opened, and careful and catlike steps drew near along the hall. Challoner, supposing he was to be instantly admitted, produced his letter, and, as well as he was able, prepared a smiling face. To his indescribable surprise, however, the footsteps ceased, and then, after a pause and with the like stealthiness, withdrew once more, and died away in the interior of the house. A second time the young man rang violently at the bell; a second time, to his keen hearkening, a certain bustle of discreet footing moved upon the hollow boards of the old villa; and again the fainthearted garrison only drew near to retreat. The cup of the visitor's endurance was now full to overflowing; and, committing the whole family of Fonblanque to every mood and shade of condemnation, he turned upon his heel and redescended the steps. Perhaps the mover in the house was watching from a window, and plucked up courage at the sight of this desistance; or perhaps, where he lurked trembling in the back parts of the villa, reason in its own right had conquered his alarms. Challoner, at least, had scarce set foot upon the pavement when he was arrested by the sound of the withdrawal of an inner bolt; one followed another, rattling in their sockets; the key turned harshly in the lock; the door opened; and there appeared upon the threshold a man of a very stalwart figure in his shirt sleeves. He was a person neither of great manly beauty nor of a refined exterior; he was not the man, in ordinary moods, to attract the eyes of the observer; but as he now stood in the doorway, he was marked so legibly with the extreme passion of terror that Challoner stood wonder-struck. For a fraction of a minute they gazed upon each other in silence; and then the man of the house, with ashen lips and gasping voice, inquired the business of his visitor. Challoner replied, in tones from which he strove to banish his surprise, that he was the bearer of a letter to a certain Miss Fonblanque. At this name, as at a talisman, the man fell back and impatiently invited him to enter; and no sooner had the adventurer crossed the threshold, than the door was closed behind him and his retreat cut off.

It was already long past eight at night; and though the late twilight of the north still lingered in the streets, in the passage it was already groping dark. The man led Challoner directly to a parlour looking on the garden to the back. Here he had apparently been supping; for by the light of a tallow dip the table was seen to be covered with a napkin, and set out with a quart of bottled ale and the heel of a Gouda cheese. The room, on the other hand, was furnished with faded solidity, and the walls were lined with scholarly and costly volumes in glazed cases. The house must have been taken furnished; for it had no congruity with this man of the shirt sleeves and the mean supper. As for the earl's daughter, the earl and the visionary consulships in foreign cities, they had long ago begun to fade in Challoner's imagination. Like Doctor Grierson and the Mormon angels, they were plainly woven of the stuff of dreams. Not an illusion remained to the knight-errant; not a hope was left him, but to be speedily relieved from this disreputable business.

The man had continued to regard his visitor with undisguised anxiety, and began once more to press him for his errand.

'I am here,' said Challoner, 'simply to do a service between two ladies; and I must ask you, without further delay, to summon Miss Fonblanque, into whose hands alone I am authorised to deliver the letter that I bear.'

A growing wonder began to mingle on the man's face with the lines of solicitude. 'I am Miss Fonblanque,' he said; and then, perceiving the effect of this communication, 'Good God!' he cried, 'what are you staring at? I tell you, I am Miss Fonblanque.'

Seeing the speaker wore a chin-beard of considerable length, and the remainder of his face was blue with shaving, Challoner could only suppose himself the subject of a jest. He was no longer under the spell of the young lady's presence; and with men, and above all with his inferiors, he was capable of some display of spirit.

'Sir,' said he, pretty roundly, 'I have put myself to great inconvenience for persons of whom I know too little, and I begin to be weary of the business. Either you shall immediately summon Miss Fonblanque, or I leave this house and put myself under the direction of the police.'

'This is horrible!' exclaimed the man. 'I declare before Heaven I am the person meant, but how shall I convince you? It must have been Clara, I perceive, that sent you on this errand—a madwoman, who jests with the most deadly interests; and here we are incapable, perhaps, of an agreement, and Heaven knows what may depend on our delay!'

He spoke with a really startling earnestness; and at the same time there flashed upon the mind of Challoner the ridiculous jingle which was to serve as password. 'This may, perhaps, assist you,' he said, and then, with some embarrassment, '"Nigger, nigger, never die."'

A light of relief broke upon the troubled countenance of the man with the chin-beard. '"Black face and shining eye"— give me the letter,' he panted, in one gasp.

'Well,' said Challoner, though still with some reluctance, 'I suppose I must regard you as the proper recipient; and though I may justly complain of the spirit in which I have been treated, I am only too glad to be done with all responsibility. Here it is,' and he produced the envelope.

The man leaped upon it like a beast, and with hands that trembled in a manner painful to behold, tore it open and unfolded the letter. As he read, terror seemed to mount upon him to the pitch of nightmare. He struck one hand upon his brow, while with the other, as if unconsciously, he crumpled the paper to a ball. 'My gracious powers!' he cried; and then, dashing to the window, which stood open on the garden, he clapped forth his head and shoulders, and whistled long and shrill. Challoner fell back into a corner, and resolutely grasping his staff, prepared for the most desperate events; but the thoughts of the man with the chin-beard were far removed from violence. Turning again into the room, and once more beholding his visitor, whom he appeared to have forgotten, he fairly danced with trepidation. 'Impossible!' he cried.

'Oh, quite impossible! O Lord, I have lost my head.' And then, once more striking his hand upon his brow, 'The money!' he exclaimed. 'Give me the money.'

'My good friend,' replied Challoner, 'this is a very painful exhibition; and until I see you reasonably master of yourself, I decline to proceed with any business.'

'You are quite right,' said the man. 'I am of a very nervous habit; a long course of the dumb ague has undermined my consti- tution. But I know you have money; it may be still the saving of me; and oh, dear young gentleman, in pity's name be expeditious!' Challoner, sincerely uneasy as he was, could scarce refrain from laughter; but he was himself in a hurry to be gone, and without more delay produced the money. 'You will find the sum, I trust, correct,' he observed 'and let me ask you to give me a receipt.'

But the man heeded him not. He seized the money, and disre- garding the sovereigns that rolled loose upon the floor, thrust the bundle of notes into his pocket.

'A receipt,' repeated Challoner, with some asperity. 'I insist on a receipt.'

'Receipt?' repeated the man, a little wildly. 'A receipt? Imme- diately! Await me here.'

Challoner, in reply, begged the gentleman to lose no unneces- sary time, as he was himself desirous of catching a particular train.

'Ah, by God, and so am I!' exclaimed the man with the chin- beard; and with that he was gone out of the room, and had rattled upstairs, four at a time, to the upper story of the villa.

'This is certainly a most amazing business,' thought Chal- loner; 'certainly a most disquieting affair; and I cannot conceal from myself that I have become mixed up with either lunatics or malefactors. I may truly thank my stars that I am so nearly and so creditably done with it.' Thus thinking, and perhaps remembering the episode of the whistle, he turned to the open window. The gar- den was still faintly clear; he could distinguish the stairs and ter- races with which the small domain had been adorned by former owners, and the blackened bushes and dead trees that had once afforded shelter to the country birds; beyond these he saw the strong retaining wall, some thirty feet in height, which enclosed the garden to the back; and again above that, the pile of dingy buildings rearing its frontage high into the night. A peculiar object lying stretched upon the lawn for some time baffled his eyesight; but at length he had made it out to be a long ladder, or series of ladders bound into one; and he was still wondering of what service so great an instrument could be in such a scant enclosure, when he was recalled to himself by the noise of some one running violently down the stairs. This was followed by the sudden, clamorous banging of the house door; and that again, by rapid and retreating footsteps in the street.

Challoner sprang into the passage. He ran from room to room, upstairs and downstairs; and in that old dingy and worm-eaten house, he found himself alone. Only in one apartment, looking to the front, were there any traces of the late inhabitant: a bed that had been recently slept in and not made, a chest of drawers disordered by a hasty search, and on the floor a roll of crumpled paper. This he picked up. The light in this upper story looking to the front was considerably brighter than in the parlour; and he was able to make out that the paper bore the mark of the hotel at Euston, and even, by peering closely, to decipher the following lines in a very elegant and careful female hand:

'DEAR M'GUIRE,—
It is certain your retreat is known. We have just had another failure, clockwork thirty hours too soon, with the usual humiliating result. Zero is quite disheartened. We are all scattered, and I could find no one but the SOLEMN ASS who brings you this and the money. I would love to see your meeting.—Ever yours,
SHINING EYE.'

Challoner was stricken to the heart. He perceived by what facility, by what unmanly fear of ridicule, he had been brought down to be the gull of this intriguer; and his wrath flowed forth in almost equal measure against himself, against the woman, and against Somerset, whose idle counsels had impelled him to embark on that adventure. At the same time a great and troubled curiosity, and a certain chill of fear, possessed his spirit. The conduct of the man with the chin-beard, the terms of the letter, and the explosion of the early morning, fitted together like parts in some obscure and mischievous imbroglio. Evil was certainly afoot; evil, secrecy, terror, and falsehood were the conditions and the passions of the people among whom he had begun to move, like a blind puppet; and he who began as a puppet, his experience told him, was often doomed to perish as a victim.

From the stupor of deep thought into which he had glided with the letter in his hand, he was awakened by the clatter of the bell. He glanced from the window; and, conceive his horror and surprise when he beheld, clustered on the steps, in the front garden and on the pavement of the street, a formidable posse of police! He started to the full possession of his powers and courage. Escape, and escape at any cost, was the one idea that possessed him. Swiftly and silently he redescended the creaking stairs; he was already in the passage when a second and more imperious summons from the door awoke the echoes of the empty house; nor had the bell ceased to jangle before he had bestridden the window-sill of the parlour and was lowering himself into the garden. His coat was hooked upon the iron flower-basket; for a moment he hung dependent heels and head below; and then, with the noise of rending cloth, and followed by several pots, he dropped upon the sod. Once more the bell was rung, and now with furious and repeated peals. The desperate Challoner turned his eyes on every side. They fell upon the ladder, and he ran to it, and with strenuous but unavailing effort sought to raise it from the ground. Suddenly the weight, which was thus resisting his whole strength, began to lighten in his hands; the ladder, like a thing of life, reared its bulk from off the sod; and Challoner, leaping back with a cry of almost superstitious terror, beheld the whole structure mount, foot by foot, against the face of the retaining wall. At the same time, two heads were dimly visible above the parapet, and he was hailed by a guarded whistle. Something in its modulation recalled, like an echo, the whistle of the man with the chin-beard,

Had he chanced upon a means of escape prepared beforehand by those very miscreants whose messenger and gull he had become? Was this, indeed, a means of safety, or but the starting-point of further complication and disaster? He paused not to reflect. Scarce was the ladder reared to its full length than he had sprung already on the rounds; hand over hand, swift as an ape, he scaled the tottering stairway. Strong arms received, embraced, and helped him; he was lifted and set once more upon the earth; and with the spasm of his alarm yet unsubsided, found himself in the company of two rough-looking men, in the paved back yard of one of the tall houses that crowned the summit of the hill. Meanwhile, from below, the note of the bell had been succeeded by the sound of vigorous and redoubling blows.

'Are you all out?' asked one of his companions; and, as soon as he had babbled an answer in the affirmative, the rope was cut from the top round, and the ladder thrust roughly back into the garden, where it fell and broke with clattering reverberations. Its fall was hailed with many broken cries; for the whole of Richard Street was now in high emotion, the people crowding to the windows or clambering on the garden walls. The same man who had already addressed Challoner seized him by the arm; whisked him through the basement of the house and across the street upon the other side; and before the unfortunate adventurer had time to realise his situation, a door was opened, and he was thrust into a low and dark compartment.

'Bedad,' observed his guide, 'there was no time to lose. Is M'Guire gone, or was it you that whistled?

'M'Guire is gone,' said Challoner.

The guide now struck a light. 'Ah,' said he, 'this will never do. You dare not go upon the streets in such a figure. Wait quietly here and I will bring you something decent.'

With that the man was gone, and Challoner, his attention thus rudely awakened, began ruefully to consider the havoc that had been worked in his attire. His hat was gone; his trousers were cruelly ripped; and the best part of one tail of his very elegant frock-coat had been left hanging from the iron crockets of the window. He had scarce had time to measure these disasters when his host re-entered the apartment and proceeded, without a word, to envelop the refined and urbane Challoner in a long ulster of the cheapest material, and of a pattern so gross and vulgar that his spirit sickened at the sight. This calumnious disguise was crowned and completed by a soft felt hat of the Tyrolese design, and several sizes too small. At another moment Challoner would simply have refused to issue forth upon the world thus travestied; but the desire to escape from Glasgow was now too strongly and too exclusively impressed upon his mind. With one haggard glance at the spotted tails of his new coat, he inquired what was to pay for this accoutrement. The man assured him that the whole expense was easily met from funds in his possession, and begged him, instead of wasting time, to make his best speed out of the neighbourhood.

The young man was not loath to take the hint. True to his usual courtesy, he thanked the speaker and complimented him upon his taste in greatcoats; and leaving the man somewhat abashed by these remarks and the manner of their delivery, he hurried forth into the lamplit city. The last train was gone ere, after many deviations, he had reached the terminus. Attired as he was he dared not present himself at any reputable inn; and he felt keenly that the unassuming dignity of his demeanour would serve to attract attention, perhaps mirth and possibly suspicion, in any humbler hostelry. He was thus condemned to pass the solemn and uneventful hours of a whole night in pacing the streets of Glasgow; supperless; a figure of fun for all beholders; waiting the dawn, with hope indeed, but with unconquerable shrinkings; and above all things, filled with a profound sense of the folly and weakness of his conduct. It may be conceived with what curses he assailed the memory of the fair narrator of Hyde Park; her parting laughter rang in his ears all night with damning mockery and iteration; and when he could spare a thought from this chief artificer of his confusion, it was to expend his wrath on Somerset and the career of the amateur detective. With the coming of day, he found in a shy milk-shop the means to appease his hunger. There were still many hours to wait before the departure of the South express; these he passed wandering with indescribable fatigue in the obscurer by-streets of the city; and at length slipped quietly into the station and took his place in the darkest corner of a third-class carriage. Here, all day long, he jolted on the bare boards, distressed by heat and continually reawakened from uneasy slumbers. By the half return ticket in his purse, he was entitled to make the journey on the easy cushions and with the ample space of the first-class;

but alas! in his absurd attire, he durst not, for decency, commingle with his equals; and this small annoyance, coming last in such a series of disasters, cut him to the heart.

That night, when, in his Putney lodging, he reviewed the expense, anxiety, and weariness of his adventure; when he beheld the ruins of his last good trousers and his last presentable coat; and above all, when his eye by any chance alighted on the Tyrolese hat or the degrading ulster, his heart would overflow with bitterness, and it was only by a serious call on his philosophy that he maintained the dignity of his demeanour.

Somerset's Adventure: The Superfluous Mansion

MR. PAUL SOMERSET was a young gentleman of a lively and fiery imagination, with very small capacity for action. He was one who lived exclusively in dreams and in the future: the creature of his own theories, and an actor in his own romances. From the cigar divan he proceeded to parade the streets, still heated with the fire of his eloquence, and scouting upon every side for the offer of some fortunate adventure. In the continual stream of passers-by, on the sealed fronts of houses, on the posters that covered the hoardings, and in every lineament and throb of the great city, he saw a mysterious and hopeful hieroglyph. But although the elements of adventure were streaming by him as thick as drops of water in the Thames, it was in vain that, now with a beseeching, now with something of a braggadocio air, he courted and provoked the notice of the passengers; in vain that, putting fortune to the touch, he even thrust himself into the way and came into direct collision with those of the more promising demeanour. Persons brimful of secrets, persons pining for affection, persons perishing for lack of help or counsel, he was sure he could perceive on every side; but by some contrariety of fortune, each passed upon his way without remarking the young gentleman, and went farther (surely to fare worse!) in quest of the confidant, the friend, or the adviser. To thousands he must have turned an appealing countenance, and yet not one regarded him.

A light dinner, eaten to the accompaniment of his impetuous aspirations, broke in upon the series of his attempts on fortune; and when he returned to the task, the lamps were already lighted, and the nocturnal crowd was dense upon the pavement. Before a certain restaurant, whose name will readily occur to any student of our Babylon, people were already packed so closely that passage had grown difficult; and Somerset, standing in the kennel, watched, with a hope that was beginning to grow somewhat weary, the faces and the manners of the crowd. Suddenly he was startled by a gentle touch upon the shoulder, and facing about, he was aware of a very plain and elegant brougham, drawn by a pair of powerful horses, and driven by a man in sober livery. There were no arms upon the panel; the window was open, but the interior was obscure; the driver yawned behind his palm; and the young man was already beginning to suppose himself the dupe of his own fancy, when a hand, no larger than a child's and smoothly gloved in white, appeared in a corner of the window and privily beckoned him to approach. He did so, and looked in. The carriage was occupied by a single small and very dainty figure, swathed head and shoulders in impenetrable folds of white lace; and a voice, speaking low and silvery, addressed him in these words—

'Open the door and get in.'

'It must be,' thought the young man with an almost unbearable thrill, 'it must be that duchess at last!' Yet, although the moment was one to which he had long looked forward, it was with a certain share of alarm that he opened the door, and, mounting into the brougham, took his seat beside the lady of the lace. Whether or no she had touched a spring, or given some other signal, the young man had hardly closed the door before the carriage, with considerable swiftness, and with a very luxurious and easy movement on its springs, turned and began to drive towards the west.

Somerset, as I have written, was not unprepared; it had long been his particular pleasure to rehearse his conduct in the most unlikely situations; and this, among others, of the patrician ravisher, was one he had familiarly studied. Strange as it may seem, however, he could find no apposite remark; and as the lady, on her side, vouchsafed no further sign, they continued to drive in silence through the streets. Except for alternate flashes from the passing lamps, the carriage was plunged in obscurity; and beyond the fact that the fittings were luxurious, and that the lady was singularly small and slender in person, and, all but one gloved hand, still swathed in her costly veil, the young man could decipher no detail of an inspiring nature. The suspense began to grow unbearable. Twice he cleared his throat, and twice the whole resources of the language failed him. In similar scenes, when he had forecast them on the theatre of fancy, his presence of mind had always been complete, his eloquence remarkable; and at this disparity between the rehearsal and the performance, he began to be seized with a panic of apprehension. Here, on the very threshold of adventure, suppose him ignominiously to fail; suppose that after ten, twenty, or sixty seconds of still uninterrupted silence, the lady should touch the check-string and re-deposit him, weighed and found wanting, on the common street! Thousands of persons of no mind at all, he reasoned, would be found more equal to the part; could, that very instant, by some decisive step, prove the lady's choice to have been well inspired, and put a stop to this intolerable silence.

His eye, at this point, lighted on the hand. It was better to fall by desperate councils than to continue as he was; and with one tremulous swoop he pounced on the gloved fingers and drew them to himself. One overt step, it had appeared to him, would dissolve the spell of his embarrassment; in act, he found it otherwise: he found himself no less incapable of speech or further progress; and with the lady's hand in his, sat helpless. But worse was in store. A peculiar quivering began to agitate the form of his companion; the hand that lay unresistingly in Somerset's trembled as with ague; and presently there broke forth, in the shadow of the carriage, the bubbling and musical sound of laughter, resisted but triumphant. The young man dropped his prize; had it been possible, he would have bounded from the carriage. The lady, meanwhile, lying back upon the cushions, passed on from trill to trill of the most heart-felt, high-pitched, clear and fairy-sounding merriment.

'You must not be offended,' she said at last, catching an opportunity between two paroxysms. 'If you have been mistaken in the warmth of your attentions, the fault is solely mine; it does not flow from your presumption, but from my eccentric manner of recruiting friends; and, believe me, I am the last person in the world to think the worse of a young man for showing spirit. As for to-night, it is my intention to entertain you to a little supper; and if I shall continue to be as much pleased with your manners as I was taken with your face, I may perhaps end by making you an advantageous offer.'

Somerset sought in vain to find some form of answer, but his discomfiture had been too recent and complete.

'Come,' returned the lady, 'we must have no display of temper; that is for me the one disqualifying fault; and as I perceive we are drawing near our destination, I shall ask you to descend and offer me your arm.'

Indeed, at that very moment the carriage drew up before a stately and severe mansion in a spacious square; and Somerset, who was possessed of an excellent temper, with the best grace in the world assisted the lady to alight. The door was opened by an old woman of a grim appearance, who ushered the pair into a dining-room somewhat dimly lighted, but already laid for supper, and occupied by a prodigious company of large and valuable cats. Here, as soon as they were alone, the lady divested herself of the lace in which she was enfolded; and Somerset was relieved to find, that although still bearing the traces of great beauty, and still distinguished by the fire and colour of her eye, her hair was of a silvery whiteness and her face lined with years.

'And now, MON PREUX,' said the old lady, nodding at him with a quaint gaiety, 'you perceive that I am no longer in my first youth. You will soon find that I am all the better company for that.'

As she spoke, the maid re-entered the apartment with a light but tasteful supper. They sat down, accordingly, to table, the cats with savage pantomime surrounding the old lady's chair; and what with the excellence of the meal and the gaiety of his entertainer, Somerset was soon completely at his ease. When they had well eaten and drunk, the old lady leaned back in her chair, and taking a cat upon her lap, subjected her guest to a prolonged but evidently mirthful scrutiny.

'I fear, madam,' said Somerset, 'that my manners have not risen to the height of your preconceived opinion.'

'My dear young man,' she replied, 'you were never more mistaken in your life. I find you charming, and you may very well have lighted on a fairy godmother. I am not one of those who are given to change their opinions, and short of substantial demerit, those who have once gained my favour continue to enjoy it; but I have a singular swiftness of decision, read my fellow men and women with a glance, and have acted throughout life on first impressions. Yours, as I tell you, has been favourable; and if, as I suppose, you are a young fellow of somewhat idle habits, I think it not improbable that we may strike a bargain.'

'Ah, madam,' returned Somerset, 'you have divined my situation. I am a man of birth, parts, and breeding; excellent company, or at least so I find myself; but by a peculiar iniquity of fate, destitute alike of trade or money. I was, indeed, this evening upon the quest of an adventure, resolved to close with any offer of interest, emolument, or pleasure; and your summons, which I profess I am still at some loss to understand, jumped naturally with the inclination of my mind. Call it, if you will, impudence; I am here, at least, prepared for any proposition you can find it in your heart to make, and resolutely determined to accept.'

'You express yourself very well,' replied the old lady, 'and are certainly a droll and curious young man. I should not care to affirm that you were sane, for I have never found any one entirely so besides myself; but at least the nature of your madness entertains me, and I will reward you with some description of my character and life.'

Thereupon the old lady, still fondling the cat upon her lap, proceeded to narrate the following particulars.

Narrative of the Spirited Old Lady

I WAS the eldest daughter of the Reverend Bernard Fanshawe, who held a valuable living in the diocese of Bath and Wells. Our family, a very large one, was noted for a sprightly and incisive wit, and came of a good old stock where beauty was an heirloom. In Christian grace of character we were unhappily deficient. From my earliest years I saw and deplored the defects of those relatives whose age and position should have enabled them to conquer my esteem; and while I was yet a child, my father married a second wife, in whom (strange to say) the Fanshawe failings were exaggerated to a monstrous and almost laughable degree. Whatever may be said against me, it cannot be denied I was a pattern daughter; but it was in vain that, with the most touching patience, I submitted to my stepmother's demands; and from the hour she entered my father's house, I may say that I met with nothing but injustice and ingratitude.

I stood not alone, however, in the sweetness of my disposition; for one other of the family besides myself was free from any violence of character. Before I had reached the age of sixteen, this cousin, John by name, had conceived for me a sincere but silent passion; and although the poor lad was too timid to hint at the nature of his feelings, I had soon divined and begun to share them. For some days I pondered on the odd situation created for me by the bashfulness of my admirer; and at length, perceiving that he began, in his distress, rather to avoid than seek my company, I determined to take the matter into my own hands. Finding him alone in a retired part of the rectory garden, I told him that I had divined his amiable secret, that I knew with what disfavour our union was sure to be regarded; and that, under the circumstances, I was prepared to flee with him at once. Poor John was literally paralysed with joy; such was the force of his emotions, that he could find no words in which to thank me; and that I, seeing him thus helpless, was obliged to arrange, myself, the details of our flight, and of the stolen marriage which was immediately to crown it. John had been at that time projecting a visit to the metropolis. In this I bade him persevere, and promised on the following day to join him at the Tavistock Hotel.

True, on my side, to every detail of our arrangement, I arose, on the day in question, before the servants, packed a few necessaries in a bag, took with me the little money I possessed, and bade farewell for ever to the rectory. I walked with good spirits to a town some thirty miles from home, and was set down the next morning in this great city of London. As I walked from the coach-office to the hotel, I could not help exulting in the pleasant change that had befallen me; beholding, meanwhile, with innocent delight, the traffic of the streets, and depicting, in all the colours of fancy, the reception that awaited me from John. But alas! when I inquired for Mr. Fanshawe, the porter assured me there was no such gentleman among the guests. By what channel our secret had leaked out, or what pressure had been brought to bear on the too facile John, I could never fathom. Enough that my family had triumphed; that I found myself alone in London, tender in years, smarting under the most sensible mortification, and by every sentiment of pride and self-respect debarred for ever from my father's house.

I rose under the blow, and found lodgings in the neighbourhood of Euston Road, where, for the first time in my life, I tasted the joys of independence. Three days afterwards, an advertisement in the TIMES directed me to the office of a solicitor whom I knew to be in my father's confidence. There I was given the promise of a very moderate allowance, and a distinct intimation that I must never look to be received at home. I could not but resent so cruel a desertion, and I told the lawyer it was a meeting I desired as little as themselves. He smiled at my courageous spirit, paid me the first quarter of my income, and gave me the remainder of my personal effects, which had been sent to me, under his care, in a couple of rather ponderous boxes. With these I returned in triumph to my lodgings, more content with my position than I should have thought possible a week before, and fully determined to make the best of the future.

All went well for several months; and, indeed, it was my own fault alone that ended this pleasant and secluded episode of life. I have, I must confess, the fatal trick of spoiling my inferiors. My landlady, to whom I had as usual been overkind, impertinently called me in fault for some particular too small to mention; and I, annoyed that I had allowed her the freedom upon which she thus presumed, ordered her to leave my presence. She stood a moment dumb, and then, recalling her self-possession, 'Your bill,' said she, 'shall be ready this evening, and to-morrow, madam, you shall leave my house. See,' she added, 'that you are able to pay what you owe me; for if I do not receive the uttermost farthing, no box of yours shall pass my threshold.'

I was confounded at her audacity, but as a whole quarter's income was due to me, not otherwise affected by the threat. That afternoon, as I left the solicitor's door, carrying in one hand, and done up in a paper parcel, the whole amount of my fortune, there befell me one of those decisive incidents that sometimes shape a life. The lawyer's office was situate in a street that opened at the upper end upon the Strand, and was closed at the lower, at the time of which I speak, by a row of iron railings looking on the Thames. Down this street, then, I beheld my stepmother advancing to meet me, and doubtless bound to the very house I had just left. She was attended by a maid whose face was new to me, but her own was too clearly printed on my memory; and the sight of it, even from a distance, filled me with generous indignation. Flight was impossible. There was nothing left but to retreat against the railing, and with my back turned to the street, pretend to be admiring the barges on the river or the chimneys of transpontine London.

I was still so standing, and had not yet fully mastered the turbulence of my emotions, when a voice at my elbow addressed me with a trivial question. It was the maid whom my stepmother, with characteristic hardness, had left to await her on the street, while she transacted her business with the family solicitor. The girl did not know who I was; the opportunity too golden to be lost; and I was soon hearing the latest news of my father's rectory and parish. It did not surprise me to find that she detested her employers; and yet the terms in which she spoke of them were hard to bear, hard to let pass unchallenged. I heard them, however, without dissent, for my self-command is wonderful; and we might have parted as we met, had she not proceeded, in an evil hour, to criticise the rector's missing daughter, and with the most shocking perversions, to narrate the story of her flight. My nature is so essentially generous that I can never pause to reason. I flung up my hand sharply, by way, as well as I remember, of indignant protest; and, in the act, the packet slipped from my fingers, glanced between the railings, and fell and sunk in the river. I stood a moment petrified, and then, struck by the drollery of the incident, gave way to peals of laughter. I was still laughing when my stepmother reappeared, and the maid, who doubtless considered me insane, ran off to join her; nor had I yet recovered my gravity when I presented myself before the lawyer to solicit a fresh advance. His answer made me serious enough, for it was a flat refusal; and it was not until I had besought him even with tears, that he consented to lend me ten pounds from his own pocket. 'I am a poor man,' said he, 'and you must look for nothing farther at my hands.'

The landlady met me at the door. 'Here, madam,' said she, with a curtsey insolently low, 'here is my bill. Would it inconvenience you to settle it at once?'

'You shall be paid, madam,' said I, 'in the morning, in the proper course.' And I took the paper with a very high air, but inwardly quaking.

I had no sooner looked at it than I perceived myself to be lost. I had been short of money and had allowed my debt to mount; and it had now reached the sum, which I shall never forget, of twelve pounds thirteen and fourpence halfpenny. All evening I sat by the fire considering my situation. I could not pay the bill; my landlady would not suffer me to remove my boxes; and without either baggage or money, how was I to find another lodging? For three months, unless I could invent some remedy, I was condemned to be without a roof and without a penny. It can surprise no one that I decided on immediate flight; but even here I was confronted by a difficulty, for I had no sooner packed my boxes than I found I was not strong enough to move, far less to carry them.

In this strait I did not hesitate a moment, but throwing on a shawl and bonnet, and covering my face with a thick veil, I betook myself to that great bazaar of dangerous and smiling chances, the pavement of the city. It was already late at night, and the weather being wet and windy, there were few abroad besides policemen. These, on my present mission, I had wit enough to know for enemies; and wherever I perceived their moving lanterns, I made haste to turn aside and choose another thoroughfare. A few miserable women still walked the pavement; here and there were young fellows returning drunk, or ruffians of the lowest class lurking in the mouths of alleys; but of any one to whom I might appeal in my distress, I began almost to despair.

At last, at the corner of a street, I ran into the arms of one who was evidently a gentleman, and who, in all his appointments, from his furred great-coat to the fine cigar which he was smoking, comfortably breathed of wealth. Much as my face has changed from its original beauty, I still retain (or so I tell myself) some traces of the youthful lightness of my figure. Even veiled as I then was, I could perceive the gentleman was struck by my appearance: and this emboldened me for my adventure.

'Sir,' said I, with a quickly beating heart, 'sir, are you one in whom a lady can confide?'

'Why, my dear,' said he, removing his cigar, 'that depends on circumstances. If you will raise your veil—'

'Sir,' I interrupted, 'let there be no mistake. I ask you, as a gentleman, to serve me, but I offer no reward.'

'That is frank,' said he; 'but hardly tempting. And what, may I inquire, is the nature of the service?'

But I knew well enough it was not my interest to tell him on so short an interview. 'If you will accompany me,' said I, 'to a house not far from here, you can see for yourself.'

He looked at me awhile with hesitating eyes; and then, tossing away his cigar, which was not yet a quarter smoked, 'Here goes!' said he, and with perfect politeness offered me his arm. I was wise enough to take it; to prolong our walk as far as possible, by more than one excursion from the shortest line; and to beguile the way with that sort of conversation which should prove to him indubitably from what station in society I sprang. By the time we reached the door of my lodging, I felt sure I had confirmed his interest, and might venture, before I turned the pass-key, to beseech him to moderate his voice and to tread softly. He promised to obey me: and I admitted him into the passage and thence into my sitting-room, which was fortunately next the door.

'And now,' said he, when with trembling fingers I had lighted a candle, 'what is the meaning of all this?'

'I wish you,' said I, speaking with great difficulty, 'to help me out with these boxes—and I wish nobody to know.'

He took up the candle. 'And I wish to see your face,' said he.

I turned back my veil without a word, and looked at him with every appearance of resolve that I could summon up. For some time he gazed into my face, still holding up the candle. 'Well,' said he at last, 'and where do you wish them taken?'

I knew that I had gained my point; and it was with a tremor in my voice that I replied. 'I had thought we might carry them between us to the corner of Euston Road,' said I, 'where, even at this late hour, we may still find a cab.'

'Very good,' was his reply; and he immediately hoisted the heavier of my trunks upon his shoulder, and taking one handle of the second, signed to me to help him at the other end. In this order we made good our retreat from the house, and without the least adventure, drew pretty near to the corner of Euston Road. Before a house, where there was a light still burning, my companion paused. 'Let us here,' said he, 'set down our boxes, while we go forward to the end of the street in quest of a cab. By doing so, we can still keep an eye upon their safety, and we avoid the very extraordinary figure we should otherwise present—a young man, a young lady, and a mass of baggage, standing castaway at midnight on the streets of London.' So it was done, and the event proved him to be wise; for long before there was any word of a cab, a policeman appeared upon the scene, turned upon us the full glare of his lantern, and hung suspiciously behind us in a doorway.

'There seem to be no cabs about, policeman,' said my champion, with affected cheerfulness. But the constable's answer was ungracious; and as for the offer of a cigar, with which this rebuff was most unwisely followed up, he refused it point-blank, and without the least civility. The young gentleman looked at me with a warning grimace, and there we continued to stand, on the edge of the pavement, in the beating rain, and with the policeman still silently watching our movements from the doorway.

At last, and after a delay that seemed interminable, a four-wheeler appeared lumbering along in the mud, and was instantly hailed by my companion. 'Just pull up here, will you?' he cried. 'We have some baggage up the street.'

And now came the hitch of our adventure; for when the policeman, still closely following us, beheld my two boxes lying in the rain, he arose from mere suspicion to a kind of certitude of something evil. The light in the house had been extinguished; the whole frontage of the street was dark; there was nothing to explain the presence of these unguarded trunks; and no two innocent people were ever, I believe, detected in such questionable circumstances.

'Where have these things come from?' asked the policeman, flashing his light full into my champion's face.

'Why, from that house, of course,' replied the young gentleman, hastily shouldering a trunk.

The policeman whistled and turned to look at the dark windows; he then took a step towards the door, as though to knock, a course which had infallibly proved our ruin; but seeing us already hurrying down the street under our double burthen, thought better or worse of it, and followed in our wake.

'For God's sake,' whispered my companion, 'tell me where to drive to.'

'Anywhere,' I replied with anguish. 'I have no idea. Anywhere you like.'

Thus it befell that, when the boxes had been stowed, and I had already entered the cab, my deliverer called out in clear tones the address of the house in which we are now seated. The policeman, I could see, was staggered. This neighbourhood, so retired, so aristocratic, was far from what he had expected. For all that, he took the number of the cab, and spoke for a few seconds and with a decided manner in the cabman's ear.

'What can he have said?' I gasped, as soon as the cab had rolled away.

'I can very well imagine,' replied my champion; 'and I can assure you that you are now condemned to go where I have said;

for, should we attempt to change our destination by the way, the jarvey will drive us straight to a police-office. Let me compliment you on your nerves,' he added. 'I have had, I believe, the most horrible fright of my existence.'

But my nerves, which he so much misjudged, were in so strange a disarray that speech was now become impossible; and we made the drive thenceforward in unbroken silence. When we arrived before the door of our destination, the young gentleman alighted, opened it with a pass-key like one who was at home, bade the driver carry the trunks into the hall, and dismissed him with a handsome fee. He then led me into this dining-room, looking nearly as you behold it, but with certain marks of bachelor occupancy, and hastened to pour out a glass of wine, which he insisted on my drinking. As soon as I could find my voice, 'In God's name,' I cried, 'where am I?'

He told me I was in his house, where I was very welcome, and had no more urgent business than to rest myself and recover my spirits. As he spoke he offered me another glass of wine, of which, indeed, I stood in great want, for I was faint, and inclined to be hysterical. Then he sat down beside the fire, lit another cigar, and for some time observed me curiously in silence.

'And now,' said he, 'that you have somewhat restored yourself, will you be kind enough to tell me in what sort of crime I have become a partner? Are you murderer, smuggler, thief, or only the harmless and domestic moonlight flitter?'

I had been already shocked by his lighting a cigar without permission, for I had not forgotten the one he threw away on our first meeting; and now, at these explicit insults, I resolved at once to reconquer his esteem. The judgment of the world I have consistently despised, but I had already begun to set a certain value on the good opinion of my entertainer. Beginning with a note of pathos, but soon brightening into my habitual vivacity and humour, I rapidly narrated the circumstances of my birth, my flight, and subsequent misfortunes. He heard me to an end in silence, gravely smoking. 'Miss Fanshawe,' said he, when I had done, 'you are a very comical and most enchanting creature; and I can see nothing for it but that I should return to-morrow morning and satisfy your landlady's demands.'

'You strangely misinterpret my confidence,' was my reply; 'and if you had at all appreciated my character, you would understand that I can take no money at your hands.'

'Your landlady will doubtless not be so particular,' he returned; 'nor do I at all despair of persuading even your unconquerable self. I desire you to examine me with critical indulgence. My name is Henry Luxmore, Lord Southwark's second son. I possess nine thousand a year, the house in which we are now sitting, and seven others in the best neighbourhoods in town. I do not believe I am repulsive to the eye, and as for my character, you have seen me under trial. I think you simply the most original of created beings; I need not tell you what you know very well, that you are ravishingly pretty; and I have nothing more to add, except that, foolish as it may appear, I am already head over heels in love with you.'

'Sir,' said I, 'I am prepared to be misjudged; but while I continue to accept your hospitality that fact alone should be enough to protect me from insult.'

'Pardon me,' said he: 'I offer you marriage.' And leaning back in his chair he replaced his cigar between his lips.

I own I was confounded by an offer, not only so unprepared, but couched in terms so singular. But he knew very well how to obtain his purposes, for he was not only handsome in person, but his very coolness had a charm; and to make a long story short, a fortnight later I became the wife of the Honourable Henry Luxmore.

For nearly twenty years I now led a life of almost perfect quiet. My Henry had his weaknesses; I was twice driven to flee from his roof, but not for long; for though he was easily overexcited, his nature was placable below the surface, and with all his faults, I loved him tenderly. At last he was taken from me; and such is the power of self-deception, and so strange are the whims of the dying, he actually assured me, with his latest breath, that he forgave the violence of my temper!

There was but one pledge of the marriage, my daughter Clara. She had, indeed, inherited a shadow of her father's failing; but in all things else, unless my partial eyes deceived me, she derived her qualities from me, and might be called my moral image. On my side, whatever else I may have done amiss, as a mother I was above reproach. Here, then, was surely every promise for the future; here, at last, was a relation in which I might hope to taste repose. But it was not to be. You will hardly credit me when I inform you that she ran away from home; yet such was the case. Some whim about oppressed nationalities—Ireland, Poland, and the like —has turned her brain; and if you should anywhere encounter a young lady (I must say, of remarkable attractions) answering to the name of Luxmore, Lake, or Fonblanque (for I am told she uses these indifferently, as well as many others), tell her, from me, that I forgive her cruelty, and though I will never more behold her face, I am at any time prepared to make her a liberal allowance.

On the death of Mr. Luxmore, I sought oblivion in the details of business. I believe I have mentioned that seven mansions, besides this, formed part of Mr. Luxmore's property: I have found them seven white elephants. The greed of tenants, the dishonesty of solicitors, and the incapacity that sits upon the bench, have combined together to make these houses the burthen of my life. I had no sooner, indeed, begun to look into these matters for myself, than I discovered so many injustices and met with so much studied incivility, that I was plunged into a long series of lawsuits, some of which are pending to this day. You must have heard my name already; I am the Mrs. Luxmore of the Law Reports: a strange destiny, indeed, for one born with an almost cowardly desire for peace! But I am of the stamp of those who, when they have once begun a task, will rather die than leave their duty unfulfilled. I have met with every obstacle: insolence and ingratitude from my own lawyers; in my adversaries, that fault of obstinacy which is to me perhaps the most distasteful in the calendar; from the bench, civility indeed —always, I must allow, civility—but never a spark of independence, never that knowledge of the law and love of justice which we have a right to look for in a judge, the most august of human officers. And still, against all these odds, I have undissuadably persevered.

It was after the loss of one of my innumerable cases (a subject on which I will not dwell) that it occurred to me to make a melancholy pilgrimage to my various houses. Four were at that time tenantless and closed, like pillars of salt, commemorating the corruption of the age and the decline of private virtue. Three were occupied by persons who had wearied me by every conceivable unjust demand and legal subterfuge—persons whom, at that very hour, I was moving heaven and earth to turn into the street. This was perhaps the sadder spectacle of the two; and my heart grew hot within me to behold them occupying, in my very teeth, and with an insolent ostentation, these handsome structures which were as much mine as the flesh upon my body.

One more house remained for me to visit, that in which we now are. I had let it (for at that period I lodged in a hotel, the life that I have always preferred) to a Colonel Geraldine, a gentleman attached to Prince Florizel of Bohemia, whom you must certainly have heard of; and I had supposed, from the character and position of my tenant, that here, at least, I was safe against annoyance. What was my surprise to find this house also shuttered and apparently deserted! I will not deny that I was offended; I conceived that a house, like a yacht, was better to be kept in commission; and I promised myself to bring the matter before my solicitor the following morning. Meanwhile the sight recalled my fancy naturally to the past; and yielding to the tender influence of sentiment, I sat down opposite the door upon the garden parapet. It was August, and a sultry afternoon, but that spot is sheltered, as you may observe by daylight, under the branches of a spreading chestnut; the square, too, was deserted; there was a sound of distant music in the air; and all combined to plunge me into that most agreeable of states, which is neither happiness nor sorrow, but shares the poignancy of both.

From this I was recalled by the arrival of a large van, very handsomely appointed, drawn by valuable horses, mounted by several men of an appearance more than decent, and bearing on its panels, instead of a trader's name, a coat-of-arms too modest to be deciphered from where I sat. It drew up before my house, the door of which was immediately opened by one of the men. His companions—I counted seven of them in all— proceeded, with disciplined activity, to take from the van and carry into the house a variety of hampers, bottle-baskets, and boxes, such as are designed for plate and napery. The windows of the dining-room were thrown widely open, as though to air it; and I saw some of those within laying the table for a meal. Plainly, I concluded, my tenant was about to return; and while still determined to submit to no aggression on my rights, I was gratified by the number and discipline of his attendants, and the quiet profusion that appeared to reign in his establishment. I was still so thinking when, to my extreme surprise, the windows and shutters of the dining-room were once more closed; the men began to reappear from the interior and resume their stations on the van; the last closed the door behind his exit; the van drove away; and the house was once more left to itself, looking blindly on the square with shuttered windows, as though the whole affair had been a vision.

It was no vision, however; for, as I rose to my feet, and thus brought my eyes a little nearer to the level of the fanlight over the door, I saw that, though the day had still some hours to run, the hall lamps had been lighted and left burning. Plainly, then, guests were expected, and were not expected before night. For whom, I asked myself with indignation, were such secret preparations likely to be made? Although no prude, I am a woman of decided views upon morality; if my house, to which my husband had brought me, was to serve in the character of a PETITE MAISON, I saw myself forced, however unwillingly, into a new course of litigation; and, determined to return and know the worst, I hastened to my hotel for dinner.

I was at my post by ten. The night was clear and quiet; the moon rode very high and put the lamps to shame; and the shadow below the chestnut was black as ink. Here, then, I ensconced myself on the low parapet, with my back against the railings, face to face with the moonlit front of my old home, and ruminating gently on the past. Time fled; eleven struck on all the city clocks; and presently after I was aware of the approach of a gentleman of stately and agreeable demeanour. He was smoking as he walked; his light paletot, which was open, did not conceal his evening clothes; and he bore himself with a serious grace that immediately awakened my attention. Before the door of this house he took a pass-key from his pocket, quietly admitted himself, and disappeared into the lamplit hall.

He was scarcely gone when I observed another and a much younger man approaching hastily from the opposite side of the square. Considering the season of the year and the genial mildness of the night, he was somewhat closely muffled up; and as he came, for all his hurry, he kept looking nervously behind him. Arrived before my door, he halted and set one foot upon the step, as though about to enter; then, with a sudden change, he turned and began to hurry away; halted a second time, as if in painful indecision; and lastly, with a violent gesture, wheeled about, returned straight to the door, and rapped upon the knocker. He was almost immediately admitted by the first arrival.

My curiosity was now broad awake. I made myself as small as I could in the very densest of the shadow, and waited for the sequel. Nor had I long to wait. From the same side of the square a second young man made his appearance, walking slowly and softly, and like the first, muffled to the nose. Before the house he paused, looked all about him with a swift and comprehensive glance; and seeing the square lie empty in the moon and lamplight, leaned far across the area railings and appeared to listen to what was passing in the house. From the dining-room there came the report of a champagne cork, and following upon that, the sound of rich and manly laughter. The listener took heart of grace, produced a key, unlocked the area gate, shut it noiselessly behind him, and descended the stair. Just when his head had reached the level of the pavement, he turned half round and once more raked the square with a suspicious eyeshot. The mufflings had fallen lower round his neck; the moon shone full upon him; and I was startled to observe the pallor and passionate agitation of his face.

I could remain no longer passive. Persuaded that something deadly was afoot, I crossed the roadway and drew near the area railings. There was no one below; the man must therefore have entered the house, with what purpose I dreaded to imagine. I have at no part of my career lacked courage; and now, finding the area gate was merely laid to, I pushed it gently open and descended the stairs. The kitchen door of the house, like the area gate, was closed but not fastened. It flashed upon me that the criminal was thus preparing his escape; and the thought, as it confirmed the worst of my suspicions, lent me new resolve. I entered the house; and being now quite reckless of my life, I shut and locked the door.

From the dining-room above I could hear the pleasant tones of a voice in easy conversation. On the ground floor all was not only profoundly silent, but the darkness seemed to weigh upon my eyes. Here, then, I stood for some time, having thrust myself uncalled into the utmost peril, and being destitute of any power to help or interfere. Nor will I deny that fear had begun already to assail me, when I became aware, all at once and as though by some immediate but silent incandescence, of a certain glimmering of light upon the passage floor. Towards this I groped my way with infinite precaution; and having come at length as far as the angle of the corridor, beheld the door of the butler's pantry standing just ajar and a narrow thread of brightness falling from the chink. Creeping still closer, I put my eye to the aperture. The man sat within upon a chair, listening, I could see, with the most rapt attention. On a table before him he had laid a watch, a pair of steel revolvers, and a bull's-eye lantern. For one second many contradictory theories and projects whirled together in my head; the next, I had slammed the door and turned the key upon the malefactor. Surprised at my own decision, I stood and panted, leaning on the wall. From within the pantry not a sound was to be heard; the man, whatever he was, had accepted his fate without a struggle, and now, as I hugged myself to fancy, sat frozen with terror and looking for the worst to follow. I promised myself that he should not be disappointed; and the better to complete my task, I turned to ascend the stairs.

The situation, as I groped my way to the first floor, appealed to me suddenly by my strong sense of humour. Here was I, the owner of the house, burglariously present in its walls; and there, in the dining-room, were two gentlemen, unknown to me, seated complacently at supper, and only saved by my promptitude from some surprising or deadly interruption. It were strange if I could not manage to extract the matter of amusement from so unusual a situation.

Behind this dining-room, there is a small apartment intended for a library. It was to this that I cautiously groped my way; and you will see how fortune had exactly served me. The weather, I have said, was sultry; in order to ventilate the dining-room and yet preserve the uninhabited appearance of the mansion to the front, the window of the library had been widely opened, and the door of communication between the two apartments left ajar. To this interval I now applied my eye.

Wax tapers, set in silver candlesticks, shed their chastened brightness on the damask of the tablecloth and the remains of a cold collation of the rarest delicacy. The two gentlemen had finished supper, and were now trifling with cigars and maraschino; while in a silver spirit lamp, coffee of the most captivating fragrance was preparing in the fashion of the East. The elder of the two, he who had first arrived, was placed directly facing me; the other was set on his left hand. Both, like the man in the butler's pantry, seemed to be intently listening; and on the face of the second I thought I could perceive the marks of fear. Oddly enough, however, when they came to speak, the parts were found to be reversed.

'I assure you,' said the elder gentleman, 'I not only heard the slamming of a door, but the sound of very guarded footsteps.'

'Your highness was certainly deceived,' replied the other. 'I am endowed with the acutest hearing, and I can swear that not a mouse has rustled.' Yet the pallor and contraction of his features were in total discord with the tenor of his words.

His highness (whom, of course, I readily divined to be Prince Florizel) looked at his companion for the least fraction of a second; and though nothing shook the easy quiet of his attitude, I could see that he was far from being duped. 'It is well,' said he; 'let us dismiss the topic. And now, sir, that I have very freely explained the sentiments by which I am directed, let me ask you, according to your promise, to imitate my frankness.'

'I have heard you,' replied the other, 'with great interest.'

'With singular patience,' said the prince politely.

'Ay, your highness, and with unlooked-for sympathy,' returned the young man. 'I know not how to tell the change that has befallen me. You have, I must suppose, a charm, to which even your enemies are subject.' He looked at the clock on the mantel-piece and visibly blanched. 'So late!' he cried. 'Your highness—God knows I am now speaking from the heart— before it be too late, leave this house!'

The prince glanced once more at his companion, and then very deliberately shook the ash from his cigar. 'That is a strange remark,' said he; 'and A PROPOS DE BOTTES, I never continue a cigar when once the ash is fallen; the spell breaks, the soul of the flavour flies away, and there remains but the dead body of tobacco; and I make it a rule to throw away that husk and choose another.' He suited the action to the words.

'Do not trifle with my appeal,' resumed the young man, in tones that trembled with emotion. 'It is made at the price of my honour and to the peril of my life. Go—go now! lose not a moment; and if you have any kindness for a young man, miserably deceived indeed, but not devoid of better sentiments, look not behind you as you leave.'

'Sir,' said the prince, 'I am here upon your honour; assure you upon mine that I shall continue to rely upon that safeguard. The coffee is ready; I must again trouble you, I fear.' And with a courteous movement of the hand, he seemed to invite his companion to pour out the coffee.

The unhappy young man rose from his seat. 'I appeal to you,' he cried, 'by every holy sentiment, in mercy to me, if not in pity to yourself, begone before it is too late.'

'Sir,' replied the prince, 'I am not readily accessible to fear; and if there is one defect to which I must plead guilty, it is that of a curious disposition. You go the wrong way about to make me leave this house, in which I play the part of your entertainer; and, suffer me to add, young man, if any peril threaten us, it was of your contriving, not of mine.'

'Alas, you do not know to what you condemn me,' cried the other. 'But I at least will have no hand in it.' With these words he carried his hand to his pocket, hastily swallowed the contents of a phial, and, with the very act, reeled back and fell across his chair upon the floor. The prince left his place and came and stood above him, where he lay convulsed upon the carpet. 'Poor moth!' I heard his highness murmur. 'Alas, poor moth! must we again inquire which is the more fatal—weakness or wickedness? And can a sympathy with ideas, surely not ignoble in themselves, conduct a man to this dishonourable death?'

By this time I had pushed the door open and walked into the room. 'Your highness,' said I, 'this is no time for moralising; with a little promptness we may save this creature's life; and as for the other, he need cause you no concern, for I have him safely under lock and key.'

The prince had turned about upon my entrance, and regarded me certainly with no alarm, but with a profundity of wonder which almost robbed me of my self-possession. 'My dear madam,' he cried at last, 'and who the devil are you?'

I was already on the floor beside the dying man. I had, of course, no idea with what drug he had attempted his life, and I was forced to try him with a variety of antidotes. Here were both oil and vinegar, for the prince had done the young man the honour of compounding for him one of his celebrated salads; and of each of these I administered from a quarter to half a pint, with no apparent efficacy. I next plied him with the hot coffee, of which there may have been near upon a quart.

'Have you no milk?' I inquired.

'I fear, madam, that milk has been omitted,' returned the prince.

'Salt, then,' said I; 'salt is a revulsive. Pass the salt.'

'And possibly the mustard?' asked his highness, as he offered me the contents of the various salt-cellars poured together on a plate.

'Ah,' cried I, 'the thought is excellent! Mix me about half a pint of mustard, drinkably dilute.'

Whether it was the salt or the mustard, or the mere combination of so many subversive agents, as soon as the last had been poured over his throat, the young sufferer obtained relief.

'There!' I exclaimed, with natural triumph, 'I have saved a life!'

'And yet, madam,' returned the prince, 'your mercy may be cruelty disguised. Where the honour is lost, it is, at least, superfluous to prolong the life.'

'If you had led a life as changeable as mine, your highness,' I replied, 'you would hold a very different opinion. For my part, and after whatever extremity of misfortune or disgrace, I should still count to-morrow worth a trial.'

'You speak as a lady, madam,' said the prince; 'and for such you speak the truth. But to men there is permitted such a field of license, and the good behaviour asked of them is at once so easy and so little, that to fail in that is to fall beyond the reach of pardon. But will you suffer me to repeat a question, put to you at first, I am afraid, with some defect of courtesy; and to ask you once more, who you are and how I have the honour of your company?'

'I am the proprietor of the house in which we stand,' said I.

'And still I am at fault,' returned the prince.

But at that moment the timepiece on the mantel-shelf began to strike the hour of twelve; and the young man, raising himself upon one elbow, with an expression of despair and horror that I have never seen excelled, cried lamentably, 'Midnight! oh, just God!' We stood frozen to our places, while the tingling hammer of the timepiece measured the remaining strokes; nor had we yet stirred, so tragic had been the tones of the young man, when the various bells of London began in turn to declare the hour. The timepiece was inaudible beyond the walls of the chamber where we stood; but the second pulsation of Big Ben had scarcely throbbed into the night, before a sharp detonation rang about the house. The prince sprang for the door by which I had entered; but quick as he was, I yet contrived to intercept him.

'Are you armed?' I cried.

'No, madam,' replied he. 'You remind me appositely; I will take the poker.'

'The man below,' said I, 'has two revolvers. Would you confront him at such odds?'

He paused, as though staggered in his purpose.

'And yet, madam,' said he, 'we cannot continue to remain in ignorance of what has passed.'

'No!' cried I. 'And who proposes it? I am as curious as yourself, but let us rather send for the police; or, if your highness dreads a scandal, for some of your own servants.'

'Nay, madam,' he replied, smiling, 'for so brave a lady, you surprise me. Would you have me, then, send others where I fear to go myself?'

'You are perfectly right,' said I, 'and I was entirely wrong. Go, in God's name, and I will hold the candle!'

Together, therefore, we descended to the lower story, he carrying the poker, I the light; and together we approached and opened the door of the butler's pantry. In some sort, I believe, I was prepared for the spectacle that met our eyes; I was prepared, that is, to find the villain dead, but the rude details of such a violent suicide I was unable to endure. The prince, unshaken by horror as he had remained unshaken by alarm, assisted me with the most respectful gallantry to regain the dining-room.

There we found our patient, still, indeed, deadly pale, but vastly recovered and already seated on a chair. He held out both his hands with a most pitiful gesture of interrogation.

'He is dead,' said the prince.

'Alas!' cried the young man, 'and it should be I! What do I do, thus lingering on the stage I have disgraced, while he, my sure comrade, blameworthy indeed for much, but yet the soul of fidelity, has judged and slain himself for an involuntary fault? Ah, sir,' said he, 'and you too, madam, without whose cruel help I should be now beyond the reach of my accusing conscience, you behold in me the victim equally of my own faults and virtues. I was born a hater of injustice; from my most tender years my blood boiled against heaven when I beheld the sick, and against men when I witnessed the sorrows of the poor; the pauper's crust stuck in my throat when I sat down to eat my dainties, and the cripple child has set me weeping. What was there in that but what was noble? and yet observe to what a fall these thoughts have led me! Year after year this passion for the lost besieged me closer. What hope was there in kings? what hope in these well-feathered classes that now roll in money? I had observed the course of history; I knew the burgess, our ruler of to-day, to be base, cowardly, and dull; I saw him, in every age, combine to pull down that which was immediately above and to prey upon those that were below; his dulness, I knew, would ultimately bring about his ruin; I knew his days were numbered, and yet how was I to wait? how was I to let the poor child shiver in the rain? The better days, indeed, were coming, but the child would die before that. Alas, your highness, in surely no ungenerous impatience I enrolled myself among the enemies of this unjust and doomed society; in surely no unnatural desire to keep the fires of my philanthropy alight, I bound myself by an irrevocable oath.

'That oath is all my history. To give freedom to posterity I had forsworn my own. I must attend upon every signal; and soon my father complained of my irregular hours and turned me from his house. I was engaged in betrothal to an honest girl; from her also I had to part, for she was too shrewd to credit my inventions and too innocent to be entrusted with the truth. Behold me, then, alone with conspirators! Alas! as the years went on, my illusions left me. Surrounded as I was by the fervent disciples and apologists of revolution, I beheld them daily advance in confidence and desperation; I beheld myself, upon the other hand, and with an almost equal regularity, decline in faith. I had sacrificed all to further that cause in which I still believed; and daily I began to grow in doubts if we were advancing it indeed. Horrible was the society with which we warred, but our own means were not less horrible.

'I will not dwell upon my sufferings; I will not pause to tell you how, when I beheld young men still free and happy, married, fathers of children, cheerfully toiling at their work, my heart reproached me with the greatness and vanity of my unhappy sacrifice. I will not describe to you how, worn by poverty, poor lodging, scanty food, and an unquiet conscience, my health began to fail, and in the long nights, as I wandered bedless in the rainy streets, the most cruel sufferings of the body were added to the tortures of my mind. These things are not personal to me; they are common to all unfortunates in my position. An oath, so light a thing to swear, so grave a thing to break: an oath, taken in the heat of youth, repented with what sobbings of the heart, but yet in vain repented, as the years go on: an oath, that was once the very utterance of the truth of God, but that falls to be the symbol of a meaningless and empty slavery; such is the yoke that many young men joyfully assume, and under whose dead weight they live to suffer worse than death.

'It is not that I was patient. I have begged to be released; but I knew too much, and I was still refused. I have fled; ay, and for the time successfully. I reached Paris. I found a lodging in the Rue St. Jacques, almost opposite the Val de Grace. My room was mean and bare, but the sun looked into it towards evening; it commanded a peep of a green garden; a bird hung by a neighbour's window and made the morning beautiful; and I, who was sick, might lie in bed and rest myself: I, who was in full revolt against the principles that I had served, was now no longer at the beck of the council, and was no longer charged with shameful and revolting tasks. Oh! what an interval of peace was that! I still dream, at times, that I can hear the note of my neighbour's bird.

'My money was running out, and it became necessary that I should find employment. Scarcely had I been three days upon the search, ere I thought that I was being followed. I made certain of the features of the man, which were quite strange to me, and turned into a small cafe, where I whiled away an hour, pretending to read the papers, but inwardly convulsed with terror. When I came forth again into the street, it was quite empty, and I breathed again; but alas, I had not turned three corners, when I once more observed the human hound pursuing me. Not an hour was to be lost; timely submission might yet preserve a life which otherwise was forfeit and dishonoured; and I fled, with what speed you may conceive, to the Paris agency of the society I served.

'My submission was accepted. I took up once more the hated burthen of that life; once more I was at the call of men whom I despised and hated, while yet I envied and admired them. They at least were wholehearted in the things they purposed; but I, who had once been such as they, had fallen from the brightness of my faith, and now laboured, like a hireling, for the wages of a loathed existence. Ay, sir, to that I was condemned; I obeyed to continue to live, and lived but to obey.

'The last charge that was laid upon me was the one which has to-night so tragically ended. Boldly telling who I was, I was to request from your highness, on behalf of my society, a private audience, where it was designed to murder you. If one thing remained to me of my old convictions, it was the hate of kings; and when this task was offered me, I took it gladly. Alas, sir, you triumphed. As we supped, you gained upon my heart. Your character, your talents, your designs for our unhappy country, all had been misrepresented. I began to forget you were a prince; I began, all too feelingly, to remember that you were a man. As I saw the hour approach, I suffered agonies untold; and when, at last, we heard the slamming of the door which announced in my unwilling ears the arrival of the partner of my crime, you will bear me out with what instancy I besought you to depart. You would not, alas! and what could I? Kill you, I could not; my heart revolted, my hand turned back from such a deed. Yet it was impossible that I should suffer you to stay; for when the hour struck and my companion came, true to his appointment, and he, at least, true to our design, I could neither suffer you to be killed nor yet him to be arrested. From such a tragic passage, death, and death alone, could save me; and it is no fault of mine if I continue to exist.

'But you, madam,' continued the young man, addressing himself more directly to myself, 'were doubtless born to save the prince and to confound our purposes. My life you have prolonged; and by turning the key on my companion, you have made me the author of his death. He heard the hour strike; he was impotent to help; and thinking himself forfeit to honour, thinking that I should fall alone upon his highness and perish for lack of his support, he has turned his pistol on himself.'

'You are right,' said Prince Florizel: 'it was in no ungenerous spirit that you brought these burthens on yourself; and when I see you so nobly to blame, so tragically punished, I stand like one reproved. For is it not strange, madam, that you and I, by practising accepted and inconsiderable virtues, and commonplace but still unpardonable faults, should stand here, in the sight of God, with what we call clean hands and quiet consciences; while this poor youth, for an error that I could almost envy him, should be sunk beyond the reach of hope?

'Sir,' resumed the prince, turning to the young man, 'I cannot help you; my help would but unchain the thunderbolt that overhangs you; and I can but leave you free.'

'And, sir,' said I, 'as this house belongs to me, I will ask you to have the kindness to remove the body. You and your conspirators, it appears to me, can hardly in civility do less.'

'It shall be done,' said the young man, with a dismal accent.

'And you, dear madam,' said the prince, 'you, to whom I owe my life, how can I serve you?'

'Your highness,' I said, 'to be very plain, this is my favourite house, being not only a valuable property, but endeared to me by various associations. I have endless troubles with tenants of the ordinary class: and at first applauded my good fortune when I found one of the station of your Master of the Horse. I now begin to think otherwise: dangers set a siege about great personages; and I do not wish my tenement to share these risks. Procure me the resiliation of the lease, and I shall feel myself your debtor.'

'I must tell you, madam,' replied his highness, 'that Colonel Geraldine is but a cloak for myself; and I should be sorry indeed to think myself so unacceptable a tenant.'

'Your highness,' said I, 'I have conceived a sincere admiration for your character; but on the subject of house property, I cannot allow the interference of my feelings. I will, however, to prove to you that there is nothing personal in my request, here solemnly engage my word that I will never put another tenant in this house.'

'Madam,' said Florizel, 'you plead your cause too charmingly to be refused.'

Thereupon we all three withdrew. The young man, still reeling in his walk, departed by himself to seek the assistance of his fellow-conspirators; and the prince, with the most attentive gallantry, lent me his escort to the door of my hotel. The next day, the lease was cancelled; nor from that hour to this, though sometimes regretting my engagement, have I suffered a tenant in this house.

The Superfluous Mansion (continued)

AS soon as the old lady had finished her relation, Somerset made haste to offer her his compliments.

'Madam,' said he, 'your story is not only entertaining but instructive; and you have told it with infinite vivacity. I was much affected towards the end, as I held at one time very liberal opinions, and should certainly have joined a secret society if I had been able to find one. But the whole tale came home to me; and I was the better able to feel for you in your various perplexities, as I am myself of somewhat hasty temper.'

'I do not understand you,' said Mrs. Luxmore, with some marks of irritation. 'You must have strangely misinterpreted what I have told you. You fill me with surprise.'

Somerset, alarmed by the old lady's change of tone and manner, hurried to recant.

'Dear Mrs. Luxmore,' said he, 'you certainly misconstrue my remark. As a man of somewhat fiery humour, my conscience repeatedly pricked me when I heard what you had suffered at the hands of persons similarly constituted.'

'Oh, very well indeed,' replied the old lady; 'and a very proper spirit. I regret that I have met with it so rarely.'

'But in all this,' resumed the young man, 'I perceive nothing that concerns myself.'

'I am about to come to that,' she returned. 'And you have already before you, in the pledge I gave Prince Florizel, one of the elements of the affair. I am a woman of the nomadic sort, and when I have no case before the courts I make it a habit to visit continental spas: not that I have ever been ill; but then I am no longer young, and I am always happy in a crowd. Well, to come more shortly to the point, I am now on the wing for Evian; this incubus of a house, which I must leave behind and dare not let, hangs heavily upon my hands; and I propose to rid myself of that concern, and do you a very good turn into the bargain, by lending you the mansion, with all its fittings, as it stands. The idea was sudden; it appealed to me as humorous: and I am sure it will cause my relatives, if they should ever hear of it, the keenest possible chagrin.

Here, then, is the key; and when you return at two to-morrow afternoon, you will find neither me nor my cats to disturb you in your new possession.'

So saying, the old lady arose, as if to dismiss her visitor; but Somerset, looking somewhat blankly on the key, began to protest.

'Dear Mrs. Luxmore,' said he, 'this is a most unusual proposal. You know nothing of me, beyond the fact that I displayed both impudence and timidity. I may be the worst kind of scoundrel; I may sell your furniture—'

'You may blow up the house with gunpowder, for what I care!' cried Mrs. Luxmore. 'It is in vain to reason. Such is the force of my character that, when I have one idea clearly in my head, I do not care two straws for any side consideration. It amuses me to do it, and let that suffice. On your side, you may do what you please—let apartments, or keep a private hotel; on mine, I promise you a full month's warning before I return, and I never fail religiously to keep my promises.'

The young man was about to renew his protest, when he observed a sudden and significant change in the old lady's countenance.

'If I thought you capable of disrespect!' she cried.

'Madam,' said Somerset, with the extreme fervour of asseveration, 'madam, I accept. I beg you to understand that I accept with joy and gratitude.'

'Ah well,' returned Mrs. Luxmore, 'if I am mistaken, let it pass. And now, since all is comfortably settled, I wish you a good-night.'

Thereupon, as if to leave him no room for repentance, she hurried Somerset out of the front door, and left him standing, key in hand, upon the pavement.

The next day, about the hour appointed, the young man found his way to the square, which I will here call Golden Square, though that was not its name. What to expect, he knew not; for a man may live in dreams, and yet be unprepared for their realisation. It was already with a certain pang of surprise that he beheld the mansion, standing in the eye of day, a solid among solids. The key, upon trial, readily opened the front door; he entered that great house, a privileged burglar; and, escorted by the echoes of

desertion, rapidly reviewed the empty chambers. Cats, servant, old
lady, the very marks of habitation, like writing on a slate, had been
in these few hours obliterated. He wandered from floor to floor,
and found the house of great extent; the kitchen offices commodious and well appointed; the rooms many and large; and the drawing-room, in particular, an apartment of princely size and tasteful
decoration. Although the day without was warm, genial, and
sunny, with a ruffling wind from the quarter of Torquay, a chill, as
it were, of suspended animation inhabited the house. Dust and
shadows met the eye; and but for the ominous procession of the
echoes, and the rumour of the wind among the garden trees, the
ear of the young man was stretched in vain.

Behind the dining-room, that pleasant library, referred to the
old lady in her tale, looked upon the flat roofs and netted
cupolas of the kitchen quarters; and on a second visit, this room
appeared to greet him with a smiling countenance. He might as
well, he thought, avoid the expense of lodging: the library, fitted
with an iron bedstead which he had remarked, in one of the upper
chambers, would serve his purpose for the night; while in the dining-room, which was large, airy, and lightsome, looking on the
square and garden, he might very agreeably pass his days, cook his
meals, and study to bring himself to some proficiency in that art
of painting which he had recently determined to adopt. It did not
take him long to make the change: he had soon returned to the
mansion with his modest kit; and the cabman who brought him
was readily induced, by the young man's pleasant manner and a
small gratuity, to assist him in the installation of the iron bed. By
six in the evening, when Somerset went forth to dine, he was able
to look back upon the mansion with a sense of pride and property.
Four-square it stood, of an imposing frontage, and flanked on
either side by family hatchments. His eye, from where he stood
whistling in the key, with his back to the garden railings, reposed
on every feature of reality; and yet his own possession seemed as
flimsy as a dream.

In the course of a few days, the genteel inhabitants of the
square began to remark the customs of their neighbour. The sight
of a young gentleman discussing a clay pipe, about four o'clock of

the afternoon, in the drawing-room balcony of so discreet a mansion; and perhaps still more, his periodical excursion to a decent tavern in the neighbourhood, and his unabashed return, nursing the full tankard: had presently raised to a high pitch the interest and indignation of the liveried servants of the square. The disfavour of some of these gentlemen at first proceeded to the length of insult; but Somerset knew how to be affable with any class of men; and a few rude words merrily accepted, and a few glasses amicably shared, gained for him the right of toleration.

The young man had embraced the art of Raphael, partly from a notion of its ease, partly from an inborn distrust of offices. He scorned to bear the yoke of any regular schooling; and proceeded to turn one half of the dining-room into a studio for the reproduction of still life. There he amassed a variety of objects, indiscriminately chosen from the kitchen, the drawing-room, and the back garden; and there spent his days in smiling assiduity. Meantime, the great bulk of empty building overhead lay, like a load, upon his imagination. To hold so great a stake and to do nothing, argued some defect of energy; and he at length determined to act upon the hint given by Mrs. Luxmore herself, and to stick, with wafers, in the window of the dining-room, a small handbill announcing furnished lodgings. At half-past six of a fine July morning, he affixed the bill, and went forth into the square to study the result. It seemed, to his eye, promising and unpretentious; and he returned to the drawing-room balcony, to consider, over a studious pipe, the knotty problem of how much he was to charge.

Thereupon he somewhat relaxed in his devotion to the art of painting. Indeed, from that time forth, he would spend the best part of the day in the front balcony, like the attentive angler poring on his float; and the better to support the tedium, he would frequently console himself with his clay pipe. On several occasions, passers-by appeared to be arrested by the ticket, and on several others ladies and gentlemen drove to the very doorstep by the carriageful; but it appeared there was something repulsive in the appearance of the house; for with one accord, they would cast but one look upward, and hastily resume their onward progress or direct the driver to proceed. Somerset had thus the mortification of actually meeting the eye of a large number of lodging-seekers; and though he hastened to withdraw his pipe, and to compose his features to an air of invitation, he was never rewarded by so much as an inquiry. 'Can there,' he thought, 'be anything repellent in myself?' But a candid examination in one of the pier-glasses of the drawing-room led him to dismiss the fear.

Something, however, was amiss. His vast and accurate calculations on the fly-leaves of books, or on the backs of playbills, appeared to have been an idle sacrifice of time. By these, he had variously computed the weekly takings of the house, from sums as modest as five-and-twenty shillings, up to the more majestic figure of a hundred pounds; and yet, in despite of the very elements of arithmetic, here he was making literally nothing.

This incongruity impressed him deeply and occupied his thoughtful leisure on the balcony; and at last it seemed to him that he had detected the error of his method. 'This,' he reflected, 'is an age of generous display: the age of the sandwich-man, of Griffiths, of Pears' legendary soap, and of Eno's fruit salt, which, by sheer brass and notoriety, and the most disgusting pictures I ever remember to have seen, has overlaid that comforter of my childhood, Lamplough's pyretic saline. Lamplough was genteel, Eno was omnipresent; Lamplough was trite, Eno original and abominably vulgar; and here have I, a man of some pretensions to knowledge of the world, contented myself with half a sheet of note-paper, a few cold words which do not directly address the imagination, and the adornment (if adornment it may be called) of four red wafers! Am I, then, to sink with Lamplough, or to soar with Eno? Am I to adopt that modesty which is doubtless becoming in a duke? or to take hold of the red facts of life with the emphasis of the tradesman and the poet?'

Pursuant upon these meditations, he procured several sheets of the very largest size of drawing-paper; and laying forth his paints, proceeded to compose an ensign that might attract the eye, and at the same time, in his own phrase, directly address the imagination of the passenger. Something taking in the way of colour, a good, savoury choice of words, and a realistic design setting forth the life a lodger might expect to lead within the walls of that palace of delight: these, he perceived, must be the elements of his advertisement. It was possible, upon the one hand, to depict the sober pleasures of domestic life, the evening fire, blond-headed urchins and the hissing urn; but on the other, it was possible (and he almost felt as if it were more suited to his muse) to set forth the charms of an existence somewhat wider in its range or, boldly say, the paradise of the Mohammedan. So long did the artist waver between these two views, that, before he arrived at a conclusion, he had finally conceived and completed both designs. With the proverbially tender heart of the parent, he found himself unable to sacrifice either of these offsprings of his art; and decided to expose them on alternate days. 'In this way,' he thought, 'I shall address myself indifferently to all classes of the world.'

The tossing of a penny decided the only remaining point; and the more imaginative canvas received the suffrages of fortune, and appeared first in the window of the mansion. It was of a high fancy, the legend eloquently writ, the scheme of colour taking and bold; and but for the imperfection of the artist's drawing, it might have been taken for a model of its kind. As it was, however, when viewed from his favourite point against the garden railings, and with some touch of distance, it caused a pleasurable rising of the artist's heart. 'I have thrown away,' he ejaculated, 'an invaluable motive; and this shall be the subject of my first academy picture.'

The fate of neither of these works was equal to its merit. A crowd would certainly, from time to time, collect before the area-railings; but they came to jeer and not to speculate; and those who pushed their inquiries further, were too plainly animated by the spirit of derision. The racier of the two cartoons displayed, indeed, no symptom of attractive merit; and though it had a certain share of that success called scandalous, failed utterly of its effect. On the day, however, of the second appearance of the companion work, a real inquirer did actually present himself before the eyes of Somerset.

This was a gentlemanly man, with some marks of recent merriment, and his voice under inadequate control.

'I beg your pardon,' said he, 'but what is the meaning of your extraordinary bill?'

'I beg yours,' returned Somerset hotly. 'Its meaning is sufficiently explicit.' And being now, from dire experience, fearful of
ridicule, he was preparing to close the door, when the gentleman
thrust his cane into the aperture.

'Not so fast, I beg of you,' said he. 'If you really let apartments,
here is a possible tenant at your door; and nothing would give me
greater pleasure than to see the accommodation and to learn your
terms.'

His heart joyously beating, Somerset admitted the visitor,
showed him over the various apartments, and, with some return
of his persuasive eloquence, expounded their attractions. The gentleman was particularly pleased by the elegant proportions of the
drawing-room.

'This,' he said, 'would suit me very well. What, may I ask,
would be your terms a week, for this floor and the one above it?'

'I was thinking,' returned Somerset, 'of a hundred pounds.'

'Surely not,' exclaimed the gentleman.

'Well, then,' returned Somerset, 'fifty.'

The gentleman regarded him with an air of some amazement.
'You seem to be strangely elastic in your demands,' said he. 'What
if I were to proceed on your own principle of division, and offer
twenty-five?'

'Done!' cried Somerset; and then, overcome by a sudden
embarrassment, 'You see,' he added apologetically, 'it is all found
money for me.'

'Really?' said the stranger, looking at him all the while with
growing wonder. 'Without extras, then?'

'I—I suppose so,' stammered the keeper of the lodging-
house.

'Service included?' pursued the gentleman.

'Service?' cried Somerset. 'Do you mean that you expect me
to empty your slops?'

The gentleman regarded him with a very friendly interest.
'My dear fellow,' said he, 'if you take my advice, you will give up
this business.' And thereupon he resumed his hat and took himself
away.

This smarting disappointment produced a strong effect on
the artist of the cartoons; and he began with shame to eat up his

rosier illusions. First one and then the other of his great works was condemned, withdrawn from exhibition, and relegated, as a mere wall-picture, to the decoration of the dining-room. Their place was taken by a replica of the original wafered announcement, to which, in particularly large letters, he had added the pithy rubric: 'NO SERVICE.' Meanwhile he had fallen into something as nearly bordering on low spirits as was consistent with his disposition; depressed, at once by the failure of his scheme, the laughable turn of his late interview, and the judicial blindness of the public to the merit of the twin cartoons.

Perhaps a week had passed before he was again startled by the note of the knocker. A gentleman of a somewhat foreign and somewhat military air, yet closely shaven and wearing a soft hat, desired in the politest terms to visit the apartments. He had (he explained) a friend, a gentleman in tender health, desirous of a sedate and solitary life, apart from interruptions and the noises of the common lodging-house. 'The unusual clause,' he continued, 'in your announcement, particularly struck me. "This," I said, "is the place for Mr. Jones." You are yourself, sir, a professional gentleman?' concluded the visitor, looking keenly in Somerset's face.

'I am an artist,' replied the young man lightly.

'And these,' observed the other, taking a side glance through the open door of the dining-room, which they were then passing, 'these are some of your works. Very remarkable.' And he again and still more sharply peered into the countenance of the young man.

Somerset, unable to suppress a blush, made the more haste to lead his visitor upstairs and to display the apartments.

'Excellent,' observed the stranger, as he looked from one of the back windows. 'Is that a mews behind, sir? Very good. Well, sir: see here. My friend will take your drawing-room floor; he will sleep in the back drawing-room; his nurse, an excellent Irish widow, will attend on all his wants and occupy a garret; he will pay you the round sum of ten dollars a week; and you, on your part, will engage to receive no other lodger? I think that fair.'

Somerset had scarcely words in which to clothe his gratitude and joy.

'Agreed,' said the other; 'and to spare you trouble, my friend will bring some men with him to make the changes. You will find him a retiring inmate, sir; receives but few, and rarely leaves the house, except at night.'

'Since I have been in this house,' returned Somerset, 'I have myself, unless it were to fetch beer, rarely gone abroad except in the evening. But a man,' he added, 'must have some amusement.'

An hour was then agreed on; the gentleman departed; and Somerset sat down to compute in English money the value of the figure named. The result of this investigation filled him with amazement and disgust; but it was now too late; nothing remained but to endure; and he awaited the arrival of his tenant, still trying, by various arithmetical expedients, to obtain a more favourable quotation for the dollar. With the approach of dusk, however, his impatience drove him once more to the front balcony. The night fell, mild and airless; the lamps shone around the central darkness of the garden; and through the tall grove of trees that intervened, many warmly illuminated windows on the farther side of the square, told their tale of white napery, choice wine, and genial hospitality. The stars were already thickening overhead, when the young man's eyes alighted on a procession of three four-wheelers, coasting round the garden railing and bound for the Superfluous Mansion. They were laden with formidable boxes; moved in a military order, one following another; and, by the extreme slowness of their advance, inspired Somerset with the most serious ideas of his tenant's malady.

By the time he had the door open, the cabs had drawn up beside the pavement; and from the two first, there had alighted the military gentleman of the morning and two very stalwart porters. These proceeded instantly to take possession of the house; with their own hands, and firmly rejecting Somerset's assistance, they carried in the various crates and boxes; with their own hands dismounted and transferred to the back drawing-room the bed in which the tenant was to sleep; and it was not until the bustle of arrival had subsided, and the arrangements were complete, that there descended, from the third of the three vehicles, a gentleman of great stature and broad shoulders, leaning on the shoulder of a woman in a widow's dress, and himself covered by a long cloak and muffled in a coloured comforter.

Somerset had but a glimpse of him in passing; he was soon shut into the back drawing-room; the other men departed; silence redescended on the house; and had not the nurse appeared a little before half-past ten, and, with a strong brogue, asked if there were a decent public-house in the neighbourhood, Somerset might have still supposed himself to be alone in the Superfluous Mansion.

Day followed day; and still the young man had never come by speech or sight of his mysterious lodger. The doors of the drawing-room flat were never open; and although Somerset could hear him moving to and fro, the tall man had never quitted the privacy of his apartments. Visitors, indeed, arrived; sometimes in the dusk, sometimes at intempestuous hours of night or morning; men, for the most part; some meanly attired, some decently; some loud, some cringing; and yet all, in the eyes of Somerset, displeasing. A certain air of fear and secrecy was common to them all; they were all voluble, he thought, and ill at ease; even the military gentleman proved, on a closer inspection, to be no gentleman at all; and as for the doctor who attended the sick man, his manners were not suggestive of a university career. The nurse, again, was scarcely a desirable house-fellow. Since her arrival, the fall of whisky in the young man's private bottle was much accelerated; and though never communicative, she was at times unpleasantly familiar. When asked about the patient's health, she would dolorously shake her head, and declare that the poor gentleman was in a pitiful condition.

Yet somehow Somerset had early begun to entertain the notion that his complaint was other than bodily. The ill-looking birds that gathered to the house, the strange noises that sounded from the drawing-room in the dead hours of night, the careless attendance and intemperate habits of the nurse, the entire absence of correspondence, the entire seclusion of Mr. Jones himself, whose face, up to that hour, he could not have sworn to in a court of justice—all weighed unpleasantly upon the young man's mind. A sense of something evil, irregular and underhand, haunted and depressed him; and this uneasy sentiment was the more firmly rooted in his mind, when, in the fulness of time, he had an opportunity of observing the features of his tenant. It fell in this way.

The young landlord was awakened about four in the morning by a noise in the hall. Leaping to his feet, and opening the door of the library, he saw the tall man, candle in hand, in earnest conversation with the gentleman who had taken the rooms. The faces of both were strongly illuminated; and in that of his tenant, Somerset could perceive none of the marks of disease, but every sign of health, energy, and resolution. While he was still looking, the visitor took his departure; and the invalid, having carefully fastened the front door, sprang upstairs without a trace of lassitude.

That night upon his pillow, Somerset began to kindle once more into the hot fit of the detective fever; and the next morning resumed the practice of his art with careless hand and an abstracted mind. The day was destined to be fertile in surprises; nor had he long been seated at the easel ere the first of these occurred. A cab laden with baggage drew up before the door; and Mrs. Luxmore in person rapidly mounted the steps and began to pound upon the knocker. Somerset hastened to attend the summons.

'My dear fellow,' she said, with the utmost gaiety, 'here I come dropping from the moon. I am delighted to find you faithful; and I have no doubt you will be equally pleased to be restored to liberty.'

Somerset could find no words, whether of protest or welcome; and the spirited old lady pushed briskly by him and paused on the threshold of the dining-room. The sight that met her eyes was one well calculated to inspire astonishment. The mantelpiece was arrayed with saucepans and empty bottles; on the fire some chops were frying; the floor was littered from end to end with books, clothes, walking-canes and the materials of the painter's craft; but what far outstripped the other wonders of the place was the corner which had been arranged for the study of still-life. This formed a sort of rockery; conspicuous upon which, according to the principles of the art of composition, a cabbage was relieved against a copper kettle, and both contrasted with the mail of a boiled lobster.

'My gracious goodness!' cried the lady of the house; and then, turning in wrath on the young man, 'From what rank in life are you sprung?' she demanded. 'You have the exterior of a gentleman; but from the astonishing evidences before me, I should say you can only be a greengrocer's man. Pray, gather up your vegetables, and let me see no more of you.'

'Madam,' babbled Somerset, 'you promised me a month's warning.'

'That was under a misapprehension,' returned the old lady. 'I now give you warning to leave at once.'

'Madam,' said the young man, 'I wish I could; and indeed, as far as I am concerned, it might be done. But then, my lodger!'

'Your lodger?' echoed Mrs. Luxmore.

'My lodger: why should I deny it?' returned Somerset. 'He is only by the week.'

The old lady sat down upon a chair. 'You have a lodger?—you?' she cried. 'And pray, how did you get him?'

'By advertisement,' replied the young man. 'O madam, I have not lived unobservantly. I adopted'—his eyes involuntarily shifted to the cartoons—'I adopted every method.'

Her eyes had followed his; for the first time in Somerset's experience, she produced a double eye-glass; and as soon as the full merit of the works had flashed upon her, she gave way to peal after peal of her trilling and soprano laughter.

'Oh, I think you are perfectly delicious!' she cried. 'I do hope you had them in the window. M'Pherson,' she continued, crying to her maid, who had been all this time grimly waiting in the hall, 'I lunch with Mr. Somerset. Take the cellar key and bring some wine.'

In this gay humour she continued throughout the luncheon; presented Somerset with a couple of dozen of wine, which she made M'Pherson bring up from the cellar—'as a present, my dear,' she said, with another burst of tearful merriment, 'for your charming pictures, which you must be sure to leave me when you go;' and finally, protesting that she dared not spoil the absurdest houseful of madmen in the whole of London, departed (as she vaguely phrased it) for the continent of Europe.

She was no sooner gone, than Somerset encountered in the corridor the Irish nurse; sober, to all appearance, and yet a prey to singularly strong emotion. It was made to appear, from her account, that Mr. Jones had already suffered acutely in his health from Mrs. Luxmore's visit, and that nothing short of a full explanation could allay the invalid's uneasiness. Somerset, somewhat staring, told what he thought fit of the affair.

'Is that all?' cried the woman. 'As God sees you, is that all?'

'My good woman,' said the young man, 'I have no idea what you can be driving at. Suppose the lady were my friend's wife, suppose she were my fairy godmother, suppose she were the Queen of Portugal; and how should that affect yourself or Mr. Jones?'

'Blessed Mary!' cried the nurse, 'it's he that will be glad to hear it!'

And immediately she fled upstairs.

Somerset, on his part, returned to the dining-room, and with a very thoughtful brow and ruminating many theories, disposed of the remainder of the bottle. It was port; and port is a wine, sole among its equals and superiors, that can in some degree support the competition of tobacco. Sipping, smoking, and theorising, Somerset moved on from suspicion to suspicion, from resolve to resolve, still growing braver and rosier as the bottle ebbed. He was a sceptic, none prouder of the name; he had no horror at command, whether for crimes or vices, but beheld and embraced the world, with an immoral approbation, the frequent consequence of youth and health. At the same time, he felt convinced that he dwelt under the same roof with secret malefactors; and the unregenerate instinct of the chase impelled him to severity. The bottle had run low; the summer sun had finally withdrawn; and at the same moment, night and the pangs of hunger recalled him from his dreams.

He went forth, and dined in the Criterion: a dinner in consonance, not so much with his purse, as with the admirable wine he had discussed. What with one thing and another, it was long past midnight when he returned home. A cab was at the door; and entering the hall, Somerset found himself face to face with one of the most regular of the few who visited Mr. Jones: a man of powerful figure, strong lineaments, and a chin-beard in the American fashion. This person was carrying on one shoulder a black portmanteau, seemingly of considerable weight. That he should find a visitor removing baggage in the dead of night, recalled some odd stories to the young man's memory; he had heard of lodgers who thus gradually drained away, not only their own effects, but the very furniture and fittings of the house that sheltered them; and now, in a mood between pleasantry and suspicion, and aping the manner of a drunkard, he roughly bumped against the man with the chin-beard and knocked the portmanteau from his shoulder to the floor. With a face struck suddenly as white as paper, the man with the chin-beard called lamentably on the name of his maker, and fell in a mere heap on the mat at the foot of the stairs. At the same time, though only for a single instant, the heads of the sick lodger and the Irish nurse popped out like rabbits over the banisters of the first floor; and on both the same scare and pallor were apparent.

The sight of this incredible emotion turned Somerset to stone, and he continued speechless, while the man gathered himself together, and, with the help of the handrail and audibly thanking God, scrambled once more upon his feet.

'What in Heaven's name ails you?' gasped the young man as soon as he could find words and utterance.

'Have you a drop of brandy?' returned the other. 'I am sick.'

Somerset administered two drams, one after the other, to the man with the chin-beard; who then, somewhat restored, began to confound himself in apologies for what he called his miserable nervousness, the result, he said, of a long course of dumb ague; and having taken leave with a hand that still sweated and trembled, he gingerly resumed his burthen and departed.

Somerset retired to bed but not to sleep. What, he asked himself, had been the contents of the black portmanteau? Stolen goods? the carcase of one murdered? or—and at the thought he sat upright in bed—an infernal machine? He took a solemn vow that he would set these doubts at rest; and with the next morning, installed himself beside the dining-room window, vigilant with eye; and ear, to await and profit by the earliest opportunity.

The hours went heavily by. Within the house there was no circumstance of novelty; unless it might be that the nurse more frequently made little journeys round the corner of the square, and before afternoon was somewhat loose of speech and gait. A little after six, however, there came round the corner of the gardens a

very handsome and elegantly dressed young woman, who paused
a little way off, and for some time, and with frequent sighs, contemplated the front of the Superfluous Mansion. It was not the
first time that she had thus stood afar and looked upon it, like our
common parents at the gates of Eden; and the young man had
already had occasion to remark the lively slimness of her carriage,
and had already been the butt of a chance arrow from her eye. He
hailed her coming, then, with pleasant feelings, and moved a little
nearer to the window to enjoy the sight. What was his surprise,
however, when, as if with a sensible effort, she drew near, mounted
the steps and tapped discreetly at the door! He made haste to get
before the Irish nurse, who was not improbably asleep, and had
the satisfaction to receive this gracious visitor in person.

She inquired for Mr. Jones; and then, without transition,
asked the young man if he were the person of the house (and at
the words, he thought he could perceive her to be smiling),
'because,' she added, 'if you are, I should like to see some of the
other rooms.' Somerset told her he was under an engagement to
receive no other lodgers; but she assured him that would be no
matter, as these were friends of Mr. Jones's. 'And,' she continued,
moving suddenly to the dining-room door, 'let us begin here.'
Somerset was too late to prevent her entering, and perhaps he
lacked the courage to essay. 'Ah!' she cried, 'how changed it is!'

'Madam,' cried the young man, 'since your entrance, it is I
who have the right to say so.'

She received this inane compliment with a demure and conscious droop of the eyelids, and gracefully steering her dress
among the mingled litter, now with a smile, now with a sigh,
reviewed the wonders of the two apartments. She gazed upon the
cartoons with sparkling eyes, and a heightened colour, and in a
somewhat breathless voice, expressed a high opinion of their merits. She praised the effective disposition of the rockery, and in the
bedroom, of which Somerset had vainly endeavoured to defend
the entry, she fairly broke forth in admiration. 'How simple and
manly!' she cried: 'none of that effeminacy of neatness, which is so
detestable in a man!' Hard upon this, telling him, before he had
time to reply, that she very well knew her way, and would trouble

him no further, she took her leave with an engaging smile, and ascended the staircase alone.

For more than an hour the young lady remained closeted with Mr. Jones; and at the end of that time, the night being now come completely, they left the house in company. This was the first time since the arrival of his lodger, that Somerset had found himself alone with the Irish widow; and without the loss of any more time than was required by decency, he stepped to the foot of the stairs and hailed her by her name. She came instantly, wreathed in weak smiles and with a nodding head; and when the young man politely offered to introduce her to the treasures of his art, she swore that nothing could afford her greater pleasure, for, though she had never crossed the threshold, she had frequently observed his beautiful pictures through the door. On entering the dining-room, the sight of a bottle and two glasses prepared her to be a gentle critic; and as soon as the pictures had been viewed and praised, she was easily persuaded to join the painter in a single glass. 'Here,' she said, 'are my respects; and a pleasure it is, in this horrible house, to see a gentleman like yourself, so affable and free, and a very nice painter, I am sure.' One glass so agreeably prefaced, was sure to lead to the acceptance of a second; at the third, Somerset was free to cease from the affectation of keeping her company; and as for the fourth, she asked it of her own accord. 'For indeed,' said she, 'what with all these clocks and chemicals, without a drop of the creature life would be impossible entirely. And you seen yourself that even M'Guire was glad to beg for it. And even himself, when he is downhearted with all these cruel disappointments, though as temperate a man as any child, will be sometimes crying for a glass of it. And I'll thank you for a thimbleful to settle what I got.' Soon after, she began with tears to narrate the deathbed dispositions and lament the trifling assets of her husband. Then she declared she heard 'the master' calling her, rose to her feet, made but one lurch of it into the still-life rockery, and with her head upon the lobster, fell into stertorous slumbers.

Somerset mounted at once to the first story, and opened the door of the drawing-room, which was brilliantly lit by several lamps. It was a great apartment; looking on the square with three

tall windows, and joined by a pair of ample folding-doors to the
next room; elegant in proportion, papered in sea-green, furnished
in velvet of a delicate blue, and adorned with a majestic mantel-
piece of variously tinted marbles. Such was the room that Somerset remembered; that which he now beheld was changed in almost
every feature: the furniture covered with a figured chintz; the walls
hung with a rhubarb-coloured paper, and diversified by the curtained recesses for no less than seven windows. It seemed to himself that he must have entered, without observing the transition,
into the adjoining house. Presently from these more specious
changes, his eye condescended to the many curious objects with
which the floor was littered. Here were the locks of dismounted
pistols; clocks and clockwork in every stage of demolition, some
still busily ticking, some reduced to their dainty elements; a great
company of carboys, jars and bottles; a carpenter's bench and a
laboratory-table.

The back drawing-room, to which Somerset proceeded, had
likewise undergone a change. It was transformed to the exact
appearance of a common lodging-house bedroom; a bed with
green curtains occupied one corner; and the window was blocked
by the regulation table and mirror. The door of a small closet here
attracted the young man's attention; and striking a vesta, he
opened it and entered. On a table several wigs and beards were
lying spread; about the walls hung an incongruous display of suits
and overcoats; and conspicuous among the last the young man
observed a large overall of the most costly sealskin. In a flash his
mind reverted to the advertisement in the STANDARD newspa-
per. The great height of his lodger, the disproportionate breadth of
his shoulders, and the strange particulars of his instalment, all
pointed to the same conclusion.

The vesta had now burned to his fingers; and taking the coat
upon his arm, Somerset hastily returned to the lighted drawing-
room. There, with a mixture of fear and admiration, he pored
upon its goodly proportions and the regularity and softness of the
pile. The sight of a large pier-glass put another fancy in his head.
He donned the fur-coat; and standing before the mirror in an attitude suggestive of a Russian prince, he thrust his hands into the
ample pockets. There his fingers encountered a folded journal. He

drew it out, and recognised the type and paper of the STAN-DARD; and at the same instant, his eyes alighted on the offer of two hundred pounds. Plainly then, his lodger, now no longer mysterious, had laid aside his coat on the very day of the appearance of the advertisement.

He was thus standing, the tell-tale coat upon his back, the incriminating paper in his hand, when the door opened and the tall lodger, with a firm but somewhat pallid face, stepped into the room and closed the door again behind him. For some time, the two looked upon each other in perfect silence; then Mr. Jones moved forward to the table, took a seat, and still without once changing the direction of his eyes, addressed the young man.

'You are right,' he said. 'It is for me the blood money is offered. And now what will you do?'

It was a question to which Somerset was far from being able to reply. Taken as he was at unawares, masquerading in the man's own coat, and surrounded by a whole arsenal of diabolical explosives, the keeper of the lodging-house was silenced.

'Yes,' resumed the other, 'I am he. I am that man, whom with impotent hate and fear, they still hunt from den to den, from disguise to disguise. Yes, my landlord, you have it in your power, if you be poor, to lay the basis of your fortune; if you be unknown, to capture honour at one snatch. You have hocussed an innocent widow; and I find you here in my apartment, for whose use I pay you in stamped money, searching my wardrobe, and your hand—shame, sir!—your hand in my very pocket. You can now complete the cycle of your ignominious acts, by what will be at once the simplest, the safest, and the most remunerative.' The speaker paused as if to emphasise his words; and then, with a great change of tone and manner, thus resumed: 'And yet, sir, when I look upon your face, I feel certain that I cannot be deceived: certain that in spite of all, I have the honour and pleasure of speaking to a gentleman. Take off my coat, sir—which but cumbers you. Divest yourself of this confusion: that which is but thought upon, thank God, need be no burthen to the conscience; we have all harboured guilty thoughts: and if it flashed into your mind to sell my flesh and blood, my anguish in the dock, and the sweat of my death agony—it was a thought, dear sir, you were as incapable of acting on, as I of any further question of your honour.' At these words, the speaker, with a very open, smiling countenance, like a forgiving father, offered Somerset his hand.

It was not in the young man's nature to refuse forgiveness or dissect generosity. He instantly, and almost without thought, accepted the proffered grasp.

'And now,' resumed the lodger, 'now that I hold in mine your loyal hand, I lay by my apprehensions, I dismiss suspicion, I go further—by an effort of will, I banish the memory of what is past. How you came here, I care not: enough that you are here—as my guest. Sit ye down; and let us, with your good permission, improve acquaintance over a glass of excellent whisky.'

So speaking, he produced glasses and a bottle: and the pair pledged each other in silence.

'Confess,' observed the smiling host, 'you were surprised at the appearance of the room.'

'I was indeed,' said Somerset; 'nor can I imagine the purpose of these changes.'

'These,' replied the conspirator, 'are the devices by which I continue to exist. Conceive me now, accused before one of your unjust tribunals; conceive the various witnesses appearing, and the singular variety of their reports! One will have visited me in this drawing-room as it originally stood; a second finds it as it is to-night; and to-morrow or next day, all may have been changed. If you love romance (as artists do), few lives are more romantic than that of the obscure individual now addressing you. Obscure yet famous. Mine is an anonymous, infernal glory. By infamous means, I work towards my bright purpose. I found the liberty and peace of a poor country, desperately abused; the future smiles upon that land; yet, in the meantime, I lead the existence of a hunted brute, work towards appalling ends, and practice hell's dexterities.'

Somerset, glass in hand, contemplated the strange fanatic before him, and listened to his heated rhapsody, with indescribable bewilderment. He looked him in the face with curious particularity; saw there the marks of education; and wondered the more profoundly.

'Sir,' he said—'for I know not whether I should still address you as Mr. Jones—'

'Jones, Breitman, Higginbotham, Pumpernickel, Daviot, Henderland, by all or any of these you may address me,' said the plotter; 'for all I have at some time borne. Yet that which I most prize, that which is most feared, hated, and obeyed, is not a name to be found in your directories; it is not a name current in post-offices or banks; and, indeed, like the celebrated clan M'Gregor, I may justly describe myself as being nameless by day. But,' he continued, rising to his feet, 'by night, and among my desperate followers, I am the redoubted Zero.'

Somerset was unacquainted with the name, but he politely expressed surprise and gratification. 'I am to understand,' he continued, 'that, under this alias, you follow the profession of a dynamiter?'

The plotter had resumed his seat and now replenished the glasses.

'I do,' he said. 'In this dark period of time, a star—the star of dynamite—has risen for the oppressed; and among those who practise its use, so thick beset with dangers and attended by such incredible difficulties and disappointments, few have been more assiduous, and not many—' He paused, and a shade of embarrassment appeared upon his face—'not many have been more successful than myself.'

'I can imagine,' observed Somerset, 'that, from the sweeping consequences looked for, the career is not devoid of interest. You have, besides, some of the entertainment of the game of hide and seek. But it would still seem to me—I speak as a layman—that nothing could be simpler or safer than to deposit an infernal machine and retire to an adjacent county to await the painful consequences.'

'You speak, indeed,' returned the plotter, with some evidence of warmth, 'you speak, indeed, most ignorantly. Do you make nothing, then, of such a peril as we share this moment? Do you think it nothing to occupy a house like this one, mined, menaced, and, in a word, literally tottering to its fall?'

'Good God!' ejaculated Somerset.

'And when you speak of ease,' pursued Zero, 'in this age of scientific studies, you fill me with surprise. Are you not aware that chemicals are proverbially fickle as woman, and clockwork as capricious as the very devil? Do you see upon my brow these furrows of anxiety? Do you observe the silver threads that mingle with my hair? Clockwork, clockwork has stamped them on my brow—chemicals have sprinkled them upon my locks! No, Mr. Somerset,' he resumed, after a moment's pause, his voice still quivering with sensibility, 'you must not suppose the dynamiter's life to be all gold. On the contrary, you cannot picture to yourself the bloodshot vigils and the staggering disappointments of a life like mine. I have toiled (let us say) for months, up early and down late; my bag is ready, my clock set; a daring agent has hurried with white face to deposit the instrument of ruin; we await the fall of England, the massacre of thousands, the yell of fear and execration; and lo! a snap like that of a child's pistol, an offensive smell, and the entire loss of so much time and plant! If,' he concluded, musingly, 'we had been merely able to recover the lost bags, I believe with but a touch or two, I could have remedied the peccant engine. But what with the loss of plant and the almost insuperable scientific difficulties of the task, our friends in France are almost ready to desert the chosen medium. They propose, instead, to break up the drainage system of cities and sweep off whole populations with the devastating typhoid pestilence: a tempting and a scientific project: a process, indiscriminate indeed, but of idyllical simplicity. I recognise its elegance; but, sir, I have something of the poet in my nature; something, possibly, of the tribune. And, for my small part, I shall remain devoted to that more emphatic, more striking, and (if you please) more popular method, of the explosive bomb. Yes,' he cried, with unshaken hope, 'I will still continue, and, I feel it in my bosom, I shall yet succeed.'

'Two things I remark,' said Somerset. 'The first somewhat staggers me. Have you, then—in all this course of life, which you have sketched so vividly—have you not once succeeded?'

'Pardon me,' said Zero. 'I have had one success. You behold in me the author of the outrage of Red Lion Court.'

'But if I remember right,' objected Somerset, 'the thing was a FIASCO. A scavenger's barrow and some copies of the WEEKLY BUDGET—these were the only victims.'

'You will pardon me again,' returned Zero with positive asperity: 'a child was injured.'

'And that fitly brings me to my second point,' said Somerset. 'For I observed you to employ the word "indiscriminate." Now, surely, a scavenger's barrow and a child (if child there were) represent the very acme and top pin-point of indiscriminate, and, pardon me, of ineffectual reprisal.'

'Did I employ the word?' asked Zero. 'Well, I will not defend it. But for efficiency, you touch on graver matters; and before entering upon so vast a subject, permit me once more to fill our glasses. Disputation is dry work,' he added, with a charming gaiety of manner.

Once more accordingly the pair pledged each other in a stalwart grog; and Zero, leaning back with an air of some complacency, proceeded more largely to develop his opinions.

'The indiscriminate?' he began. 'War, my dear sir, is indiscriminate. War spares not the child; it spares not the barrow of the harmless scavenger. No more,' he concluded, beaming, 'no more do I. Whatever may strike fear, whatever may confound or paralyse the activities of the guilty nation, barrow or child, imperial Parliament or excursion steamer, is welcome to my simple plans. You are not,' he inquired, with a shade of sympathetic interest, 'you are not, I trust, a believer?'

'Sir, I believe in nothing,' said the young man.

'You are then,' replied Zero, 'in a position to grasp my argument. We agree that humanity is the object, the glorious triumph of humanity; and being pledged to labour for that end, and face to face with the banded opposition of kings, parliaments, churches, and the members of the force, who am I —who are we, dear sir— to affect a nicety about the tools employed? You might, perhaps, expect us to attack the Queen, the sinister Gladstone, the rigid Derby, or the dexterous Granville; but there you would be in error. Our appeal is to the body of the people; it is these that we would touch and interest. Now, sir, have you observed the English house-maid?'

'I should think I had,' cried Somerset.

'From a man of taste and a votary of art, I had expected it,' returned the conspirator politely. 'A type apart; a very charming figure; and thoroughly adapted to our ends. The neat cap, the clean print, the comely person, the engaging manner; her position between classes, parents in one, employers in another; the probability that she will have at least one sweet-heart, whose feelings we shall address: — yes, I have a leaning—call it, if you will, a weakness— for the housemaid. Not that I would be understood to despise the nurse. For the child is a very interesting feature: I have long since marked out the child as the sensitive point in society.' He wagged his head, with a wise, pensive smile. 'And talking, sir, of children and of the perils of our trade, let me now narrate to you a little incident of an explosive bomb, that fell out some weeks ago under my own observation. It fell out thus.'

And Zero, leaning back in his chair, narrated the following simple tale.

Zero's Tale of The Explosive Bomb

I DINED by appointment with one of our most trusted agents, in a private chamber at St. James's Hall. You have seen the man: it was M'Guire, the most chivalrous of creatures, but not himself expert in our contrivances. Hence the necessity of our meeting; for I need not remind you what enormous issues depend upon the nice adjustment of the engine. I set our little petard for half an hour, the scene of action being hard by; and the better to avert miscarriage, employed a device, a recent invention of my own, by which the opening of the Gladstone bag in which the bomb was carried, should instantly determine the explosion. M'Guire was somewhat dashed by this arrangement, which was new to him: and pointed out, with excellent, clear good sense, that should he be arrested, it would probably involve him in the fall of our opponents. But I was not to be moved, made a strong appeal to his patriotism, gave him a good glass of whisky, and despatched him on his glorious errand.

Our objective was the effigy of Shakespeare in Leicester Square: a spot, I think, admirably chosen; not only for the sake of the dramatist, still very foolishly claimed as a glory by the English race, in spite of his disgusting political opinions; but from the fact that the seats in the immediate neighbourhood are often thronged by children, errand-boys, unfortunate young ladies of the poorer class and infirm old men—all classes making a direct appeal to public pity, and therefore suitable with our designs. As M'Guire drew near his heart was inflamed by the most noble sentiment of triumph. Never had he seen the garden so crowded; children, still stumbling in the impotence of youth, ran to and fro, shouting and playing, round the pedestal; an old, sick pensioner sat upon the nearest bench, a medal on his breast, a stick with which he walked (for he was disabled by wounds) reclining on his knee. Guilty England would thus be stabbed in the most delicate quarters; the moment had, indeed, been well selected; and M'Guire, with a radiant provision of the event, drew merrily nearer. Suddenly his eye alighted on the burly form of a policeman, standing hard by the effigy in an attitude of watch. My bold companion paused; he looked about him closely; here and there, at different points of the enclosure, other men stood or loitered, affecting an abstraction, feigning to gaze upon the shrubs, feigning to talk, feigning to be weary and to rest upon the benches. M'Guire was no child in these affairs; he instantly divined one of the plots of the Machiavellian Gladstone.

A chief difficulty with which we have to deal, is a certain nervousness in the subaltern branches of the corps; as the hour of some design draws near, these chicken-souled conspirators appear to suffer some revulsion of intent; and frequently despatch to the authorities, not indeed specific denunciations, but vague anonymous warnings. But for this purely accidental circumstance, England had long ago been an historical expression. On the receipt of such a letter, the Government lay a trap for their adversaries, and surround the threatened spot with hirelings. My blood sometimes boils in my veins, when I consider the case of those who sell themselves for money in such a cause. True, thanks to the generosity of our supporters, we patriots receive a very comfortable stipend; I myself, of course, touch a salary which puts me quite beyond the reach of any peddling, mercenary thoughts; M'Guire, again, ere he joined our ranks, was on the brink of starving, and now, thank God! receives a decent income. That is as it should be; the patriot must not be diverted from his task by any base consideration; and the distinction between our position and that of the police is too obvious to be stated.

Plainly, however, our Leicester Square design had been divulged; the Government had craftily filled the place with minions; even the pensioner was not improbably a hireling in disguise; and our emissary, without other aid or protection than the simple apparatus in his bag, found himself confronted by force; brutal force; that strong hand which was a character of the ages of oppression. Should he venture to deposit the machine, it was almost certain that he would be observed and arrested; a cry would arise; and there was just a fear that the police might not be present in sufficient force, to protect him from the savagery of the mob. The scheme must be delayed. He stood with his bag on his arm, pretending to survey the front of the Alhambra, when there flashed into his mind a thought to appal the bravest. The machine was set; at the appointed hour, it must explode; and how, in the interval, was he to be rid of it?

Put yourself, I beseech you, into the body of that patriot. There he was, friendless and helpless; a man in the very flower of life, for he is not yet forty; with long years of happiness before him; and now condemned, in one moment, to a cruel and revolting death by dynamite! The square, he said, went round him like a thaumatrope; he saw the Alhambra leap into the air like a balloon; and reeled against the railing. It is probable he fainted.

When he came to himself, a constable had him by the arm.

'My God!' he cried.

'You seem to be unwell, sir,' said the hireling.

'I feel better now,' cried poor M'Guire: and with uneven steps, for the pavement of the square seemed to lurch and reel under his footing, he fled from the scene of this disaster. Fled? Alas, from what was he fleeing? Did he not carry that from which he fled along with him? and had he the wings of the eagle, had he the swiftness of the ocean winds, could he have been rapt into the uttermost quarters of the earth, how should he escape the ruin that he carried? We have heard of living men who have been fettered to the dead; the grievance, soberly considered, is no more than sentimental; the case is but a flea-bite to that of him who should be linked, like poor M'Guire, to an explosive bomb.

A thought struck him in Green Street, like a dart through his liver: suppose it were the hour already. He stopped as though he had been shot, and plucked his watch out. There was a howling in his ears, as loud as a winter tempest; his sight was now obscured as if by a cloud, now, as by a lightning flash, would show him the very dust upon the street. But so brief were these intervals of vision, and so violently did the watch vibrate in his hands, that it was impossible to distinguish the numbers on the dial. He covered his eyes for a few seconds; and in that space, it seemed to him that he had fallen to be a man of ninety. When he looked again, the watch-plate had grown legible: he had twenty minutes. Twenty minutes, and no plan!

Green Street, at that time, was very empty; and he now observed a little girl of about six drawing near to him, and as she came, kicking in front of her, as children will, a piece of wood. She sang, too; and something in her accent recalling him to the past, produced a sudden clearness in his mind. Here was a God-sent opportunity!

'My dear,' said he, 'would you like a present of a pretty bag?'

The child cried aloud with joy and put out her hands to take it. She had looked first at the bag, like a true child; but most unfortunately, before she had yet received the fatal gift, her eyes fell directly on M'Guire; and no sooner had she seen the poor gentleman's face, than she screamed out and leaped backward, as though she had seen the devil. Almost at the same moment a woman appeared upon the threshold of a neighbouring shop, and called upon the child in anger. 'Come here, colleen,' she said, 'and don't be plaguing the poor old gentleman!' With that she re-entered the house, and the child followed her, sobbing aloud.

With the loss of this hope M'Guire's reason swooned within him. When next he awoke to consciousness, he was standing before St. Martin's-in-the-Fields, wavering like a drunken man;

the passers-by regarding him with eyes in which he read, as in a glass, an image of the terror and horror that dwelt within his own.

'I am afraid you are very ill, sir,' observed a woman, stopping and gazing hard in his face. 'Can I do anything to help you?'

'Ill?' said M'Guire. 'O God!' And then, recovering some shadow of his self-command, 'Chronic, madam,' said he: 'a long course of the dumb ague. But since you are so compassionate—an errand that I lack the strength to carry out,' he gasped—'this bag to Portman Square. Oh, compassionate woman, as you hope to be saved, as you are a mother, in the name of your babes that wait to welcome you at home, oh, take this bag to Portman Square! I have a mother, too,' he added, with a broken voice. 'Number 19, Portman Square.'

I suppose he had expressed himself with too much energy of voice; for the woman was plainly taken with a certain fear of him. 'Poor gentleman!' said she. 'If I were you, I would go home.' And she left him standing there in his distress.

'Home!' thought M'Guire, 'what a derision!' What home was there for him, the victim of philanthropy? He thought of his old mother, of his happy youth; of the hideous, rending pang of the explosion; of the possibility that he might not be killed, that he might be cruelly mangled, crippled for life, condemned to lifelong pains, blinded perhaps, and almost surely deafened. Ah, you spoke lightly of the dynamiter's peril; but even waiving death, have you realised what it is for a fine, brave young man of forty, to be smitten suddenly with deafness, cut off from all the music of life, and from the voice of friendship, and love? How little do we realise the sufferings of others! Even your brutal Government, in the heyday of its lust for cruelty, though it scruples not to hound the patriot with spies, to pack the corrupt jury, to bribe the hangman, and to erect the infamous gallows, would hesitate to inflict so horrible a doom: not, I am well aware, from virtue, not from philanthropy, but with the fear before it of the withering scorn of the good.

But I wander from M'Guire. From this dread glance into the past and future, his thoughts returned at a bound upon the present. How had he wandered there? and how long—oh, heavens! how long had he been about it? He pulled out his watch; and found that but three minutes had elapsed. It seemed too bright a

thing to be believed. He glanced at the church clock; and sure
enough, it marked an hour four minutes faster than the watch.

Of all that he endured, M'Guire declares that pang was the
most desolate. Till then, he had had one friend, one counsellor, in
whom he plenarily trusted; by whose advertisement, he numbered
the minutes that remained to him of life; on whose sure testimony,
he could tell when the time was come to risk the last adventure, to
cast the bag away from him, and take to flight. And now in what
was he to place reliance? His watch was slow; it might be losing
time; if so, in what degree? What limit could he set to its derange-
ment? and how much was it possible for a watch to lose in thirty
minutes? Five? ten? fifteen? It might be so; already, it seemed years
since he had left St. James's Hall on this so promising enterprise; at
any moment, then, the blow was to be looked for.

In the face of this new distress, the wild disorder of his pulses
settled down; and a broken weariness succeeded, as though he had
lived for centuries and for centuries been dead. The buildings and
the people in the street became incredibly small, and far-away, and
bright; London sounded in his ears stilly, like a whisper; and the
rattle of the cab that nearly charged him down, was like a sound
from Africa. Meanwhile, he was conscious of a strange abstraction
from himself; and heard and felt his footfalls on the ground, as
those of a very old, small, debile and tragically fortuned man,
whom he sincerely pitied.

As he was thus moving forward past the National Gallery, in a
medium, it seemed, of greater rarity and quiet than ordinary air,
there slipped into his mind the recollection of a certain entry in
Whitcomb Street hard by, where he might perhaps lay down his
tragic cargo unremarked. Thither, then, he bent his steps, seeming,
as he went, to float above the pavement; and there, in the mouth of
the entry, he found a man in a sleeved waistcoat, gravely chewing a
straw. He passed him by, and twice patrolled the entry, scouting
for the barest chance; but the man had faced about and continued
to observe him curiously.

Another hope was gone. M'Guire reissued from the entry, still
followed by the wondering eyes of the man in the sleeved waistcoat. He once more consulted his watch: there were but fourteen
minutes left to him. At that, it seemed as if a sudden, genial heat

were spread about his brain; for a second or two, he saw the world as red as blood; and thereafter entered into a complete possession of himself, with an incredible cheerfulness of spirits, prompting him to sing and chuckle as he walked. And yet this mirth seemed to belong to things external; and within, like a black and leaden-heavy kernel, he was conscious of the weight upon his soul.

I care for nobody, no, not I, And nobody cares for me, he sang, and laughed at the appropriate burthen, so that the passengers stared upon him on the street. And still the warmth seemed to increase and to become more genial. What was life? he considered, and what he, M'Guire? What even Erin, our green Erin? All seemed so incalculably little that he smiled as he looked down upon it. He would have given years, had he possessed them, for a glass of spirits; but time failed, and he must deny himself this last indulgence.

At the corner of the Haymarket, he very jauntily hailed a hansom cab; jumped in; bade the fellow drive him to a part of the Embankment, which he named; and as soon as the vehicle was in motion, concealed the bag as completely as he could under the vantage of the apron, and once more drew out his watch. So he rode for five interminable minutes, his heart in his mouth at every jolt, scarce able to possess his terrors, yet fearing to wake the attention of the driver by too obvious a change of plan, and willing, if possible, to leave him time to forget the Gladstone bag.

At length, at the head of some stairs on the Embankment, he hailed; the cab was stopped; and he alighted—with how glad a heart! He thrust his hand into his pocket. All was now over; he had saved his life; nor that alone, but he had engineered a striking act of dynamite; for what could be more pictorial, what more effective, than the explosion of a hansom cab, as it sped rapidly along the streets of London. He felt in one pocket; then in another. The most crushing seizure of despair descended on his soul; and struck into abject dumbness, he stared upon the driver. He had not one penny.

'Hillo,' said the driver, 'don't seem well.'

'Lost my money,' said M'Guire, in tones so faint and strange that they surprised his hearing.

The man looked through the trap. 'I dessay,' said he: 'you've left your bag.'

M'Guire half unconsciously fetched it out; and looking on that black continent at arm's length, withered inwardly and felt his features sharpen as with mortal sickness.

'This is not mine,' said he. 'Your last fare must have left it. You had better take it to the station.'

'Now look here,' returned the cabman: 'are you off your chump? or am I?'

'Well, then, I'll tell you what,' exclaimed M'Guire; 'you take it for your fare!'

'Oh, I dessay,' replied the driver. 'Anything else? What's IN your bag? Open it, and let me see.'

'No, no,' returned M'Guire. 'Oh no, not that. It's a surprise; it's prepared expressly: a surprise for honest cabmen.'

'No, you don't,' said the man, alighting from his perch, and coming very close to the unhappy patriot. 'You're either going to pay my fare, or get in again and drive to the office.'

It was at this supreme hour of his distress, that M'Guire spied the stout figure of one Godall, a tobacconist of Rupert Street, drawing near along the Embankment. The man was not unknown to him; he had bought of his wares, and heard him quoted for the soul of liberality; and such was now the nearness of his peril, that even at such a straw of hope, he clutched with gratitude.

'Thank God!' he cried. 'Here comes a friend of mine. I'll borrow.' And he dashed to meet the tradesman. 'Sir,' said he, 'Mr. Godall, I have dealt with you—you doubtless know my face—calamities for which I cannot blame myself have overwhelmed me. Oh, sir, for the love of innocence, for the sake of the bonds of humanity, and as you hope for mercy at the throne of grace, lend me two-and-six!'

'I do not recognise your face,' replied Mr. Godall; 'but I remember the cut of your beard, which I have the misfortune to dislike. Here, sir, is a sovereign; which I very willingly advance to you, on the single condition that you shave your chin.'

M'Guire grasped the coin without a word; cast it to the cabman, calling out to him to keep the change; bounded down the

steps, flung the bag far forth into the river, and fell headlong after
it. He was plucked from a watery grave, it is believed, by the hands
of Mr. Godall. Even as he was being hoisted dripping to the shore,
a dull and choked explosion shook the solid masonry of the
Embankment, and far out in the river a momentary fountain rose
and disappeared.

The Superfluous Mansion (continued)

SOMERSET in vain strove to attach a meaning to these words. He
had, in the meanwhile, applied himself assiduously to the flagon;
the plotter began to melt in twain, and seemed to expand and hover
on his seat; and with a vague sense of nightmare, the young man
rose unsteadily to his feet, and, refusing the proffer of a third grog,
insisted that the hour was late and he must positively get to bed.

'Dear me,' observed Zero, 'I find you very temperate. But I
will not be oppressive. Suffice it that we are now fast friends; and,
my dear landlord, AU REVOIR!'

So saying the plotter once more shook hands; and with the
politest ceremonies, and some necessary guidance, conducted the
bewildered young gentleman to the top of the stair.

Precisely, how he got to bed, was a point on which Somerset
remained in utter darkness; but the next morning when, at a blow,
he started broad awake, there fell upon his mind a perfect hurricane
of horror and wonder. That he should have suffered himself to be
led into the semblance of intimacy with such a man as his abominable lodger, appeared, in the cold light of day, a mystery of human
weakness. True, he was caught in a situation that might have tested
the aplomb of Talleyrand. That was perhaps a palliation; but it was
no excuse. For so wholesale a capitulation of principle, for such a
fall into criminal familiarity, no excuse indeed was possible; nor any
remedy, but to withdraw at once from the relation.

As soon as he was dressed, he hurried upstairs, determined on
a rupture. Zero hailed him with the warmth of an old friend.

'Come in,' he cried, 'dear Mr. Somerset! Come in, sit down,
and, without ceremony, join me at my morning meal.'

'Sir,' said Somerset, 'you must permit me first to disengage my honour. Last night, I was surprised into a certain appearance of complicity; but once for all, let me inform you that I regard you and your machinations with unmingled horror and disgust, and I will leave no stone unturned to crush your vile conspiracy.'

'My dear fellow,' replied Zero, with an air of some complacency, 'I am well accustomed to these human weaknesses. Disgust? I have felt it myself; it speedily wears off. I think none the worse, I think the more of you, for this engaging frankness. And in the meanwhile, what are you to do? You find yourself, if I interpret rightly, in very much the same situation as Charles the Second (possibly the least degraded of your British sovereigns) when he was taken into the confidence of the thief. To denounce me, is out of the question; and what else can you attempt? No, dear Mr. Somerset, your hands are tied; and you find yourself condemned, under pain of behaving like a cad, to be that same charming and intellectual companion who delighted me last night.'

'At least,' cried Somerset, 'I can, and do, order you to leave this house.'

'Ah!' cried the plotter, 'but there I fail to follow you. You may, if you please, enact the part of Judas; but if, as I suppose, you recoil from that extremity of meanness, I am, on my side, far too intelligent to leave these lodgings, in which I please myself exceedingly, and from which you lack the power to drive me. No, no, dear sir; here I am, and here I propose to stay.'

'I repeat,' cried Somerset, beside himself with a sense of his own weakness, 'I repeat that I give you warning. I am the master of this house; and I emphatically give you warning.'

'A week's warning?' said the imperturbable conspirator. 'Very well: we will talk of it a week from now. That is arranged; and in the meanwhile, I observe my breakfast growing cold. Do, dear Mr. Somerset, since you find yourself condemned, for a week at least, to the society of a very interesting character, display some of that open favour, some of that interest in life's obscurer sides, which stamp the character of the true artist. Hang me, if you will, to-morrow; but to-day show yourself divested of the scruples of the burgess, and sit down pleasantly to share my meal.'

'Man!' cried Somerset, 'do you understand my sentiments?'

'Certainly,' replied Zero; 'and I respect them! Would you be outdone in such a contest? will you alone be partial? and in this nineteenth century, cannot two gentlemen of education agree to differ on a point of politics? Come, sir: all your hard words have left me smiling; judge then, which of us is the philosopher!'

Somerset was a young man of a very tolerant disposition and by nature easily amenable to sophistry. He threw up his hands with a gesture of despair, and took the seat to which the conspirator invited him. The meal was excellent; the host not only affable, but primed with curious information. He seemed, indeed, like one who had too long endured the torture of silence, to exult in the most wholesale disclosures. The interest of what he had to tell was great; his character, besides, developed step by step; and Somerset, as the time fled, not only outgrew some of the discomfort of his false position, but began to regard the conspirator with a familiarity that verged upon contempt. In any circumstances, he had a singular inability to leave the society in which he found himself; company, even if distasteful, held him captive like a limed sparrow; and on this occasion, he suffered hour to follow hour, was easily persuaded to sit down once more to table, and did not even attempt to withdraw till, on the approach of evening, Zero, with many apologies, dismissed his guest. His fellow-conspirators, the dynamiter handsomely explained, as they were unacquainted with the sterling qualities of the young man, would be alarmed at the sight of a strange face.

As soon as he was alone, Somerset fell back upon the humour of the morning. He raged at the thought of his facility; he paced the dining-room, forming the sternest resolutions for the future; he wrung the hand which had been dishonoured by the touch of an assassin; and among all these whirling thoughts, there flashed in from time to time, and ever with a chill of fear, the thought of the confounded ingredients with which the house was stored. A powder magazine seemed a secure smoking-room alongside of the Superfluous Mansion.

He sought refuge in flight, in locomotion, in the flowing bowl. As long as the bars were open, he travelled from one to another, seeking light, safety, and the companionship of human faces; when these resources failed him, he fell back on the belated baked-potato man; and at length, still pacing the streets, he was goaded to fraternise with the police. Alas, with what a sense of guilt he conversed with these guardians of the law; how gladly had he wept upon their ample bosoms; and how the secret fluttered to his lips and was still denied an exit! Fatigue began at last to triumph over remorse; and about the hour of the first milkman, he returned to the door of the mansion; looked at it with a horrid expectation, as though it should have burst that instant into flames; drew out his key, and when his foot already rested on the steps, once more lost heart and fled for repose to the grisly shelter of a coffee-shop.

It was on the stroke of noon when he awoke. Dismally searching in his pockets, he found himself reduced to half-a-crown; and when he had paid the price of his distasteful couch, saw himself obliged to return to the Superfluous Mansion. He sneaked into the hall and stole on tiptoe to the cupboard where he kept his money. Yet half a minute, he told himself, and he would be free for days from his obseding lodger, and might decide at leisure on the course he should pursue. But fate had otherwise designed: there came a tap at the door and Zero entered.

'Have I caught you?' he cried, with innocent gaiety. 'Dear fellow, I was growing quite impatient.' And on the speaker's somewhat stolid face, there came a glow of genuine affection. 'I am so long unused to have a friend,' he continued, 'that I begin to be afraid I may prove jealous.' And he wrung the hand of his landlord.

Somerset was, of all men, least fit to deal with such a greeting. To reject these kind advances was beyond his strength. That he could not return cordiality for cordiality, was already almost more than he could carry. That inequality between kind sentiments which, to generous characters, will always seem to be a sort of guilt, oppressed him to the ground; and he stammered vague and lying words.

'That is all right,' cried Zero—'that is as it should be— say no more! I had a vague alarm; I feared you had deserted me; but I now own that fear to have been unworthy, and apologise. To doubt of your forgiveness were to repeat my sin. Come, then; dinner waits; join me again and tell me your adventures of the night.'

Kindness still sealed the lips of Somerset; and he suffered himself once more to be set down to table with his innocent and criminal acquaintance. Once more, the plotter plunged up to the neck in damaging disclosures: now it would be the name and biography of an individual, now the address of some important centre, that rose, as if by accident, upon his lips; and each word was like another turn of the thumbscrew to his unhappy guest. Finally, the course of Zero's bland monologue led him to the young lady of two days ago: that young lady, who had flashed on Somerset for so brief a while but with so conquering a charm; and whose engaging grace, communicative eyes, and admirable conduct of the sweeping skirt, remained imprinted on his memory.

'You saw her?' said Zero. 'Beautiful, is she not? She, too, is one of ours: a true enthusiast: nervous, perhaps, in presence of the chemicals; but in matters of intrigue, the very soul of skill and daring. Lake, Fonblanque, de Marly, Valdevia, such are some of the names that she employs; her true name—but there, perhaps, I go too far. Suffice it, that it is to her I owe my present lodging, and, dear Somerset, the pleasure of your acquaintance. It appears she knew the house. You see dear fellow, I make no concealment: all that you can care to hear, I tell you openly.'

'For God's sake,' cried the wretched Somerset, 'hold your tongue! You cannot imagine how you torture me!'

A shade of serious discomposure crossed the open countenance of Zero.

'There are times,' he said, 'when I begin to fancy that you do not like me. Why, why, dear Somerset, this lack of cordiality? I am depressed; the touchstone of my life draws near; and if I fail'—he gloomily nodded—'from all the height of my ambitious schemes, I fall, dear boy, into contempt. These are grave thoughts, and you may judge my need of your delightful company. Innocent prattler, you relieve the weight of my concerns. And yet . . . and yet . . .' The speaker pushed away his plate, and rose from table. 'Follow me,' said he, 'follow me. My mood is on; I must have air, I must behold the plain of battle.'

So saying, he led the way hurriedly to the top flat of the mansion, and thence, by ladder and trap, to a certain leaded platform, sheltered at one end by a great stalk of chimneys and occupying the actual summit of the roof. On both sides, it bordered, without parapet or rail, on the incline of slates; and, northward above all, commanded an extensive view of housetops, and rising through the smoke, the distant spires of churches.

'Here,' cried Zero, 'you behold this field of city, rich, crowded, laughing with the spoil of continents; but soon, how soon, to be laid low! Some day, some night, from this coign of vantage, you shall perhaps be startled by the detonation of the judgment gun— not sharp and empty like the crack of cannon, but deep-mouthed and unctuously solemn. Instantly thereafter, you shall behold the flames break forth. Ay,' he cried, stretching forth his hand, 'ay, that will be a day of retribution. Then shall the pallid constable flee side by side with the detected thief. Blaze!' he cried, 'blaze, derided city! Fall, flatulent monarchy, fall like Dagon!'

With these words his foot slipped upon the lead; and but for Somerset's quickness, he had been instantly precipitated into space. Pale as a sheet, and limp as a pocket-handkerchief, he was dragged from the edge of downfall by one arm; helped, or rather carried, down the ladder; and deposited in safety on the attic landing. Here he began to come to himself, wiped his brow, and at length, seizing Somerset's hand in both of his, began to utter his acknowledgments.

'This seals it,' said he. 'Ours is a life and death connection. You have plucked me from the jaws of death; and if I were before attracted by your character, judge now of the ardour of my gratitude and love! But I perceive I am still greatly shaken. Lend me, I beseech you, lend me your arm as far as my apartment.'

A dram of spirits restored the plotter to something of his customary self-possession; and he was standing, glass in hand and genially convalescent, when his eye was attracted by the dejection of the unfortunate young man.

'Good heavens, dear Somerset,' he cried, 'what ails you? Let me offer you a touch of spirits.'

But Somerset had fallen below the reach of this material comfort.

'Let me be,' he said. 'I am lost; you have caught me in the toils. Up to this moment, I have lived all my life in the most reckless manner, and done exactly what I pleased, with the most perfect innocence. And now—what am I? Are you so blind and wooden that you do not see the loathing you inspire me with? Is it possible you can suppose me willing to continue to exist upon such terms? To think,' he cried, 'that a young man, guilty of no fault on earth but amiability, should find himself involved in such a damned imbroglio!' And placing his knuckles in his eyes, Somerset rolled upon the sofa.

'My God,' said Zero, 'is this possible? And I so filled with tenderness and interest! Can it be, dear Somerset, that you are under the empire of these out-worn scruples? or that you judge a patriot by the morality of the religious tract? I thought you were a good agnostic.'

'Mr. Jones,' said Somerset, 'it is in vain to argue. I boast myself a total disbeliever, not only in revealed religion, but in the data, method, and conclusions of the whole of ethics. Well! what matters it? what signifies a form of words? I regard you as a reptile, whom I would rejoice, whom I long, to stamp under my heel. You would blow up others? Well then, understand: I want, with every circumstance of infamy and agony, to blow up you!'

'Somerset, Somerset!' said Zero, turning very pale, 'this is wrong; this is very wrong. You pain, you wound me, Somerset.'

'Give me a match!' cried Somerset wildly. 'Let me set fire to this incomparable monster! Let me perish with him in his fall!'

'For God's sake,' cried Zero, clutching hold of the young man, 'for God's sake command yourself! We stand upon the brink; death yawns around us; a man—a stranger in this foreign land—one whom you have called your friend—'

'Silence!' cried Somerset, 'you are no friend, no friend of mine. I look on you with loathing, like a toad: my flesh creeps with physical repulsion; my soul revolts against the sight of you.'

Zero burst into tears. 'Alas!' he sobbed, 'this snaps the last link that bound me to humanity. My friend disowns—he insults me. I am indeed accurst.'

Somerset stood for an instant staggered by this sudden change of front. The next moment, with a despairing gesture, he fled from the room and from the house. The first dash of his escape carried him hard upon half-way to the next police-office: but presently began to droop; and before he reached the house of lawful intervention, he fell once more among doubtful counsels. Was he an agnostic? had he a right to act? Away with such nonsense, and let Zero perish! ran his thoughts. And then again: had he not promised, had he not shaken hands and broken bread? and that with open eyes? and if so how could he take action, and not forfeit honour? But honour? what was honour? A figment, which, in the hot pursuit of crime, he ought to dash aside. Ay, but crime? A figment, too, which his enfranchised intellect discarded. All day, he wandered in the parks, a prey to whirling thoughts; all night, patrolled the city; and at the peep of day he sat down by the wayside in the neighbourhood of Peckham and bitterly wept. His gods had fallen. He who had chosen the broad, daylit, unencumbered paths of universal scepticism, found himself still the bondslave of honour. He who had accepted life from a point of view as lofty as the predatory eagle's, though with no design to prey; he who had clearly recognised the common moral basis of war, of commercial competition, and of crime; he who was prepared to help the escaping murderer or to embrace the impenitent thief, found, to the overthrow of all his logic, that he objected to the use of dynamite. The dawn crept among the sleeping villas and over the smokeless fields of city; and still the unfortunate sceptic sobbed over his fall from consistency.

At length, he rose and took the rising sun to witness. 'There is no question as to fact,' he cried; 'right and wrong are but figments and the shadow of a word; but for all that, there are certain things that I cannot do, and there are certain others that I will not stand.' Thereupon he decided to return to make one last effort of persuasion, and, if he could not prevail on Zero to desist from his infernal trade, throw delicacy to the winds, give the plotter an hour's start, and denounce him to the police. Fast as he went, being winged by this resolution, it was already well on in the morning when he came in sight of the Superfluous Mansion. Tripping down the steps, was the young lady of the various aliases; and he was surprised to see upon her countenance the marks of anger and concern.

'Madam,' he began, yielding to impulse and with no clear knowledge of what he was to add.

But at the sound of his voice she seemed to experience a shock of fear or horror; started back; lowered her veil with a sudden movement; and fled, without turning, from the square.

Here then, we step aside a moment from following the fortunes of Somerset, and proceed to relate the strange and romantic episode of THE BROWN BOX.

Desborough's Adventure: The Brown Box

MR. HARRY DESBOROUGH lodged in the fine and grave old quarter of Bloomsbury, roared about on every side by the high tides of London, but itself rejoicing in romantic silences and city peace. It was in Queen Square that he had pitched his tent, next door to the Children's Hospital, on your left hand as you go north: Queen Square, sacred to humane and liberal arts, whence homes were made beautiful, where the poor were taught, where the sparrows were plentiful and loud, and where groups of patient little ones would hover all day long before the hospital, if by chance they might kiss their hand or speak a word to their sick brother at the window. Desborough's room was on the first floor and fronted to the square; but he enjoyed besides, a right by which he often profited, to sit and smoke upon a terrace at the back, which looked down upon a fine forest of back gardens, and was in turn commanded by the windows of an empty room.

On the afternoon of a warm day, Desborough sauntered forth upon this terrace, somewhat out of hope and heart, for he had been now some weeks on the vain quest of situations, and prepared for melancholy and tobacco. Here, at least, he told himself that he would be alone; for, like most youths, who are neither rich, nor witty, nor successful, he rather shunned than courted the society of other men. Even as he expressed the thought, his eye alighted on the window of the room that looked upon the terrace; and to his surprise and annoyance, he beheld it curtained with a silken hanging. It was like his luck, he thought; his privacy was gone, he could no longer brood and sigh unwatched, he could no longer suffer his discouragement to find a vent in words or soothe himself with sentimental whistling; and in the irritation of the moment, he struck his pipe upon the rail with unnecessary force. It was an old, sweet, seasoned briar-root, glossy and dark with long employment, and justly dear to his fancy. What, then, was his chagrin, when the head snapped from the stem, leaped airily in space, and fell and disappeared among the lilacs of the garden?

He threw himself savagely into the garden chair, pulled out the story-paper which he had brought with him to read, tore off a fragment of the last sheet, which contains only the answers to correspondents, and set himself to roll a cigarette. He was no master of the art; again and again, the paper broke between his fingers and the tobacco showered upon the ground; and he was already on the point of angry resignation, when the window swung slowly inward, the silken curtain was thrust aside, and a lady, somewhat strangely attired, stepped forth upon the terrace.

'Senorito,' said she, and there was a rich thrill in her voice, like an organ note, 'Senorito, you are in difficulties. Suffer me to come to your assistance.'

With the words, she took the paper and tobacco from his unresisting hands; and with a facility that, in Desborough's eyes, seemed magical, rolled and presented him a cigarette. He took it, still seated, still without a word; staring with all his eyes upon that apparition. Her face was warm and rich in colour; in shape, it was that piquant triangle, so innocently sly, so saucily attractive, so rare in our more northern climates; her eyes were large, starry, and visited by changing lights; her hair was partly covered by a lace mantilla, through which her arms, bare to the shoulder, gleamed white; her figure, full and soft in all the womanly contours, was yet alive and active, light with excess of life, and slender by grace of some divine proportion.

'You do not like my cigarrito, Senor?' she asked. 'Yet it is better made than yours.' At that she laughed, and her laughter trilled in his ear like music; but the next moment her face fell. 'I see,' she cried. 'It is my manner that repels you. I am too constrained, too cold. I am not,' she added, with a more engaging air, 'I am not the simple English maiden I appear.'

'Oh!' murmured Harry, filled with inexpressible thoughts.

'In my own dear land,' she pursued, 'things are differently ordered. There, I must own, a girl is bound by many and rigorous restrictions; little is permitted her; she learns to be distant, she learns to appear forbidding. But here, in free England—oh, glorious liberty!' she cried, and threw up her arms with a gesture of inimitable grace—'here there are no fetters; here the woman may dare to be herself entirely, and the men, the chivalrous men—is it not written on the very shield of your nation, HONI SOIT? Ah, it is hard for me to learn, hard for me to dare to be myself. You must not judge me yet awhile; I shall end by conquering this stiffness, I shall end by growing English. Do I speak the language well?'

'Perfectly—oh, perfectly!' said Harry, with a fervency of conviction worthy of a graver subject.

'Ah, then,' she said, 'I shall soon learn; English blood ran in my father's veins; and I have had the advantage of some training in your expressive tongue. If I speak already without accent, with my thorough English appearance, there is nothing left to change except my manners.'

'Oh no,' said Desborough. 'Oh pray not! I—madam—'

'I am,' interrupted the lady, 'the Senorita Teresa Valdevia. The evening air grows chill. Adios, Senorito.' And before Harry could stammer out a word, she had disappeared into her room.

He stood transfixed, the cigarette still unlighted in his hand. His thoughts had soared above tobacco, and still recalled and beautified the image of his new acquaintance. Her voice re-echoed in his memory; her eyes, of which he could not tell the colour, haunted his soul. The clouds had risen at her coming, and he beheld a new-created world. What she was, he could not fancy, but he adored her. Her age, he durst not estimate; fearing to find her older than himself, and thinking sacrilege to couple that fair favour with the thought of mortal changes. As for her character, beauty to the young is always good. So the poor lad lingered late upon the terrace, stealing timid glances at the curtained window, sighing to the gold laburnums, rapt into the country of romance; and when at length he entered and sat down to dine, on cold boiled mutton and a pint of ale, he feasted on the food of gods.

Next day when he returned to the terrace, the window was a little ajar, and he enjoyed a view of the lady's shoulder, as she sat patiently sewing and all unconscious of his presence. On the next, he had scarce appeared when the window opened, and the Senorita tripped forth into the sunlight, in a morning disorder, delicately neat, and yet somehow foreign, tropical, and strange. In one hand she held a packet.

'Will you try,' she said, 'some of my father's tobacco—from dear Cuba? There, as I suppose you know, all smoke, ladies as well as gentlemen. So you need not fear to annoy me. The fragrance will remind me of home. My home, Senor, was by the sea.' And as she uttered these few words, Desborough, for the first time in his life, realised the poetry of the great deep. 'Awake or asleep, I dream of it: dear home, dear Cuba!'

'But some day,' said Desborough, with an inward pang, 'some day you will return?'

' Never!' she cried; 'ah, never, in Heaven's name!'

'Are you then resident for life in England?' he inquired, with a strange lightening of spirit.

'You ask too much, for you ask more than I know,' she answered sadly; and then, resuming her gaiety of manner: 'But you have not tried my Cuban tobacco,' she said.

'Senorita,' said he, shyly abashed by some shadow of coquetry in her manner, 'whatever comes to me—you—I mean,' he concluded, deeply flushing, 'that I have no doubt the tobacco is delightful.'

'Ah, Senor,' she said, with almost mournful gravity, 'you seemed so simple and good, and already you are trying to pay compliments—and besides,' she added, brightening, with a quick upward glance, into a smile, 'you do it so badly! English gentlemen, I used to hear, could be fast friends, respectful, honest friends; could be companions, comforters, if the need arose, or champions, and yet never encroach. Do not seek to please me by copying the graces of my countrymen. Be yourself: the frank, kindly, honest English gentleman that I have heard of since my childhood and still longed to meet.'

Harry, much bewildered, and far from clear as to the manners of the Cuban gentlemen, strenuously disclaimed the thought of plagiarism.

'Your national seriousness of bearing best becomes you, Senor,' said the lady. 'See!' marking a line with her dainty, slippered foot, 'thus far it shall be common ground; there, at my window-sill, begins the scientific frontier. If you choose, you may drive me to my forts; but if, on the other hand, we are to be real English friends, I may join you here when I am not too sad; or, when I am yet more graciously inclined, you may draw your chair beside the window and teach me English customs, while I work. You will find me an apt scholar, for my heart is in the task.' She laid her hand lightly upon Harry's arm, and looked into his eyes. 'Do you know,' said she, 'I am emboldened to believe that I have already caught something of your English aplomb? Do you not perceive a change, Senor? Slight, perhaps, but still a change? Is my deportment not more open, more free, more like that of the dear "British Miss" than when you saw me first?' She gave a radiant smile; withdrew her hand from Harry's arm; and before the young man could for-mulate in words the eloquent emotions that ran riot through his brain—with an 'Adios, Senor: good-night, my English friend,' she vanished from his sight behind the curtain.

The next day Harry consumed an ounce of tobacco in vain upon the neutral terrace; neither sight nor sound rewarded him, and the dinner-hour summoned him at length from the scene of disap-pointment. On the next it rained; but nothing, neither business nor weather, neither prospective poverty nor present hardship, could now divert the young man from the service of his lady; and wrapt in a long ulster, with the collar raised, he took his stand against the balustrade, awaiting fortune, the picture of damp and discomfort to the eye, but glowing inwardly with tender and delightful ardours. Presently the window opened, and the fair Cuban, with a smile imperfectly dissembled, appeared upon the sill.

'Come here,' she said, 'here, beside my window. The small verandah gives a belt of shelter.' And she graciously handed him a folding-chair.

As he sat down, visibly aglow with shyness and delight, a certain bulkiness in his pocket reminded him that he was not come empty-handed.

'I have taken the liberty,' said he, 'of bringing you a little book. I thought of you, when I observed it on the stall, because I saw it was in Spanish. The man assured me it was by one of the best authors, and quite proper.' As he spoke, he placed the little volume in her hand. Her eyes fell as she turned the pages, and a flush rose and died again upon her cheeks, as deep as it was fleeting. 'You are angry,' he cried in agony. 'I have presumed.'

'No, Senor, it is not that,' returned the lady. 'I—' and a flood of colour once more mounted to her brow—'I am confused and ashamed because I have deceived you. Spanish,' she began, and paused—'Spanish is, of course, my native tongue,' she resumed, as though suddenly taking courage; 'and this should certainly put the highest value on your thoughtful present; but alas, sir, of what use is it to me? And how shall I confess to you the truth—the humiliating truth—that I cannot read?'

As Harry's eyes met hers in undisguised amazement, the fair Cuban seemed to shrink before his gaze. 'Read?' repeated Harry. 'You!'

She pushed the window still more widely open with a large and noble gesture. 'Enter, Senor,' said she. 'The time has come to which I have long looked forward, not without alarm; when I must either fear to lose your friendship, or tell you without disguise the story of my life.'

It was with a sentiment bordering on devotion, that Harry passed the window. A semi-barbarous delight in form and colour had presided over the studied disorder of the room in which he found himself. It was filled with dainty stuffs, furs and rugs and scarves of brilliant hues, and set with elegant and curious trifles-fans on the mantelshelf, an antique lamp upon a bracket, and on the table a silver-mounted bowl of cocoa-nut about half full of unset jewels. The fair Cuban, herself a gem of colour and the fit masterpiece for that rich frame, motioned Harry to a seat, and sinking herself into another, thus began her history.

Story of the Fair Cuban

I AM not what I seem. My father drew his descent, on the one hand, from grandees of Spain, and on the other, through the maternal line, from the patriot Bruce. My mother, too, was the descendant of a line of kings; but, alas! these kings were African. She was fair as the day: fairer than I, for I inherited a darker strain of blood from the veins of my European father; her mind was noble, her manners queenly and accomplished; and seeing her more than the equal of her neighbours, and surrounded by the most considerate affection and respect, I grew up to adore her, and when the time came, received her last sigh upon my lips, still ignorant that she was a slave, and alas! my father's mistress. Her death, which befell me in my sixteenth year, was the first sorrow I had known: it left our home bereaved of its attractions, cast a shade of melancholy on my youth, and wrought in my father a tragic and durable change. Months went by; with the elasticity of my years, I regained some of the simple mirth that had before distinguished me; the plantation smiled with fresh crops; the negroes on the estate had already forgotten my mother and transferred their simple obedience to myself; but still the cloud only darkened on the brows of Senor Valdevia. His absences from home had been frequent even in the old days, for he did business in precious gems in the city of Havana; they now became almost continuous; and when he returned, it was but for the night and with the manner of a man crushed down by adverse fortune.

The place where I was born and passed my days was an isle set in the Caribbean Sea, some half-hour's rowing from the coasts of Cuba. It was steep, rugged, and, except for my father's family and plantation, uninhabited and left to nature. The house, a low building surrounded by spacious verandahs, stood upon a rise of ground and looked across the sea to Cuba. The breezes blew about it gratefully, fanned us as we lay swinging in our silken hammocks, and tossed the boughs and flowers of the magnolia. Behind and to the left, the quarter of the negroes and the waving fields of the plantation covered an eighth part of the surface of the isle. On the right and closely bordering on the garden, lay a vast and deadly swamp, densely covered with wood, breathing fever, dotted with profound sloughs, and inhabited by poisonous oysters, man-eating crabs, snakes, alligators, and sickly fishes. Into the recesses of that jungle, none could penetrate but those of African descent; an invisible, unconquerable foe lay there in wait for the European; and the air was death.

One morning (from which I must date the beginning of my ruinous misfortune) I left my room a little after day, for in that warm climate all are early risers, and found not a servant to attend upon my wants. I made the circuit of the house, still calling: and my surprise had almost changed into alarm, when coming at last into a large verandahed court, I found it thronged with negroes. Even then, even when I was amongst them, not one turned or paid the least regard to my arrival. They had eyes and ears for but one person: a woman, richly and tastefully attired; of elegant carriage, and a musical speech; not so much old in years, as worn and marred by self-indulgence: her face, which was still attractive, stamped with the most cruel passions, her eye burning with the greed of evil. It was not from her appearance, I believe, but from some emanation of her soul, that I recoiled in a kind of fainting terror; as we hear of plants that blight and snakes that fascinate, the woman shocked and daunted me. But I was of a brave nature; trod the weakness down; and forcing my way through the slaves, who fell back before me in embarrassment, as though in the presence of rival mistresses, I asked, in imperious tones: 'Who is this person?'

A slave girl, to whom I had been kind, whispered in my ear to have a care, for that was Madam Mendizabal; but the name was new to me.

In the meanwhile the woman, applying a pair of glasses to her eyes, studied me with insolent particularity from head to foot.

'Young woman,' said she, at last, 'I have had a great experience in refractory servants, and take a pride in breaking them. You really tempt me; and if I had not other affairs, and these of more importance, on my hand, I should certainly buy you at your father's sale.'

'Madam—' I began, but my voice failed me.

'Is it possible that you do not know your position?' she returned, with a hateful laugh. 'How comical! Positively, I must buy her. Accomplishments, I suppose?' she added, turning to the servants.

Several assured her that the young mistress had been brought up like any lady, for so it seemed in their inexperience.

'She would do very well for my place of business in Havana,' said the Senora Mendizabal, once more studying me through her glasses; 'and I should take a pleasure,' she pursued, more directly addressing myself, 'in bringing you acquainted with a whip.' And she smiled at me with a savoury lust of cruelty upon her face.

At this, I found expression. Calling by name upon the servants, I bade them turn this woman from the house, fetch her to the boat, and set her back upon the mainland. But with one voice, they protested that they durst not obey, coming close about me, pleading and beseeching me to be more wise; and, when I insisted, rising higher in passion and speaking of this foul intruder in the terms she had deserved, they fell back from me as from one who had blasphemed. A superstitious reverence plainly encircled the stranger; I could read it in their changed demeanour, and in the paleness that prevailed upon the natural colour of their faces; and their fear perhaps reacted on myself. I looked again at Madam Mendizabal. She stood perfectly composed, watching my face through her glasses with a smile of scorn; and at the sight of her assured superiority to all my threats, a cry broke from my lips, a cry of rage, fear, and despair, and I fled from the verandah and the house.

I ran I knew not where, but it was towards the beach. As I went, my head whirled; so strange, so sudden, were these events and insults. Who was she? what, in Heaven's name, the power she wielded over my obedient negroes? Why had she addressed me as a slave? why spoken of my father's sale? To all these tumultuary questions I could find no answer; and in the turmoil of my mind, nothing was plain except the hateful leering image of the woman.

I was still running, mad with fear and anger, when I saw my father coming to meet me from the landing-place; and with a cry that I thought would have killed me, leaped into his arms and broke into a passion of sobs and tears upon his bosom. He made me sit down below a tall palmetto that grew not far off; comforted me, but with some abstraction in his voice; and as soon as I regained the least command upon my feelings, asked me, not without harshness, what this grief betokened. I was surprised by his tone into a still greater measure of composure; and in firm tones, though still interrupted by sobs, I told him there was a stranger in the island, at which I thought he started and turned pale; that the servants would not obey me; that the stranger's name was Madam Mendizabal, and, at that, he seemed to me both troubled and relieved; that she had insulted me, treated me as a slave (and here my father's brow began to darken), threatened to buy me at a sale, and questioned my own servants before my face; and that, at last, finding myself quite helpless and exposed to these intolerable liberties, I had fled from the house in terror, indignation, and amazement.

'Teresa,' said my father, with singular gravity of voice, 'I must make to-day a call upon your courage; much must be told you, there is much that you must do to help me; and my daughter must prove herself a woman by her spirit. As for this Mendizabal, what shall I say? or how am I to tell you what she is? Twenty years ago, she was the loveliest of slaves; to-day she is what you see her—prematurely old, disgraced by the practice of every vice and every nefarious industry, but free, rich, married, they say, to some reputable man, whom may Heaven assist! and exercising among her ancient mates, the slaves of Cuba, an influence as unbounded as its reason is mysterious. Horrible rites, it is supposed, cement her empire: the rites of Hoodoo. Be that as it may, I would have you dismiss the thought of this incomparable witch; it is not from her that danger threatens us; and into her hands, I make bold to promise, you shall never fall.'

'Father!' I cried. 'Fall? Was there any truth, then, in her words? Am I—O father, tell me plain; I can bear anything but this suspense.'

'I will tell you,' he replied, with merciful bluntness. 'Your mother was a slave; it was my design, so soon as I had saved a competence, to sail to the free land of Britain, where the law would suffer me to marry her: a design too long procrastinated; for death, at the last moment, intervened. You will now understand the heaviness with which your mother's memory hangs about my neck.'

I cried out aloud, in pity for my parents; and in seeking to console the survivor, I forgot myself.

'It matters not,' resumed my father. 'What I have left undone can never be repaired, and I must bear the penalty of my remorse. But, Teresa, with so cutting a reminder of the evils of delay, I set myself at once to do what was still possible: to liberate yourself.'

I began to break forth in thanks, but he checked me with a sombre roughness.

'Your mother's illness,' he resumed, 'had engaged too great a portion of my time; my business in the city had lain too long at the mercy of ignorant underlings; my head, my taste, my unequalled knowledge of the more precious stones, that art by which I can distinguish, even on the darkest night, a sapphire from a ruby, and tell at a glance in what quarter of the earth a gem was disinterred—all these had been too long absent from the conduct of affairs. Teresa, I was insolvent.'

'What matters that?' I cried. 'What matters poverty, if we be left together with our love and sacred memories?'

'You do not comprehend,' he said gloomily. 'Slave, as you are, young—alas! scarce more than child!—accomplished, beautiful with the most touching beauty, innocent as an angel —all these qualities that should disarm the very wolves and crocodiles, are, in the eyes of those to whom I stand indebted, commodities to buy and sell. You are a chattel; a marketable thing; and worth—heavens, that I should say such words!—worth money. Do you begin to see? If I were to give you freedom, I should defraud my creditors; the manumission would be certainly annulled; you would be still a slave, and I a criminal.'

I caught his hand in mine, kissed it, and moaned in pity for myself, in sympathy for my father.

'How I have toiled,' he continued, 'how I have dared and striven to repair my losses, Heaven has beheld and will remember.

Its blessing was denied to my endeavours, or, as I please myself by thinking, but delayed to descend upon my daughter's head. At length, all hope was at an end; I was ruined beyond retrieve; a heavy debt fell due upon the morrow, which I could not meet; I should be declared a bankrupt, and my goods, my lands, my jewels that I so much loved, my slaves whom I have spoiled and rendered happy, and oh! tenfold worse, you, my beloved daughter, would be sold and pass into the hands of ignorant and greedy traffickers. Too long, I saw, had I accepted and profited by this great crime of slavery; but was my daughter, my innocent unsullied daughter, was SHE to pay the price? I cried out—no!—I took Heaven to witness my temptation; I caught up this bag and fled. Close upon my track are the pursuers; perhaps to-night, perhaps to-morrow, they will land upon this isle, sacred to the memory of the dear soul that bore you, to consign your father to an ignominious prison, and yourself to slavery and dishonour. We have not many hours before us. Off the north coast of our isle, by strange good fortune, an English yacht has for some days been hovering. It belongs to Sir George Greville, whom I slightly know, to whom ere now I have rendered unusual services, and who will not refuse to help in our escape. Or if he did, if his gratitude were in default, I have the power to force him. For what does it mean, my child—what means this Englishman, who hangs for years upon the shores of Cuba, and returns from every trip with new and valuable gems?'

'He may have found a mine,' I hazarded.

'So he declares,' returned my father; 'but the strange gift I have received from nature, easily transpierced the fable. He brought me diamonds only, which I bought, at first, in innocence; at a second glance, I started; for of these stones, my child, some had first seen the day in Africa, some in Brazil; while others, from their peculiar water and rude workmanship, I divined to be the spoil of ancient temples. Thus put upon the scent, I made inquiries. Oh, he is cunning, but I was cunninger than he. He visited, I found, the shop of every jeweller in town; to one he came with rubies, to one with emeralds, to one with precious beryl; to all, with this same story of the mine. But in what mine, what rich epitome of the earth's surface, were there conjoined the rubies of

Ispahan, the pearls of Coromandel, and the diamonds of Golconda? No, child, that man, for all his yacht and title, that man must fear and must obey me. To-night, then, as soon as it is dark, we must take our way through the swamp by the path which I shall presently show you; thence, across the highlands of the isle, a track is blazed, which shall conduct us to the haven on the north; and close by the yacht is riding. Should my pursuers come before the hour at which I look to see them, they will still arrive too late; a trusty man attends on the mainland; as soon as they appear, we shall behold, if it be dark, the redness of a fire, if it be day, a pillar of smoke, on the opposing headland; and thus warned, we shall have time to put the swamp between ourselves and danger. Meantime, I would conceal this bag; I would, before all things, be seen to arrive at the house with empty hands; a blabbing slave might else undo us. For see!' he added; and holding up the bag, which he had already shown me, he poured into my lap a shower of unmounted jewels, brighter than flowers, of every size and colour, and catching, as they fell, upon a million dainty facets, the ardour of the sun.

I could not restrain a cry of admiration.

'Even in your ignorant eyes,' pursued my father, 'they command respect. Yet what are they but pebbles, passive to the tool, cold as death? Ingrate!' he cried. 'Each one of these—miracles of nature's patience, conceived out of the dust in centuries of microscopical activity, each one is, for you and me, a year of life, liberty, and mutual affection. How, then, should I cherish them! and why do I delay to place them beyond reach! Teresa, follow me.'

He rose to his feet, and led me to the borders of the great jungle, where they overhung, in a wall of poisonous and dusky foliage, the declivity of the hill on which my father's house stood planted. For some while he skirted, with attentive eyes, the margin of the thicket. Then, seeming to recognise some mark, for his countenance became immediately lightened of a load of thought, he paused and addressed me. 'Here,' said he, 'is the entrance of the secret path that I have mentioned, and here you shall await me. I but pass some hundreds of yards into the swamp to bury my poor treasure; as soon as that is safe, I will return.' It was in vain that I sought to dissuade him, urging the dangers of the place; in vain that I begged to be allowed to follow, pleading the black blood that I now knew to circulate in my veins: to all my appeals he turned a deaf ear, and, bending back a portion of the screen of bushes, disappeared into the pestilential silence of the swamp.

At the end of a full hour, the bushes were once more thrust aside; and my father stepped from out the thicket, and paused and almost staggered in the first shock of the blinding sunlight. His face was of a singular dusky red; and yet for all the heat of the tropical noon, he did not seem to sweat.

'You are tired,' I cried, springing to meet him. 'You are ill.'

'I am tired,' he replied; 'the air in that jungle stifles one; my eyes, besides, have grown accustomed to its gloom, and the strong sunshine pierces them like knives. A moment, Teresa, give me but a moment. All shall yet be well. I have buried the hoard under a cypress, immediately beyond the bayou, on the left-hand margin of the path; beautiful, bright things, they now lie whelmed in slime; you shall find them there, if needful. But come, let us to the house; it is time to eat against our journey of the night: to eat and then to sleep, my poor Teresa: then to sleep.' And he looked upon me out of bloodshot eyes, shaking his head as if in pity.

We went hurriedly, for he kept murmuring that he had been gone too long, and that the servants might suspect; passed through the airy stretch of the verandah; and came at length into the grateful twilight of the shuttered house. The meal was spread; the house servants, already informed by the boatmen of the master's return, were all back at their posts, and terrified, as I could see, to face me. My father still murmuring of haste with weary and feverish pertinacity, I hurried at once to take my place at table; but I had no sooner left his arm than he paused and thrust forth both his hands with a strange gesture of groping. 'How is this?' he cried, in a sharp, unhuman voice. 'Am I blind?' I ran to him and tried to lead him to the table; but he resisted and stood stiffly where he was, opening and shutting his jaws, as if in a painful effort after breath. Then suddenly he raised both hands to his temples, cried out, 'My head, my head!' and reeled and fell against the wall.

I knew too well what it must be. I turned and begged the servants to relieve him. But they, with one accord, denied the possibility of hope; the master had gone into the swamp, they said, the master must die; all help was idle. Why should I dwell upon his sufferings? I had him carried to a bed, and watched beside him. He lay still, and at times ground his teeth, and talked at times unintelligibly, only that one word of hurry, hurry, coming distinctly to my ears, and telling me that, even in the last struggle with the powers of death, his mind was still tortured by his daughter's peril. The sun had gone down, the darkness had fallen, when I perceived that I was alone on this unhappy earth. What thought had I of flight, of safety, of the impending dangers of my situation? Beside the body of my last friend, I had forgotten all except the natural pangs of my bereavement.

The sun was some four hours above the eastern line, when I was recalled to a knowledge of the things of earth, by the entrance of the slave-girl to whom I have already referred. The poor soul was indeed devotedly attached to me; and it was with streaming tears that she broke to me the import of her coming. With the first light of dawn a boat had reached our landing-place, and set on shore upon our isle (till now so fortunate) a party of officers bearing a warrant to arrest my father's person, and a man of a gross body and low manners, who declared the island, the plantation, and all its human chattels, to be now his own. 'I think,' said my slave-girl, 'he must be a politician or some very powerful sorcerer; for Madam Mendizabal had no sooner seen them coming, than she took to the woods.'

'Fool,' said I, 'it was the officers she feared; and at any rate why does that beldam still dare to pollute the island with her presence? And O Cora,' I exclaimed, remembering my grief, 'what matter all these troubles to an orphan?'

'Mistress,' said she, 'I must remind you of two things. Never speak as you do now of Madam Mendizabal; or never to a person of colour; for she is the most powerful woman in this world, and her real name even, if one durst pronounce it, were a spell to raise the dead. And whatever you do, speak no more of her to your unhappy Cora; for though it is possible she may be afraid of the police (and indeed I think that I have heard she is in hiding), and though I know that you will laugh and not believe, yet it is true, and proved, and known that she hears every word that people utter in this whole vast world; and your poor Cora is already deep enough in her black books. She looks at me, mistress, till my blood turns ice. That is the first I had to say; and now for the second: do, pray, for Heaven's sake, bear in mind that you are no longer the poor Senor's daughter. He is gone, dear gentleman; and now you are no more than a common slave-girl like myself. The man to whom you belong calls for you; oh, my dear mistress, go at once! With your youth and beauty, you may still, if you are winning and obedient, secure yourself an easy life.'

For a moment I looked on the creature with the indignation you may conceive; the next, it was gone: she did but speak after her kind, as the bird sings or cattle bellow. 'Go,' said I. 'Go, Cora. I thank you for your kind intentions. Leave me alone one moment with my dead father; and tell this man that I will come at once.'

She went: and I, turning to the bed of death, addressed to those deaf ears the last appeal and defence of my beleaguered innocence. 'Father,' I said, 'it was your last thought, even in the pangs of dissolution, that your daughter should escape disgrace. Here, at your side, I swear to you that purpose shall be carried out; by what means, I know not; by crime, if need be; and Heaven forgive both you and me and our oppressors, and Heaven help my helplessness!' Thereupon I felt strengthened as by long repose; stepped to the mirror, ay, even in that chamber of the dead; hastily arranged my hair, refreshed my tear-worn eyes, breathed a dumb farewell to the originator of my days and sorrows; and composing my features to a smile, went forth to meet my master.

He was in a great, hot bustle, reviewing that house, once ours, to which he had but now succeeded; a corpulent, sanguine man of middle age, sensual, vulgar, humorous, and, if I judged rightly, not ill-disposed by nature. But the sparkle that came into his eye as he observed me enter, warned me to expect the worst.

'Is this your late mistress?' he inquired of the slaves; and when he had learnt it was so, instantly dismissed them. 'Now, my dear,' said he, 'I am a plain man: none of your damned Spaniards, but a true blue, hard-working, honest Englishman. My name is Caulder.'

'Thank you, sir,' said I, and curtsied very smartly as I had seen the servants.

'Come,' said he, 'this is better than I had expected; and if you
choose to be dutiful in the station to which it has pleased God to
call you, you will find me a very kind old fellow. I like your looks,'
he added, calling me by my name, which he scandalously mispro-
nounced. 'Is your hair all your own?' he then inquired with a certain sharpness, and coming up to me, as though I were a horse, he
grossly satisfied his doubts. I was all one flame from head to foot,
but I contained my righteous anger and submitted. 'That is very
well,' he continued, chucking me good humouredly under the
chin. 'You will have no cause to regret coming to old Caulder, eh?
But that is by the way. What is more to the point is this: your late
master was a most dishonest rogue, and levanted with some valuable property that belonged of rights to me. Now, considering
your relation to him, I regard you as the likeliest person to know
what has become of it; and I warn you, before you answer, that my
whole future kindness will depend upon your honesty. I am an
honest man myself, and expect the same in my servants.'

'Do you mean the jewels?' said I, sinking my voice into a
whisper.

'That is just precisely what I do,' said he, and chuckled.

'Hush!' said I.

'Hush?' he repeated. 'And why hush? I am on my own place, I
would have you to know, and surrounded by my own lawful servants.'

'Are the officers gone?' I asked; and oh! how my hopes hung
upon the answer!

'They are,' said he, looking somewhat disconcerted. 'Why do
you ask?'

'I wish you had kept them,' I answered, solemnly enough,
although my heart at that same moment leaped with exultation.
'Master, I must not conceal from you the truth. The servants on
this estate are in a dangerous condition, and mutiny has long been
brewing.'

'Why,' he cried, 'I never saw a milder-looking lot of niggers in
my life.' But for all that he turned somewhat pale.

'Did they tell you,' I continued, 'that Madam Mendizabal is on
the island? that, since her coming, they obey none but her? that if,

this morning, they have received you with even decent civility, it was only by her orders—issued with what after-thought I leave you to consider?'

'Madam Jezebel?' said he. 'Well, she is a dangerous devil; the police are after her, besides, for a whole series of murders; but after all, what then? To be sure, she has a great influence with you coloured folk. But what in fortune's name can be her errand here?'

'The jewels,' I replied. 'Ah, sir, had you seen that treasure, sapphire and emerald and opal, and the golden topaz, and rubies red as the sunset—of what incalculable worth, of what unequalled beauty to the eye!—had you seen it, as I have, and alas! as SHE has—you would understand and tremble at your danger.'

'She has seen them!' he cried, and I could see by his face, that my audacity was justified by its success.

I caught his hand in mine. 'My master,' said I, 'I am now yours; it is my duty, it should be my pleasure, to defend your interests and life. Hear my advice, then; and, I conjure you, be guided by my prudence. Follow me privily; let none see where we are going; I will lead you to the place where the treasure has been buried; that once disinterred, let us make straight for the boat, escape to the mainland, and not return to this dangerous isle without the countenance of soldiers.'

What free man in a free land would have credited so sudden a devotion? But this oppressor, through the very arts and sophistries he had abused, to quiet the rebellion of his conscience and to convince himself that slavery was natural, fell like a child into the trap I laid for him. He praised and thanked me; told me I had all the qualities he valued in a servant; and when he had questioned me further as to the nature and value of the treasure, and I had once more artfully inflamed his greed, bade me without delay proceed to carry out my plan of action.

From a shed in the garden, I took a pick and shovel; and thence, by devious paths among the magnolias, led my master to the entrance of the swamp. I walked first, carrying, as I was now in duty bound, the tools, and glancing continually behind me, lest we should be spied upon and followed. When we were come as far as the beginning of the path, it flashed into my mind I had forgotten meat; and leaving Mr. Caulder in the shadow of a tree, I returned alone to the house for a basket of provisions. Were they for him? I asked myself. And a voice within me answered, No. While we were face to face, while I still saw before my eyes the man to whom I belonged as the hand belongs to the body, my indignation held me bravely up. But now that I was alone, I conceived a sickness at myself and my designs that I could scarce endure; I longed to throw myself at his feet, avow my intended treachery, and warn him from that pestilential swamp, to which I was decoying him to die; but my vow to my dead father, my duty to my innocent youth, prevailed upon these scruples; and though my face was pale and must have reflected the horror that oppressed my spirits, it was with a firm step that I returned to the borders of the swamp, and with smiling lips that I bade him rise and follow me.

The path on which we now entered was cut, like a tunnel, through the living jungle. On either hand and overhead, the mass of foliage was continuously joined; the day sparingly filtered through the depth of super-impending wood; and the air was hot like steam, and heady with vegetable odours, and lay like a load upon the lungs and brain. Underfoot, a great depth of mould received our silent footprints; on each side, mimosas, as tall as a man, shrank from my passing skirts with a continuous hissing rustle; and but for these sentient vegetables, all in that den of pestilence was motionless and noiseless.

We had gone but a little way in, when Mr. Caulder was seized with sudden nausea, and must sit down a moment on the path. My heart yearned, as I beheld him; and I seriously begged the doomed mortal to return upon his steps. What were a few jewels in the scales with life? I asked. But no, he said; that witch Madam Jezebel would find them out; he was an honest man, and would not stand to be defrauded, and so forth, panting the while, like a sick dog. Presently he got to his feet again, protesting he had conquered his uneasiness; but as we again began to go forward, I saw in his changed countenance, the first approaches of death.

'Master,' said I, 'you look pale, deathly pale; your pallor fills me with dread. Your eyes are bloodshot; they are red like the rubies that we seek.'

'Wench,' he cried, 'look before you; look at your steps. I declare to Heaven, if you annoy me once again by looking back, I shall remind you of the change in your position.'

A little after, I observed a worm upon the ground, and told, in a whisper, that its touch was death. Presently a great green serpent, vivid as the grass in spring, wound rapidly across the path; and once again I paused and looked back at my companion, with a horror in my eyes. 'The coffin snake,' said I, 'the snake that dogs its victim like a hound.'

But he was not to be dissuaded. 'I am an old traveller,' said he. 'This is a foul jungle indeed; but we shall soon be at an end.'

'Ay,' said I, looking at him, with a strange smile, 'what end?'

Thereupon he laughed again and again, but not very heartily; and then, perceiving that the path began to widen and grow higher, 'There!' said he. 'What did I tell you? We are past the worst.'

Indeed, we had now come to the bayou, which was in that place very narrow and bridged across by a fallen trunk; but on either hand we could see it broaden out, under a cavern of great arms of trees and hanging creepers: sluggish, putrid, of a horrible and sickly stench, floated on by the flat heads of alligators, and its banks alive with scarlet crabs.

'If we fall from that unsteady bridge,' said I, 'see, where the caiman lies ready to devour us! If, by the least divergence from the path, we should be snared in a morass, see, where those myriads of scarlet vermin scour the border of the thicket! Once helpless, how they would swarm together to the assault! What could man do against a thousand of such mailed assailants? And what a death were that, to perish alive under their claws.'

'Are you mad, girl?' he cried. 'I bid you be silent and lead on.'

Again I looked upon him, half relenting; and at that he raised the stick that was in his hand and cruelly struck me on the face. 'Lead on!' he cried again. 'Must I be all day, catching my death in this vile slough, and all for a prating slave-girl?'

I took the blow in silence, I took it smiling; but the blood welled back upon my heart. Something, I know not what, fell at that moment with a dull plunge in the waters of the lagoon, and I told myself it was my pity that had fallen.

On the farther side, to which we now hastily scrambled, the wood was not so dense, the web of creepers not so solidly convolved. It was possible, here and there, to mark a patch of somewhat brighter daylight, or to distinguish, through the lighter web of parasites, the proportions of some soaring tree. The cypress on the left stood very visibly forth, upon the edge of such a clearing; the path in that place widened broadly; and there was a patch of open ground, beset with horrible ant-heaps, thick with their artificers. I laid down the tools and basket by the cypress root, where they were instantly blackened over with the crawling ants; and looked once more in the face of my unconscious victim. Mosquitoes and foul flies wove so close a veil between us that his features were obscured; and the sound of their flight was like the turning of a mighty wheel.

'Here,' I said, 'is the spot. I cannot dig, for I have not learned to use such instruments; but, for your own sake, I beseech you to be swift in what you do.'

He had sunk once more upon the ground, panting like a fish; and I saw rising in his face the same dusky flush that had mantled on my father's. 'I feel ill,' he gasped, 'horribly ill; the swamp turns around me; the drone of these carrion flies confounds me. Have you not wine?'

I gave him a glass, and he drank greedily. 'It is for you to think,' said I, 'if you should further persevere. The swamp has an ill name.' And at the word I ominously nodded.

'Give me the pick,' said he. 'Where are the jewels buried?'

I told him vaguely; and in the sweltering heat and closeness, and dim twilight of the jungle, he began to wield the pickaxe, swinging it overhead with the vigour of a healthy man. At first, there broke forth upon him a strong sweat, that made his face to shine, and in which the greedy insects settled thickly.

'To sweat in such a place,' said I. 'O master, is this wise? Fever is drunk in through open pores.'

'What do you mean?' he screamed, pausing with the pick buried in the soil. 'Do you seek to drive me mad? Do you think I do not understand the danger that I run?'

'That is all I want,' said I: 'I only wish you to be swift.' And then, my mind flitting to my father's deathbed, I began to murmur, scarce above my breath, the same vain repetition of words, 'Hurry, hurry, hurry.'

Presently, to my surprise, the treasure-seeker took them up; and while he still wielded the pick, but now with staggering and uncertain blows, repeated to himself, as it were the burthen of a song, 'Hurry, hurry, hurry;' and then again, 'There is no time to lose; the marsh has an ill name, ill name;' and then back to 'Hurry, hurry, hurry,' with a dreadful, mechanical, hurried, and yet wearied utterance, as a sick man rolls upon his pillow. The sweat had disappeared; he was now dry, but all that I could see of him, of the same dull brick red. Presently his pick unearthed the bag of jewels; but he did not observe it, and continued hewing at the soil.

'Master,' said I, 'there is the treasure.' He seemed to waken from a dream. 'Where?' he cried; and then, seeing it before his eyes, 'Can this be possible?' he added. 'I must be light-headed. Girl,' he cried suddenly, with the same screaming tone of voice that I had once before observed, 'what is wrong? is this swamp accursed?'

'It is a grave,' I answered. 'You will not go out alive; and as for me, my life is in God's hands.'

He fell upon the ground like a man struck by a blow, but whether from the effect of my words, or from sudden seizure of the malady, I cannot tell. Pretty soon, he raised his head. 'You have brought me here to die,' he said; 'at the risk of your own days, you have condemned me. Why?'

'To save my honour,' I replied. 'Bear me out that I have warned you. Greed of these pebbles, and not I, has been your undoer.'

He took out his revolver and handed it to me. 'You see,' he said, 'I could have killed you even yet. But I am dying, as you say; nothing could save me; and my bill is long enough already. Dear me, dear me,' he said, looking in my face with a curious, puzzled, and pathetic look, like a dull child at school, 'if there be a judgment afterwards, my bill is long enough.'

At that, I broke into a passion of weeping, crawled at his feet, kissed his hands, begged his forgiveness, put the pistol back into his grasp and besought him to avenge his death; for indeed, if with my life I could have bought back his, I had not balanced at the cost. But he was determined, the poor soul, that I should yet more bitterly regret my act.

'I have nothing to forgive,' said he. 'Dear heaven, what a thing is an old fool! I thought, upon my word, you had taken quite a fancy to me.'

He was seized, at the same time, with a dreadful, swimming dizziness, clung to me like a child, and called upon the name of some woman. Presently this spasm, which I watched with choking tears, lessened and died away; and he came again to the full possession of his mind. 'I must write my will,' he said. 'Get out my pocket-book.' I did so, and he wrote hurriedly on one page with a pencil. 'Do not let my son know,' he said; 'he is a cruel dog, is my son Philip; do not let him know how you have paid me out;' and then all of a sudden, 'God,' he cried, 'I am blind,' and clapped both hands before his eyes; and then again, and in a groaning whisper, 'Don't leave me to the crabs!' I swore I would be true to him so long as a pulse stirred; and I redeemed my promise. I sat there and watched him, as I had watched my father, but with what different, with what appalling thoughts! Through the long afternoon, he gradually sank. All that while, I fought an uphill battle to shield him from the swarms of ants and the clouds of mosquitoes: the prisoner of my crime. The night fell, the roar of insects instantly redoubled in the dark arcades of the swamp; and still I was not sure that he had breathed his last. At length, the flesh of his hand, which I yet held in mine, grew chill between my fingers, and I knew that I was free.

I took his pocket-book and the revolver, being resolved rather to die than to be captured, and laden besides with the basket and the bag of gems, set forward towards the north. The swamp, at that hour of the night, was filled with a continuous din: animals and insects of all kinds, and all inimical to life, contributing their parts. Yet in the midst of this turmoil of sound, I walked as though my eyes were bandaged, beholding nothing. The soil sank under my foot, with a horrid, slippery consistence, as though I were walking among toads; the touch of the thick wall of foliage, by which alone I guided myself, affrighted me like the touch of serpents; the darkness checked my breathing like a gag; indeed, I have never suffered such extremes of fear as during that nocturnal walk, nor have I ever known a more sensible relief than when I found the path beginning to mount and to grow firmer under foot, and saw, although still some way in front of me, the silver brightness of the moon.

Presently, I had crossed the last of the jungle, and come forth amongst noble and lofty woods, clean rock, the clean, dry dust, the aromatic smell of mountain plants that had been baked all day in sunlight, and the expressive silence of the night. My negro blood had carried me unhurt across that reeking and pestiferous morass; by mere good fortune, I had escaped the crawling and stinging vermin with which it was alive; and I had now before me the easier portion of my enterprise, to cross the isle and to make good my arrival at the haven and my acceptance on the English yacht. It was impossible by night to follow such a track as my father had described; and I was casting about for any landmark, and, in my ignorance, vainly consulting the disposition of the stars, when there fell upon my ear, from somewhere far in front, the sound of many voices hurriedly singing.

I scarce knew upon what grounds I acted; but I shaped my steps in the direction of that sound; and in a quarter of an hour's walking, came unperceived to the margin of an open glade. It was lighted by the strong moon and by the flames of a fire. In the midst, there stood a little low and rude building, surmounted by a cross: a chapel, as I then remembered to have heard, long since desecrated and given over to the rites of Hoodoo. Hard by the steps of entrance was a black mass, continually agitated and stirring to and fro as if with inarticulate life; and this I presently perceived to be a heap of cocks, hares, dogs, and other birds and animals, still struggling, but helplessly tethered and cruelly tossed one upon another. Both the fire and the chapel were surrounded by a ring of kneeling Africans, both men and women. Now they would raise their palms half-closed to heaven, with a peculiar, passionate gesture of supplication; now they would bow their heads and spread their hands before them on the ground. As the double movement passed and repassed along the line, the heads kept rising and falling, like waves upon the sea; and still, as if in time to these gesticulations, the hurried chant continued. I stood spellbound, knowing that my life depended by a hair, knowing that I had stumbled on a celebration of the rites of Hoodoo.

Presently, the door of the chapel opened, and there came forth a tall negro, entirely nude, and bearing in his hand the sacrificial knife. He was followed by an apparition still more strange and shocking: Madam Mendizabal, naked also, and carrying in both hands and raised to the level of her face, an open basket of wicker. It was filled with coiling snakes; and these, as she stood there with the uplifted basket, shot through the osier grating and curled about her arms. At the sight of this, the fervour of the crowd seemed to swell suddenly higher; and the chant rose in pitch and grew more irregular in time and accent. Then, at a sign from the tall negro, where he stood, motionless and smiling, in the moon and firelight, the singing died away, and there began the second stage of this barbarous and bloody celebration. From different parts of the ring, one after another, man or woman, ran forth into the midst; ducked, with that same gesture of the thrown-up hand, before the priestess and her snakes; and with various adjurations, uttered aloud the blackest wishes of the heart. Death and disease were the favours usually invoked: the death or the disease of enemies or rivals; some calling down these plagues upon the nearest of their own blood, and one, to whom I swear I had been never less than kind, invoking them upon myself. At each petition, the tall negro, still smiling, picked up some bird or animal from the heaving mass upon his left, slew it with the knife, and tossed its body on the ground. At length, it seemed, it reached the turn of the high-priestess. She set down the basket on the steps, moved into the centre of the ring, grovelled in the dust before the reptiles, and still grovelling lifted up her voice, between speech and singing, and with so great, with so insane a fervour of excitement, as struck a sort of horror through my blood.

'Power,' she began, 'whose name we do not utter; power that is neither good nor evil, but below them both; stronger than good, greater than evil—all my life long I have adored and served thee. Who has shed blood upon thine altars? whose voice is broken with the singing of thy praises? whose limbs are faint before their age with leaping in thy revels? Who has slain the child of her body? I,' she cried, 'I, Metamnbogu! By my own name, I name myself. I tear away the veil. I would be served or perish. Hear me, slime of the fat swamp, blackness of the thunder, venom of the serpent's udder—

hear or slay me! I would have two things, O shapeless one, O horror of emptiness—two things, or die! The blood of my white-faced husband; oh! give me that; he is the enemy of Hoodoo; give me his blood! And yet another, O racer of the blind winds, O germinator in the ruins of the dead, O root of life, root of corruption! I grow old, I grow hideous; I am known, I am hunted for my life: let thy servant then lay by this outworn body; let thy chief priestess turn again to the blossom of her days, and be a girl once more, and the desired of all men, even as in the past! And, O lord and master, as I here ask a marvel not yet wrought since we were torn from the old land, have I not prepared the sacrifice in which thy soul delighteth—the kid without the horns?'

Even as she uttered the words, there was a great rumour of joy through all the circle of worshippers; it rose, and fell, and rose again; and swelled at last into rapture, when the tall negro, who had stepped an instant into the chapel, reappeared before the door, carrying in his arms the body of the slave-girl, Cora. I know not if I saw what followed. When next my mind awoke to a clear knowledge, Cora was laid upon the steps before the serpents; the negro with the knife stood over her; the knife rose; and at this I screamed out in my great horror, bidding them, in God's name, to pause.

A stillness fell upon the mob of cannibals. A moment more, and they must have thrown off this stupor, and I infallibly have perished. But Heaven had designed to save me. The silence of these wretched men was not yet broken, when there arose, in the empty night, a sound louder than the roar of any European tempest, swifter to travel than the wings of any Eastern wind. Blackness engulfed the world; blackness, stabbed across from every side by intricate and blinding lightning. Almost in the same second, at one world-swallowing stride, the heart of the tornado reached the clearing. I heard an agonising crash, and the light of my reason was overwhelmed.

When I recovered consciousness, the day was come. I was unhurt; the trees close about me had not lost a bough; and I might have thought at first that the tornado was a feature in a dream. It was otherwise indeed; for when I looked abroad, I perceived I had escaped destruction by a hand's-breadth. Right through the forest, which here covered hill and dale, the storm had ploughed a lane of ruin. On either hand, the trees waved uninjured in the air of the morning; but in the forthright course of its advance, the hurricane had left no trophy standing. Everything, in that line, tree, man, or animal, the desecrated chapel and the votaries of Hoodoo, had been subverted and destroyed in that brief spasm of anger of the powers of air. Everything, but a yard or two beyond the line of its passage, humble flower, lofty tree, and the poor vulnerable maid who now knelt to pay her gratitude to heaven, awoke unharmed in the crystal purity and peace of the new day.

To move by the path of the tornado was a thing impossible to man, so wildly were the wrecks of the tall forest piled together by that fugitive convulsion. I crossed it indeed; with such labour and patience, with so many dangerous slips and falls, as left me, at the further side, bankrupt alike of strength and courage. There I sat down awhile to recruit my forces; and as I ate (how should I bless the kindliness of Heaven!) my eye, flitting to and fro in the colonnade of the great trees, alighted on a trunk that had been blazed. Yes, by the directing hand of Providence, I had been conducted to the very track I was to follow. With what a light heart I now set forth, and walking with how glad a step, traversed the uplands of the isle!

It was hard upon the hour of noon, when I came, all tattered and wayworn, to the summit of a steep descent, and looked below me on the sea. About all the coast, the surf, roused by the tornado of the night, beat with a particular fury and made a fringe of snow. Close at my feet, I saw a haven, set in precipitous and palm-crowned bluffs of rock. Just outside, a ship was heaving on the surge, so trimly sparred, so glossily painted, so elegant and point-device in every feature, that my heart was seized with admiration. The English colours blew from her masthead; and from my high station, I caught glimpses of her snowy planking, as she rolled on the uneven deep, and saw the sun glitter on the brass of her deck furniture. There, then, was my ship of refuge; and of all my difficulties only one remained: to get on board of her.

Half an hour later, I issued at last out of the woods on the margin of a cove, into whose jaws the tossing and blue billows entered, and along whose shores they broke with a surprising loudness. A wooded promontory hid the yacht; and I had walked some distance round the beach, in what appeared to be a virgin solitude, when my eye fell on a boat, drawn into a natural harbour, where it rocked in safety, but deserted. I looked about for those who should have manned her; and presently, in the immediate entrance of the wood, spied the red embers of a fire, and, stretched around in various attitudes, a party of slumbering mariners. To these I drew near: most were black, a few white; but all were dressed with the conspicuous decency of yachtsmen; and one, from his peaked cap and glittering buttons, I rightly divined to be an officer. Him, then, I touched upon the shoulder. He started up; the sharpness of his movement woke the rest; and they all stared upon me in surprise.

'What do you want?' inquired the officer.

'To go on board the yacht,' I answered.

I thought they all seemed disconcerted at this; and the officer, with something of sharpness, asked me who I was. Now I had determined to conceal my name until I met Sir George; and the first name that rose to my lips was that of the Senora Mendizabal. At the word, there went a shock about the little party of seamen; the negroes stared at me with indescribable eagerness, the whites themselves with something of a scared surprise; and instantly the spirit of mischief prompted me to add, 'And if the name is new to your ears, call me Metamnbogu.'

I had never seen an effect so wonderful. The negroes threw their hands into the air, with the same gesture I remarked the night before about the Hoodoo camp-fire; first one, and then another, ran forward and kneeled down and kissed the skirts of my torn dress; and when the white officer broke out swearing and calling to know if they were mad, the coloured seamen took him by the shoulders, dragged him on one side till they were out of hearing, and surrounded him with open mouths and extravagant pantomime. The officer seemed to struggle hard; he laughed aloud, and I saw him make gestures of dissent and protest; but in the end, whether overcome by reason or simply weary of resistance, he gave in—approached me civilly enough, but with something of a sneering manner underneath—and touching his cap, 'My lady,' said he, 'if that is what you are, the boat is ready.'

My reception on board the NEMOROSA (for so the yacht was named) partook of the same mingled nature. We were scarcely within hail of that great and elegant fabric, where she lay rolling gunwale under and churning the blue sea to snow, before the bulwarks were lined with the heads of a great crowd of sea-men, black, white, and yellow; and these and the few who manned the boat began exchanging shouts in some LINGUA FRANCA incomprehensible to me. All eyes were directed on the passenger; and once more I saw the negroes toss up their hands to heaven, but now as if with passionate wonder and delight.

At the head of the gangway, I was received by another officer, a gentlemanly man with blond and bushy whiskers; and to him I addressed my demand to see Sir George.

'But this is not—' he cried, and paused.

'I know it,' returned the other officer, who had brought me from the shore. 'But what the devil can we do? Look at all the niggers!'

I followed his direction; and as my eye lighted upon each, the poor ignorant Africans ducked, and bowed, and threw their hands into the air, as though in the presence of a creature half divine. Apparently the officer with the whiskers had instantly come round to the opinion of his subaltern; for he now addressed me with every signal of respect.

'Sir George is at the island, my lady,' said he: 'for which, with your ladyship's permission, I shall immediately make all sail. The cabins are prepared. Steward, take Lady Greville below.'

Under this new name, then, and so captivated by surprise that I could neither think nor speak, I was ushered into a spacious and airy cabin, hung about with weapons and surrounded by divans. The steward asked for my commands; but I was by this time so wearied, bewildered, and disturbed, that I could only wave him to leave me to myself, and sink upon a pile of cushions. Presently, by the changed motion of the ship, I knew her to be under way; my thoughts, so far from clarifying, grew the more distracted and confused; dreams began to mingle and confound them; and at length, by insensible transition, I sank into a dreamless slumber.

When I awoke, the day and night had passed, and it was once more morning. The world on which I reopened my eyes swam strangely up and down; the jewels in the bag that lay beside me chinked together ceaselessly; the clock and the barometer wagged to and fro like pendulums; and overhead, seamen were singing out at their work, and coils of rope clattering and thumping on the deck. Yet it was long before I had divined that I was at sea; long before I had recalled, one after another, the tragical, mysterious, and inexplicable events that had brought me where was.

When I had done so, I thrust the jewels, which I was surprised to find had been respected, into the bosom of my dress; and seeing a silver bell hard by upon a table, rang it loudly. The steward instantly appeared; I asked for food; and he proceeded to lay the table, regarding me the while with a disquieting and pertinacious scrutiny. To relieve myself of my embarrassment, I asked him, with as fair a show of ease as I could muster, if it were usual for yachts to carry so numerous a crew?

'Madam,' said he, 'I know not who you are, nor what mad fancy has induced you to usurp a name and an appalling destiny that are not yours. I warn you from the soul. No sooner arrived at the island—'

At this moment he was interrupted by the whiskered officer, who had entered unperceived behind him, and now laid a hand upon his shoulder. The sudden pallor, the deadly and sick fear, that was imprinted on the steward's face, formed a startling addition to his words.

'Parker!' said the officer, and pointed towards the door.

'Yes, Mr. Kentish,' said the steward. 'For God's sake, Mr. Kentish!' And vanished, with a white face, from the cabin.

Thereupon the officer bade me sit down, and began to help me, and join in the meal. 'I fill your ladyship's glass,' said he, and handed me a tumbler of neat rum.

'Sir,' cried I, 'do you expect me to drink this?'

He laughed heartily. 'Your ladyship is so much changed,' said he, 'that I no longer expect any one thing more than any other.'

Immediately after, a white seaman entered the cabin, saluted both Mr. Kentish and myself, and informed the officer there was a sail in sight, which was bound to pass us very close, and that Mr. Harland was in doubt about the colours.

'Being so near the island?' asked Mr. Kentish.

'That was what Mr. Harland said, sir,' returned the sailor, with a scrape.

'Better not, I think,' said Mr. Kentish. 'My compliments to Mr. Harland; and if she seem a lively boat, give her the stars and stripes; but if she be dull, and we can easily outsail her, show John Dutchman. That is always another word for incivility at sea; so we can disregard a hail or a flag of distress, without attracting notice.'

As soon as the sailor had gone on deck, I turned to the officer in wonder. 'Mr. Kentish, if that be your name,' said I, 'are you ashamed of your own colours?'

'Your ladyship refers to the JOLLY ROGER?' he inquired, with perfect gravity; and immediately after, went into peals of laughter. 'Pardon me,' said he; 'but here for the first time I recognise your ladyship's impetuosity.' Nor, try as I pleased, could I extract from him any explanation of this mystery, but only oily and commonplace evasion.

While we were thus occupied, the movement of the NEMOROSA gradually became less violent; its speed at the same time diminished; and presently after, with a sullen plunge, the anchor was discharged into the sea. Kentish immediately rose, offered his arm, and conducted me on deck; where I found we were lying in a roadstead among many low and rocky islets, hovered about by an innumerable cloud of sea-fowl. Immediately under our board, a somewhat larger isle was green with trees, set with a few low buildings and approached by a pier of very crazy workmanship; and a little inshore of us, a smaller vessel lay at anchor.

I had scarce time to glance to the four quarters, ere a boat was lowered. I was handed in, Kentish took place beside me, and we pulled briskly to the pier. A crowd of villainous, armed loiterers, both black and white, looked on upon our landing; and again the word passed about among the negroes, and again I was received with prostrations and the same gesture of the flung-up hand. By this, what with the appearance of these men, and the lawless, sea-girt spot in which I found myself, my courage began a little to decline, and clinging to the arm of Mr. Kentish, I begged him to tell me what it meant?

'Nay, madam,' he returned, 'YOU know.' And leading me smartly through the crowd, which continued to follow at a considerable distance, and at which he still kept looking back, I thought, with apprehension, he brought me to a low house that stood alone in an encumbered yard, opened the door, and begged me to enter.

'But why?' said I. 'I demand to see Sir George.'

'Madam,' returned Mr. Kentish, looking suddenly as black as thunder, 'to drop all fence, I know neither who nor what you are; beyond the fact that you are not the person whose name you have assumed. But be what you please, spy, ghost, devil, or most ill-judging jester, if you do not immediately enter that house, I will cut you to the earth.' And even as he spoke, he threw an uneasy glance behind him at the following crowd of blacks.

I did not wait to be twice threatened; I obeyed at once, and with a palpitating heart; and the next moment, the door was locked from the outside and the key withdrawn. The interior was long, low, and quite unfurnished, but filled, almost from end to end, with sugar-cane, tar-barrels, old tarry rope, and other incongruous and highly inflammable material; and not only was the door locked, but the solitary window barred with iron.

I was by this time so exceedingly bewildered and afraid, that I would have given years of my life to be once more the slave of Mr. Caulder. I still stood, with my hands clasped, the image of despair, looking about me on the lumber of the room or raising my eyes to heaven; when there appeared outside the window bars, the face of a very black negro, who signed to me imperiously to draw near. I did so, and he instantly, and with every mark of fervour, addressed me a long speech in some unknown and barbarous tongue.

'I declare,' I cried, clasping my brow, 'I do not understand one syllable.'

'Not?' he said in Spanish. 'Great, great, are the powers of Hoodoo! Her very mind is changed! But, O chief priestess, why have you suffered yourself to be shut into this cage? why did you not call your slaves at once to your defence? Do you not see that all has been prepared to murder you? at a spark, this flimsy house will go in flames; and alas! who shall then be the chief priestess? and what shall be the profit of the miracle?'

'Heavens!' cried I, 'can I not see Sir George? I must, I must, come by speech of him. Oh, bring me to Sir George!' And, my terror fairly mastering my courage, I fell upon my knees and began to pray to all the saints.

'Lordy!' cried the negro, 'here they come!' And his black head was instantly withdrawn from the window.

'I never heard such nonsense in my life,' exclaimed a voice.

'Why, so we all say, Sir George,' replied the voice of Mr. Kentish. 'But put yourself in our place. The niggers were near two to one. And upon my word, if you'll excuse me, sir, considering the notion they have taken in their heads, I regard it as precious fortunate for all of us that the mistake occurred.'

'This is no question of fortune, sir,' returned Sir George. 'It is a question of my orders, and you may take my word for it, Kentish, either Harland, or yourself, or Parker—or, by George, all three of you!—shall swing for this affair. These are my sentiments. Give me the key and be off.'

Immediately after, the key turned in the lock; and there appeared upon the threshold a gentleman, between forty and fifty, with a very open countenance, and of a stout and personable figure.

'My dear young lady,' said he, 'who the devil may you be?'

I told him all my story in one rush of words. He heard me, from the first, with an amazement you can scarcely picture, but when I came to the death of the Senora Mendizabal in the tornado, he fairly leaped into the air.

'My dear child,' he cried, clasping me in his arms, 'excuse a man who might be your father! This is the best news I ever had since I was born; for that hag of a mulatto was no less a person than my wife.' He sat down upon a tar-barrel, as if unmanned by joy. 'Dear me,' said he, 'I declare this tempts me to believe in Providence. And what,' he added, 'can I do for you?'

'Sir George,' said I, 'I am already rich: all that I ask is your protection.'

'Understand one thing,' he said, with great energy. 'I will never marry.'

'I had not ventured to propose it,' I exclaimed, unable to restrain my mirth; 'I only seek to be conveyed to England, the natural home of the escaped slave.'

'Well,' returned Sir George, 'frankly I owe you something for this exhilarating news; besides, your father was of use to me. Now, I have made a small competence in business—a jewel mine, a sort of naval agency, et caetera, and I am on the point of breaking up my company, and retiring to my place in Devonshire to pass a plain old age, unmarried. One good turn deserves another: if you swear to hold your tongue about this island, these little bonfire arrangements, and the whole episode of my unfortunate marriage, why, I'll carry you home aboard the NEMOROSA.' I eagerly accepted his conditions.

'One thing more,' said he. 'My late wife was some sort of a sorceress among the blacks; and they are all persuaded she has come alive again in your agreeable person. Now, you will have the goodness to keep up that fancy, if you please; and to swear to them, on the authority of Hoodoo or whatever his name may be, that I am from this moment quite a sacred character.'

'I swear it,' said I, 'by my father's memory; and that is a vow that I will never break.'

'I have considerably better hold on you than any oath,' returned Sir George, with a chuckle; 'for you are not only an escaped slave, but have, by your own account, a considerable amount of stolen property.'

I was struck dumb; I saw it was too true; in a glance, I recognised that these jewels were no longer mine; with similar quickness, I decided they should be restored, ay, if it cost me the liberty that I had just regained. Forgetful of all else, forgetful of Sir George, who sat and watched me with a smile, I drew out Mr. Caulder's pocket-book and turned to the page on which the dying man had scrawled his testament. How shall I describe the agony of happiness and remorse with which I read it! for my victim had not only set me free, but bequeathed to me the bag of jewels.

My plain tale draws towards a close. Sir George and I, in my character of his rejuvenated wife, displayed ourselves arm-in-arm among the negroes, and were cheered and followed to the place of embarkation. There, Sir George, turning about, made a speech to his old companions, in which he thanked and bade them farewell with a very manly spirit; and towards the end of which he fell on some expressions which I still remember. 'If any of you gentry lose your money,' he said, 'take care you do not come to me; for in the first place, I shall do my best to have you murdered; and if that fails, I hand you over to the law. Blackmail won't do for me. I'll rather risk all upon a cast, than be pulled to pieces by degrees. I'll rather be found out and hang, than give a doit to one man-jack of you.' That same night we got under way and crossed to the port of New Orleans, whence, as a sacred trust, I sent the pocket-book to Mr. Caulder's son. In a week's time, the men were all paid off; new hands were shipped; and the NEMOROSA weighed her anchor for Old England.

A more delightful voyage it were hard to fancy. Sir George, of course, was not a conscientious man; but he had an unaffected gaiety of character that naturally endeared him to the young; and it was interesting to hear him lay out his projects for the future, when he should be returned to Parliament, and place at the service of the nation his experience of marine affairs. I asked him, if his notion of piracy upon a private yacht were not original. But he told me, no. 'A yacht, Miss Valdevia,' he observed, 'is a chartered nuisance. Who smuggles? Who robs the salmon rivers of the West of Scotland? Who cruelly beats the keepers if they dare to intervene? The crews and the proprietors of yachts. All I have done is to extend the line a trifle, and if you ask me for my unbiassed opinion, I do not suppose that I am in the least alone.'

In short, we were the best of friends, and lived like father and daughter; though I still withheld from him, of course, that respect which is only due to moral excellence.

We were still some days' sail from England, when Sir George obtained, from an outward-bound ship, a packet of newspapers; and from that fatal hour my misfortunes recommenced. He sat, the same evening, in the cabin, reading the news, and making savoury comments on the decline of England and the poor condition of the navy, when I suddenly observed him to change countenance.

'Hullo!' said he, 'this is bad; this is deuced bad, Miss Valdevia. You would not listen to sound sense, you would send that pocket-book to that man Caulder's son.'

'Sir George,' said I, 'it was my duty.'

'You are prettily paid for it, at least,' says he; 'and much as I regret it, I, for one, am done with you. This fellow Caulder demands your extradition.'

'But a slave,' I returned, 'is safe in England.'

'Yes, by George!' replied the baronet; 'but it's not a slave, Miss Valdevia, it's a thief that he demands. He has quietly destroyed the will; and now accuses you of robbing your father's bankrupt estate of jewels to the value of a hundred thousand pounds.'

I was so much overcome by indignation at this hateful charge and concern for my unhappy fate that the genial baronet made haste to put me more at ease.

'Do not be cast down,' said he. 'Of course, I wash my hands of you myself. A man in my position—baronet, old family, and all that—cannot possibly be too particular about the company he keeps. But I am a deuced good-humoured old boy, let me tell you, when not ruffled; and I will do the best I can to put you right. I will lend you a trifle of ready money, give you the address of an excellent lawyer in London, and find a way to set you on shore unsuspected.'

He was in every particular as good as his word. Four days later, the NEMOROSA sounded her way, under the cloak of a dark night, into a certain haven of the coast of England; and a boat, rowing with muffled oars, set me ashore upon the beach within a stone's throw of a railway station. Thither, guided by Sir George's directions, I groped a devious way; and finding a bench upon the platform, sat me down, wrapped in a man's fur great-coat, to await the coming of the day. It was still dark when a light was struck behind one of the windows of the building; nor had the east begun to kindle to the warmer colours of the dawn, before a porter carrying a lantern, issued from the door and found himself face to face with the unfortunate Teresa. He looked all about him; in the grey twilight of the dawn, the haven was seen to lie deserted, and the yacht had long since disappeared.

'Who are you?' he cried.

'I am a traveller,' said I.

'And where do you come from?' he asked.

'I am going by the first train to London,' I replied.

In such manner, like a ghost or a new creation, was Teresa with her bag of jewels landed on the shores of England; in this silent fashion, without history or name, she took her place among the millions of a new country.

Since then, I have lived by the expedients of my lawyer, lying concealed in quiet lodgings, dogged by the spies of Cuba, and not knowing at what hour my liberty and honour may be lost.

The Brown Box (concluded)

THE effect of this tale on the mind of Harry Desborough was instant and convincing. The Fair Cuban had been already the loveliest, she now became, in his eyes, the most romantic, the most innocent, and the most unhappy of her sex. He was bereft of words to utter what he felt: what pity, what admiration, what youthful envy of a career so vivid and adventurous. 'O madam!' he began; and finding no language adequate to that apostrophe, caught up her hand and wrung it in his own. 'Count upon me,' he added, with bewildered fervour; and getting somehow or other out of the apartment and from the circle of that radiant sorceress, he found himself in the strange out-of-doors, beholding dull houses, wondering at dull passers-by, a fallen angel. She had smiled upon him as he left, and with how significant, how beautiful a smile! The memory lingered in his heart; and when he found his way to a certain restaurant where music was performed, flutes (as it were of Paradise) accompanied his meal. The strings went to the melody of that parting smile; they paraphrased and glossed it in the sense that he desired; and for the first time in his plain and somewhat dreary life, he perceived himself to have a taste for music.

The next day, and the next, his meditations moved to that delectable air. Now he saw her, and was favoured; now saw her not at all; now saw her and was put by. The fall of her foot upon the stair entranced him; the books that he sought out and read were books on Cuba, and spoke of her indirectly; nay, and in the very landlady's parlour, he found one that told of precisely such a hurricane, and, down to the smallest detail, confirmed (had confirmation been required) the truth of her recital. Presently he began to fall into that prettiest mood of a young love, in which the lover scorns himself for his presumption. Who was he, the dull one, the commonplace unemployed, the man without adventure, the impure, the untruthful, to aspire to such a creature made of fire and air, and hallowed and adorned by such incomparable passages of life? What should he do, to be more worthy? by what devotion, call down the notice of these eyes to so terrene a being as himself?

He betook himself, thereupon, to the rural privacy of the square, where, being a lad of a kind heart, he had made himself a circle of acquaintances among its shy frequenters, the half-domestic cats and the visitors that hung before the windows of the Children's Hospital. There he walked, considering the depth of his demerit and the height of the adored one's super-excellence; now lighting upon earth to say a pleasant word to the brother of some infant invalid; now, with a great heave of breath, remembering the queen of women, and the sunshine of his life.

What was he to do? Teresa, he had observed, was in the habit of leaving the house towards afternoon: she might, perchance, run danger from some Cuban emissary, when the presence of a friend might turn the balance in her favour: how, then, if he should follow her? To offer his company would seem like an intrusion; to dog her openly were a manifest impertinence; he saw himself reduced to a more stealthy part, which, though in some ways distasteful to his mind, he did not doubt that he could practise with the skill of a detective.

The next day he proceeded to put his plan in action. At the corner of Tottenham Court Road, however, the Senorita suddenly turned back, and met him face to face, with every mark of pleasure and surprise.

'Ah, Senor, I am sometimes fortunate!' she cried. 'I was looking for a messenger;' and with the sweetest of smiles, she despatched him to the East End of London, to an address which he was unable to find. This was a bitter pill to the knight-errant; but when he returned at night, worn out with fruitless wandering and dismayed by his FIASCO, the lady received him with a friendly gaiety, protesting that all was for the best, since she had changed her mind and long since repented of her message.

Next day he resumed his labours, glowing with pity and courage, and determined to protect Teresa with his life. But a painful shock awaited him. In the narrow and silent Hanway Street, she turned suddenly about and addressed him with a manner and a light in her eyes that were new to the young man's experience.

'Do I understand that you follow me, Senor?' she cried. 'Are these the manners of the English gentleman?'

Harry confounded himself in the most abject apologies and prayers to be forgiven, vowed to offend no more, and was at length dismissed, crestfallen and heavy of heart. The check was final; he gave up that road to service; and began once more to hang about the square or on the terrace, filled with remorse and love, admirable and idiotic, a fit object for the scorn and envy of older men. In these idle hours, while he was courting fortune for a sight of the beloved, it fell out naturally that he should observe the manners and appearance of such as came about the house. One person alone was the occasional visitor of the young lady: a man of considerable stature, and distinguished only by the doubtful ornament of a chin-beard in the style of an American deacon. Something in his appearance grated upon Harry; this distaste grew upon him in the course of days; and when at length he mustered courage to inquire of the Fair Cuban who this was, he was yet more dismayed by her reply.

'That gentleman,' said she, a smile struggling to her face, 'that gentleman, I will not attempt to conceal from you, desires my hand in marriage, and presses me with the most respectful ardour. Alas, what am I to say? I, the forlorn Teresa, how shall I refuse or accept such protestations?'

Harry feared to say more; a horrid pang of jealousy transfixed him; and he had scarce the strength of mind to take his leave with decency. In the solitude of his own chamber, he gave way to every manifestation of despair. He passionately adored the Senorita; but it was not only the thought of her possible union with another that distressed his soul, it was the indefeasible conviction that her suitor was unworthy. To a duke, a bishop, a victorious general, or any man adorned with obvious qualities, he had resigned her with a sort of bitter joy; he saw himself follow the wedding party from a great way off; he saw himself return to the poor house, then robbed of its jewel; and while he could have wept for his despair, he felt he could support it nobly. But this affair looked otherwise. The man was patently no gentleman; he had a startled, skulking, guilty bearing; his nails were black, his eyes evasive; his love perhaps was a pretext; he was perhaps, under this deep disguise, a Cuban emissary!

Harry swore that he would satisfy these doubts; and the next evening, about the hour of the usual visit, he posted himself at a spot whence his eye commanded the three issues of the square.

Presently after, a four-wheeler rumbled to the door, and the man with the chin-beard alighted, paid off the cabman, and was seen by Harry to enter the house with a brown box hoisted on his back. Half an hour later, he came forth again without the box, and struck eastward at a rapid walk; and Desborough, with the same skill and caution that he had displayed in following Teresa, proceeded to dog the steps of her admirer. The man began to loiter, studying with apparent interest the wares of the small fruiterer or tobacconist; twice he returned hurriedly upon his former course; and then, as though he had suddenly conquered a moment's hesitation, once more set forth with resolute and swift steps in the direction of Lincoln's Inn. At length, in a deserted by-street, he turned; and coming up to Harry with a countenance which seemed to have become older and whiter, inquired with some severity of speech if he had not had the pleasure of seeing the gentleman before.

'You have, sir,' said Harry, somewhat abashed, but with a good show of stoutness; 'and I will not deny that I was following you on purpose. Doubtless,' he added, for he supposed that all men's minds must still be running on Teresa, 'you can divine my reason.'

At these words, the man with the chin-beard was seized with a palsied tremor. He seemed, for some seconds, to seek the utterance which his fear denied him; and then whipping sharply about, he took to his heels at the most furious speed of running.

Harry was at first so taken aback that he neglected to pursue; and by the time he had recovered his wits, his best expedition was only rewarded by a glimpse of the man with the chin-beard mounting into a hansom, which immediately after disappeared into the moving crowds of Holborn.

Puzzled and dismayed by this unusual behaviour, Harry returned to the house in Queen Square, and ventured for the first time to knock at the fair Cuban's door. She bade him enter, and he found her kneeling with rather a disconsolate air beside a brown wooden trunk.

'Senorita,' he broke out, 'I doubt whether that man's character is what he wishes you to believe. His manner, when he found, and indeed when I admitted that I was following him, was not the manner of an honest man.'

'Oh!' she cried, throwing up her hands as in desperation, 'Don Quixote, Don Quixote, have you again been tilting against windmills?' And then, with a laugh, 'Poor soul!' she added, 'how you must have terrified him! For know that the Cuban authorities are here, and your poor Teresa may soon be hunted down. Even yon humble clerk from my solicitor's office may find himself at any moment the quarry of armed spies.'

'A humble clerk!' cried Harry, 'why, you told me yourself that he wished to marry you!'

'I thought you English like what you call a joke,' replied the lady calmly. 'As a matter of fact, he is my lawyer's clerk, and has been here to-night charged with disastrous news. I am in sore straits, Senor Harry. Will you help me?'

At this most welcome word, the young man's heart exulted; and in the hope, pride, and self-esteem that kindled with the very thought of service, he forgot to dwell upon the lady's jest. 'Can you ask?' he cried. 'What is there that I can do? Only tell me that.'

With signs of an emotion that was certainly unfeigned, the fair Cuban laid her hand upon the box. 'This box,' she said, 'contains my jewels, papers, and clothes; all, in a word, that still connects me with Cuba and my dreadful past. They must now be smuggled out of England; or, by the opinion of my lawyer, I am lost beyond remedy. To-morrow, on board the Irish packet, a sure hand awaits the box: the problem still unsolved, is to find some one to carry it as far as Holyhead, to see it placed on board the steamer, and instantly return to town. Will you be he? Will you leave to-morrow by the first train, punctually obey orders, bear still in mind that you are surrounded by Cuban spies; and without so much as a look behind you, or a single movement to betray your interest, leave the box where you have put it and come straight on shore? Will you do this, and so save your friend?'

'I do not clearly understand . . .' began Harry.

'No more do I,' replied the Cuban. 'It is not necessary that we should, so long as we obey the lawyer's orders.'

'Senorita,' returned Harry gravely, 'I think this, of course, a very little thing to do for you, when I would willingly do all. But suffer me to say one word. If London is unsafe for your treasures, it cannot long be safe for you; and indeed, if I at all fathom the plan of your solicitor, I fear I may find you already fled on my return. I am not considered clever, and can only speak out plainly what is in my heart: that I love you, and that I cannot bear to lose all knowledge of you. I hope no more than to be your servant; I ask no more than just that I shall hear of you. Oh, promise me so much!'

'You shall,' she said, after a pause. 'I promise you, you shall.' But though she spoke with earnestness, the marks of great embarrassment and a strong conflict of emotions appeared upon her face.

'I wish to tell you,' resumed Desborough, 'in case of accidents. . . .'

'Accidents!' she cried: 'why do you say that?'

'I do not know,' said he, 'you may be gone before my return, and we may not meet again for long. And so I wished you to know this: That since the day you gave me the cigarette, you have never once, not once, been absent from my mind; and if it will in any way serve you, you may crumple me up like that piece of paper, and throw me on the fire. I would love to die for you.'

'Go!' she said. 'Go now at once. My brain is in a whirl. I scarce know what we are talking. Go; and good-night; and oh, may you come safe!'

Once back in his own room a fearful joy possessed the young man's mind; and as he recalled her face struck suddenly white and the broken utterance of her last words, his heart at once exulted and misgave him. Love had indeed looked upon him with a tragic mask; and yet what mattered, since at least it was love—since at least she was commoved at their division? He got to bed with these parti-coloured thoughts; passed from one dream to another all night long, the white face of Teresa still haunting him, wrung with unspoken thoughts; and in the grey of the dawn, leaped suddenly out of bed, in a kind of horror. It was already time for him to rise. He dressed, made his breakfast on cold food that had been laid for him the night before; and went down to the room of his idol for the box. The door was open; a strange disorder reigned within; the furniture all pushed aside, and the centre of the room left bare of impediment, as though for the pacing of a creature with a tortured mind. There lay the box, however, and upon the lid a paper with these words: 'Harry, I hope to be back before you go. Teresa.'

He sat down to wait, laying his watch before him on the table. She had called him Harry: that should be enough, he thought, to fill the day with sunshine; and yet somehow the sight of that disordered room still poisoned his enjoyment. The door of the bedchamber stood gaping open; and though he turned aside his eyes as from a sacrilege, he could not but observe the bed had not been slept in. He was still pondering what this should mean, still trying to convince himself that all was well, when the moving needle of his watch summoned him to set forth without delay. He was before all things a man of his word; ran round to Southampton Row to fetch a cab; and taking the box on the front seat, drove off towards the terminus.

The streets were scarcely awake; there was little to amuse the eye; and the young man's attention centred on the dumb companion of his drive. A card was nailed upon one side, bearing the superscription: 'Miss Doolan, passenger to Dublin. Glass. With care.' He thought with a sentimental shock that the fair idol of his heart was perhaps driven to adopt the name of Doolan; and as he still studied the card, he was aware of a deadly, black depression settling steadily upon his spirits. It was in vain for him to contend against the tide; in vain that he shook himself or tried to whistle: the sense of some impending blow was not to be averted. He looked out; in the long, empty streets, the cab pursued its way without a trace of any follower. He gave ear; and over and above the jolting of the wheels upon the road, he was conscious of a certain regular and quiet sound that seemed to issue from the box.

He put his ear to the cover; at one moment, he seemed to perceive a delicate ticking: the next, the sound was gone, nor could his closest hearkening recapture it. He laughed at himself; but still the gloom continued; and it was with more than the common relief of an arrival, that he leaped from the cab before the station.

Probably enough on purpose, Teresa had named an hour some thirty minutes earlier than needful; and when Harry had given the box into the charge of a porter, who sat it on a truck, he proceeded briskly to pace the platform. Presently the bookstall opened; and the young man was looking at the books when he was seized by the arm. He turned, and, though she was closely veiled, at once recognised the Fair Cuban.

'Where is it?' she asked; and the sound of her voice surprised him.

'It?' he said. 'What?'

'The box. Have it put on a cab instantly. I am in fearful haste.'

He hurried to obey, marvelling at these changes, but not daring to trouble her with questions; and when the cab had been brought round, and the box mounted on the front, she passed a little way off upon the pavement and beckoned him to follow.

'Now,' said she, still in those mechanical and hushed tones that had at first affected him, 'you must go on to Holyhead alone; go on board the steamer; and if you see a man in tartan trousers and a pink scarf, say to him that all has been put off: if not,' she added, with a sobbing sigh, 'it does not matter. So, good-bye.'

'Teresa,' said Harry, 'get into your cab, and I will go along with you. You are in some distress, perhaps some danger; and till I know the whole, not even you can make me leave you.'

'You will not?' she asked. 'O Harry, it were better!'

'I will not,' said Harry stoutly.

She looked at him for a moment through her veil; took his hand suddenly and sharply, but more as if in fear than tenderness; and still holding him, walked to the cab-door.

'Where are we to drive?' asked Harry.

'Home, quickly,' she answered; 'double fare!' And as soon as they had both mounted to their places, the vehicle crazily trundled from the station.

Teresa leaned back in a corner. The whole way Harry could perceive her tears to flow under her veil; but she vouchsafed no explanation. At the door of the house in Queen Square, both alighted; and the cabman lowered the box, which Harry, glad to display his strength, received upon his shoulders.

'Let the man take it,' she whispered. 'Let the man take it.'

'I will do no such thing,' said Harry cheerfully; and having paid the fare, he followed Teresa through the door which she had opened with her key. The landlady and maid were gone upon their morning errands; the house was empty and still; and as the rattling of the cab died away down Gloucester Street, and Harry continued to ascend the stair with his burthen, he heard close against his shoulders the same faint and muffled ticking as before. The lady, still preceding him, opened the door of her room, and helped him to lower the box tenderly in the corner by the window.

'And now,' said Harry, 'what is wrong?'

'You will not go away?' she cried, with a sudden break in her voice and beating her hands together in the very agony of impatience. 'O Harry, Harry, go away! Oh, go, and leave me to the fate that I deserve!'

'The fate?' repeated Harry. 'What is this?'

'No fate,' she resumed. 'I do not know what I am saying. But I wish to be alone. You may come back this evening, Harry; come again when you like; but leave me now, only leave me now!' And then suddenly, 'I have an errand,' she exclaimed; 'you cannot refuse me that!'

'No,' replied Harry, 'you have no errand. You are in grief or danger. Lift your veil and tell me what it is.'

'Then,' she said, with a sudden composure, 'you leave but one course open to me.' And raising the veil, she showed him a countenance from which every trace of colour had fled, eyes marred with weeping, and a brow on which resolve had conquered fear. 'Harry,' she began, 'I am not what I seem.'

'You have told me that before,' said Harry, 'several times.'

'O Harry, Harry,' she cried, 'how you shame me! But this is the God's truth. I am a dangerous and wicked girl. My name is Clara Luxmore. I was never nearer Cuba than Penzance. From first to last I have cheated and played with you. And what I am I dare not even name to you in words. Indeed, until to-day, until the sleepless watches of last night, I never grasped the depth and foulness of my guilt.'

The young man looked upon her aghast. Then a generous current poured along his veins. 'That is all one,' he said. 'If you be all you say, you have the greater need of me.'

'Is it possible,' she exclaimed, 'that I have schemed in vain? And will nothing drive you from this house of death?'

'Of death?' he echoed.

'Death!' she cried: 'death! In that box that you have dragged about London and carried on your defenceless shoulders, sleep, at the trigger's mercy, the destroying energies of dynamite.'

'My God!' cried Harry.

'Ah!' she continued wildly, 'will you flee now? At any moment you may hear the click that sounds the ruin of this building. I was sure M'Guire was wrong; this morning, before day, I flew to Zero; he confirmed my fears; I beheld you, my beloved Harry, fall a victim to my own contrivances. I knew then I loved you—Harry, will you go now? Will you not spare me this unwilling crime?'

Harry remained speechless, his eyes fixed upon the box: at last he turned to her.

'Is it,' he asked hoarsely, 'an infernal machine?'

Her lips formed the word 'Yes,' which her voice refused to utter.

With fearful curiosity, he drew near and bent above the box; in that still chamber, the ticking was distinctly audible; and at the measured sound, the blood flowed back upon his heart.

'For whom?' he asked.

'What matters it,' she cried, seizing him by the arm. 'If you may still be saved, what matter questions?'

'God in heaven!' cried Harry. 'And the Children's Hospital! At whatever cost, this damned contrivance must be stopped!'

'It cannot,' she gasped. 'The power of man cannot avert the blow. But you, Harry—you, my beloved—you may still—'

And then from the box that lay so quietly in the corner, a sudden catch was audible, like the catch of a clock before it strikes the hour. For one second the two stared at each other with lifted brows and stony eyes. Then Harry, throwing one arm over his face, with the other clutched the girl to his breast and staggered against the wall.

A dull and startling thud resounded through the room; their eyes blinked against the coming horror; and still clinging together like drowning people, they fell to the floor. Then followed a prolonged and strident hissing as from the indignant pit; an offensive stench seized them by the throat; the room was filled with dense and choking fumes.

Presently these began a little to disperse: and when at length they drew themselves, all limp and shaken, to a sitting posture, the first object that greeted their vision was the box reposing uninjured in its corner, but still leaking little wreaths of vapour round the lid.

'Oh, poor Zero!' cried the girl, with a strange sobbing laugh. 'Alas, poor Zero! This will break his heart!'

The Superfluous Mansion (concluded)

SOMERSET ran straight upstairs; the door of the drawing-room, contrary to all custom, was unlocked; and bursting in, the young man found Zero seated on a sofa in an attitude of singular dejection. Close beside him stood an untasted grog, the mark of strong preoccupation. The room besides was in confusion: boxes had been tumbled to and fro; the floor was strewn with keys and other implements; and in the midst of this disorder lay a lady's glove.

'I have come,' cried Somerset, 'to make an end of this. Either you will instantly abandon all your schemes, or (cost what it may) I will denounce you to the police.'

'Ah!' replied Zero, slowly shaking his head. 'You are too late, dear fellow! I am already at the end of all my hopes, and fallen to be a laughing-stock and mockery. My reading,' he added, with a gentle despondency of manner, 'has not been much among romances; yet I recall from one a phrase that depicts my present state with critical exactitude; and you behold me sitting here "like a burst drum."'

'What has befallen you?' cried Somerset.

'My last batch,' returned the plotter wearily, 'like all the others, is a hollow mockery and a fraud. In vain do I combine the elements; in vain adjust the springs; and I have now arrived at such a pitch of disconsideration that (except yourself, dear fellow) I do not know a soul that I can face. My subordinates themselves have turned upon me. What language have I heard to-day, what illiberality of sentiment, what pungency of expression! She came once; I could have pardoned that, for she was moved; but she returned, returned to announce to me this crushing blow; and, Somerset, she was very inhumane. Yes, dear fellow, I have drunk a bitter cup; the speech of females is remarkable for . . . well, well! Denounce me, if you will; you but denounce the dead. I am extinct. It is strange how, at this supreme crisis of my life, I should be haunted by quotations from works of an inexact and even fanciful description; but here,' he added, 'is another: "Othello's occupation's gone." Yes, dear Somerset, it is gone; I am no more a dynamiter; and how, I ask you, after having tasted of these joys, am I to condescend to a less glorious life?'

'I cannot describe how you relieve me,' returned Somerset, sitting down on one of several boxes that had been drawn out into the middle of the floor. 'I had conceived a sort of maudlin toleration for your character; I have a great distaste, besides, for anything in the nature of a duty; and upon both grounds, your news delights me. But I seem to perceive,' he added, 'a certain sound of ticking in this box.'

'Yes,' replied Zero, with the same slow weariness of manner, 'I have set several of them going.'

'My God!' cried Somerset, bounding to his feet.

'Machines?'

'Machines!' returned the plotter bitterly. 'Machines indeed! I blush to be their author. Alas!' he said, burying his face in his hands, 'that I should live to say it!'

'Madman!' cried Somerset, shaking him by the arm. 'What am I to understand? Have you, indeed, set these diabolical contrivances in motion? and do we stay here to be blown up?'

'"Hoist with his own petard?"' returned the plotter musingly. 'One more quotation: strange! But indeed my brain is struck with numbness. Yes, dear boy, I have, as you say, put my contrivance in motion. The one on which you are sitting, I have timed for half an hour. Yon other—'

'Half an hour!—' echoed Somerset, dancing with trepidation. 'Merciful Heavens, in half an hour?'

'Dear fellow, why so much excitement?' inquired Zero. 'My dynamite is not more dangerous than toffy; had I an only child, I would give it him to play with. You see this brick?' he continued, lifting a cake of the infernal compound from the laboratory-table. 'At a touch it should explode, and that with such unconquerable energy as should bestrew the square with ruins. Well now, behold! I dash it on the floor.'

Somerset sprang forward, and with the strength of the very ecstasy of terror, wrested the brick from his possession. 'Heavens!' he cried, wiping his brow; and then with more care than ever mother handled her first-born withal, gingerly transported the explosive to the far end of the apartment: the plotter, his arms once more fallen to his side, dispiritedly watching him.

'It was entirely harmless,' he sighed. 'They describe it as burning like tobacco.'

'In the name of fortune,' cried Somerset, 'what have I done to you, or what have you done to yourself, that you should persist in this insane behaviour? If not for your own sake, then for mine, let us depart from this doomed house, where I profess I have not the heart to leave you; and then, if you will take my advice, and if your determination be sincere, you will instantly quit this city, where no further occupation can detain you.'

'Such, dear fellow, was my own design,' replied the plotter. 'I have, as you observe, no further business here; and once I have packed a little bag, I shall ask you to share a frugal meal, to go with me as far as to the station, and see the last of a broken-hearted man. And yet,' he added, looking on the boxes with a lingering regret, 'I should have liked to make quite certain. I cannot but suspect my underlings of some mismanagement; it may be fond, but yet I cherish that idea: it may be the weakness of a man of science, but yet,' he cried, rising into some energy, 'I will never, I cannot if I try, believe that my poor dynamite has had fair usage!'

'Five minutes!' said Somerset, glancing with horror at the timepiece. 'If you do not instantly buckle to your bag, I leave you.'

'A few necessaries,' returned Zero, 'only a few necessaries, dear Somerset, and you behold me ready.'

He passed into the bedroom, and after an interval which seemed to draw out into eternity for his unfortunate companion, he returned, bearing in his hand an open Gladstone bag. His movements were still horribly deliberate, and his eyes lingered gloatingly on his dear boxes, as he moved to and fro about the drawing-room, gathering a few small trifles. Last of all, he lifted one of the squares of dynamite.

'Put that down!' cried Somerset. 'If what you say be true, you have no call to load yourself with that ungodly contraband.'

'Merely a curiosity, dear boy,' he said persuasively, and slipped the brick into his bag; 'merely a memento of the past —ah, happy past, bright past! You will not take a touch of spirits? no? I find you very abstemious. Well,' he added, 'if you have really no curiosity to await the event—'

'I!' cried Somerset. 'My blood boils to get away.'

'Well, then,' said Zero, 'I am ready; I would I could say, willing; but thus to leave the scene of my sublime endeavours —'

Without further parley, Somerset seized him by the arm, and dragged him downstairs; the hall-door shut with a clang on the deserted mansion; and still towing his laggardly companion, the young man sped across the square in the Oxford Street direction. They had not yet passed the corner of the garden, when they were arrested by a dull thud of an extraordinary amplitude of sound, accompanied and followed by a shattering FRACAS. Somerset turned in time to see the mansion rend in twain, vomit forth flames and smoke, and instantly collapse into its cellars. At the same moment, he was thrown violently to the ground. His first glance was towards Zero. The plotter had but reeled against the garden rail; he stood there, the Gladstone bag clasped tight upon his heart, his whole face radiant with relief and gratitude; and the young man heard him murmur to himself: 'NUNC DIMITTIS, NUNC DIMITTIS!'

The consternation of the populace was indescribable; the whole of Golden Square was alive with men, women, and children, running wildly to and fro, and like rabbits in a warren, dashing in and out of the house doors. And under favour of this confusion, Somerset dragged away the lingering plotter.

'It was grand,' he continued to murmur: 'it was indescribably grand. Ah, green Erin, green Erin, what a day of glory! and oh, my calumniated dynamite, how triumphantly hast thou prevailed!'

Suddenly a shade crossed his face; and pausing in the middle of the footway, he consulted the dial of his watch.

'Good God!' he cried, 'how mortifying! seven minutes too early! The dynamite surpassed my hopes; but the clockwork, fickle clockwork, has once more betrayed me. Alas, can there be no success unmixed with failure? and must even this red-letter day be chequered by a shadow?'

'Incomparable ass!' said Somerset, 'what have you done? Blown up the house of an unoffending old lady, and the whole earthly property of the only person who is fool enough to befriend you!'

'You do not understand these matters,' replied Zero, with an air of great dignity. 'This will shake England to the heart. Gladstone, the truculent old man, will quail before the pointing finger of revenge. And now that my dynamite is proved effective—'

'Heavens, you remind me!' ejaculated Somerset. 'That brick in your bag must be instantly disposed of. But how? If we could throw it in the river—'

'A torpedo,' cried Zero, brightening, 'a torpedo in the Thames! Superb, dear fellow! I recognise in you the marks of an accomplished anarch.'

'True!' returned Somerset. 'It cannot so be done; and there is no help but you must carry it away with you. Come on, then, and let me at once consign you to a train.'

'Nay, nay, dear boy,' protested Zero. 'There is now no call for me to leave. My character is now reinstated; my fame brightens; this is the best thing I have done yet; and I see from here the ovations that await the author of the Golden Square Atrocity.'

'My young friend,' returned the other, 'I give you your choice. I will either see you safe on board a train or safe in gaol.'

'Somerset, this is unlike you!' said the chymist. 'You surprise me, Somerset.'

'I shall considerably more surprise you at the next police office,' returned Somerset, with something bordering on rage. 'For on one point my mind is settled: either I see you packed off to America, brick and all, or else you dine in prison.'

'You have perhaps neglected one point,' returned the unoffended Zero: 'for, speaking as a philosopher, I fail to see what means you can employ to force me. The will, my dear fellow—'

'Now, see here,' interrupted Somerset. 'You are ignorant of anything but science, which I can never regard as being truly knowledge; I, sir, have studied life; and allow me to inform you that I have but to raise my hand and voice—here in this street— and the mob—'

'Good God in heaven, Somerset,' cried Zero, turning deadly white and stopping in his walk, 'great God in heaven, what words are these? Oh, not in jest, not even in jest, should they be used! The brutal mob, the savage passions . . . . Somerset, for God's sake, a public-house!'

Somerset considered him with freshly awakened curiosity. 'This is very interesting,' said he. 'You recoil from such a death?'

'Who would not?' asked the plotter.

'And to be blown up by dynamite,' inquired the young man, 'doubtless strikes you as a form of euthanasia?'

'Pardon me,' returned Zero: 'I own, and since I have braved it daily in my professional career, I own it even with pride: it is a death unusually distasteful to the mind of man.'

'One more question,' said Somerset: 'you object to Lynch Law? why?'

'It is assassination,' said the plotter calmly, but with eyebrows a little lifted, as in wonder at the question.

'Shake hands with me,' cried Somerset. 'Thank God, I have now no ill-feeling left; and though you cannot conceive how I burn to see you on the gallows, I can quite contentedly assist at your departure.'

'I do not very clearly take your meaning,' said Zero, 'but I am sure you mean kindly. As to my departure, there is another point to be considered. I have neglected to supply myself with funds; my little all has perished in what history will love to relate under the name of the Golden Square Atrocity; and without what is coarsely if vigorously called stamps, you must be well aware it is impossible for me to pass the ocean.'

'For me,' said Somerset, 'you have now ceased to be a man. You have no more claim upon me than a door scraper; but the touching confusion of your mind disarms me from extremities. Until to-day, I always thought stupidity was funny; I now know otherwise; and when I look upon your idiot face, laughter rises within me like a deadly sickness, and the tears spring up into my eyes as bitter as blood. What should this portend? I begin to doubt; I am losing faith in scepticism. Is it possible,' he cried, in a kind of horror of himself—'is it conceivable that I believe in right and wrong? Already I have found myself, with incredulous surprise, to be the victim of a prejudice of personal honour. And must this change proceed? Have you robbed me of my youth? Must I fall, at my time of life, into the Common Banker? But why should I address that head of wood? Let this suffice. I dare not let you stay among women and children; I lack the courage to denounce you, if by any means I may avoid it; you have no money: well then, take mine, and go; and if ever I behold your face after to-day, that day will be your last.'

'Under the circumstances,' replied Zero, 'I scarce see my way to refuse your offer. Your expressions may pain, they cannot surprise me; I am aware our point of view requires a little training, a little moral hygiene, if I may so express it; and one of the points that has always charmed me in your character is this delightful frankness. As for the small advance, it shall be remitted you from Philadelphia.'

'It shall not,' said Somerset.

'Dear fellow, you do not understand,' returned the plotter. 'I shall now be received with fresh confidence by my superiors; and my experiments will be no longer hampered by pitiful conditions of the purse.'

'What I am now about, sir, is a crime,' replied Somerset; 'and were you to roll in wealth like Vanderbilt, I should scorn to be reimbursed of money I had so scandalously misapplied. Take it,

and keep it. By George, sir, three days of you have transformed me
to an ancient Roman.'

With these words, Somerset hailed a passing hansom; and the
pair were driven rapidly to the railway terminus. There, an oath
having been exacted, the money changed hands.

'And now,' said Somerset, 'I have bought back my honour
with every penny I possess. And I thank God, though there is
nothing before me but starvation, I am free from all entanglement
with Mr. Zero Pumpernickel Jones.'

'To starve?' cried Zero. 'Dear fellow, I cannot endure the
thought.'

'Take your ticket!' returned Somerset.

'I think you display temper,' said Zero.

'Take your ticket,' reiterated the young man.

'Well,' said the plotter, as he returned, ticket in hand, 'your
attitude is so strange and painful, that I scarce know if I should ask
you to shake hands.'

'As a man, no,' replied Somerset; 'but I have no objection to
shake hands with you, as I might with a pump-well that ran poi-
son or bell-fire.'

'This is a very cold parting,' sighed the dynamiter; and still
followed by Somerset, he began to descend the platform. This was
now bustling with passengers; the train for Liverpool was just
about to start, another had but recently arrived; and the double
tide made movement difficult. As the pair reached the neighbourhood of the bookstall, however, they came into an open space; and
here the attention of the plotter was attracted by a STANDARD
broadside bearing the words: 'Second Edition: Explosion in
Golden Square.' His eye lighted; groping in his pocket for the necessary coin, he sprang forward—his bag knocked sharply on the
corner of the stall—and instantly, with a formidable report, the
dynamite exploded. When the smoke cleared away the stall was
seen much shattered, and the stall keeper running forth in terror
from the ruins; but of the Irish patriot or the Gladstone bag no
adequate remains were to be found.

In the first scramble of the alarm, Somerset made good his
escape, and came out upon the Euston Road, his head spinning,

his body sick with hunger, and his pockets destitute of coin. Yet as
he continued to walk the pavements, he wondered to find in his
heart a sort of peaceful exultation, a great content, a sense, as it
were, of divine presence and the kindliness of fate; and he was able
to tell himself that even if the worst befell, he could now starve
with a certain comfort since Zero was expunged.

 Late in the afternoon, he found himself at the door of Mr.
Godall's shop; and being quite unmanned by his long fast, and
scarce considering what he did, he opened the glass door and
entered.

 'Ha!' said Mr. Godall, 'Mr. Somerset! Well, have you met with
an adventure? Have you the promised story? Sit down, if you
please; suffer me to choose you a cigar of my own special brand;
and reward me with a narrative in your best style.'

 'I must not take a cigar,' said Somerset.

 'Indeed!' said Mr. Godall. 'But now I come to look at you
more closely, I perceive that you are changed. My poor boy, I hope
there is nothing wrong?'

 Somerset burst into tears.

Epilogue of the Cigar Divan

ON a certain day of lashing rain in the December of last year, and
between the hours of nine and ten in the morning, Mr. Edward
Challoner pioneered himself under an umbrella to the door of the
Cigar Divan in Rupert Street. It was a place he had visited but once
before: the memory of what had followed on that visit and the fear
of Somerset having prevented his return. Even now, he looked in
before he entered; but the shop was free of customers.

 The young man behind the counter was so intently writing in
a penny version-book, that he paid no heed to Challoner's arrival.
On a second glance, it seemed to the latter that he recognised him.

 'By Jove,' he thought, 'unquestionably Somerset!'

 And though this was the very man he had been so sedulously
careful to avoid, his unexplained position at the receipt of custom
changed distaste to curiosity.

'"Or opulent rotunda strike the sky,"' said the shopman to himself, in the tone of one considering a verse. 'I suppose it would be too much to say "orotunda," and yet how noble it were! "Or opulent orotunda strike the sky." But that is the bitterness of arts; you see a good effect, and some nonsense about sense continually intervenes.'

'Somerset, my dear fellow,' said Challoner, 'is this a masquerade?'

'What? Challoner!' cried the shopman. 'I am delighted to see you. One moment, till I finish the octave of my sonnet: only the octave.' And with a friendly waggle of the hand, he once more buried himself in the commerce of the Muses. 'I say,' he said presently, looking up, 'you seem in wonderful preservation: how about the hundred pounds?'

'I have made a small inheritance from a great aunt in Wales,' replied Challoner modestly.

'Ah,' said Somerset, 'I very much doubt the legitimacy of inheritance. The State, in my view, should collar it. I am now going through a stage of socialism and poetry,' he added apologetically, as one who spoke of a course of medicinal waters.

'And are you really the person of the—establishment?' inquired Challoner, deftly evading the word 'shop.'

'A vendor, sir, a vendor,' returned the other, pocketing his poesy. 'I help old Happy and Glorious. Can I offer you a weed?'

'Well, I scarcely like . . .' began Challoner.

'Nonsense, my dear fellow,' cried the shopman. 'We are very proud of the business; and the old man, let me inform you, besides being the most egregious of created beings from the point of view of ethics, is literally sprung from the loins of kings. "DE GODALL JE SUIS LE FERVENT." There is only one Godall.—By the way,' he added, as Challoner lit his cigar, 'how did you get on with the detective trade?'

'I did not try,' said Challoner curtly.

'Ah, well, I did,' returned Somerset, 'and made the most incomparable mess of it: lost all my money and fairly covered myself with odium and ridicule. There is more in that business, Challoner, than meets the eye; there is more, in fact, in all businesses. You must believe in them, or get up the belief that you believe. Hence,' he added, 'the recognised inferiority of the plumber, for no one could believe in plumbing.'

'A PROPOS,' asked Challoner, 'do you still paint?'

'Not now,' replied Paul; 'but I think of taking up the violin.'

Challoner's eye, which had been somewhat restless since the trade of the detective had been named, now rested for a moment on the columns of the morning paper, where it lay spread upon the counter.

'By Jove,' he cried, 'that's odd!'

'What is odd?' asked Paul.

'Oh, nothing,' returned the other: 'only I once met a person called M'Guire.'

'So did I!' cried Somerset. 'Is there anything about him?'

Challoner read as follows: 'MYSTERIOUS DEATH IN STEPNEY. An inquest was held yesterday on the body of Patrick M'Guire, described as a carpenter. Doctor Dovering stated that he had for some time treated the deceased as a dispensary patient, for sleeplessness, loss of appetite, and nervous depression. There was no cause of death to be found. He would say the deceased had sunk. Deceased was not a temperate man, which doubtless accelerated death. Deceased complained of dumb ague, but witness had never been able to detect any positive disease. He did not know that he had any family. He regarded him as a person of unsound intellect, who believed himself a member and the victim of some secret society. If he were to hazard an opinion, he would say deceased had died of fear.'

'And the doctor would be right,' cried Somerset; 'and my dear Challoner, I am so relieved to hear of his demise, that I will—Well, after all,' he added, 'poor devil, he was well served.'

The door at this moment opened, and Desborough appeared upon the threshold. He was wrapped in a long waterproof, imperfectly supplied with buttons; his boots were full of water, his hat greasy with service; and yet he wore the air of one exceeding well content with life. He was hailed by the two others with exclamations of surprise and welcome.

'And did you try the detective business?' inquired Paul.

'No,' returned Harry. 'Oh yes, by the way, I did though: twice, and got caught out both times. But I thought I should find my—my wife here?' he added, with a kind of proud confusion.

'What? are you married?' cried Somerset.

'Oh yes,' said Harry, 'quite a long time: a month at least.'

'Money?' asked Challoner.

'That's the worst of it,' Desborough admitted. 'We are deadly hard up. But the Pri-Mr. Godall is going to do something for us. That is what brings us here.'

'Who was Mrs. Desborough?' said Challoner, in the tone of a man of society.

'She was a Miss Luxmore,' returned Harry. 'You fellows will be sure to like her, for she is much cleverer than I. She tells wonderful stories, too; better than a book.'

And just then the door opened, and Mrs. Desborough entered. Somerset cried out aloud to recognise the young lady of the Superfluous Mansion, and Challoner fell back a step and dropped his cigar as he beheld the sorceress of Chelsea.

'What!' cried Harry, 'do you both know my wife?'

'I believe I have seen her,' said Somerset, a little wildly.

'I think I have met the gentleman,' said Mrs. Desborough sweetly; 'but I cannot imagine where it was.'

'Oh no,' cried Somerset fervently: 'I have no notion—I cannot conceive—where it could have been. Indeed,' he continued, growing in emphasis, 'I think it highly probable that it's a mistake.'

'And you, Challoner?' asked Harry, 'you seemed to recognise her too.'

'These are both friends of yours, Harry?' said the lady. 'Delighted, I am sure. I do not remember to have met Mr. Challoner.'

Challoner was very red in the face, perhaps from having groped after his cigar. 'I do not remember to have had the pleasure,' he responded huskily.

'Well, and Mr. Godall?' asked Mrs. Desborough.

'Are you the lady that has an appointment with old—' began Somerset, and paused blushing. 'Because if so,' he resumed, 'I was to announce you at once.'

And the shopman raised a curtain, opened a door, and passed into a small pavilion which had been added to the back of the house. On the roof, the rain resounded musically. The walls were lined with maps and prints and a few works of reference. Upon a table was a large-scale map of Egypt and the Soudan, and another of Tonkin, on which, by the aid of coloured pins, the progress of the different wars was being followed day by day. A light, refreshing odour of the most delicate tobacco hung upon the air; and a fire, not of foul coal, but of clear-flaming resinous billets, chattered upon silver dogs. In this elegant and plain apartment, Mr. Godall sat in a morning muse, placidly gazing at the fire and hearkening to the rain upon the roof.

'Ha, my dear Mr. Somerset,' said he, 'and have you since last night adopted any fresh political principle?'

'The lady, sir,' said Somerset, with another blush.

'You have seen her, I believe?' returned Mr. Godall; and on Somerset's replying in the affirmative, 'You will excuse me, my dear sir,' he resumed, 'if I offer you a hint. I think it not improbable this lady may desire entirely to forget the past. From one gentleman to another, no more words are necessary.'

A moment after, he had received Mrs. Desborough with that grave and touching urbanity that so well became him.

'I am pleased, madam, to welcome you to my poor house,' he said; 'and shall be still more so, if what were else a barren courtesy and a pleasure personal to myself, shall prove to be of serious benefit to you and Mr. Desborough.'

'Your Highness,' replied Clara, 'I must begin with thanks; it is like what I have heard of you, that you should thus take up the case of the unfortunate; and as for my Harry, he is worthy of all that you can do.' She paused.

'But for yourself?' suggested Mr. Godall—'it was thus you were about to continue, I believe.'

'You take the words out of my mouth,' she said. 'For myself, it is different.'

'I am not here to be a judge of men,' replied the Prince; 'still less of women. I am now a private person like yourself and many million others; but I am one who still fights upon the side of quiet. Now, madam, you know better than I, and God better than you, what you have done to mankind in the past; I pause not to inquire; it is with the future I concern myself, it is for the future I demand security. I would not willingly put arms into the hands of a disloyal combatant; and I dare not restore to wealth one of the levyers of a private and a barbarous war. I speak with some severity, and yet I pick my terms. I tell myself continually that you are a woman; and a voice continually reminds me of the children whose lives and limbs you have endangered. A woman,' he repeated solemnly—'and children. Possibly, madam, when you are yourself a mother, you will feel the bite of that antithesis: possibly when you kneel at night beside a cradle, a fear will fall upon you, heavier than any shame; and when your child lies in the pain and danger of disease, you shall hesitate to kneel before your Maker.'

'You look at the fault,' she said, 'and not at the excuse. Has your own heart never leaped within you at some story of oppression? But, alas, no! for you were born upon a throne.'

'I was born of woman,' said the Prince; 'I came forth from my mother's agony, helpless as a wren, like other nurselings. This, which you forgot, I have still faithfully remembered. Is it not one of your English poets, that looked abroad upon the earth and saw vast circumvallations, innumerable troops manoeuvring, warships at sea and a great dust of battles on shore; and casting anxiously about for what should be the cause of so many and painful preparations, spied at last, in the centre of all, a mother and her babe? These, madam, are my politics; and the verses, which are by Mr. Coventry Patmore, I have caused to be translated into the Bohemian tongue. Yes, these are my politics: to change what we can, to better what we can; but still to bear in mind that man is but a devil weakly fettered by some generous beliefs and impositions, and for no word however nobly sounding, and no cause however just and pious, to relax the stricture of these bonds.'

There was a silence of a moment.

'I fear, madam,' resumed the Prince, 'that I but weary you. My views are formal like myself; and like myself, they also begin to grow old. But I must still trouble you for some reply.'

'I can say but one thing,' said Mrs. Desborough: 'I love my husband.'

'It is a good answer,' returned the Prince; 'and you name a good influence, but one that need not be conterminous with life.'

'I will not play at pride with such a man as you,' she answered. 'What do you ask of me? not protestations, I am sure. What shall I say? I have done much that I cannot defend and that I would not do again. Can I say more? Yes: I can say this: I never abused myself with the muddle-headed fairy tales of politics. I was at least prepared to meet reprisals. While I was levying war myself—or levying murder, if you choose the plainer term—I never accused my adversaries of assassination. I never felt or feigned a righteous horror, when a price was put upon my life by those whom I attacked. I never called the policeman a hireling. I may have been a criminal, in short; but I never was a fool.'

'Enough, madam,' returned the Prince: 'more than enough! Your words are most reviving to my spirits; for in this age, when even the assassin is a sentimentalist, there is no virtue greater in my eyes than intellectual clarity. Suffer me, then, to ask you to retire; for by the signal of that bell, I perceive my old friend, your mother, to be close at hand. With her I promise you to do my utmost.'

And as Mrs. Desborough returned to the Divan, the Prince, opening a door upon the other side, admitted Mrs. Luxmore.

'Madam and my very good friend,' said he, 'is my face so much changed that you no longer recognise Prince Florizel in Mr. Godall?'

'To be sure!' she cried, looking at him through her glasses. 'I have always regarded your Highness as a perfect man; and in your altered circumstances, of which I have already heard with deep regret, I will beg you to consider my respect increased instead of lessened.'

'I have found it so,' returned the Prince, 'with every class of my acquaintance. But, madam, I pray you to be seated. My business is of a delicate order, and regards your daughter.'

'In that case,' said Mrs. Luxmore, 'you may save yourself the trouble of speaking, for I have fully made up my mind to have nothing to do with her. I will not hear one word in her defence; but as I value nothing so particularly as the virtue of justice, I think it my duty to explain to you the grounds of my complaint.

She deserted me, her natural protector; for years, she has consorted with the most disreputable persons; and to fill the cup of her offence, she has recently married. I refuse to see her, or the being to whom she has linked herself. One hundred and twenty pounds a year, I have always offered her: I offer it again. It is what I had myself when I was her age.'

'Very well, madam,' said the Prince; 'and be that so! But to touch upon another matter: what was the income of the Reverend Bernard Fanshawe?'

'My father?' asked the spirited old lady. 'I believe he had seven hundred pounds in the year.'

'You were one, I think, of several?' pursued the Prince.

'Of four,' was the reply. 'We were four daughters; and painful as the admission is to make, a more detestable family could scarce be found in England.'

'Dear me!' said the Prince. 'And you, madam, have an income of eight thousand?'

'Not more than five,' returned the old lady; 'but where on earth are you conducting me?'

'To an allowance of one thousand pounds a year,' replied Florizel, smiling. 'For I must not suffer you to take your father for a rule. He was poor, you are rich. He had many calls upon his poverty: there are none upon your wealth. And indeed, madam, if you will let me touch this matter with a needle, there is but one point in common to your two positions: that each had a daughter more remarkable for liveliness than duty.'

'I have been entrapped into this house,' said the old lady, getting to her feet. 'But it shall not avail. Not all the tobacconists in Europe . . .'

'Ah, madam,' interrupted Florizel, 'before what is referred to as my fall, you had not used such language! And since you so much object to the simple industry by which I live, let me give you a friendly hint. If you will not consent to support your daughter, I shall be constrained to place that lady behind my counter, where I doubt not she would prove a great attraction; and your son-in-law shall have a livery and run the errands. With such young blood my business might be doubled, and I might be bound in common gratitude to place the name of Luxmore beside that of Godall.'

'Your Highness,' said the old lady, 'I have been very rude, and you are very cunning. I suppose the minx is on the premises. Produce her.'

'Let us rather observe them unperceived,' said the Prince; and so saying he rose and quietly drew back the curtain.

Mrs. Desborough sat with her back to them on a chair; Somerset and Harry were hanging on her words with extraordinary interest; Challoner, alleging some affair, had long ago withdrawn from the detested neighbourhood of the enchantress.

'At that moment,' Mrs. Desborough was saying, 'Mr Gladstone detected the features of his cowardly assailant. A cry rose to his lips: a cry of mingled triumph . . .'

'That is Mr. Somerset!' interrupted the spirited old lady, in the highest note of her register. 'Mr. Somerset, what have you done with my house-property?'

'Madam,' said the Prince, 'let it be mine to give the explanation; and in the meanwhile, welcome your daughter.'

'Well, Clara, how do you do?' said Mrs. Luxmore. 'It appears I am to give you an allowance. So much the better for you. As for Mr. Somerset, I am very ready to have an explanation; for the whole affair, though costly, was eminently humorous. And at any rate,' she added, nodding to Paul, 'he is a young gentleman for whom I have a great affection, and his pictures were the funniest I ever saw.'

'I have ordered a collation,' said the Prince. 'Mr. Somerset, as these are all your friends, I propose, if you please, that you should join them at table. I will take the shop.'